C000175374

THE LUCK

Kathy Biggs is originally from Yorkshire. She took a summer job in Mid Wales in 1985 – and never left. She has two grown children and lives with her husband, Paul. After studying a number of Creative Writing courses linked to Aberystwyth University, she discovered a talent for writing. *The Luck* is her first novel.

THE LUCK

Kathy Biggs

HONNO MODERN FICTION

First published in Great Britain in 2022 by Honno Press
D41, Hugh Owen Building, Aberystwyth University, Ceredigion, SY23 3DY

1 2 3 4 5 6 7 8 9 10

Copyright © Kathy Biggs 2022

The right of Kathy Biggs to be identified as the Author of the Work has been asserted in accordance with the Copyright, Designs and Patents Act 1988. All rights reserved. No part of the book may be reproduced, stored in a retrieval system, or transmitted in any form, or by any means, electronic, mechanical, photocopying, recording or otherwise without the prior permission of the copyright owner.

A catalogue record for this book is available from the British Library.

Published with the financial support of the Books Council of Wales.

ISBN 9781912905621 (paperback)
ISBN 9781912905638 (ebook)
Cover design: Kari Brownlie
Text design: Elaine Sharples
Printed by 4edge Ltd

All characters in this publication are fictitious and any resemblance to real persons, living or dead, is purely coincidental.

This book is dedicated to my mum, Lucy Little of West Cornforth and my grandmothers, Dora Hodgson of Cassop and Annie O'Grady of Cappaduff, Co Clare

Chapter 1

Darragh leaned in and gave the instrument panel a light tap. *Due west,* Carter had said. *Follow the river till it drops out of sight, then stick due west. You'll see it.* He peered out the window. He couldn't see a damn thing. Another wasted trip. A quarter tank of fuel down and nothing to show for it.

He might have turned round there and then, this is what he reasoned afterwards: gone back to the base, haggled with Carter, tried again next day. But he didn't. He never could explain what pulled him on: whether it was the quality of the light, a low pink wash that spoke of some warm, cosy room, made him want to kick off his shoes and cruise a while longer, taking in the lie of the land below him. Empty, some might have said: a wide expanse of empty. Or so it seemed.

It caught his eye like someone signalling with a torch. A sharp glint: on, off, and then a dazzling burst that swelled towards him, glancing off the windshield like he was some chosen thing then reeling itself back in like it knew he was already caught. He dipped the Annie O'Grady into a soft curving arc and followed it like a moth to a flame.

It wasn't a place, more the possibility of a place. This is what he told Carter hours later. It was like looking down on a giant puzzle. All the right pieces were there: a river, like a twist of rope, a stand of oak sitting like a crown on the north bank of a lake, a loose sprawl of half-flattened buildings and pasture ... pasture as far as his eye could see.

'Sounds to me like you got yourself right off track, son.'

This was Carter's usual explanation when his directions fell short of getting you to the place you were aiming for. His way of getting you in the mood for the fact that, despite the wasted fuel, you'd be getting no money off him.

'You know where it might be, then?'

'A lake, you say?'

'That's right. And oak, a good planting of oak.'

Carter hobbled over to the desk and pulled a length of cord. It parted a pair of old curtains strung up on the wall behind the desk. His maps. The glare of the sun played havoc with the ink. He took the pointing stick from its spot in the corner and considered for a moment.

'So ... this is where you were headed ... supposed to be headed ...' He tapped the wall lightly, indicating, as far as Darragh could see, some wide open space that had no bearing at all on where he was supposed to have been heading.

'No road?'

'Not that I saw.'

'And the buildings?'

'I don't know. Fallen in, I guess. Maybe a small barn, a couple of sheds or perhaps a shack. I couldn't take too long, the fuel ...' It was worth a go.

Carter ignored it. 'Mmhh ... I can't be sure, but ... no road, you say ... but a lake, yes?'

'A lake, yes. That's what drew my eye, the sun coming off the water.'

Carter pulled the chair out from behind the desk and stepped up onto it. He pulled his glasses out of his top pocket and peered at the map.

'There an island in that lake by any chance?'

'I daresay there was,' Darragh said, sliding himself sideways behind the desk. 'You found it?'

Carter didn't answer. He climbed carefully down, using the top of Darragh's head to steady himself, pulled the curtains closed then returned the pointing stick to the corner.

'Sounds you was likely in the region of Stig Petersen's old place.' He pulled the chair back into place and sat down on it.

'Stig Petersen? I reckon I don't know the feller.'

'Well, seeing as you only just showed up round here a few months back, and bearing in mind the man is no longer with us, I'd say that was no surprise.' Carter pushed his chair back a few inches and pulled open one of the drawers. Got out his order book.

'So?'

'What?'

'Stig Petersen, you were saying about him ...'

Carter had the book open, his finger tracing the brittle pages. He gave Darragh a sideways glance.

'Well ... ' He leaned back in his chair. 'I only know what I've been told ... and it was a sorry tale. He settled the place, what, must be fifty years back. Could be more. Foreigner I believe. Brought his wife and children with him, set the place up, then ...'

Darragh waited.

'Then, well. I only know how the story goes and, strictly speaking, no one knows what happened because they were out there by themselves. Some kind of accident with the boat, that's what got said. A storm maybe? Anyways, whatever it was, they all ended up dead. His wife, his children. Drowned. The lot of them.'

'Drowned? In the lake, you mean?'

'That's what folks said. His family came over, I believe, emptied the place and took Stig back with them. Been empty ever since.'

'But his wife ... and ...'

Carter gave a small shrug. 'Still there as far as I know.'

'What? In the ...'

'Yep. In the lake.'

Darragh perched on the edge of Carter's desk. He pulled back the curtain and gazed up at the map.

'And no one's ever taken the place on?'

Carter shook his head. 'I wouldn't know. Never had call to go out that way. There's some place set up not too far from there now, one of them one-street towns. Might be someone there knows about it but ... well, I guess some places just need to be left alone.'

Darragh was only half listening. His eye was tracking the path he'd taken earlier, scanning the empty inches, seeking out the ribbon twist of river, the lake, the oaks. Seeking out the shape of the place.

Like a picture puzzle. That's what he'd said to Carter. What he hadn't said was that it had seemed to him there was a piece of the puzzle missing and he had a strong conviction he might be just the feller to fit the gap.

Buying the place turned out to be the easiest thing he'd done in months.

Easier than leaving Ireland – three weeks at sea, his stomach roaming round like it had forgotten which part of his body it belonged to.

Easier than setting eyes on his brother, his hopes dashed before he even got on to the dockside.

Easier than lying to his mother.

'Write me as soon as you get there, son. Let me know how he is.'

Too much hope in her eyes. Sean. Her best boy really. Born to let her down. Darragh had spotted him from the queue, staggering along the quayside, his two feet barely lined up one in front of the other. He'd watched the stream of disembarking passengers stepping out of his way.

'Sean's doing real good, Ma.' That's what he wrote, knowing she would see through it. Real good at what? The drinking, the horses, the dogs. Real good at all the wrong things.

Just like his father.

He'd stayed as long as he could, as long as he'd dared, then he'd cut loose and left without saying he was going.

He wasn't up to the drama of another goodbye, he reasoned. The truth was different to that. He'd got back from his shift on the docks one night, his back near cut in two from hauling cotton bales and found his mattress thrown on its side, the bedclothes strewn about the floor. Of Sean there was no sign other than a half-finished plate of food in the kitchen sink. He'd quickly slid the wardrobe forward, his mouth swilling with acid, then prised up a floorboard and, ready for nothing but disappointment, felt in the cavity below. His bundle of money was where he'd left it. He'd let out a short sob then thrown it into his suitcase and left.

Headed west.

He kept going till the railroad ran out and the land turned green then golden, on and on, taking work where he could, adding to his bundle of money until eventually he was ready: ready to pursue the dream that had rattled his poor bones across the Atlantic in the first place.

Crop spraying.

It would be fair to say that Darragh's dream didn't initially fit with the reality. This, he reasoned, was likely the fault of the films – and Lyle Carter.

'What in God's name ...'

Darragh had brought the plane down on the strip with what he thought was a certain finesse. Fair enough he'd misjudged it first attempt, but second time round she'd kissed the ground with barely a bounce. He'd hauled himself out of the cockpit and crossed the dusty strip, his goggles perched aloft, his scarf flapping behind. He'd held his hand out to the approaching Carter and watched as the man limped past him and up to the Annie O'Grady.

'I said, what in God's good name do you call that?'

Darragh strode after him, his hand still outstretched. 'Darragh O'Grady, sir. I hear you're looking to hire?'

Carter was walking round the plane, scratching his head. He was got up like a man set for safari: a frayed shirt the colour of dust and sand, kitted out with an impressive range of pockets and epaulettes, a pair of pants that stopped short below the knees and a set of boots that didn't match.

'What the hell colour is that? Thought you was a damn canary coming at me.'

'Oh, I ... ' Darragh had painted the thing himself.

'And this ... what the hell is this?' Carter was tracing the lettering – a bold red – hand painted along the fuselage.

'The Annie O'Grady, sir. My mother. Back in Ireland.'

Carter clapped his hand over his eyes. 'Ireland? Oh my lord. Don't tell me you flew that thing from Ireland.'

'Well, no ... I don't think ...'

'Joking, son. Just joking. So, you know anything about crop spraying?'

It turned out that he did know a thing or two about crop spraying – enough at any rate for Carter to hire him on. That first night, his face flushed from the wind and sun and his unexpected success, Darragh dragged his camp bed outside and pitched it beside the Annie O'Grady. He penned a short note to his mother then lay himself down. The sky spun out above him, a flood of blue that lapped at the horizon then absorbed it, deepening, deepening until, like an orchestra waiting quietly in the wings, a million stars appeared and pulsed their silent music down and over him till he no longer knew whether he was waking or sleeping, whether he was on the earth or in the sky.

By the end of the first month Carter reckoned he'd struck gold. The young Irish feller had a hellish approach to work. Like a packhorse he might have said, except the lad could fly a plane like he was part of the damn thing.

'Sure you've not got feathers underneath that jacket?'

O'Grady was grinning – as usual – eight hours solid in the air and nothing to show for it but a grin. Carter had taken to watching for him, dragging his office chair out to the side of the strip just so he could watch the lad bring the plane in.

By the end of the sixth month Carter was considering expansion. A couple of outfits further east were buying up old mail carriers – 1934 Stearmans – and rigging them out as dusters. He figured there was nothing to stop him doing the same, not with O'Grady on the team. He was working on a way to bring it up with the lad, maybe talk him into some portion of *investment.* Not a *partnership* as such, more of an interest that might offer some financial gain.

This is how his thoughts were running the evening the lad came back from his trip with a strange look on his face. First off Carter reckoned the lad was *piqued* because he'd not managed to find where he was aimed. *Lost his bearings.* Then he started in asking questions.

Chapter 2

Darragh took to farming as easy as he took to flying. Strictly speaking this was no great surprise, him coming from a line of Irish farmers, but he'd insist, years later, that his skill or lack of it was of no significance at all because the land he'd bought was nothing but good: all he'd done was encourage it. *And give it a name.*

Darragh liked to tell himself that he hadn't given too much thought to the naming of the place. This wasn't really true.

He'd written home at the end of the first week, too weary to make much of a letter, but feeling the need to let his mother know where he was.

'I'm going to name the place for the horse, Ma,' he'd said. He knew she'd smile at that. Their secret.

O'Grady's Luck. His father's one good mare. A stalwart in the races, a sure bet at the bookies. His mother's face had coloured up when she'd handed over the small roll of cash. Her winnings. She'd pushed it into his jacket pocket before his father came in from the wash house.

What he hadn't admitted, either to her or himself, was that the name would surely offer some kind of assurance. Some protection. He had allowed himself to conclude that Stig Petersen, if the man ever really existed, had fallen short as a father, failed in his duty to look after his family. His imagination had the man lying drunk in his bed, neglecting his work, raging and cursing at his cowed wife.

O'Grady's Luck. He'd painted the name on a short plank of oak and nailed it to the gate at the end of the track. He'd tapped the last nail home then waited. He was being nothing but an eejit, he knew that: chances were Carter's story was just a nonsense – the feller in the land office certainly made no mention of Stig Petersen – but all week it had been all he could think of. Every shovel of earth he moved, every plank of timber he levered off had him holding his breath, afraid he might suddenly unearth something that told him he was wrong, that he should never have come, that he'd made a mistake.

But, whether it was the nailing up of the sign or just the passage of time – or just plain bone weariness – by the time he had his mother's reply he knew he'd made no mistake. It was plain as the grass was green: he'd managed to secure one of the best parcels of land in the county. The sun, it seemed, lingered there longer and the wind whipping in from the east had an obliging tendency to rise as it approached, passing just low enough to set his shirts jigging on the line. It wasn't so much that he took to farming as the farm seemed to take to him, like every bit of work he put in came back tenfold. And the land: every inch of it had an itch to grow. Not just the crops – he reckoned he could plant beans in the evening and they'd be up by morning – but the farm itself. It sprang back up around him and he tended it till it gleamed like a thing made of gold.

For two years Darragh thought of nothing else. He rose with the sun, worked till dark, ate, slept, rose with the sun – like the happiest man that ever lived.

It was the start of the third year that things changed. Sometime round February. There was some *quietness* about the place he'd not noticed before. The clock seemed to tick more loudly when he sat down to eat and the sight of his mug sitting on the draining board gave him a hollowed out feeling.

He determined to be more sociable but the habit of working hard and late and alone had ground its way into his bones: once or twice he called on neighbours – folks who had settled the land around him – the Rileys, the Creasys, but he had to stop. All the talking. He'd lost the knack.

He took to lying longer in bed, gazing at the ceiling, then at the pillow beside him. *Empty.* Eventually he wrote a long letter home, asking after his father, his sisters, his nephews and nieces. His mother saw straight through it.

'Sounds like you're ready for settling down, son,' she'd written. He'd put the letter down on the table and puzzled for a few moments. He *was* settled down. She surely knew that already. He read on a few more lines then lay the page down again.

A wife?

He gave a small snort. A wife and him only just twenty-one? What was his mother thinking of? He pushed the letter in the drawer and thought no more of it till he got to bed. He lay for a while letting his gaze scan the room, thinking of his mother's words. Eventually, there being nothing to look at other than his work clothes draped at the end of the bed, he turned on his side and considered the empty pillow.

A wife.

An idea is a powerful thing. Even if it belongs to someone else. Once it's said, *offered*, it becomes another thing altogether. A challenge maybe or a possibility. Perhaps a dream, something to aim for. In Darragh's case his mother's words, her suggestion, settled in his mind like a seed. By autumn the thing had taken on a life of its own, branched upwards and outwards in all directions until it was all he could do to contain it. A wife. It was the only thing he could think of.

It has to be said that Darragh had a certain kind of woman in mind and evenings, when he put his tools down and sat out back, he would let himself picture her: dark curls lifting slightly as she walked towards him, an easy smile on her lips and a light in her eye for him, a simple dress scribing her supple waist. Had he thought about this in something other than a romantic light he might have realised that this ideal woman was in fact a young version of his own mother: the girl in the wedding photograph at the back of the dresser, her face lit up and hopeful. Consequently it was a great surprise to him (and to most other folk) when in fact he fell for Beattie Darling, the only daughter of a far neighbour.

Beattie was considered by most as spinster material. This was not just due to her age – twenty-two being considered a tad old – but also to the fact that she had a gimpy leg. Truth was it wasn't a gimpy leg at all – it was a wooden leg fashioned by her father after a bout of brain fever in early childhood necessitated the hasty removal of her own. As a consequence she wore men's trousers and walked in a stomping crooked fashion. This misfortune however was not the thing that she was known for, nor the thing that made O'Grady notice her in the first place.

One morning, early, he had discovered halfway through the job that he was short of a length of fencing wire. He'd walked back down to the farm and investigated the lean-to at the back of the barn – the most likely place he might find a useable length. Fortune was on his side – a small roll slotted up on the rafters got him out of the fix and he finished the job. Later that morning, though, as he sat at the table jawing through a plate of tough bread and ham, the thought of the patched fence started to bother him. He went to the back porch and scanned the top field. He was right: even from a distance the neat evenness of the fencing was marred by the slight thickening of the lines where he'd twisted the two lengths together. He left the bread and ham where it was, tucked a few dollars in his jacket and pointed the truck in the direction of Picker's Flag.

He arrived just after midday and, having secured a roll of fencing, decided to visit The Ponderosa – the only eating place in town. Eating out wasn't something he was accustomed to doing but a fleeting vision of the stale bread and ham sitting on the kitchen table surely getting tougher by the minute, took him through the door – and into the midst of some table-thumping hilarity that he first mistook for a fracas. He chose a table by the fire and glanced over at the rowdy group: four men helpless with laughter, the one of them talking low, clearly relating some tale, the other three in degrees of mirthful helplessness. When the waitress came for his order, he nodded over to the group with a questioning smile.

'Oh, that Beattie,' the girl said, smiling, but otherwise throwing no light his way at all. 'What a storyteller!'

She walked away just as the story came to some climax and the group exploded into a foot-stamping finale. One of the group got up and walked towards the bar, passing his table on the way. He saw, with some surprise, that it was no man but a woman in men's britches. On top of that she carried some kind of ailment that gave her a floor-stomping limp. Her face was flushed and damp with tears. She glanced at him as she passed, wiping her eyes – a look of such fun on her face he caught himself watching her as she came back from the bar. Not only watching but hastily trying to think of something he might say to her. He found that he needn't have worried; she stopped beside him and stuck her hand out towards his.

'Beattie Darling,' she said, pushing her straw-coloured hair off her forehead. Her hand was the best thing he had ever had the good fortune to touch. Rough and calloused like a man's, it fit into his own like an egg in a nest. He smiled his best smile and stood up.

'Darragh O'Grady,' he said, his voice not quite his own. She understood him nonetheless.

'Well, very pleased to meet you, Mr O'Grady,' she said, eyes shining, and stomped off to rejoin her buddies, leaving him in a fizz that curbed his appetite entirely.

The following Saturday O'Grady found that he was suddenly short of fencing staples. This was largely due to the fact that he was wilfully disregarding the box, stowed for such emergencies, beneath the bench in the barn. He jumped in the truck, pointed it once again in the direction of Picker's Flag. Half a mile down the track he spun the truck round, jogged back to the farm and grabbed his good jacket and his better hat. He walked into The Ponderosa with a tap dance going on in his chest. He headed for the same table by the fire, nodding at the group who were mopping their eyes and breathing heavy.

'Mr O'Grady.' It was Beattie's voice. 'Come and join us.'

Darragh never dreamed of dark curls and cotton dresses again: his every waking thought was of Beattie and his sleep, such as he got, took him on such flights of fancy that he woke sweating – even when the stove was out. It drove him crazy; generally a decisive man he was paralysed with his feelings for her. He couldn't live without her but he couldn't work out how to tell her. The first problem was getting her on her own – she was always surrounded by people, generally at the centre of some hilarity. The second problem was that he wasn't sure of her feelings for him; she seemed to approach everyone in the same jovial manner, singled no one out for special treatment. As the weeks went by he wore himself out with dithering until, the week of Christmas, Beattie herself stepped in.

Although he'd become a regular at the Saturday table, he'd never presumed to take the seat next to Beattie, nor engage her in any conversation that didn't include the others. So, the Saturday before Christmas, when she took hold of his arm as he was getting up to leave and asked him quietly if he would consider joining her and her pa for Christmas dinner he almost choked with relief and joy. He agreed quickly and got himself out of The Ponderosa and into the pickup where he burst into a sweat of disbelief.

By Christmas Eve Darragh was unable to sit or stand or sleep without thinking about Beattie. He worked on the farm until he was worn out then, after heating up some water and scrubbing himself in the tub, dropped onto his bed and fell gratefully asleep. He woke early, twisted in the sheets to the sudden realisation that he didn't have a Christmas gift to take. He lay for a few minutes in something of a sweat, his mind roaming the cabin and farm for something that might be deemed suitable.

The idea came as he was boiling water for coffee: staring absent-mindedly out of the window, watching the birds quarrelling around the feeding station he'd rigged up for them. A feeding station. That surely might be a thing to consider? There was a pile of good timber in the barn and enough time to fashion something acceptable. He poured his coffee and, with a spring of relief in his step, took it across to the barn.

Darragh's feeding station hit the jackpot on two accounts: unknown to him Beattie's childhood passion – kindled by the long hours of being bedbound – was birds. Few things gave her the pleasure she derived from watching them. She gasped with delight when O'Grady handed it over then burst into peals of laughter when he produced the 'feeding balls' he'd fashioned from tallow and corn and threaded with twine. She stomped her way to the house where her pa was waiting on the porch and thrust the station into his hands.

'Look, Pa, look what O'Grady has made.'

Tom Darling ran his hands over the construction.

'You know something about wood then, son,' he said.

'Well, I wouldn't strictly ...'

'Pa's a real keen wood man, aren't you, Pa?'

'Well ...'

'Oh, you are, you are. Look ... look at this, O'Grady.' To Darragh's amazement Beattie started hauling up the leg of her britches. 'My pa ... he made it for me.'

Darragh gazed down at her bared leg. It was made of wood.

'Pine,' Tom Darling said. 'Oak's a tad heavy.'

'See how it works,' Beattie said, slipping her shoe off. The leg was hinged at the ankle. She waggled the foot up and down with her hand.

'It's marvellous,' Darragh said.

Tom Darling knew there and then. That's what he told Beattie once Darragh had left. *He's the man for you, Beatt.* That's what he'd said. He'd stared into the fire and let the words roll around in his mind then loosed them into the air. He'd had to get up and make some pretence of stoking the wood. The tears had come of their own accord and he couldn't stop them. A man for Beattie. He'd thought he would never see the day. It lifted like a leaf in the wind. The load he'd carried for half his life, suddenly weightless. The *guilt*. It wasn't his fault, the doctors told him over and over. And she'd survived. A miracle, they'd said. An out-and-out miracle. But still, the guilt.

He'd sought redemption in wood, fashioning limbs for her,

started when she was two years old: a small peg formed from an oak sapling – a simple affair that she quickly outgrew and was put to use for planting taters. And now, Darragh O'Grady. Another miracle.

They married on Valentine's Day. Come Easter, Beattie was expecting.

Chapter 3

Conrad O'Grady was born during a January storm. Wind and rain had lashed the farm till water was running in one end of the barn and out the other. The cattle – brought in from the field – huddled together chewing hay, watching the steady stream pour past. For three days Darragh was running from one emergency to the next, and for three days Beattie was praying the baby would not come. The fourth day, when they both thought things could not get worse, the wind blew a sheet of metal off the barn roof. It flew across the yard, smashing the windshield of the pickup as it hurtled past and Beattie went into labour.

She was watching Darragh from the kitchen window – his hair blasted back off his head as he wrestled a couple of boulders on top of the metal sheet. She was wondering whether they should try to get over to check on her pa, perhaps take a couple of pies over. The weather had kept her in and she had baked till the pantry door could hardly close. Darragh was head down now, forging his way to the barn, his back bent, coat soaked and flapping. Like a drenched crow.

The first sign was small. A quiet nudge at the front of her belly. A couple of minutes later, something of a stout kick – followed by a sudden release of hot water between her legs. She let out a gasp – then a small laugh. Seven hours later the boy was born and, aside from Beattie's yelling, the sound of rain drumming on the roof was the first thing he heard. Whether that had put something into the boy's make-up became the topic of many conversations because, from an early age Conrad O'Grady had an unnatural attraction to water.

'I reckon you gave birth to a damn otter, Beattie.'

Darragh was bathing the boy in the small washbasin, gently

swilling water over his belly. Beattie had the kettle heating on the stove – rewarming the bathwater every few minutes. It was gone midnight. They'd paced back and forth with the squawking infant for hours until Beattie had hit on the idea. The moment she placed him in the water he fell silent. His tight belly relaxed and he settled into a peaceful doze. Each time Darragh raised him up to let her add hot water he struck up again.

They eventually learned that the same effect could be achieved by parking him by the kitchen sink and leaving the tap running lightly. The first good night's sleep they had was several weeks later when another storm hit. Darragh and Beattie, drooped with fatigue by then, spent a good portion of the day in bed – Conrad sleeping sound beside them, the rain drumming on the roof. They got to watching the sky, hopeful for dark clouds.

As the months went by things improved – or maybe they just got used to it. Either way the boy settled, they all started sleeping better and, as winter approached, life had resumed a degree of peaceful order. It didn't last long.

It was a Sunday. They'd finished the after-church socialising and were fixing to go over to see Beattie's pa. Conrad was just off crawling, happiest on the ground, specially outside. Beattie was finishing off talking with the minister and Darragh had his head together with Clarence Picker – farm talk. Conrad was sitting at his feet, nose in a tump of dry grass. All of a sudden a yell went up and folks started running. Darragh stooped down to pick up the boy – and discovered him gone. He yelled over to Beattie who was craning her neck to see what the fuss was about. She took one look at his face and joined the rush.

Mabel Picker caught him. Managed to swoop him up before he crawled into the church pond.

'Never seen a child move so fast,' Mabel gasped. 'Like he was on rollers ...'

He became a town legend. Nothing could keep him from water. After a couple more incidents Darragh quit sleeping – getting up in the night to check on the boy then, if sleep did come, waking in a blind panic after some dreamed drowning.

It was Tom Darling came to the rescue. He appeared one morning – after another close call involving the cattle trough – with a wooden pen. Beattie was at the window when he pulled into the yard. She pulled Conrad out of the bathtub and wrapped him in a blanket and headed out to her pa.

'What you got there?' she said, Conrad squirming in her arms like a young trout.

'I've made a pen for the boy,' Tom said and despite herself Beattie burst out laughing.

'A pen?' she said. 'I reckon this boy might be better suited to a tank.'

Tom just nodded and set about unloading the contraption off the truck. They hauled it up onto the porch where he set it up, Conrad quiet and watchful.

It was like a miracle. Beattie found she could set him up on the porch with a basin of water and a tin cup and snatch enough time in the day to get her chores done. By spring Tom was there most days. Come summer he and the boy were inseparable.

'Been thinking, Beattie,' Darragh said one night. They were in bed, Conrad flat out exhausted by a day down at the farm pond with Tom. 'Your pa. Reckon we ought to find room for him here?'

They tackled the subject over breakfast – Tom generally being parked up in the yard before they got the kettle on the stove.

'What do you say, Pa? Move in here with us. Plenty of room and it ...'

Tom shook his head. 'I'm content with things as they are, girl. Couldn't ask for more.' He paused a moment or two to tear a piece of bread for the boy. 'I do have something to ask, though.'

Beattie and Darragh looked at him.

He cleared his throat. 'I reckon this youngster would take to fishing real quick, you know, when he's more grown ... so ... I was wondering. Well, you might not think it a good idea ...'

'Come on, Pa, spit it out.'

'Well I was figuring I might build us a nice little fishing shack. You know, for me and the boy.' He shot them an embarrassed grin. Tom Darling was not big on asking for much, never had been. Preferred to get by under his own steam – if he hankered after a thing he made it himself or did without.

'A fishing shack? Where?'

'Well,' Tom looked down at the table. 'I was thinking the best spot would be over on the island. We could set ourselves up – you know, when the lad is older of course, might even do a spot of camping out there. What do you think?'

Beattie looked to Darragh. He wasn't smiling.

'The island?' he said. He put his cup down on the table. 'So you'd have to ... you'd have to row across ...'

'Well, yes,' Tom said, glancing at Beattie. 'But not now, of course, not now. When the boy is older I mean. I wouldn't take him across yet. I just meant I could get the place built, ready as it were.'

'Well ...' Darragh began, then discovered the words would not come. *Tom row across to the island with the boy? Across the lake?*

'Pa, it's a grand idea, isn't it, Darragh? Darragh.' She kicked his boot under the table. 'It's a grand idea, isn't it? You could help out, get Pa started with the groundwork.'

He was watching her mouth move but couldn't rightly hear what she was saying. *Tom and Conrad on the lake?* They didn't go to the lake, Beattie knew that. As far as she was concerned it was on account of the boy and his hankering for the water. That and the fact that Darragh was no swimmer. But it was more than that of course.

Stig Petersen.

Darragh had done his best to banish thoughts of the man from his mind. Of his drowned family. He'd visited the lake when he was newly arrived, walked himself down, figuring on choosing some building timber. A warm day, him in his shirt sleeves, thinking of nothing other than the task in hand, considering how many poles he might need, what length. He'd stopped suddenly, unsure why. First off he thought it was the wind. A trick it was playing as it wound through the trees. Sounded like voices. He'd stood at the water's edge listening, making sure, and was turning to continue on his way when suddenly, clear as day, he heard it. A shout that made his heart run queer.

'Papa ...'

He'd put his hands to his mouth and hollered back.

There was no reply.

He'd kicked off his boots and waded into the water to his knees, then stopped and hollered again. And that's when he felt it, some kind of magnet pull that urged him forward, up to his thighs, the seat of his pants, his waist. Like someone was reeling him in. He never knew what stopped him but it was like he suddenly woke, the water lapping cold around his chest, a feeling in his heart like something was lost ...

He'd avoided the place ever since. Told Beattie it was because he couldn't swim, because of the boy.

'Darragh.'

He picked his cup back up from the table and took a small mouthful of coffee. 'Well I don't ...'

'You don't see why not,' Beattie said. 'Exactly!' The excitement of the idea had revved her up, put some colour in her cheeks. 'When are you thinking of getting started, Pa?'

Tom was studying Darragh's face. 'Well maybe it's not such a good idea ...'

Beattie's elbow found Darragh's ribs. 'Darragh, tell him ...'

'No,' Darragh said. 'Do it, Tom. Beattie's right. It's a grand idea. It's ...' The words stuck there. A grand idea? What in God's name was he saying? What if, what if the boat ... He went to the sink. Drew a glass of water and swallowed it down, closed his eyes against the picture playing in front of his face. A capsized boat, Tom and Conrad in the water, him on the shore, helpless. He ran his hand across his face and turned back to face them. He was being an eejit.

'No, do it, Tom,' he said. 'Do it. When ... when do you think you might get started?'

'Well,' Tom put down his fork and winked at Conrad. 'I happen to have some timber and nails in the truck now. Thought I might row over directly.'

Chapter 4

From then on Conrad O'Grady's life was bound to water, as if his milestones were measured by marker buoys as opposed to notches on a doorpost: he was swimming before he was two years old, had his own small boat – crafted by Tom – before he started school, was selling his catch to the general store by the time he was eight. He was happiest on the island with Tom – the two of them camped out, sending smoke signals up through the trees. He was a willing hand at home but by the time he was sixteen it was evident to Darragh and Beattie the boy was no farmer.

It was the spring of '49 that everything changed.

The war in Europe had left many shortages and Tom Darling – after a brief tussle with pneumonia, untreated because of a lack of antibiotics – died. Beattie had seen it coming for months: she'd found her pa snoozing on the porch on more than one occasion, noticed his pace had fallen off. But Conrad fell like an oak. After the funeral he rowed himself out to the island and stayed there till Beattie got worried and went out to fetch him. By morning he'd gone back – a thin trail of woodsmoke out on the island like a message.

'He'll do it his own way, Beattie,' Darragh said. She was out on the porch, watching the soft twist of the smoke curling away to nothing.

'I guess I know that for sure,' she said. She didn't know what else to say.

'He'll be back in his own time, he's just working things through.'

'Well, I hope he don't take too long.'

He took a week. Darragh came down one morning to find the boy in the kitchen, working his way through a pot of coffee and what appeared to be most of the food in the house.

'Looks like you didn't get a whole lot to eat out there, son,' he said, salvaging the end of the loaf while he still had the opportunity.

'Ate everything me and Grandpa had stashed in the food cellar, cooked a few fish.' He looked up at Darragh, his chin dripping honey. 'I got lonesome. Wasn't the same without him.' He turned his face from Darragh and wiped his eyes on his shirt sleeve. He cranked his voice a notch. 'So – thought I'd better get back over here, get some work done.' He stood up, still avoiding Darragh's eye. 'I'll see you out in the yard.' And he was gone.

It didn't last long. The lad laboured on the farm all day, then, come suppertime, took off on his own. Sometimes it was the island – the thin trail of smoke granting Beattie some peace of mind. Other times he borrowed the truck and went into town, coming back late and loud, knocking into furniture, stumbling and cursing on the stairs.

They never said anything to him but it was like the boy was spoiling for a fight – always prodding and poking for some reaction. He reared up at the smallest thing – a lame ewe, a broken fence – like it was a jibe aimed right at him. He took to staying over at the island, not turning in for farmwork, then showing up half drunk, mean and sparky.

Summer brought about an improvement: the long days of farmwork drawing most of the heat from his blood, granting Darragh and Beattie a degree of peace and some hope that he was on the mend. Come fall, though, things were deteriorating again – spiralling to a head. It was a Friday morning, early. Conrad was in the yard, splitting wood. There had been a row about the truck the night before, Darragh had refused to let him take it into town. So he'd walked there – or hitched. Whatever, he'd come back late, banging up the stairs, singing to himself, laughing. Now he was out in the yard, splitting wood. He wasn't going to settle without another fight: Darragh could see it in the set of the boy's shoulders as he hefted the axe then kicked the split logs to one side. He knew Beattie could see it too, she was mixing the batter more fierce than was needed. As far as he could see there was only one thing for it: the very thought cast a lump in his chest.

'Beattie,' he said, sidling over to her. 'We both know there's only one answer to this ...' He paused and waited for her tears to stop. 'And we both know it's the answer the two of us don't want. We have to let him go.'

She stepped away from him and looked out of the window, at Conrad, her only son, hefting logs like a condemned man. 'He's all we have, Darragh,' she said. 'We can't let him go.'

'We have each other, Beattie. And he'll come back, you'll see. He just needs to be loosed – it'll take the fight out of him – and he'll come back. He shaped the words carefully so she wouldn't detect the hollow centre of each one. The only future he could see was one with dust and weed blowing through it. He stood at the window with Beattie awhile, watching, fixing the picture in his mind.

'I'll take him over to the island tonight ...'

'I'll get you some food packed up, then,' Beattie said, shaking herself free of his arm. 'How long you think you'll be over there?'

Conrad pulled on the oars like they were extensions of his own arms, he rowed through the water like he was flying: it was one of life's pleasures to watch him. Darragh's announcement that they were going to camp out awhile had lightened the boy a cinch but the knot still showed on his forehead. Darragh waited till they were camped up, the fire shooting dry wood sparks into the night.

'Your ma and I have been thinking, son.'

Conrad poked at the fire with a stick, shoulders perked ready to rise up against whatever Darragh was about to announce. Some dumb scheme to keep him tied no doubt: fencing the corral, cutting the top field, dredging the goddamn pond.

'We thought it might be time you went off ...' Darragh's voice would not take him to the end of what he was going to say. Like a man at a funeral, his throat closed round the words and would not allow them.

Conrad quit messing with the fire. 'What's that you say, Pa?'

Darragh ran at it quick. 'Thought it might be time for you to go, son. Leave the farm to me and your ma for a while. Go see the world.' He had to turn away. Later, he would tell Beattie how the boy protested, how he had to press him to go. He didn't say how the knot dropped from his forehead and a smile like the sun itself split his face in two, that he just about heard the damn shackles fall off his feet.

He was gone by the end of the week: fixed a ride west with one of his trucker buddies. Left them standing on the porch, watching him jaunt down the track, a small pack bouncing on his back. He looked back once, shielding his eyes against the sun breaking like blood over the top field, and waved. A wave so loose with relief it took the strength from Darragh's legs.

'He'll be back in a month or two,' Darragh said, as Beattie stomped into the house.

He was wrong.

Chapter 5

After three or four months Beattie let off waiting for the mail. Darragh was relieved. The hopefulness in the set of her shoulders each morning as she stood by the gate; the short chat with Henry, the mailman; the way she sort of drooped forward then headed back up the track, her lovely head bent low: Darragh had watched it all and it had near broken him. After a couple of years they quit talking about the boy, choosing instead to lay awake conjuring solitary answers to questions they didn't speak out loud. Daytimes they sweated it out side by side on the farm, the pair of them skirting carefully around the hole he'd left behind for fear of falling in. It sometimes seemed to Darragh that all the colour had been drained from their lives – and taken Beattie's laughter with it.

Darragh was in the middle field, checking the ewes, when the rumble of wheels on dirt alerted him to some imminent arrival. He straightened up and saw a strange-looking vehicle heading up the track towards the farm. The dust cloud it was raising didn't disguise the fact that it was decorated like a flower garden. Some kind of bus. He could hear the music from where he stood. He started down towards the farm, watching as the driver got out and unlatched the gate. Darragh put his hand up against the sun and peered as the young man – tall, limber, smiling – jumped back into the van.

'Conrad.' The boy's name flew from his mouth like a bird from a cage. He took the field at a trot, some sudden space in his heart like a tight belt had been unexpectedly loosened.

'Conrad ... Conrad.' Darragh knew he couldn't be heard, but the relief of speaking the boy's name at last – it bubbled out of him like water from a spring.

He lengthened his stride and got into the yard just as the van was pulling up in front of the barn. Beattie was already on the front porch – a wooden mixing spoon still in her hand.

'It's Conrad,' he shouted as he strode past her, but it didn't need saying because the boy – the man – was running across the yard towards them, arms outstretched, smiling like a sunny day. How long the three of them stood there, hugging and weeping would be hard to measure because time itself slipped away. Darragh cleaved to his son like he was a magnet: the feel of his boy's arms around his shoulders loosing some wild feeling in his heart like his two feet might suddenly leave the ground. Beattie was making a noise some way between a groan and a laugh. Almost animal.

It was a small voice that suddenly brought them to their senses.

'Papa.'

Beattie spun round. A young woman, pale as drift wood, hair like gold falling to her waist, was standing beside them, holding a youngster.

'Papa.'

Conrad broke away and the child leaned towards him. 'Look who I've brought,' Conrad said, taking the child in his arms, his face lit up. 'This here is Olive – our daughter – and this here is my wife, Vida, and this ...' he gently rounded his hand over the firm swell of her belly, 'this is our youngest!' The young woman stepped forward like a whisper, her long thin dress trailing over the stones of the yard, so quiet and insubstantial that Beattie had an overwhelming urge to touch her. She put out an awkward hand and placed it on the girl's head. Her hair was soft and warm and fell about her bony shoulders like something royal. The girl swept it back and smiled at Beattie.

'What do you think, Ma?' Conrad said.

Beattie turned to him. 'What do I think, son? I think it must be Christmas!' She held her hand out to touch her son and the youngster in his arms leaned forward and swung across to her as if she'd known her all her life. Beattie let out a cry some way between surprise and delight, hitched the child onto her hip and let rip a peal of laughter that mended every goddamn thing that ever needed mending.

It lasted best part of two weeks, Darragh and Beattie's idyll. Late nights sitting up on the back porch, warm days rowing across to the island, trips into town to show off their good fortune and Olive, always Olive riding Beattie's hip like a small limpet, her hands tangled and clinging. These were the memories they stored up, the things they repeated to one another in bed, laying them down firm, like blankets in a chest, for it was obvious to them that it wouldn't last long: Conrad might have returned, but he wasn't going to stay. It seemed that neither his time at sea – for that is where his journeying had taken him: long months working the Pacific trawlers; longer, colder months on the Nova Scotia salmon – nor his young wife and daughter had been able to wash the salt from his blood and tie him to dry land.

'Why not stay here awhile, son?' Darragh said one night. The two of them were on the back porch, sky watching. The stars were at their best, the moon hanging low and heavy, its light picking out the ewes on the middle field, the slanting gleam of the barn roof. Conrad didn't answer at first, but his sigh spoke for him. Darragh held fast.

'You could stay till the new one is born ... imagine your ma.' He gave a small laugh which, even to his own ears, had a pitch of desperation.

'I can't, Pa. I'm signed up for another ship beginning of the week. Vida's sister is expecting us ... we've got it all organised.'

'Beginning of the week? Which week?'

'Next week, Pa. We aim to leave day after tomorrow. I'm sorry.'

Darragh got up from the bench. 'I better go and tell your ma.'

'Tell her not to worry. We'll be back – I promise we'll be back as soon as I'm home.'

The day after tomorrow came too soon and had Beattie and Darragh known that they would never see their son again they would not have let him go. They might instead have barred his way or chased down the track after him or even fallen to their sorry knees and begged him to stay. But no, they waved him off, his promise of an early return pasting hopeful smiles on their faces and propping up their slumped hearts. They managed to keep it up for a couple of months, until the smiling and constant cheeriness began to get them both down and Darragh – after the third night of lying awake wondering – spoke up.

'Beattie,' he whispered. She didn't answer, although her breathing told him she was awake.

'Beattie.'

'I don't want to talk about it, Darragh,' she said.

'We've got to talk about it,' he said. 'We're going round like a pair of ghosts. Wherever he is, he's living his life. We've got to live ours ...'

She sighed and turned towards him in the bed.

'I know that, Darragh. But the child ...' She sighed again. 'She's our granddaughter, Darragh. What if he doesn't come back. What if we never see her again?'

It hung in the air between them, a subject they seldom raised: Conrad had turned out to be their only child. Beattie had claimed the blame, chastising herself – usually between the dark hour between 3am and 4am – for wearing men's britches, riding horses, swilling ale, whatever it was that she'd done to stop herself up. And Darragh had left her alone with it, some quiet and shameful relief that his ability as a father had not been tested further than he was able to deliver.

The bed springs creaked as Beattie rolled onto her back. He didn't need to look at her to know what she was thinking.

'The new baby,' she said, her voice tripping over the thought. 'It must be born by now. Dammit, Darragh, why doesn't he write?'

'He's at sea, Beattie – we know that. The boy was shipping off again ...'

'Yes. But a short trip. He told us that. More or less said he'd be back within a month.'

'Beattie, love, there's nothing we can do. We've just got to sit tight and be patient.'

In the dark, Beattie sighed and considered his advice. Then she did what any desperate mother would do. She decided to ignore it.

When Darragh woke next morning she'd gone. He came down to an empty kitchen, a note propped up on the table. His eyes flicked to the yard: she'd taken the truck.

'Damn it, Beattie,' he said out loud, then plucked up the note and stomped outside with it.

Darragh dear

I'll not be long. I won't rest until I have looked for him. Will leave truck in rail yard and will contact Henry in the mail office when I get to San Francisco. Don't worry

Beattie

He screwed the note in a ball and hurled it across the yard then, for good measure, kicked out at the dog dishes and sent them the same way. One of the dogs came out from under the barn door and gave him a queer look.

'I know, I know,' he muttered, turning his back on the dog. 'I should have gone. I should have gone myself.'

Chapter 6

Beattie knew about San Francisco in the way folks knew about Mickey Mouse: that he existed in books and films, but wasn't actually real. So the feeling she got, when she clambered down from the train and joined the wave of travellers swelling towards the exit, then found herself swept out into the bright sunshine of the busy street, was of disbelief and surprise. Then fear. She was lost within minutes. She walked with the crowd – the only indication of which direction to take – until the numbers thinned out and the pace slowed and she found herself in what she judged to be the centre of town. She sat on a bench and watched folks hurrying by in numbers she'd never knew possible. Hordes of them. She took a long look round and fixed on a swanky building across the street: *The Sheridan Hotel* written in fancy script above two glass doors that were swinging lightly and sending bursts of light across the road. She hoisted her suitcase and navigated the traffic with a naïve recklessness that somehow got her safely to the other side and into the foyer.

By the time the mail van came into view Darragh had near worn a hole in the bottom of his boots. He started off down the road towards it, hailing Henry down with an impatient wave.

'Woah, there Darragh,' Henry said, as he stepped on the brake. 'Thought you was going to jump right out in front of me.'

'You got a message from Beattie?'

'Sure have, feller. Yes. She says ... um ... She says ...'

'What, Henry? What does she say?'

'Erm, hold on a minute there, let me just recollect.' He cleared his throat and put his two hands together like a youngster at a school recital. 'Miss Beattie called and said for you to pick her up in the truck – from the railroad station.'

Darragh bided his time. 'Did she say when?'

Henry's considered the question for a moment, his eyes wandering up to the sky. Darragh held his breath.

'Eight o'clock.'

'Eight o'clock?'

'Yup.' Henry gave a nod of satisfaction.

'Eight o'clock tonight or eight o'clock in the morning?'

Henry's face clouded over. He pulled a huge handkerchief out of his trouser pocket and wiped his face with it. Darragh waited.

'Um ... let me see. What did she say?'

Henry scratched his head and Darragh had to hold himself back: it was like watching someone unwind a ball of wool. Slowly.

'It's OK, Henry,' he said. 'I'll go down to the railyard tonight and if she's not there I'll go back in the morning.'

Henry blew out a long breath and smiled – his face soft with relief. 'Well, I guess that would work, Darragh, you'll catch her one way or the other, yes?' He heaved himself back into the mail van and waved his arm out of the window as he took off down the road. A couple of hundred yards down he screeched to a halt and reversed noisily back to where Darragh was still standing.

'Forgot to give you your mail,' he chortled and thrust a bundle into Darragh's hands.

Darragh inspected it as he walked back towards the farm. It was there on the back of the first envelope, scrawled in Henry's schoolboy handwriting:

Tell Darragh. Beattie 8 o'clock. Tonight.

Darragh studied Beattie's face through the carriage window as they waited for the train to stop. She was smiling but he couldn't figure if it was the genuine sort or the pasted-on sort. She looked done in that was for sure – a grimy, knocked-out look about her. She stepped down from the train and swung awkwardly into his arms.

'Sorry, love,' she said. 'But you understood, didn't you?'

He took a step back from her. 'I understood, Beattie – but you worried the hell out of me. I should have been with you. How the hell did you manage?'

She let out a loud guffaw. 'Manage? I didn't,' she said. 'I nearly got myself flattened. Do you know they have trains in the middle of the town? Nearly ended up reading about my own self in the newspaper.' She let out another peal of laughter and despite himself Darragh smiled.

'Thought we might go to The Ponderosa for a bite,' he said.

'Fine thinking, husband – I'm starved. Let's find us a quiet corner and I'll tell you what happened.'

Beattie had a whole lot to tell: she had telephoned Henry from a hotel lobby then caught a cab ride out to the port. She'd trawled the shipping offices – small and large – until she found the right one.

'Conrad O'Grady,' the man had boomed, his hair and thick whiskers red as a fox's pelt. He'd put back his head and bellowed out a laugh, then brought his fist down on the table, eyes bright with merriment. 'You are Conrad O'Grady's ma?' Then, still laughing, he'd hauled himself from behind the desk and come round to shake Beattie's hand. 'Mighty pleased to meet you, ma'am. Mighty pleased. Conrad O'Grady's ma. I'll be damned. Best boy I ever had on the boat ...'

'When are you expecting him back?' The question set him off laughing again.

'When am I expecting him back? Conrad O'Grady? You tell me. That boy, well, I never met anyone more suited to water. And he tells me he hails from farming folk ... you folks are farmers, yes?'

'We are,' Beattie said, still at a loss. 'Perhaps you know where he lives? His wife and ...'

'Ah, his wife. Yes, I know where he lives – can take you there if you like. But I doubt his wife is there. Doubt that very much.'

So he had taken her a short ride across the port and shown her the place.

'It was real lovely, Darragh,' she said. 'In a plain sort of way of course. But a proper-looking place. Small, but square, built good.'

'And was she there? Vida?'

Beattie's face dropped its liveliness. 'No. No sign of her. A neighbour came out. Said no one had been there for two or three months.'

'She must still be with her sister then.'

'That's what I figured. Neighbour didn't know where that might be.' Beattie put her hand on his arm and smiled at him. 'But it makes a difference, Darragh. I know where he lives. I've seen it with my own eyes. I feel hopeful – like it's just a matter of time till that ungodly van pulls up in the yard again – all I have to do is wait.'

Chapter 7

It was a Sunday. Beattie and Darragh were in the churchyard – the usual milling around chit-chat after the service was over. The day was warm and the two were in no hurry to get back to the farm. As they turned off the road and headed up the track they hit a problem. Five heifers – their own five heifers – loose and wandering down the lane. Darragh stopped the truck and jumped out, waving his arms. Beattie took the prod from the truck bed and stationed herself at the opposite side of the track to Darragh.

It is a well-known fact that it is nigh impossible to get a cow to walk backwards but from where they were standing it seemed like there was no other option. The five heifers were shoulder to shoulder and kept coming until they were as good as wedged between the two fences. Then they stopped and considered Darragh and Beattie.

'Any ideas?' Beattie said.

Darragh went to the back of the truck and rummaged in the toolbox. 'Pull the truck across the track, Beattie, so they can't go no further.'

She backed the truck up and watched Darragh take the wirecutters to the fence. He cut a gap through then rolled the wire back. Then he got an empty feed bucket and held it out to the cows. They considered it for a moment then followed him through the gap and into the field. Darragh joined the fence with a couple of good twists and jumped back in the truck.

'Don't understand that,' he said. 'Don't understand that at all. How the hell did they get out?'

He had his answer further up the track. The gate was swinging open.

'Who the hell ...'

Beattie let out a sudden yelp. 'Darragh – look!' She was pointing up at the farm. A long van, or was it a bus, was parked sideways in the yard. Even from a distance it was evident it was not the same one from the previous visit: the bodywork and most of the windows were covered in bright strokes of paint – no pattern to it other than what a blind man might achieve. The sight of it put a light under Beattie's feet. 'Hurry, Darragh, quick – it's Conrad. It's the van. They've come back. Oh my Lord, they've come back.'

When they crossed the yard, half choked from the dust they'd raised, the bus – for it was indeed a small bus – was seemingly empty: there was no sign of either Conrad or Vida.

'Must be in the house,' Beattie said.

They pushed in through the door, smiles fixed on their faces, but the kitchen was empty.

'Conrad?' Beattie shouted. 'Vida?' There was a small noise from upstairs, then the sound of a door closing, then Olive appeared on the landing. Beattie charged up the stairs and swept the child into her arms.

'Conrad,' she shouted and pushed open the door of his bedroom. The curtains were closed, the air heavy and sour. One side of the bed was rumpled, the other still occupied – a small shape underneath the counterpane.

'Vida. Is that you?' Beattie chinked the curtains and bent down to the bed. 'Vida?'

Vida hauled herself up. Even in the afternoon glow coming through the curtains Beattie could see the girl was white as milk. And thin: arms like sticks, eyes too big in her face. Her damp hair plastered itself across her bony shoulders.

'Hello,' she said. Her voice was a hoarse whisper.

'Where's Conrad?' Beattie said. 'I can't find him.'

Vida gave a small shrug. 'You and me both. I don't know where he is. He took off months back – signed up with some merchant ship. Big money, he said. Told him I didn't want anything to do with it – Vietnam, you know?'

'But ...' Beattie hesitated. 'The baby?' she said. 'Where's the baby?'

'The baby? Oh, she's here.' Vida reached under the sheet and took out a small bundle. Handed it to Beattie.

'I called her Rose,' Vida said. 'Conrad's not seen her.'

It took three days to get some colour in the girl's cheeks. Fourth day she was already sitting at the kitchen table when Darragh came down, still in his night clothes. She was all dressed up like she was going somewhere.

'I have a favour to ask,' she said, as he set the kettle on the range.

'What favour would that be?' He had a notion it would involve money.

'Could I leave the girls with you a couple of days?'

Beattie had been all for it, she was out of the bed like a firecracker, fixing her leg, pulling on her clothes, Darragh hovering like a backfielder. He pitched all the right objections and she returned them smart as a whip.

'But how will we feed the youngster, Beattie?'

'A feeding bottle, Darragh. We'll water down some of the milk. But she's near enough weaned, anyway.'

'And where will they sleep. What if we don't hear them?'

'Nothing wrong with Conrad's room. It's right next door. I'll fix up a cradle.'

'The farmwork – how'll we do that with a couple of youngsters?'

'We done it before, we'll do it again.'

Darragh was losing ground fast and he knew it, could feel Beattie grabbing this thing with both hands, running for base and not looking back.

'But what if Olive is upset, away from her mother?'

Beattie gave him an arch look. 'We're her kin, Darragh. She'll be settled with us.'

At this point Beattie was dragging the brush through her hair, readying for the bedroom door and Darragh was out of questions. He sat on the edge of the bed a few moments listening to the two women downstairs, the question he'd not had the courage to ask jumping in his throat.

What if she doesn't come back?

They had a short letter from her a couple of weeks later. Henry delivered it by hand to the door – the town was parched for news about the situation and Henry had been tasked with finding out what was going on. He handed the letter over then hung around on the porch, stumbling over unnecessary small talk as Beattie slit open the envelope and pulled out the letter. Her face flushed and she went into the house, leaving him standing. She leaned against the stove and read the letter again:

Dear Darragh and Beattie,

Sorry to stay away so long, it was not something I intended to do. I am fixing a place for me and the girls. Will be back soon as its ready.

Vida.

Ps hope the girls are fine. I miss them so.

Beattie turned the paper over in her hand, then sniffed at it. She examined the envelope – it had been mailed from San Diego. She went out into the yard, muttering to herself. Darragh was in the small barn.

'Look at this,' she said and stood waiting, arms folded over her chest.

'"I miss them so."' Darragh said.

Beattie nodded. 'That's what I thought. Sounds like something she heard in the movies.'

He watched her leave, stepping though the door and out into the sunshine like she was still a girl, ready to take on whatever came her way.

'Come on, Darragh,' she shouted, without looking back. He

levered himself up and followed her out, lining himself up in her slipstream, hoping he might catch a portion of her confidence and breathe it in.

Within weeks Beattie was blooming like a summer rose and whatever light had gone out in her after losing Conrad returned tenfold. This went a long way down the road to settling Darragh's mind. First off he'd skirted around the girls, fearful of getting too attached, one eye always on the lookout for Vida's bus. Eventually though he quit his worrying and got down to the business of enjoying. He took to hurrying down from the fields early just to catch a glimpse of Beattie and the girls; the baby strapped to her chest and Olive like a busy shadow, always at her side: the three of them like some painting, caught up in whatever it was they were doing, the light up and down of their chit-chat soothing as a cool breeze on a hot day. Those first few weeks after their arrival saw just about every woman from town up at the farm, clucking over the girls, exclaiming over Beattie's good fortune – landing herself a second crack at mothering. For months the very sight of them in town or church sent up flurries of excitement.

Although they became generally known as the O'Grady girls, it was evident from the get-go and over the years that followed that the two girls were as unalike, both in nature and appearance, as it is possible to be. Olive, dark-eyed and serious, was quick and impatient, ready to absorb any learning, easy to offend, her busy eyes always looking for the next thing to do. Rose, by comparison, had Beattie's fair colouring; she was a slow and dreamy child, easy to please, rarely angered and happy to shuffle along in her sister's shadow. Nonetheless the four of them together possessed an ease and contentment that made folks smile and The Luck became the place folks stopped by to visit.

Chapter 8

'I swear that girl's headed for great things.' Henry had dropped by for a visit. He and Darragh and Beattie were parked up on the front porch watching Olive lead her latest rescue mare round the corral. It was a sorry-looking sag of bone and skin – worked near to death by the dam crews out west then sent off to the auction house while it was still able to stand. The auctioneer had knocked it down to Darragh for a pittance and Olive had set to work on it the minute they arrived back at The Luck. She was leading it gently round the dusty compound, head leaning lightly against its ribby flank, some soft talk flowing from her lips. The mare was easing already.

'How the hell does she do it?' Henry said. The child was not quite eleven, and as sorry as the mare was, it was twice her height.

'Must be my pa's blood,' Darragh said. 'There was no one like him for horses – not in the whole county of Clare.'

Beattie nodded. It was a story she knew well, but still enjoyed the telling of it. The Irish part of Darragh – the unknown faraway part of him – was the thing about him she loved the best. This was chiefly because she was, at heart, a great romantic and the notion that this man had sailed the wide Atlantic, then flown himself two thousand miles west in order to find her – Beattie Darling – was something that lit a flame in her heart.

'You serious about building more stabling?' Henry said.

'Don't see why not. Sure seems to have the knack for horses. Reckon we'd be wise to encourage that some.'

Henry nodded, then sighed. He still lived at home with his mother. Suspected he was destined to live with her for the duration. Whatever that meant.

By the time Olive was thirteen folks were not just dropping by to pay neighbourly visits, but coming up – often not even bothering to seek out Darragh or Beattie – to consult with the girl on some pressing horse matter. On one occasion Beattie, out in the yard collecting eggs, saw the vet at the corral fence, head down listening intently to whatever advice Olive was delivering. After a few minutes the two of them jumped into the vet's truck and disappeared down the track. She trudged back into the kitchen a couple of hours later, stinking like a barn floor, both arms streaked with some unnameable substance, her hair sticking with straw and God knows what. She downed two glasses of water at the kitchen sink. Beattie raised a questioning eyebrow.

'Picker's mare,' Olive said, in her usual curt way. She murmured to her horses for hours but she didn't have much to say to anyone else. 'Foaling problem. Vet needed some help.'

'Supper?' Beattie said.

'Leave it on the stove – got to get the mares settled.'

Rose looked up from her book at the slamming of the door. 'She better wash up good before she comes to bed. She stinks.'

'You want to go walking?' Beattie said, smiling at the sight of her youngest granddaughter, draped on the sofa like some movie star heroine, a hand-me-down frock of thin floating fabric pooling round her and onto the floor. Her hair – silk as opposed to Beattie's straw – had the same rippling sheen as Vida's. She had a look of Vida that unnerved Beattie at times – called up fears that the woman might suddenly return, take the girls away. This was compounded by the fact that the child possessed a curiosity about her true mother that Olive did not. It left Beattie unsettled, looking for ways to knit the child closer to her.

'Later,' Rose said, turning over another page and settling herself more comfortably on the settee.

By the time she was fifteen years old Olive had a pot of money put away that rivalled most working men. Her occasional work with the vet had become a paid regularity until a lot of folks, preferring her quiet approach, bypassed the man altogether where horses were concerned and came straight to her. It was about this time that Darragh's father, no doubt enchanted by the notion that the girl was following in his footsteps, sent over a book that he considered to be as close to a horse bible as you could get. Written in his own slanting hand it detailed the treatment and care for every horse he'd ever doctored. Olive received it like it was the Holy Sacrament. She disappeared into her bedroom after supper and didn't appear again till breakfast.

'You get some good tips?' Darragh said.

Olive gave him a curt nod. 'They got barley down at the store?'

'Barley?' Darragh stashed a hunk of bread in his mouth.

She got up from the table and went up to her room. She came back down with a small sheet of paper.

'Look at this here,' Olive said. 'I reckon it's a recipe.'

Darragh took the piece of paper and felt the bread wedge behind his Adam's apple. It was a recipe, all right. His father's barley ale recipe.

'Must be in here by mistake,' he said, grabbing a glass of water and tucking the page in his shirt pocket. 'I'll send it back over to Pa next time I write.'

It was a sure thing he would send it back, or better still he might burn it. The O'Grady barley ale recipe for Christ's sake. What was his pa thinking? The man's passion for the horses was one thing but his passion for the brewing, and drinking, of his damn barley ale had been another thing altogether. He'd attributed all manner of benefits to it: his good health and vigour, his alarming head of hair, sharp eyesight, his fiddle playing – the list went on and on, depending on how much of the stuff he'd necked. The drawbacks he overlooked: the way the stuff fuelled his fists, left his mother looking for excuses to stay out of sight of the neighbours; the fact that they had to go without in order to pay for the barley and sugar. This, almost more than the beatings, dealt her a good deal of embarrassment in town and in church. The priest quoted from the safety of the pulpit. The shame of it. Darragh had the man's voice in his ears. *But if any provide not for his own and especially for those of his own house, he hath denied the faith and is worse than an infidel.* His mother, beside him on the pew, red-faced, hiding her stockingless legs beneath her skirt.

'Well, what is it?' Olive said, looking at his shirt pocket.

'Oh ... probably nothing much. But I'll let him have it back.'

She narrowed her eyes at him.

Next morning the sheet of paper was gone from his pocket and Olive was in town with Beattie.

'Buying something or other for the horses,' Rose said, book in hand.

They returned just before noon – Darragh, up on the high ground, taking a pause from his fence fixing, eyed the truck, trying to make out what kind of supplies were stashed in the back. A couple of sacks for sure. He piled up his tools and set off for the farm, practising the words as he went. 'No pastime for a young woman, Olive.' No. That wouldn't wash. 'It probably ain't legal, Olive.' No – that might be true in some places but not in Oaklake. He was wasting his time because when he got to the yard there was no sign of either Olive or Beattie. He went into the house – no Rose either. He stepped onto the porch and listened. It was Beattie's laugh pointed the way, that and the sound of metal scraping against stone. The three of them suddenly appeared from behind the small barn, Beattie walking backwards, laughing and red in the face, her hands gripping the rim of an old bathtub, the two girls giggling and staggering at the other end trying to hoist the thing off the ground.

'Darragh. Thank God!' Beattie shouted, letting her end drop with a clang. 'See what this child's got us doing ...' she was doubled up laughing. 'Come and give us a hand.'

'What's going on?' he said, eyeing up the sack of barley by the barn door.

'It's the recipe your pa sent over. Olive wants to try it out.'

A couple of months later – Darragh was at the kitchen table soaking his aching feet in a bowl of salt water – Olive sauntered into the kitchen. Beattie and Rose followed.

'Think it might be ready,' Olive said, putting a corked bottle down in front of him. Darragh eyed the bottle – it sure looked like the right colour – and pulled the cork. The scent of the stuff traced some panic in him, tugged at it like a loose thread. Home. He closed his eyes and took a sip. He let the tan liquid slide over his tongue, held it for a few seconds then let it slip down his throat. It stroked his gullet like a silk glove.

'Well,' Olive said, her small face screwed up and concentrating. 'Is it right? Is it like Grandpa's?'

Darragh took another sip. 'Mmmh,' he said, his eyebrows working like two caterpillars. 'Maybe something missing here ...' He took another sip.

'What?' Olive said. 'What does it need? Is it not right?'

'No ...' Darragh was deliberating, swirling his glass. 'I reckon it just needs ...'

'What?' Olive screeched. 'What the hell does it need?'

Darragh got up from the table, took two glasses from the cupboard, then went to the radio. The set slowly cranked into life. Beattie's face lit up.

'Just needs a bit of good fiddle music,' he said, filling the glasses and passing one to Beattie.

'Congratulations, girl,' he said, holding his glass aloft, his foot tapping along to the swell of the fiddle, 'because that is one fine O'Grady barley ale.'

Olive sweated over the recipe for another few months, adding some secret ingredient to the next brew that gave it a warm tang of a hearth fire then took a batch down to The Ponderosa to see what folks thought of it. Her idea of bottling it young, before its full kick developed, paid off and before long The Ponderosa folks took to asking for it above whiskey.

By the time she was seventeen years old it was plain that Olive was only headed in one direction: she'd acquired a head for business that left Darragh and Beattie reeling and a stack of money just asking to be invested. Her opportunity came when Hank Barnum decided to sell the general store and she decided that she'd be the person to buy it.

'Sure would be a good idea, Olive, perhaps if you was a mite older ...'

Darragh was in the barn working on the tractor – and rehearsing his words. Olive had already tackled the subject with Beattie and it had gone badly – Beattie in tears and Olive slamming out of the house. It was his turn now and he sure as hell wasn't up to it.

'I've got the money idling for some good use,' – her hands on her hips, one foot thrust forward like a challenge – 'What's the sense in waiting? Barnum's up and going. I might not get another chance.'

She was right. But she was seventeen.

'But ...' She levelled him with a glare that had him turning away. He was down without a fight.

'If you was to buy it ... ' Her face lit up some. 'Well, if you *was* to buy it ...' He was in deep water now. He ploughed through. 'Well, me and your grandma,' his voice wavered – Beattie had said nothing of the sort. 'Me and your grandma would want you to live up here at the farm. We don't want you moving into town.'

She gave him a serious look. 'Why would I be moving to town? The horses are up here.'

So it was that Olive O'Grady became the owner of the general store. First thing she did was paint it up – reckoned the sight of herself sanding down the boards, licking on fresh paint, buffing up the window glass would get the town folks used to the idea. As it was, she needn't have concerned herself: before she'd even reopened folks were stopping by to talk horse problems and by the end of her first week of trading, the opening ceremony fuelled with Beattie's beef pasties and the O'Grady barley ale, she was sold out of horse tack and ale.

Chapter 9

When Beattie looked back, a few months later – her feet never having touched the ground (so to speak), her being caught up with Olive and the store – she realised she'd missed the moment that Rose had changed, had failed to notice that her youngest granddaughter had somehow transformed from a languishing bookworm into Oaklake's own version of a movie star.

It was a Friday. Beattie was out front of the store, sweeping the boards and working up to shining the windows when she saw Darragh pull the truck up outside the mail office. Darragh strode around to the passenger door and swung it open. A woman stepped out and Beattie's heart lurched. She put down the broom and watched. Vida? Was it Vida? The length of rippling gold running down her back and the soft billow of her skirt said that it was, but as Beattie watched, the woman took hold of Darragh's arm and the pair set off towards the mail room. Rose. It was Rose. Beattie felt nothing but alarm – alarm that she'd somehow missed the transformation, that she'd neglected the child and failed to notice what must have been taking place under her very nose. She left her work and made her way across the street. She could see Rose inside the mail office handing something over to Henry. Darragh was outside on the front steps, talking to Hank Picker. As she drew level with the mail room the door opened and Rose glided out. *Glided.* It was the only way to describe it – and Beattie swore that the air itself let out a sigh and every man on the street stopped and turned to look.

'Grandma,' Rose said, her smile just about taking the shine out of the sun. The girl rushed forward, the breeze running through her hair like it just couldn't resist, lifting her light dress for the pleasure of touching her.

'Rose.' Beattie heard the awkwardness in her own voice. 'You look ... you look so lovely. So ... '

Rose swirled around, holding her dress out, laughing. 'You like it?'

'It's lovely ... I never saw it before, did I?'

'You did, Grandma! It's Mama's! It's out of Mama's box.'

The wind left Beattie's sails and she grounded somewhere stony and shallow. 'Your mama's box? But when ...'

'Oh – I found it a while back. Olive shifted a pile of stuff from the closet and it was in there – at the back!'

'Oh.' The child was so *thrilled* Beattie couldn't think what to say. She'd given the box to Olive years back, knowing that she'd pay it no attention, that it'd pose no threat. It had got pushed out of her mind but here it was, back again, unleashing its power when she wasn't prepared.

'You been in the mailroom, then?'

'Yes!' Rose was all joy. 'I found an address. It was in the box. I've mailed off a letter to Mama. Well – I reckon it won't get there of course, but ...' She broke off, her face coloured up. 'Sorry, Grandma. I should have talked to you about it first. It's just that ...'

'Well, what do you think of this young woman, then?'

It was Darragh, beaming at her. Beattie hauled a smile onto her face. Wooden and awkward, any words she might have spoken stuck crossways in her gullet.

'She ...'

'She's a real picture, no?'

Beattie swallowed hard and nodded, her cheeks aching with the effort of keeping the corners of her mouth aloft, her head like cold wind was blowing round it. *Rose had mailed a letter to Vida.*

The portion of her that could still think straight counselled that there was nothing to worry about: Vida wasn't there. She knew that for sure – for years she'd visited San Francisco – been to the shipyards, to Conrad's home, trawled the streets and bars parched for some news of him. He'd taken up with the Merchant Navy –

that's all she found out. She'd given it up in the end – settled for bringing up his girls, imagined him some place warm and homely – some place too far away to contact her.

'Well, hello there, Gil.'

Beattie swung round. Darragh was smiling hard and holding out his hand to Gil McKenzie who was heading towards the three of them – his eyes fixed on Rose.

'Afternoon to you, Mr O'Grady, Mrs O'Grady …' He paused, face lit up with something like mischief. 'And Miss O'Grady.' He gave a slight bow. Rose flushed then gave a small laugh and flushed some more.

'Don't suppose you folks would be interested in a little refreshment? I hear The Ponderosa has got a new line of sodas in?' He was looking at Rose.

Darragh jumped in, which was just as well because Beattie found herself caught in some kind of net that seemed to have wrapped itself round her throat.

'Well, Beattie and I have a few errands to do – after she's finished up here. Why don't you and Rose go along and we'll catch up with you there when we're done?'

Beattie stared at him. Had the man gone mad? Did he not know that Gil McKenzie had been trailing around after Olive these last few months – trailing but not getting anywhere? She waited till the pair were across the street.

'Darragh,' she hissed. 'What were you thinking?'

'Who was that with Gil?'

Beattie spun round. Olive was in the shop doorway, hands on bony hips, elbows pointing east and west, a scowl like a bad storm settled on her brow.

'It was Rose,' Darragh announced, smiling. Still not appreciating the situation.

'Rose?' Olive said, eyes fixed on the pair as they approached The Ponderosa, Gil pausing to hold the door open. 'Rose who?'

Darragh gave a hearty laugh – a sure sign, Beattie reckoned, that he'd felt soft ground beneath his feet.

'Our Rose, of course. We're just going over there now, isn't that right, Beatt? Gil's ordering soda for us ... you, erm, going to join us?' His voice trailed off over a cliff. He wiped a bead of sweat off his forehead.

Olive narrowed her eyes at him. Then slammed back into the store.

Beattie abandoned her cleaning cloth and hightailed Darragh across the street and into The Ponderosa. Gil and Rose were in one of the booths, deep in conversation, untouched glasses of soda parked on the table. They didn't look up until Beattie and Darragh were almost upon them. Fortunately, they'd managed to get themselves seated before Olive walked in. She'd changed her frock and loosed her hair. Gil leapt up.

'Olive. What a swell surprise. We was just sampling the new sodas. Here, have a seat. What you having?' He was all smiles.

Olive was not. She sidled past Darragh's knees and wedged herself in beside Gil, threw a glance in Rose's direction and snatched up the menu. Beattie felt the fizz go out of her soda. She nudged Darragh's foot under the table. He didn't notice.

'So, Gil,' Darragh said, settling back in his seat like he was squaring up for a good natter ...

Beattie picked up her glass and drained it. 'Maybe we should be getting along, Mr O'Grady,' she said. 'Leave these young folks to it.' Darragh gave her a blank look and didn't move. 'Yes. I was aiming to get a batch of those plums bottled,' she said, grasping at the first idea that came to her. 'Sure could use a hand, though.' She looked at Rose. Rose was gazing at Gil.

Beattie tilted the empty glass to her lips and banged it down on the table. Rose flinched but didn't quit her gazing.

'Well, I sure as hell can't help,' Olive said, planting her elbows on the table and tossing her loosed hair with something of a flourish. Store won't run itself.'

Darragh gave a small sigh. Beattie knew what was coming next. 'Did I ever tell you,' he said, his eyes already misting up, 'about the first time I saw your ...'

'Darragh.' Beattie grabbed his hat off the table and thrust it at him, her two eyebrows knit into one.

'Sorry, dear?'

'I said we should be getting along. Those plums? Bottling?'

'Oh,' he said. 'Well I was fixing to check on those new ewes. Can't rightly say I'm relishing the trek up there, mind you.'

Beattie saw her chance. 'Well what about a bit of company?' she said, flicking her in Rose's direction. 'Job's always easier with two. How about it, Rose? You up for helping?'

'Sure,' Rose said, although Beattie wasn't convinced the girl rightly knew what she was signing up for.

Beattie blew out a sigh of relief. Rose was half off her seat, smoothing her dress down, her hair slipping forward, catching the sun. Olive's face settled somewhere between a smile and a sneer. She shifted herself an inch nearer to Gil. Gil stood up.

'But you've not finished your soda,' he said, his eyes latched on Rose.

Rose pushed her glass across the table. 'You finish it for me, Olive. I'll go back and help Grandpa.'

Beattie wasted no time. She levered herself out of the booth and took Rose's arm. Gil was still on his feet.

'But ...'

For a minute Beattie thought he was going to come running after them. From where she was standing, she could just about hear his brain working.

'But ... wait. Hang on. Hey, I'm at a loose end this afternoon. Why don't I drive Rose up to The Luck? That way she can sit with me and Olive, finish her soda, then we'll come on up together. Might even lend a hand with the ewes.'

Rose hesitated, slipped her arm away from Beattie.

'If you're at a loose end, Gil McKenzie, there's a hundred and one things I need doing at the store.' Olive's voice was steel wound round silk. Threat and promise.

Gil sat back down and Beattie, muttering silent thanks, ushered Rose and Darragh out through the door.

Chapter 10

Gil McKenzie was not Oaklake born and bred – his family having upped sticks from California (too hot, too fast) and relocated to the soothing greenness of Oaklake when Gil was just approaching his twelfth birthday. Their arrival one Saturday afternoon in late August – boxes and suitcases strapped on the top of an old powder blue Caddy – had drawn long looks from the street corners and whispered conversations in Barnum's General Store.

It soon transpired that the feller who drove Mrs McKenzie into town was not her husband, but her brother. She was, in fact, a widow. The news caused a certain amount of alarm because Mimi McKenzie was a young and handsome woman. She stirred more dust up when, a few days after arriving, she put a fancy sign in her front window announcing her skills as a seamstress and dressmaker. It was ignored for several days until Gladys Fox, in a lather about a dress for her son's wedding – him living the high life in California – took the bit between her teeth and presented herself at the McKenzie house. She came back out a couple of hours later with a bag of cloth swatches and a smile on her face. It was all Mimi McKenzie needed: by the end of the week near enough every woman in town had paid her a visit and her order book was stuffed full.

If there was any doubt remaining as to the McKenzie family credentials, they were put to rest the first Monday in September when Gil, accompanied by his mother, arrived at the schoolhouse. The boy was like a gold magnet. By the time he got sat down in class every child in the school wanted to be near him. Even Miss Turbot seemed to loosen up and found herself pausing by his desk for no particular reason. It was like he had a seam of sunshine running through him: whether it was his nature or the California light in his bones, he seemed to radiate a warm attraction that no one could resist. He was simply a pleasing and pleasurable person. He settled into town like a cat in the sun, easing his way through school, acquiring a reputation for kindliness and hard work. Five years later, when his mother packed him off to college, half the town waved him away.

When he returned to Oaklake, several inches taller, handsome in a way that spoke of soft manners and good humour, he took the assistant manager's job at the woodyard, helping out part time at Barnum's store – mostly on the accounting side. It was about this time that Barnum, considering himself long in the tooth and ready for easier days, got to thinking about selling the store. He'd discussed it at some length with Mrs McKenzie – presenting it as a fine opportunity for her and her boy. By that time her reputation as a seamstress had stretched far beyond the town and she'd bought a small cabin next to the pharmacy and set up a workroom and fabric shop, so it might well have made sense. Before she had time to consider it however, news spread that Olive O'Grady from The Luck was casting her eye over it.

Gil knew of the O'Grady girls of course, but didn't rightly know them: he was a handful of years older than them and his time away at college had coincided with the years they'd started coming into town more frequently. Consequently, it would be fair to say that when he first got sight of Olive O'Grady striding across the street towards Barnum's he was somewhat taken aback. And somewhat interested. She was a striking young woman – not in terms of real beauty – but the way she bore herself: upright, intent, like she was held up with strong wires, the air parting before her as she walked. When it transpired that Olive was actually going to buy the place he'd spotted an opportunity and allowed Barnum to offer his part-time services to Olive O'Grady as part of the purchasing deal. She'd not taken up the offer. That had left him trying to find other ways of getting in her line of vision. It had not been easy. Old Barnum had given him a few conversation pointers – in particular her expertise with horses and ale – but his attempts to engage her interest had fallen on ground so stony and barren it kept him from sleeping.

Fortunately Gil McKenzie had a number of things in his favour. The first was that he was the only young man in town fool enough to even consider wooing Olive O'Grady. The second was his experience when it came to the secret workings of women. This was in no way due to romantic dalliances on his part but rather to his mother's work: the steady stream of ladies who passed through the sewing room gracing him with an education regarding the art of chit-chat and friendliness. This should have given him a head start when it came to Olive O'Grady, but it did not. If she did notice him – and he was pretty sure she didn't – it was more in the manner of a horse eyeing a troublesome fly. However the third, and most practical thing in Gil's favour, was the proximity of the woodyard to the general store: he wandered across the street most lunchtimes to peruse the merchandise – and Olive. He sidled the aisles, peering over the shelves of canned goods, made a slow show of examining whatever new tool she had in, feigned interest in the stack of seeds and beans. It was the way she moved that got him so tied up: a hasty impatience firing every task. She managed the store like she was in a race and fixing to win. The more she ignored him the more he sweated over it until his every waking moment was like some tortured play – him concocting and rehearsing small scenarios that always fell flat and left him red-faced and floundering, then, like some confounded moth going back for more, batting his head against the light in her that only he could see. Until, that is, the day he set eyes on Rose.

Rose O'Grady. She swung his gaze from Olive sure as if he was a lighthouse and she was a new ship in the bay: the lightness of her, the softness, the gold of her hair. Olive, full rattled by the threat of her sister, suddenly raised her flags, changed course and steered at top speed towards him and Gil McKenzie found himself in a fix: Olive and Rose on either side of him and him in the middle, floundering. He no longer visited the store at lunchtimes but sat on the woodyard porch instead, staring out over the town, neglecting to eat his food, a look of such bewilderment on his face that folks, amused as they were by his predicament, let him be. Olive's change of heart was clear as a news headline – hell, some days she walked over from the store and sat with him a while – the two of them casting their eyes over the street, sharing whatever piece of pie or cookie she'd brought him. But you could see his heart wasn't in it. It was with Rose: any time she appeared in town the door of the woodyard office would fly open and out he would barrel, arm raised, hailing her across the street, the two of them through the door of The Ponderosa before Olive even had chance to whip her apron off.

Then one afternoon fate intervened. Rose received a letter from Vida.

Chapter 11

The train platform was thick with luggage and the tang of fumes from the locomotives, rising to meet the throbbing heat of the noonday sun, cast a noxious, nauseating cloud over the folks waiting for the San Francisco train. Beattie was doing her damnedest not to cry, concentrating instead on the dull, pulsing pressure on the top of her head.

'Your ticket,' Beattie said. 'Sure you've got it handy, the conductor will ...'

'I have it here, Grandma.' Rose pulled it out of her travelling bag with a flourish. Smiling. She hadn't stopped smiling since Vida's letter had arrived.

'And your food, do you have ...'

'I have it. Here, look.' Rose gaped open the top of her bag – the brown package of pie there for Beattie to see, the slice of cake in wax paper from Olive. Olive. She'd handed it over with a smile on her face like she was the new queen measuring up the throne. Gil had waved from the woodyard porch and Beattie couldn't rightly fathom the expression on his face – whether Rose's departure was an agony or a relief. Darragh had taken the easy way – a cow near calving, apparently. She understood. He would not have been able to let the girl go. He would have barred her from the carriage or pulled her up out of her seat, or worse still stationed himself in front of the locomotive preventing its departure and causing an almighty embarrassment. Instead he'd poked his head round the bedroom door, early, while she was still in bed and dozing, too sleepy to notice the catch in his voice and tears in his eyes. Then he'd stomped off to the top barn and kept watch, following the trail of the truck till it was out of sight.

'You'll contact Henry as soon as you get there?'

'Yes, Grandma, look. I have the mail room number written right here.'

'And Vida is meeting you at the station?'

'She is.' Rose stepped closer to Beattie and took hold of her hands. Soft, she was so soft. 'Don't worry about me, Grandma, I'll be fine. I'll be back at the end of the week.' She leaned in and kissed Beattie's cheek, the tender scent of her unleashing the tears. No matter what the girl said Beattie knew she wouldn't be back. When Vida's letter had arrived they had read it over and over, examining every line, word, comma: everything it said lightened Rose's step and bore down on Beattie's chest. She had forced herself to face the thing she most feared – they were going to lose Rose just as they'd lost Conrad.

Vida, it transpired, was some kind of actress. The theatre. A lifestyle about which Beattie was ignorant – and mortally suspicious. She'd mailed Vida, begging her to take good care of the child, emphasising her young age, her farm upbringing, asking her to keep in contact, saying she was willing to travel out and visit – if required. If required. Truth was she wouldn't know how to address the woman, how to strike a civil conversation with her.

'Grandma ...'

Beattie looked up, suddenly aware that folks were moving, a murmur rippling through the crowd.

'The train's here.'

With Rose out of the way Olive set about convincing Gil McKenzie that she was the only O'Grady girl worth thinking about. Disregarding his distracted demeanour, his tendency to sit staring out the window saying nothing unless prompted, she plied him with her company and a whirlwind of engagements: lunches at The Ponderosa, suppers up at the farm, strolls by the lake – and trips across to the island.

'Not rightly sure I know what's going on there,' Darragh said one evening.

He and Beattie were watching Gil and Olive. The pair of them mooching down the lane, a basket of food between them. He could feel it already, the pang that started somewhere behind his breastbone and stretched itself into his throat. Like some iron pipe. Thought he'd got that one licked – or pretended he did. All those years with Conrad, he'd had no choice: learned to swim in some kind of fashion; even took the boat out on the lake with Beattie on occasion but never – never – did he have any feeling of certainty. Always the pull in his guts, the readiness for disaster taking the spit from his mouth. And now, Gil and Olive. Rowing to the island, *again*. He'd get no rest till they got back.

'You don't know or you don't approve?' Beattie said, half smiling. She'd taken off her wooden leg and was massaging her knee. She'd shed some weight since Rose's departure and the stump below the knee was showing more bone.

Darragh chuckled. 'Don't know that approval's ever come into anything as far as Olive's concerned. When her mind's set on a thing it don't seem that important to her what other people think.'

'Well, sure looks like she's got her mind set on something now.'

'Just hope he knows what he's letting himself in for.'

Beattie let out a whoop of a laugh and Darragh felt his breath come a cinch more easy – it was the first time she'd laughed since Rose had left, first bit of light he'd seen on her face.

By the end of the month it seemed that Gil had made a decision. Whether it was the fact that Rose had written from San Francisco saying she was going to stay on for a while longer, that she'd gotten a job in the wardrobe room at Vida's theatre, or that Olive's attentions had paid off, it became evident that Gil had let go of Rose and chosen Olive. Their ensuing courtship sparked much amused speculation in the town – Olive usually attracting the lion's share of interest, which, for the first few weeks of their courting boiled down to *how did she get him?* and became, as time wore on, *how does she keep him?* But keep him she did and, seeing them together in those early days – always arm in arm – his face turned down towards her in some quiet conversation, it was apparent they fit together like jigsaw pieces. In some strange way that only nature understood they were two halves that made a whole, the left and right that became a pair.

Consequently, as the weeks and months passed, Beattie found her mind wandering from its usual treadmill of worries regarding Rose's well-being to more fanciful thoughts about Olive's future. To thoughts of possible weddings, marriage. She'd struck up a friendship with Mimi and the two of them indulged flights of fancy that Olive would have snorted at.

'What if she didn't want a dress at all?' Mimi chanced one afternoon. 'What if she didn't want to get fancied up?' A slice of sun was chinking through the curtains, lighting up the dust in the air: fine motes of thread and lint suspended like they were floating in sunlit water.

'Get wed in britches you mean?' Beattie said, laughing, remembering her own wedding – her pa hiding her every pair of britches, insisting she wore her ma's wedding frock.

'What about this one?' Mimi said, pushing the pattern book over to Beattie.

'Mmmhh. More Rose than Olive I would say.'

Mimi was silent for a moment, cleared her throat quietly. 'He was smitten with her, you know. With Rose. He ...'

Beattie rested her hand atop of Mimi's. 'I know he was. But ... well. I don't know if ...' She couldn't say the words.

'You think she won't come back?'

Beattie shook her head. 'You saw her. She's got a whole lot of life in her.'

'And you don't think that would have suited Gil?' There was a bridling edge to Mimi's voice.

'No, I didn't mean that. I meant ... I don't think that would have suited staying here in Oaklake. She needed to get away. Like her father.'

Beattie's voice trailed off: seemed to her that even when you were thinking of the future the past rose up and rolled over you like some unexpected wave, knocking the breath out of you.

A few weeks later Darragh came down from the top field early. Olive and Gil were trailing behind him, hand in hand, deep in conversation, smiling. Beattie set the kettle on the stove and parked herself at the kitchen table. Waiting. She studied Darragh's face as he came in through the door.

'You're down early,' she said, anticipation of what was about to come spreading a grin on her face.

He grinned back but said nothing, stood to one side as Gil and Olive followed him in.

'Closed the store early today?' she said to Olive, who was still holding onto Gil's hand. Gil cleared his throat, but Olive spoke up before he had chance to get started.

'September 30th,' she said. 'Me and Gil are getting wed on September 30th. Grandpa agreed. Have you got Rose's address – I need to tell her.'

Beattie didn't miss the satisfaction licking round the edges of her words.

Chapter 12

It was decided, in the run-up to the wedding, that Gil would quit his job at the woodyard and start working with Olive at the store. It seemed like nothing of a decision at the time but it ended up changing everything.

When he was informed of Gil's impending departure, Danish Bridie, the manager of the woodyard, set about finding a replacement and, instead of posting advertisements, made a phone call to his brother, Griff, who ran a similar woodyard further north. The brother had an instant recommendation: a new friend, a young Irish feller recently over from Galway and keen to find office work. Experienced, good with numbers and bearing references that spoke admiringly of his skills and character. Bridie sent for him at once.

Michael Kelly, thirty-two years old and more handsome than any man had a right to be, arrived in Oaklake at the end of August. He made his way from the rail station and into town on foot which meant that by the time he hit the main street most folks, forewarned by Henry, the mailman, were out front ready to watch him walk past. He hit town like a fever. He had an easy air to him, nodding and smiling at everyone he saw, stopping briefly outside the pharmacy to ask Macy Creasy the way to the woodyard office. Her embarrassed laughter tinkled across the street as she pointed out the direction, dabbing at the hopeless heat in her cheeks with a stiff handkerchief. He shook her hand which prompted another high shriek and then a soft sigh as he strode away.

Gil looked up from the ledger book when the door to the office opened and a man, young but older than himself, walked in. Danish was down in the yard fixing the oil sump of the planing rig.

'Michael Kelly,' the man said, striding towards the desk, his hand outstretched. 'I'm here about the job. I'm to see Mr Bridie?' His voice carried the same smooth lilt as Darragh's. He looked, to Gil, like he had stepped clean out of a Hollywood movie: his skin, his eyes, his hair – everything about him was dazzling.

'Gil McKenzie,' he said, getting to his feet taking the man's hand in his own. 'Danish is down in the yard. I'll tell him you're here.' He left the office, weaving through the queue of curious town folk already loitering on the front porch. When he brought Danish back into the office, he excused himself and went over to the store.

'He's like a damn movie star, Olive, honest to God, just like a movie star.'

Olive was down on all fours, giving the floor hell with an oversized scrubbing brush.

'A movie star? Thought Danish wanted himself a bookkeeper? Anyway ... ' she dumped her brush in the bucket of soapy water and sat back on her heels, grinning up at him, 'I thought Oaklake already had its movie star ... Mr McKenzie.'

Gil felt himself colouring up but smiled back just the same. Compliments and sweet talk were not the top of Olive's list. Truth be told their after-supper talk these days was not of the upcoming wedding but of the store – how they could improve sales, increase their stock. They were planning on opening up the loft above the store and making some living space – their own home. For Gil, the more they spoke of the future the more real it became and Rose ... his memories of Rose diminished until they felt like a half-remembered dream.

'Good grief, is that the man? Is that him?' Olive was up off the floor and peering over his shoulder. Gil turned and saw Michael Kelly on the front porch of the woodyard, shaking hands with Danish.

'Well, I guess you weren't exaggerating,' Olive said, walking to the store front. 'Mmph, looks like he's heading over this way. Well, I won't be putting no goddamn red carpet out for him.' She picked up her bucket and disappeared out back.

Gil watched Kelly's approach: an athletic ease to each stride. He had the look of a man who never hurried and never had cause to worry, like he always slept well, was in a constant good humour. He ambled in through the door of the store, and Gil swore the sun came in with him. He turned his head this way and that, taking in the shelves of merchandise, the gleaming oak counter, his face lit with what appeared to be genuine pleasure.

'So this is the reason you're quitting the woodyard?' he said to Gil, his two arms held wide like he was conducting an orchestra.

'It is,' Gil said.

'And a very good reason I would say – it's a cracking good store you have here.' He was perusing the shelves, examining Olive's horse supplies.

'Well, strictly speaking, it doesn't belong to me, it ...'

The door behind the counter suddenly opened and Olive waltzed in – carrying a pile of oatmeal boxes.

'Well, hello there,' Kelly said, his smile ricocheting off the polished oak and hitting Olive full in the chops. She tripped slightly and the boxes tumbled onto the counter. Kelly sprang to action; he had them stacked before she had chance to object. She stood watching, her cheeks grazed with colour, a hank of her hair escaped and curling round her cheek.

'Michael Kelly,' he said, hand outstretched.

'Olive O'Grady,' Olive said. She jabbed her own arm towards him and shook his hand with a grip that brought water to his eyes. Then she set about rearranging the boxes of oatmeal.

'So, you worked here long, Miss O'Grady?' Kelly said, rubbing his hand.

Olive gave a small snort and ignored the question. Gil stepped forward.

'The store belongs to Miss O'Grady. When we marry – next month that is – I'll be working here too, we'll run the place together. We're going to expand. Isn't that right, Olive?' He looked over at her. She glared back.

'So, can I help you with anything, Mr Kelly?

Kelly wandered back to the shelves of horse tack and leather wear. He selected a pale, hand-tooled bridle and brought it to the counter.

'I wanted to ask you about this,' he said, his eyes fixing on hers. 'This might just be the prettiest bridle I ever saw. The toolwork here,' he fingered the soft leather like it was a woman's cheek, 'is head and shoulders the most delightful thing I ever saw.'

Olive flushed from the top of her collar to the tip of her forehead.

'Oh,' she said, clutching at her throat. 'Oh, that. Yes. No ... it's nothing. A winter hobby, you know. Quiet round here.' She gave a strangled laugh and reached for the bridle.

'Well, I daresay it might be just the thing for my youngest sister. Perhaps you could hold it for me and, when I return to take up the job ...'

'Ah, you got the job then,' Gil said, glad of the opportunity to insert himself back into the equation. He'd no sooner said it when Macy Creasy walked, or to be more accurate, almost skipped into the store. Clary and Darcy Montgomery were traipsing behind her giddy as flower girls. Kelly turned to the three of them and doffed an imaginary hat. They spluttered into high tittering, hands fluttering like small birds. Olive turned her attention back to the oatmeal boxes, then went back into the storeroom hoping its coolness would take the heat out of her cheeks.

Chapter 13

Gil spent the rest of the afternoon in quiet agitation: eyes flitting regularly from his bookwork to the window of the store. He was pretty damn sure he hadn't seen Michael Kelly leave and, though he did not consider himself a jealous kind of feller, for some reason it irked the hell out of him. Macy Creasy and her girls had teetered off a half hour earlier, but he was sure Michael Kelly was still in there with Olive. By 4pm he could no longer contain himself. He closed up his accounts and wandered, as nonchalantly as he could, over to the store. Olive was at the counter, weighing out scoops of corn for Gabriel Clodagh's wife, Pearl. Her two youngsters, twin boys if he remembered rightly, were on the counter, gazing alternately at the weighing scales to their left and the glass jar of lollies to their right. Olive looked over at him. She had a smudge of flour on the end of her nose.

'Finished early?' she said, nodding over at the clock on the wall.

'No – just thought I'd come see you. You know ...' Pearl Clodagh gave him an endearing look.

'Oh, enjoy it while you can,' she said to Olive, 'before these start coming along.' She patted her two boys on the head then rubbed the full roundness of her belly, throwing Olive what she reckoned to be a motherly beam. The woman, to Olive's eye, looked exhausted. Or unhinged.

Gil glanced quickly round the store: there was no sign of Kelly. He made some excuse for needing water and ducked behind the counter and into the back room. It was empty. He came out just as the Clodagh woman was leaving. Olive was hauling the sack of corn back under the shelf.

'God forbid I ever get like that,' she said, straightening up and wiping her hands on her apron.

'Like what?' Gil said.

'Like that. Clodagh's wife. She's like a damn brood mare.'

A small bubble of panic floated up and burst, sour and disconcerting, at the back of his throat. He swallowed it down.

'But ... don't ... You do want a family, don't you Olive? Like, we are intending to raise us a family, aren't we?'

'Oh. Yes. Of course we are. But not right now, Gil. Not while we've got the store to develop and a home to build.'

She was busying herself with the duster, her back towards him. He glanced at the door and up the street. It was quiet. He put his arms around her waist and circled around her so that he was facing her. The smudge of flour still dusted the end of her nose. He wiped it off gently with his thumb tip then kissed her – lightly at first, then pressing his lips harder. She struggled out of his arms. 'Gil, what the hell has gotten into you?'

'What say we row over to the island tonight?' he said, as she stepped away from him, straightening her dress and looking at the door.

'The island?' she said. Her face clouded over: despite Beattie and Darragh's assumptions the island trips had never involved anything more than talking and picnicking. Sure there had been a certain amount of physical endeavour on Gil's part, but she'd met it with resistance. She'd not wanted it, or she was determined to wait – she wasn't quite sure which one it was.

'We could go over,' she said, picking the duster back up, 'but it would have to be after supper. I've got horse work to do.'

'Well, you want I come up and give you a hand?'

'No. I'll get on quicker by myself. Come over around seven. Now ...' – she gave him a flick with the duster – 'get out from under my feet or I'll never get the store closed up.'

Gil got up to The Luck a mite after seven, him having got waylaid by old man Creasy. The corral was empty, neither Olive nor horses to be seen. He pulled the truck up to the fence and wandered over to the stable block. Champion and Moriah, Olive's two geldings, were out, the door to their stable wedged open, the wind blowing balls of scuddy hay round the empty stalls.

He walked toward the farmhouse: Darragh was out on the porch with a pail of paint and a brush the size of a young porcupine. He was wielding it with both hands. The upcoming wedding had sent Darragh and Beattie into something of a frenzy, the intention being that after the church ceremony folks would come up to The Luck for the reception. This had demanded a good deal of sweat and hard labour and, as far as Darragh was concerned, the sooner the damn thing was over the better. Mimi was more or less a full instalment in the kitchen – her and Beattie either hunched over some list or else strewing the place with God knows what. All he knew was the cake was made and not to be interfered with and he was, on no account, to go into Rose's bedroom because that's where the outfits were being constructed. His included. His portion of it was to paint the house front and porch railings and get the track and hedge and front yard in good order.

'You think we should get the Annie O'Grady out of her wraps?' he'd asked Beattie that evening, after the supper dishes had been cleared and the table covered afresh with wedding paraphernalia. She'd looked up from her needlework.

'What do you mean. Get her out and fly her?'

That's not what Darragh had been thinking – his flying days were long finished – he'd not been up since Conrad had been born. They'd decided, he and Beattie, that parenting didn't mix with flying. They didn't want to raise a child who was going to hanker for the sky. Never bargained for one who hankered for water.

'No,' he said. 'I mean decorate her up, let folks sit in her.'

Beattie looked over at Mimi. 'We could rig up some bunting with the bits left over. What do you think?' Mimi emerged from a heap of fancy lace cloth, loose threads hanging in her hair.

'What the hell's the Annie O'Grady?' she said, picking a pin from her teeth.

Beattie let out a low chuckle. 'It's the plane. Darragh's old Piper. From his dusting days. It's in the big barn. Been there, what, near forty years? You think it would come out, then?'

'Yep,' Darragh said, picking blue paint off his finger nails. Reckon she would come out fine. Might enjoy feeling a bit of sunshine on her old wings.'

'How's the house painting coming on? Looked to me like you still had a whole lot to do. And the yard – the yard's still to clear so's we can get the big tent up. And the track could still ...'

'Reckon I could still manage it all if I had a bit of a hand. Young Mr Kelly might have a bit of time on his hands, you know, might be able to offer a few hours.'

'Mr Kelly?' Beattie scowled over at him. 'I'd have thought Gil ought to be the man you're asking.'

Truth was Beattie was champing at the bit to give Darragh a rousting. Not only had he appeared, an hour before supper, with Michael Kelly in tow – the two of them having spent a couple of hours in The Ponderosa – he'd then taken leave of all his senses and suggested, nay insisted, that Olive take the young Irishman out on the horses. To her credit Olive made any number of excuses but finally relinquished, agreeing to a short ride to the top boundary. Beattie checked the clock. That had been over an hour ago.

'Well, I reckon I'll get back to it, then,' Darragh said, getting up from the table. Sheepish.

'Yes, you do that,' Beattie said, without looking at him. He sidled back out onto the porch and hauled the brush out of the paint pail. His stint in The Ponderosa had earned him a headache, but it was nothing like the one Beattie was going to give him over Michael Kelly.

'S'looking good, Darragh.'

Darragh turned, brush in hand. Gil was standing well back from the railings, looking up at him.

'Olive inside?'

'Olive?' Darragh said, swiping his arm across his face, spreading a smear of paint across one cheek. It hid the flush of guilty colour that had risen at the thought of Olive being out with Michael Kelly. Oh, he'd messed up good and proper. Again. 'She not down with the horses?'

'No. Thought maybe she was out riding with Beattie. Champion's out. And Moriah.'

Darragh swallowed hard. 'Oh, she must still be out with the young Irish feller, then. She was showing him ...'

'The young Irish feller? What do you mean?'

Darragh gulped then turned his back to Gil, reckoning to fill in some missing patch. 'Kelly. Michael Kelly, you know, the feller who's having your job. Yes, yes ... I met him in town and we had a couple of glasses in The Ponderosa. Grand feller ... from Galway, you know, so as you can imagine we had plenty to jaw about.' He gave a half-hearted laugh which seemed to him to drip off the end of his paint brush and land on the wooden deck. He soldiered on. 'So – I asked him up for supper. Ha. Turns out he's a hell of a horseman. Keen to see the horses.' He paused, carefully negotiating himself around his own part in the situation. 'Olive must have taken him up to the top paddock.'

'The top paddock? What do you mean, the top paddock, what ...'

Darragh didn't get chance to reply. Gil was up the porch stairs and heading for the door.

'Hold on a minute, lad,' Darragh said. 'They're on with the sewing, you better not just barge in, oh ... hang on ...'

Gil turned back. Darragh was shading his eyes and peering upland.

'I do believe this is them.'

Gil followed Darragh's gaze. Sure enough two riders, travelling at speed, were twisting a dust trail through the top paddock. Olive was easy to spot. She was in the lead, her black hair flying loose behind her, her rump out of the saddle, her body leaned forward into the horse's neck. The horses disappeared where the trail cut through the woodland and Gil's eyes traced the flank of trees seeking the spot they were most likely to emerge. He watched for a few minutes then let his eyes stray back to the place they'd disappeared. *Where in God's name were they?* A few minutes more ticked past. He was of a mind to go find them when they suddenly reappeared, both dismounted and leading their horses. Gil left Darragh and walked back down towards the stables, got there just as the two of them appeared. Olive was laughing at something Kelly was saying. Gil picked up one of the horse buckets and took it to the pump and started splashing water into it. Olive looked over, clamped her hand over her mouth, tied off her horse and hurried towards him.

'Gil,' she said. 'You're early, did you decide to ...'

'I'm not early, Olive. You're late.' He knew how he sounded: like his insides were bunched up and mean.

'Well, what time is ...'

He didn't get chance to answer – Michael Kelly, near glowing with pleasure, came up behind Olive,

'Gil. Sorry to steal this lovely woman from you ... but, by God, she's a hell of a rider.' Olive's cheeks, already flushed from the ride, lit up crimson. She stepped away from Kelly and took Gil's arm.

'I'm sorry, Gil. I didn't realise we'd been gone so long. It was Darragh, he wanted me to show Mr Kelly the farm. I didn't realise ...'

'She didn't realise she was leading a parched man to water.' Kelly said, smiling like a loon, the low sun picking out the shine of his hair. 'Riding, Mr McKenzie. Riding is the thing I love most in the world, so it is – and I haven't had a whole lot of it since I left Ireland. You might say I was dying of thirst, but now,' he paused and stretched his arms in Olive's direction, like she was some prize piece in an auction. 'Thanks to this woman, my thirst is quenched.'

'Best do the same for them horses, then,' Gil said, and thrust the bucket at him.

Chapter 14

Over the next few weeks, whether it was his imagination or just wedding nerves, Gil felt some difference in Olive. Something he couldn't rightly put his finger on: an absence in her where there shouldn't have been one, like she was off thinking about something else, even when they were alone together. Especially when they were alone together.

'You all right, Olive?' he'd chanced one night. They were rowing back from the island, the empty picnic box between them on the floor of the boat. She'd hardly spoken a word all evening – almost like she'd forgotten he was there.

'What?' she said, bringing her eyes back from the water, the sun melting out and pricking the tops of the small waves that marked the boat's passage.

'I said, are you all right?'

'All right? Of course I'm all right. Why shouldn't I be all right?' she said, her lips pursed like she was pulling soda through a straw, a small frown set between her brows.

'Well, you're mighty quiet of late.'

'Quiet?' Her voice echoed off the surface of the water, shrill as a squawking bird. 'I'm fine,' she said, lining up her two feet in the bottom of the boat as if that somehow emphasised the point.

'Well you don't seem fine,' Gil said. 'You seem ... distant. Like you're thinking of something.' He swallowed hard. 'Or somebody.'

Olive narrowed her eyes, the crease on her forehead deepening to a large V.

'Thinking of somebody? Who the hell might that be? Darn it, Gil, the only person on my mind at the moment is you. Oh, and Beattie and Darragh, and Mimi and, let's face it, near enough the entire population of Oaklake.'

'And Rose?'

'What?'

'Rose. You didn't say Rose.'

'Oh, for goodness sake,' Olive flapped her hands impatiently. 'It goes without saying. Rose. I'm thinking of Rose. For God's sake, Gil, I'm thinking of everyone. Truth is I'll be glad when this damn wedding is over, when we're just plain married. I can't abide this being in the centre of things all the time. Hell, I can't walk down the street without being accosted by some simpering woman. And if Macy Creasy hangs on my arm once more I swear I'll knock her on her backside.'

He left it for a couple of minutes. He wanted to believe that was all there was to it.

'So what do you think about Rose?'

'Rose? What about Rose?'

'Her and Michael Kelly.'

She didn't answer.

Rose's visit home had been a last-minute thing, prompted by Beattie's increasing anguish about a dress fitting. Olive had been winding up the store at the end of the day when the shop bell went. She paid no real attention and carried on with her work until she suddenly realised she was being watched.

She slid behind the counter.

'Can I help you ?' Her voice was sharp as a tack.

Michael Kelly stepped from the gloom of the shop floor, removed his hat and gave a slight bow in her direction.

'How are you, Miss O'Grady?' he said. He moistened his lips with his tongue and gave her a smile that had her holding on to the edge of the counter.

'I'm ... I'm fine. Fine, thank you. And you?'

'I'm fine too,' he said, spreading his two hands on the counter between them.

She had not seen him since the riding out incident. Fact was, she'd not stopped thinking of him either: the man had lit something in her that Gil had never even put a match to, some fire that refused to burn itself out. Gil had noticed of course and she'd fobbed him off because she couldn't seem to get the thing straight in her mind. Cold feet, Beattie would have said, had she been of a mind to talk to her about it. But she would have been wrong. She'd made the wrong decision, it was as simple as that: she'd attached herself to Gil and then Michael Kelly had come along. Come along and had her contemplating a different future, a different husband ...

'Miss O'Grady,' he said, the smooth lilt of his voice like running water. It sent a rush of blood straight to her face.

'Yes?' She leaned towards him.

'I have something to ask you.'

She realised she was already nodding, the words lining up on her tongue.

The store bell rang out and Olive glanced over as a woman walked in. The cut of her clothes showed her for a city woman – elegant lines, a simple hat atop hair that was swept up and hidden, stray strands loose and catching the colour of the late sun. She stepped forward and the pit of Olive's stomach dropped a couple of notches.

'Rose?' she said, steadying herself on the counter. The woman pulled off her hat and her hair spilled out around her face and down the length of her back in one warm gold stream. Olive heard Michael Kelly gasp.

'Rose ... I, I can't believe it. Just look at you ... you look ... ' She trailed off. It was the second time she'd failed to recognise her younger sister – but who would blame her – if she'd blossomed before she'd left Oaklake, she was the full bouquet now. 'Does Beattie know you're coming?'

'No! It's a surprise! She keeps mailing me. She's frantic about the dress fitting so I managed to get time off work. I have to go back tomorrow but, oh, it's so exciting! Just look at the store, Olive! It's divine! So quaint – and look at you – Mrs McKenzie to be!' Olive glanced down at herself then quickly up again. There was no point comparing: she looked like some dusty maiden aunt – her shoes powdered with oatmeal, her apron creased and stained. Rose gathered Olive in her arms. 'Come on,' she said. 'Let's go up to The Luck and surprise Grandma and Grandpa.' She looked over her shoulder, her hair and face glowing like she had some kind of light burning inside her. Michael Kelly beamed back then dropped into a low bow. Rose turned back to Olive.

'This is Mr Kelly,' Olive said. 'He's going to take Gil's job at the woodyard after we're ... after we're wed. Mr Kelly – my sister, Rose.

'Well, Mr Kelly, why don't you come up to The Luck with us? If you're intending to move to town you're going to need to get acquainted with The Luck.'

He didn't correct her.

'I would be honoured, Miss O'Grady,' he said, dropping into another dramatic bow. 'Most honoured.'

Olive went out back to take off her apron. By the time she got back into the shop the two of them had gone.

It didn't take much in the way of clairvoyant expertise to forecast how things were going to turn out. Rose stayed at The Luck till the next day then left, leaving Beattie a-flutter with relief and excitement on the platform edge – the relief not chiefly regarding the dress fitting, but the fact that Mr Kelly had been felled like a tree by her youngest granddaughter. He had joined them for supper but Beattie reckoned he had neither seen nor heard a thing other than Rose. He'd gazed at her so steadily during the meal that twice he'd dropped his spoon, then knocked his water tumbler clean over his apple tart.

But there was a second edge to her relief because, like Gil, she'd noticed the change in Olive. It seemed to Beattie that the girl had somehow lost her anchor, that she was drifting away and out of reach – and she was sure as hell that Michael Kelly was the reason for it. She'd broached it – carefully – one evening, Olive perched on the kitchen table, Beattie tackling the hem of the wedding gown. All she got back was a black look and a singeing reply. So, the fact that Mr Kelly's attention had suddenly been drawn elsewhere – to her other granddaughter no less – was something worth celebrating. She reckoned that Gil would agree with her.

A few days after Rose's departure Michael Kelly appeared, early, at Gil's office. Gil was only just in, not quite started his work. The yard was still quiet – the men busy loading the delivery truck, the tang of new-cut wood drifting in through the open window. It was a scent that Gil never tired of – something soothing to the mind about sap long stored then released onto the breeze. A timeless thing. This was how his mind was working when the office door opened a few inches and Michael Kelly's ever smiling face appeared.

'Gil,' he said. 'Am I too early to trouble you?'

Gil indicated the wall clock with a flick of his head. 'Not too early at all, Michael. The day's up and started. The fellers are already at it.'

'Busy day lined up?'

'Always busy, I guess. But you'll find that out soon enough. Not long before you take over now, hmm? So – what's the trouble?'

'Trouble?'

'You said you wanted to trouble me.'

Kelly gave a small laugh. 'Ah, so I did. Yes. Well. Would you have time to cut me an order of timber?'

Gil glanced down at the small pile of order papers on his desk then shuffled them over. 'It's on one of these?' he said.

'No. No, it isn't. I wanted to talk to you first – make sure you could fit it in before filling an order sheet.'

Gil sat back and considered the man. It was the constant smile that was so irksome. Something about it that spoke to Gil of insincerity. And maybe camouflage. He'd met fellers like him at college – fellers who mated up with you, then dropped you once they'd got what they needed: a leg-up with an essay, a quick loan for an evening out. Always shone up like a new dollar, always had a girl on the go.

'So who is it for?'

'It's for me,' Michael Kelly said, laying his hand flat against his heart. His fingers were long and delicate and did not speak of hard labour. 'I'm aiming to build myself a cabin – but I want to get started straight off – don't want to hang around, want to look like I'm a man worth my salt before ... erm ... before ...'

'Before Rose comes back.'

'Well ...' It gave Gil some pleasure to see Kelly stumbling over himself, 'I was going to say before the wedding or before I start the job, but yes – I would like to break ground and get something up ... ' he slid his hand up to the base of his throat and sighed loudly. 'before Rose comes back.'

'You serious about her, then?' Gil could not believe what he was saying. He sounded more like Rose's pa than the man who, only months earlier, had almost lost himself in flights of fancy and romance regarding an imagined future with her.

'Oh, I'm serious. Who wouldn't be?' He gave Gil a long, level stare, his eyes twinkling with what Gil supposed to be lovesickness.

'And you want to prove yourself to her?' Gil meant it as humour but Kelly's face dropped, shadow suddenly outlining the sharp jut of his cheekbones.

'You think she won't have me? She's already promised?' There was a vulnerability in the question, something of a young child rather than a feller of thirty-two. Gil put him out of his misery.

'From what I've heard she's as struck with you as you are with her.'

The colour returned to Kelly's face. He blew out a long, laughing breath and rubbed his two hands together. 'You think so? You think that's the truth? She likes me?'

'As I say – that's what I'm hearing.' This wasn't strictly true but it was a handy wedge in terms of keeping the feller away from Olive.

Kelly paced around in front of the desk, his hands raking through his hair, smoothing down the front of his jacket, a grin on his face that would have taken some wiping off.

'I'm going to build us a cabin,' he said, still pacing. 'Then I'm going to ask her to be my wife.' He could barely get it out for the emotion of the thought – his words crumpled and backed up in his throat. He pulled out a chair and sat himself down, took out a handkerchief and mopped his face. He pulled a folded sheet of paper out of his jacket and put it on the desk in front of Gil.

'You think you could do this for me?'

Gil regarded the note for a couple of minutes.

'A cabin, you say? Seems like an awful lot of timber for a cabin.'

'I don't necessarily need it all at once. Obviously that would be a great bonus, but if you could see your way to cutting some of it, just to get me started on the framework you know ... I want to look like a good feller.'

'Leave it with me,' Gil said, getting up from the desk. The yard below was slowly coming to life – the machines cranking up, the voices of the men already raised a notch over the growing din. 'I'll talk to Danish – he'll be in shortly.'

Chapter 15

There were two things about his wedding day that Gil knew he would never forget. One of them involved Michael Kelly.

The wedding ceremony was over and folks, eager to kick off their shoes and loosen their collars, were keen to get out of the churchyard and up to The Luck, where, if the rumour was true, Olive was fixing to break out a vintage batch of her ale, as well as loosing some of her early attempts at a stronger brew, and the celebrations would begin in earnest. Beattie, Rose and Mimi had gone on ahead to start laying out the food but Darragh, relieved of any duty other than that of walking his granddaughter up the aisle, was ambling around from group to group, enjoying the freedom. Henry had offered to run folks up to the farm in the mail van and bit by bit the crowd had dwindled until only he and Michael Kelly were left, leaning against the gateposts waiting for Henry's return. Darragh had a mind that there was some design afoot.

'You must come and see the cabin, Darragh,' Michael Kelly said. 'Now that the wedding's over.'

'Over?' Darragh said. 'To be sure lad, we've not even got started yet.'

Kelly's face clouded over. 'Of course not. That was a foolish thing I said. Sorry, Darragh. I don't know what I was thinking of.'

Darragh left it a moment or two.

'You sure about that, are you?'

'What?'

'You sure you don't know what you're thinking of? From what I hear there's only one thing – or one person – on your mind.'

There'd been *visits* according to Beattie. Three at least.

Kelly fumbled with his jacket cuffs, walked a few paces to the road edge and looked out for Henry. A breeze had picked up and wedding confetti – rose petals sent by Vida, together with her apologies for not being able to attend – 'rich, because she wasn't damn well invited' – laced the roadside with colour.

'You're right, Darragh,' Kelly said. 'Right entirely ... I ...' He rearranged his cuffs again. 'I ... well, what would you think? What would you say, would you allow it?'

'Allow it?'

'Me and Rose. Would you allow ...'

'You're talking marriage, I take it?'

Kelly nodded, a thin trickle of sweat running down the side of his face and towards his chin.

Darragh thrust his hands into his pockets. 'Well, what does Rose say? Is she of the same mind – bearing in mind it's a mighty quick courtship. And her age. She's a good deal younger than you, lad.'

'Rose? Well ... I ...'

'You have asked her?'

'Well, no. What with the wedding and her living away. And I've been so busy getting the cabin started I ...'

'Then it's no good asking me, son. Doesn't matter a darn what I think if you haven't asked Rose.'

He put his arm round Kelly's shoulders. The man was quaking like a young rabbit.

'Go on, son. You need to ask her. Don't ask me – ask her.'

It was only as Kelly was walking away, jaunty as a colt, that Darragh got the feeling he'd put his foot in it. Again.

Gil and Olive had fulfilled their first obligations as a married couple: the cake was cut – and mostly eaten – and they had led the way for the first dance, Olive fumble-footed and red in the face, pulling Gil back to their seats the moment the dance finished. She leaned against him, and he put his arms round her.

'Happy?' he said. It was as much a statement as a question.

She slipped her hand in his, the feel of the new ring on her finger sparking a grin on his face.

'Happy,' she said, simply, and turned her face up to him and kissed his mouth. The brush of her lips was like a match to touchpaper: Gil felt the colour slide from his chest, up past his collar and onto his face.

'Why, Mr McKenzie, I do believe you're blushing,' Olive said, leaning away from him and reaching for a plate of cake.

'I'm famished,' she said, squaring up a good mouthful. She pushed a piece his way and grinned. 'Better fuel up, husband. Might be needing it later.' She gave him a smile that halfway put the fear of God in him and halfway turned his insides liquid. He pulled her closer, conjuring up images of the night ahead, of the moment the two of them were alone.

It was at that point that Michael Kelly stood up and strode – a chestnut-coloured fiddle clasped to his breast – to the front of the barn. He dragged over a bale of hay and stepped up onto it, drawing a murmur of delight, then a ripple of applause from the crowd. He gave a small bow then gestured with his free arm towards someone standing at the front. It was Rose.

'Darragh and Beattie,' he said, his two arms now held wide, the fiddle and bow dangling, the promise of something to come. 'We folks have a great deal to thank you for ...' Gil blanked out the rest. He watched Kelly's mouth working, his smile on and off like an overused punctuation mark, and leaned closer to Olive until she suddenly sat up straighter, and pulled away from him, craning her neck to hear what was being said.

'I don't believe it,' she whispered.

'What?' He was only half interested, trying his best to pick up where he'd left off with the conjuring.

'Listen,' Olive said. She was off her seat now, on tiptoe. There was a murmur in the crowd, then movement, a small titter of applause and Darragh and Beattie, followed by Rose, stepped up beside Michael Kelly. The expression on Beattie's face was hard to read.

Michael Kelly said something that Gil didn't quite catch and the congregation erupted. Rose hopped up onto the haybale beside him, her smile billowing out over the crowd. Like you could touch it. Olive sat down.

'What did he say?' Gil said.

Olive didn't reply.

'What did he say?' Gil said, having to raise his voice above the cheering and clapping.

'He asked her to marry him.' Olive's voice was flat as wind-blown grass.

'He what?' Gil stood up and looked over the crowd. Michael Kelly and Rose were still at the front, his arm round her waist.

'He asked her to marry him,' Olive said. 'She said yes.'

Gil looked down at Olive. Her two hands were loose in her lap. Tears were streaming down her face.

It was Beattie saved the day. She pushed her way through the crowd, took one look at Olive and clutched the girl's face against her stomach. 'He never should have done that,' she whispered. 'Your wedding day of all days, and making an announcement like that.'

Olive wrestled herself free of Beattie's arms, her tears already drying.

'Makes no difference to me,' she said, her voice gruff as sandpaper.

'Yes, yes, I realise that,' Beattie said, chancing a look at Gil, 'but all the same, your wedding day ...'

'Our wedding day,' Olive said, slipping her hand into Gil's and getting up out of her seat. 'Come on, husband. I reckon it's high time we got ourselves home.'

'Home?' Gil said, a small buzz of excitement starting in his belly. Like a bee was trapped in there. Hell, like the whole damn hive had taken up residence.

'Home,' Olive said.

She didn't need to say it again.

If Michael Kelly's announcement had taken the shine off the evening Olive soon put it back on. They said their quick goodbyes then left, Olive starting up the truck, the skirts from her wedding frock bundled in her lap. She hurled her wedding flowers out the window at the last minute, not bothering to see who caught them, then floored the pedal and took off down the track like she was being chased.

It would be fair to say she didn't take her foot off the accelerator all night. She hit the bedroom, and Gil, like a full-on tornado. He'd not known what to expect, her being pretty immune to his courtship advances, but there came a moment sometime towards early morning, which he knew he would never forget. The sky was pointing fingers of light through the unclosed drapes, something churchlike about the motes of dust drifting in its shimmer, and he looked up at her ... her eyes half closed. Her hair damp and curling round her throat. Her thighs wrapped round him like he was a prize stallion ... and in that moment he knew he was gazing into the eye of a storm.

Chapter 16

Back at The Luck things were hopping, big time, and there was no getting away from it – Michael Kelly's fiddle-playing had a lot to do with it. He had the whole barn in the palm of his hands – belting them round breathless with a mad trio of jigs then felling them where they stood with haunting airs that left them shuffling and sighing and leaning into each other. Beattie stood on the edges, mouth set in a hard line, watching Darragh. He had been avoiding her which, in her book, meant only one thing – he was somehow behind Michael Kelly's announcement. Michael Kelly. There he was, jumped up on a couple of bales, like he was the captain of the ship, wielding the damn fiddle like it was part of his own arm. She should have admired him for it but no: she was vexed to the very pit of her stomach. Who did he think he was? Barging into their lives like they somehow needed him – like life was so dull they'd just welcome him in and thank him for livening things up?

'Come on, Beattie, come and join in!' It was Henry, red in the face and dripping sweat off the point of his chin. She managed a smile.

'Later, Henry. Need to get myself in the kitchen for a while.'

'Well, I'll be looking for you ...' and he was off, whipped back into the crowd, whooping and grinning. She watched for a little while longer then stomped off. Cattle. The whole damn lot of them, being worked like a herd of feckless cattle.

Darragh had spent an inordinate length of time on the dance floor, his concentration split between getting enough breath into his lungs and keeping an eye out for Beattie. There had been a moment, just after Michael Kelly had made his announcement, when he'd caught her eye and the joy, the elation, the sheer excitement of the evening slid off him like snow off a roof. Left him in no doubt that he was somehow responsible. He watched her talking to Henry then, as she turned and stomped off, he took his chance and slipped away from the dance floor, past the long trestles of food and ale and out into the night.

He leaned against the planking of the barn and let his breathing level out. The sky was an ink lake, rippled with night cloud and shifting stars, the fence at the top of the pasture silhouetted like in a child's drawing. The Annie O'Grady stood at the bottom of the yard, her wings partly lit with night glow, Mimi and Beattie's bunting flapping in a breeze that he couldn't feel. He pushed away from the side of the barn and wandered down, a quick look back over his shoulder to make sure Beattie hadn't spotted him. He needed to talk to her. Needed to explain himself. The very thought of it twisted a knot into his guts. He stepped up onto the wooden box he'd rigged as a makeshift step, unlatched the door and hauled himself into the plane. He settled back and took in the feel of her. The smell. The leather seat polished thin by his own backside, the faint tang of insecticide, the half-reflection of his own face in the control panel. Beattie. She was right – or she would be right when she managed to track him down: he shouldn't have led Michael Kelly on, should have dealt with the matter properly when he'd had chance at the churchyard. But who'd have expected the feller to up and propose at Olive's wedding? The thought of the crowd's elation – his own – made him cringe. But in his heart of hearts, he couldn't really see what the problem was. In his heart of hearts the young Irish man was ... no. He wasn't going to start thinking like that. Anyhow no matter what he thought – he'd seen Beattie's face sure enough and there definitely was a problem.

Darragh surveyed the view from the cockpit: The Luck, fair glowing, lit up in party colours, its walls dancing with shadows thrown from the barn, the run of the lane down to the road, good meadow on either side, fences straight and catching the moon. And the lake. He let out a long, slow breath. How was it so much time had passed and so easily? He'd been nothing but a youngster when he'd first caught sight of it, just a youngster. Like a picture puzzle. That's what he'd thought at the time. And him the missing piece. He shook his head.

The music from the barn suddenly stopped, followed by a round of clapping and shouting. He watched as folks came out through the big doors, fanning the air and loosing damp shirts, all smiling. He slipped down in his seat as the fiddle struck up again. A single note bowed lightly back and forth, back and forth, like it was drawing itself across his own heart, like it was easing open a door that had been a long time closed. He unfastened his shirt buttons, lay his chest bare against the moonlight and let the music wash over him, his heart vibrating as Michael Kelly eased the bow over the strings, each pull taking Darragh higher and higher until it seemed that the Annie O'Grady had left land and he was airborne once more. He felt himself soaring – over the farm, the lake, looking down as if he was a young man again: everything to gain and nothing to lose. *Nothing to lose.* The thought rose up to his throat and he swallowed hard, pushed it back down.

Then Kelly started in on the melody: an air so sweet and pure it came across the sky like a bird in flight and it was as though the plane banked away from the farm, over the lake and out – out across the dark land and towards the sea. The sky was thick with cloud but he was not afraid. He glanced down at the waves below, inky black and leaping, a low moon gracing the cresting water like it was showing him the way. And he followed, kept following, the music like a charm or a siren pulling him on. He was crying now, but ready. Ready to face what he'd never been able to face, for the thing that waited for him in his dreams, the thing he and Beattie couldn't bring themselves to speak of. *Conrad.*

He scanned the water, his eyes fixed on its churning surface, ready, eager, spurring him on, inspecting every dip and swell, every cross current, every leap of spray. Until, at last, he saw it.

Far below, almost invisible in the sloping rise and fall.

A ship.

He brought the Annie O'Grady round and lost some height: circled wide, his heart drumming above the sound of the waves as the clouds melted away and the moon shone down and there – surely – there he was on the deck. His lost boy, smiling and waving up at him. He stood up in the cockpit so he could get a better look and he felt the door in his heart swing open and heard the broken call spring from his own throat.

'Conrad. Conrad.'

He was waving his arms now, leaning almost double across the open window. He could sense the strain in the Annie O'Grady but it meant nothing, for here was his boy, his only ...

'Darragh O'Grady. What in God's name are you doing up there?'

Darragh straightened up at such speed the inside of his head sloshed like a bowl of water. He steadied it either side with his hands and for one precious moment he fashioned that Beattie's voice was part of the dream. He sat back heavily in his seat, his breath jagged and wretched, wiping the tears – or was it the spray – from his face. He could hear her clambering up onto the wooden crate. Her face appeared abruptly above the door, crimson with effort.

'You're missing all the fun,' she said.

She was right. Michael Kelly had struck up with the fast tunes again. The barn door was wedged wide and Darragh could see two lines of dancers charging up and down the length of the floor.

'I'm sorry ...' he said. 'I made a mess of things on Olive's wedding day. I should ... I should ...'

'You should what?' Beattie said, her voice was tender, her hand on the back of his neck warm and soft.

'Michael Kelly.' he said. 'He asked me at the churchyard and ... well, I know you're not strictly fond of him, but ... but.' He took a deep breath and let it out in one short blow.

'I understand, Darragh,' Beattie said. 'I understand.'

She'd not say any more, he knew that. All these years passed by and still no real knowing about what had happened. He'd disappeared, that's all they knew – from their lives, from the face of the earth – but never from their hearts.

Darragh nodded then turned his face away, tears blurring his vision until, for a moment, the yard disappeared again and the sea lay beneath him and Conrad was on the deck of the ship, his face lit by the moon and smiling up at him.

Chapter 17

'What's going on in there?' Gil was sitting with Darragh on the porch, the pair of them resting with their boots on the rail like a couple of old timers. Darragh had intercepted the lad on his way into the kitchen, eager for some talk that didn't leave him in fear of saying the wrong thing.

'Wedding talk,' Darragh said and let loose a sigh. Although only a couple of weeks had passed since Olive and Gil's wedding, Mimi was back at the kitchen table every night, her and Beattie flicking through magazines and catalogues, riffling through swatches of cloth that might be just the thing for Rose.

'My mother in there too?'

'What's your guess?'

Gil shook his head and took a sip of his ale. Drinking ale on a worknight was not the usual state of things, but a couple of the wedding kegs had been left unfinished and, well, loosely speaking he and Olive were still in their honeymoon period – despite the work they were putting in down at the store – and so, why not?

'Being wed suiting you then, lad?'

Darragh was grinning at him over his ale glass. Gil turned to look out at the hills to hide the rush of colour to his cheeks.

'Down to the ground,' he said, his voice cracking like a teenager.

Truth was he was feeling a little frayed round the edges, so to speak, and drinking ale with Darragh was providing a welcome breather, and a chance to get his strength up.

Olive. If their wedding night had left him staring into the eye of the storm, the days and nights that followed had him wrung out and thrown up on the sand like some hapless shipwreck, unsure of which way was up and what his name was. She was, it seemed, insatiable. Her lovemaking had a fury to it, like it was something she had to get out of her system, pummelling his chest, tearing at his hair, wrapping herself round him like a drowning swimmer. There were moments when he gasped for breath, then went under again, engulfed in the rise and flow of her, giving in and letting himself be taken to depths he had never had the imagination to consider. He was halfways in awe and halfways incredulous. That very afternoon for example, they were out in the back store, weighing bags of corn and oats and she'd suddenly come at him, lifting her dress as she launched herself onto him, pinning him against the shelves of pickle jars, her hair flying out like a deranged woman, biting at his neck, batting his face with hard kisses, tearing at his shirt, his belt, wild and moaning until she slid off him, smoothing down her dress, pinning back her hair, her eyes glazed and shining but dancing with mischief, leaving him breathless and speechless.

'So you reckon Beattie's right?' Darragh nodded his head towards the front door.

Gil hauled himself upright in the chair.

'Right? Right about what?'

'Michael Kelly. Michael Kelly and Rose. You reckon they'll wed soon?'

Gil shrugged. 'Guess so.' He didn't know one way or the other. He knew Kelly was busy building his cabin but he'd not been out to see it. Truth was, he had no time for the feller. *He's a bit of a dandy,* he'd said to Olive one evening. She'd not replied and it had irked him.

Darragh put down his ale glass and leaned towards Gil. 'Well, the man sure has a way with wood. This cabin of his? Well ...' He leaned back again, shaking his head. 'The bedroom is to have a balcony that lets down onto the garden. He plans to dam the stream and make a pond. And the kitchen. He's making it himself – table, chairs, cabinets. A rare talent indeed. Mmmh.'

'You spent a bit of time out there, then?'

'Oh. You know, when I can. Now and then – go up and give him a bit of a hand, you know.'

The fact was Darragh was at Kelly's cabin as often as he could be. Sometimes he walked halfway there and sat under a line of young oaks that marked the top end of Kelly's land, and watched the work going on below: Michael Kelly stripped to the waist and hauling timber. There was a satisfaction in watching him: his movements smooth and unhurried, an ease about him that lent a charm to the most ordinary task. But most times Darragh was working alongside the man, wrapped up in what they were doing, happy to be working with the wood, happy to be in Kelly's company.

'What will you call the place?' Darragh asked one evening. Kelly had had a full gang working all day and they'd all knocked off late. He'd accompanied Darragh back to the line of young oaks and they were looking down at the cabin. The roof trusses were in place, giving the cabin the air of an upturned boat.

'That's a very good question, Darragh. One I haven't found an answer to yet. I have a few ideas – but I think I'll let Rose settle it.'

'You should come out and see the place,' Darragh said, swinging his attention back to Gil. 'Why not walk over there with me one time? You and Olive? We could all go over on Sunday – take Beattie and Mimi?'

'Yeah, why not,' Gil said. *And why not just organise ourselves a little fan club?,* was what he wanted to say. *Get the whole town involved, maybe,* because everyone, as far as he could see, would get on board.

'I could ask her – Olive I mean. She's, you know ... busy. But yes, I'll ask her.' He turned away from Darragh. Asking Olive to visit Michael Kelly's cabin was the last thing he was going to do. He knew his own feelings about the man but, despite the heat in the bedroom, he wasn't altogether sure of Olive's.

Chapter 18

Sunday, it turned out, was the day that everything changed.

Gil had woken late, still sapped from the exertions of the night before. He opened his eyes a slit and tried to gauge if Olive was still asleep without letting on that he was awake. He listened for her breathing and crept the tips of his fingers slowly to her side of the bed.

Her space was empty.

Gil lifted his head off the pillow and looked around. Her clothes were missing from the bedside chair, her nightdress in a pile on the floor. He cocked his head and listened. There was no sound of her, either from the house or from the store below them. He swung his legs out of bed and went over to the window and looked out onto the street. Perhaps she was out on a vet call? Unlikely on a Sunday, but not impossible. He pulled on his clothes, not bothering to change into his clean shirt, slipped on his shoes and went through into the kitchen. There was no sign of her – no cup in the sink, no note on the table.

'Olive?' He called her name and immediately wished he hadn't: the sound of his voice in the empty room raised a small wave of panic from his stomach and into his throat. To his amazement, and relief, she answered.

'Gil.' Her voice was faint, like she was some distance away.

He whirled round to see where it had come from. 'Olive. Olive ... where are you?'

Gil charged down the hall, through their living room and into their small bathroom. Olive was perched on the wash basket holding her stomach.

'Must have been that fish we had,' she said, her two hands clutching the edge of the wash basin. 'I've been up since six, heaving my guts up.'

'Since six?'

'Yeah, I woke up feeling like the bed was moving, like I was on a goddamn roller coaster ...'

Gil didn't say anything. He knew the feeling.

'Then the next thing I know I'm puking up on my nightdress ... then I got to the bathroom then ... oh, wait a minute ...' She lunged forward to the toilet, retching, then loosed a spout of vomit into the bowl. She sank back onto her heels and let Gil dab at her forehead with the flannel.

'I'll go back to bed for an hour or two,' she said. 'Sleep it off. I'll be right as rain after a bit of rest.'

She was right. When she appeared in the kitchen a couple of hours later, she was fine. And starving.

'You feel up to going over to The Luck?' Gil said, watching with a mixture of concern and admiration as Olive chomped her way through half a loaf of bread, tearing it into chunks and hefting it into her mouth. Olive shook her head and carried on eating, her jaw working like it was running on new batteries.

'You not want anything on that? Butter? Syrup?'

She shook her head again and concentrated on chewing, then swallowed hard, walloping her chest bone to encourage the load of dough down her gullet.

'No,' she said, sitting back in the chair and releasing a soft belch. 'You go on – tell Beattie and Darragh I'm busy in the store. I'll be seeing them in the week anyhow. You needn't tell them I was out of sorts.'

By the time Gil reached The Luck, he'd forgotten Olive's parting words and found himself relating the morning's events to Beattie. She was putting the finishing touches to a dish of vegetables, but at the mention of Olive and vomit she swung round, her face lit up, eyebrows perched high on her forehead like she was inviting him to say more.

'Well?' she said, after he failed to go on.

'Well?' he replied, smiling but confused.

'Well, is she?'

'Is she?'

Beattie slid the dish onto the table. 'Yes. Olive. Is she ... you know ...'

Darragh chose that moment to come in from the back porch – a small bunch of Michaelmas daisies for the table clutched in his hand. He gave them to Beattie, then, realising that something was afoot, turned to look at Gil.

'Where's Olive?'

'Oh, I was just ...'

'Olive's sick,' Beattie announced, getting up from the table and taking Gil by the arm. 'I was just asking Gil about it. Just wondering ... you know, if ...'

'It was the fish,' Gil said, moving away from Beattie and nearer to Darragh.

'The fish? Hah.' Beattie beamed across at Darragh who looked as mystified as Gil.

'What was it with me, Darragh?' she said, not really waiting for an answer. 'Oh, yes. Oranges. That was the first sign for me. The next thing I knew ...'

'Sorry, Beattie. But what the hell are you talking about?'

Beattie came around the table towards him and Gil had to stifle the urge to shrug her off as she took hold of his arm again.

'Olive,' she said, softly, smile a mile wide. 'Is she in the family way? Are we ...' She glanced over at Darragh who was struggling not to bury his face in his hands. 'Are we going to be great-grandparents?' Her face was glowing hot and too close to his own. Gil took a step back.

'The family way? Is she, what? Do you mean you think she's ... aha! Goodness, Beattie, we've only been wed a few weeks. Family way. No. She's not. She's fine. I've left her in the store, restocking.' He shook his head like he was trying to loose a pea out of his ear. 'Family way,' he mused. 'No, definitely not.'

'You sure?' Beattie said, crestfallen, but unconvinced. Darragh had turned to the sink, running a glass of cold water, trying to interrupt without actually saying anything.

This was what Beattie had been running on for the last weeks – her prediction of another wedding plus 'the likelihood of a new baby' – and here she was grasping at it with both hands and embarrassing the poor feller.

'I'm sure,' Gil said, joining Darragh at the tap.

'Well, how can you be so sure?' Beattie said, determined not to be moved. 'If she was sick this morning ...'

'I told you. It was the fish. She was fine afterwards. And look ... Olive ... she doesn't want a family yet. She wants to get things steady with the store. She's got her horses, the ale, you know. She doesn't want a family yet. She said it herself, so Beattie, I'm sorry. I shouldn't have told you. She told me not to mention it.'

'She told you not to mention it?' Beattie said, the smile flicking at the corners of her mouth again.

'Yes. She said not to mention it.'

'OK,' Beattie said. That, as far as she was concerned, had clinched the matter.

The fish incident repeated itself every morning the following two weeks until Beattie, by this time too worried to be smug, stepped in. She'd been upstairs to take a peek at Olive and found the girl asleep, her lips dry and cracked, a faint crust of yellow vomit from one corner of her mouth. She looked half dead.

Olive wasn't blooming, she was fading.

'I think we better get Dr Pete to take a look at her,' Beattie said, the following afternoon. 'She can't go on like this. It's been almost three weeks, and look at her.'

Gil looked over at the counter. Olive was propped up behind it, sorting strings of beads, her hair lank and drooped over one bony shoulder.

Olive simply nodded at Beattie's suggestion, and sat, wrung out like a greasy dish cloth, in the back of the truck clutching a bowl in one hand and a cloth in the other as Gil drove them to Picker's Flag where Dr Pete confirmed Beattie's diagnosis: Olive was pregnant.

Gil was astounded, relieved and then turned into a man who couldn't stop smiling. He served in the store (Olive upstairs till at least lunchtime each day, queasy and tearful, tossing around on the bed which seemed to be afloat on rough water) like he was the star turn at a new show. Folks couldn't get enough of it – Pearl Clodagh was in almost daily, clutching some new remedy to try quell Olive's pitching stomach, Henry came whether there was post or not, to catch up on the latest developments and pass on any helpful tips he might have picked up on his rounds and Beattie – it seemed Beattie grew several inches taller: she glided around the store like a ship in full sail. She ran aground somewhat one afternoon ...

She was at the back of the store, clearing a rack of shelves ready for a delivery of winter boots. The doorbell sounded but she stayed where she was: Gil was on counter duty and she was happy where she was, mooning over thoughts of the following summer and the baby. From her post, hidden by the tall rack that held the riding tack, she became aware that whoever it was had come into the store – two or three people judging by the voices – they were now in quiet conversation just a few feet away from her on the other side of the rack. She quieted her breathing and leant in. Macy Creasey was definitely one, Pearl Clodagh the other.

'Well, I think I might be the authority on that,' she heard the Clodagh woman say. 'And I reckon it's a mite early. If you know what I mean ...'

'Well, perhaps they, you know ... they were ...'

'What?' Pearl Clodagh, said. 'You think they got started before the wedding?'

Macy Creasey didn't answer but Beattie could hear her searching in her bag for her darned handkerchief. She could just about feel the heat coming off the girl's cheeks through the back of the rack.

'Well, could be an explanation I suppose,' Pearl Clodagh said with a sniff that suggested it wasn't. 'It was a damn fast wedding. Then again ...' She lowered her voice and Beattie had to bend closer. 'There could be some truth in that rumour ...'

'The rumour?' Macy said, her voice like she'd just done a lap of a racecourse.

'Well, from what I heard she was mighty lit up by that Kelly ...'

That did it. Beattie stepped backwards and her wooden leg, never as predictable as her real one, nudged the side of the basin and sent it over. She was on the floor, cloth in hand, mopping up the damage when the two women appeared round the end of the aisle.

'Mrs O'Grady,' Pearl Clodagh said. 'You OK down there?'

'What?' Beattie said, pushing her hair away from her face. 'Oh, Pearl, Macy ... hello there. I didn't hear anyone come in. So caught up in what I was doing here ... ha. So ... can I get you ladies anything?'

'You stay right there, Mrs O'Grady. I think I saw Gil at the counter. He'll fix us up.'

Beattie held her breath, willing them to go. She picked up the cloth and carried on with the mopping up, counted slowly to twenty. Pearl Clodagh's two feet didn't budge.

'So how's Olive doing?'

Beattie threw the cloth back into the basin and sat back.

'She's fine. A rough time of it. Early days you know.'

'Early days. Oh yes,' Pearl said, stroking her own belly. 'You don't need to tell me about early days. But I guess she'll be blooming in no time.' She gave a smile that put Beattie in mind a dog she used to have.

'So when's the happy event due?' Pearl said, slinging her eyes in Macy's direction.

'Summertime,' Beattie said, picking up the cloth again and sloshing it onto the floor. Pearl took a step back, frowning at the damp soaking into the toes of her good shoes.

'Oh, sorry,' Beattie said, setting about the floor with exaggerated vigour. Pearl held her ground.

'Summer?'

Beattie yanked a huge scrubbing brush out of the bowl and smiled up at the two women. 'You got it. Now sorry, ladies,' she said, slamming the brush down. 'But I need to get on and finish this floor.'

When the pair had finally gone, Pearl dabbing at her skirt with Macy's handkerchief, Beattie relinquished her brush and sat back. Her ears rang with Pearl's words. She closed her eyes then opened them quickly – the vision of Olive and Michael Kelly at The Luck, walking up with the horses after their ride, Olive flushed and sweating, laughing out loud, the panic that flitted across the girl's face when she saw Gil – it all suddenly played out like some old film stored away, stored away like evidence. But it was evidence Beattie had filed in her own head, not spoken a word of it to anyone. So, *rumour?* What the hell was Pearl Clodagh talking about?

'You all right down there, Beattie?' Gil was smiling down at her. 'You mind watching the counter? Thought I'd go check on Olive.'

Beattie hauled herself up off the floor and watched him cross the shop. Jaunty. The very cut of him made her want to smile – so she did smile. To hell with Pearl Clodagh and to hell with rumour. Olive was wed *and* expecting, Rose was engaged to Michael Kelly and no doubt soon to be wed. What was there to worry about? Not a thing, she thought.

Not a goddamn thing.

Chapter 19

It was approaching 5am, Beattie could tell by the noise coming from the henhouse. She'd been awake half the night, worrying, directing some internal play that didn't seem to have an end – round and round it went: Olive and Michael Kelly on horseback, Gil's certainty that Olive didn't want a family, Pearl Clodagh's whispering mischief, and the timing – she was trying to get a hold on the timing. She was calculating backwards, counting on her fingers.

'What's eating at you, Beattie?' Darragh said. His voice was gravelled with sleep.

She didn't reply.

Darragh eased himself over and considered her face.

She held fast.

'Beattie,' he said. 'What's wrong?'

'Nothing,' she said, trying to maintain her count.

'Nothing? Well what you lying awake counting on your fingers for?'

Beattie clasped her two hands together and stuck them on top of the counterpane. She turned her face towards Darragh.

'Do you think it's too soon?' she whispered.

'Too soon?' Darragh lay back to contemplate her words. Here was an opportunity to take the wrong road for sure. Too soon for what?

'I don't know,' he chanced, glancing at her to see if he'd already tripped himself up.

Her hands were busy again. She was replaying Pearl Clodagh's words. Perhaps that was it – the two of them had got down to things before the wedding. Sure, Oaklake was a couple of decades behind a lot of places but hell, that didn't necessarily mean that everyone in town – especially the young folk – weren't sometimes going at their own pace behind closed doors. Think of all the evenings they rowed over to the island for example. She gave a satisfied grunt. The thought settled her.

'What did you say?' she said, looking over at Darragh, who'd read the silence as proof of a correct answer and relaxed some.

He gulped. 'I said, "I don't know" ... you know ... if it's too early.'

'Too early? Too early for what? Darragh – you must have been dreaming.' She gave her pillow a thumping, pulled the sheets up round her neck, humped over onto her side, and fell asleep.

She woke next day with the same settled feeling, annoyed with herself for being scuppered by Pearl Clodagh's nonsense. That was until around mid-morning when Gil turned up for his coffee.

'Morning, Beattie,' he said, as he came through the door.

'Everything OK?' Beattie said, biting into a slice of currant pasty. She knew he'd been up to the woodyard to see Danish about the timbers for the extra store space he and Olive were planning.

'I guess it is,' Gil said, pouring himself a mug of coffee. 'But I was just talking to Danish. And, well ... have you heard the rumour?'

Beattie stared at him goggle-eyed and swallowed hard. The currant pasty went down in one. It got as far as her voice box and lodged itself. She clutched at the button on her collar.

'Rumour?' she croaked, then took off on a bout of choking that peppered the counter with currants and pastry. Gil dashed into the storeroom and came back with a glass of water. She downed it carefully, wiping the tears from her cheeks.

'Rumour?' she tried again. 'What rumour's that?'

'Well, according to Danish, Michael Kelly's trying to negotiate some land deal with old man Riley.'

Beattie stared at him but didn't say anything. Her ears were ringing like she was submerged under water. She could see Gil's lips moving but couldn't make sense of what he was saying.

'So ... what do you think? Could it be true? Or did you already know?' Gil said.

'Know? Know what?' Beattie said.

'About the rumour – did you already know about the rumour – about Kelly?'

'Kelly?' she said. She wanted to hold out her hands to stop everything slipping through.

'Yes. Kelly and his land deal. You OK, Beattie – you need some more water?'

'Oh. Kelly and his land deal. That's the rumour? Hhhmm. News to me. No. I've not heard about no land deal. Ha. A land deal indeed.'

She refastened her collar, took a sip of coffee and set about the pasty again.

Pretty soon, Oaklake being Oaklake, and Henry being the mailman, Michael Kelly's rumoured land deal with old man Riley became common knowledge. The facts, according to Henry, were that Michael Kelly was after setting up a stud farm and he had his eye on a patch of land boundaried at its bottom edge by the river and at its top edge by the fence that marked the end of woodland above Darragh and Beattie's top meadow. It would connect to and extend his own and, turning his current patch into a very desirable parcel. It would also mean that Kelly and Darragh would become neighbours as far as farmland was concerned. When the news hit Olive it was like she'd been plugged into the electric: she was out of bed and pulling on her clothes before Gil had had chance to finish the story.

'He wants to do what?' she shrieked, pulling the brush through her greasy hair and yanking it back into a tight bunch.

'Well, Henry says it's a stud farm he wants to open ...'

'A stud farm?' she spat, more colour in her cheeks than Gil had seen for weeks.

'That's what Henry said, and he's asked old man Riley ...'

'Old man Riley?' she hollered. 'He's asked old man Riley to oblige him with the means?'

'Well, I reckon there would be money involved ... you know ... I suppose ...'

'I know there would be money involved. Of course there would be money involved.' She stamped her feet into her boots and stormed past him. He felt the heat coming off her. She yanked her coat off the peg and wrestled her arms into it.

'Where you going, Olive?'

'What?' She shot him a look, her eyes burning like two pieces of coal.

'Where you going? You know, you haven't been up for weeks.'

She straightened the back of her coat and shrugged.

'Well, I'm up now,' she said and unhooked her bag from the back of the chair.

'I'd better come with you,' Gil said, going for his own coat.

'But you don't know where I'm going, Gil.' There was an edge to her voice that unsettled him.

'Well, I'm guessing you're going to see Michael Kelly.'

'Wrong,' she said in a voice that rang out and made him think of quiz shows.

'Well ...'

'I'm going to see old man Riley,' she said. 'If he's selling that piece of land, then he'll be selling it to me.' She caught the look on Gil's face. 'I mean us, he'll be selling the land to us.'

She marched out, leaving the door to swing in Gil's face. He hesitated for a moment then took off after her.

As it turned out, old man Riley wasn't for selling: either to Michael Kelly, or Olive. Gil wasn't particularly bothered – he was still marvelling over the change in her: she was up, cooking even. It seemed he owed Michael Kelly a portion of gratitude, the incident having apparently supplied the tonic she'd been needing.

'Were you serious, though, you know, about buying it?' Gil was studying her from his seat at the kitchen table. She was all bones and sharp edges – except her belly. When she reached up to the cupboard, the new fullness of it pushed out from under her apron. Early that morning, while he was still half steeped in sleep, she'd reached for him. It had been so long that he'd hesitated: half out of concern for her and half out of surprise. She'd been different, like the wildness in her had been quelled and afterwards she'd fallen asleep, her arms thrown back across the pillow, the bed covers twisted and half on the floor. He'd looked at her then, the jut of hipbones, the sharp ridge of her pubis, the marvellous swell of her belly. Her breasts rose from her ribs, soft and swollen, inviting. He wanted to take each nipple in his mouth, feel the warmth of it, the comfort of it.

'Well, yes. I was serious. Land is land after all.'

Gil swerved away from his thoughts and looked over at her. The incident had made him unsure of her. Unsure of himself.

'But it's not like we were looking to buy any, I suppose ... you know ... until ...'

'Until Michael Kelly came along, you mean.'

'Well, yes. That's what I do mean. You'd have bought it just to stop him having it?'

'Damn right I would,' she said. 'And I'd have outbid any offer of his to do that. '

Gil waited but she didn't add anything else.

'But why?'

'Why? Because of the river. Water's king, Gil. Plus ...' she emphasised the point with the end of the wooden spoon, '... that land borders The Luck, so if it's going to be joined to any other farm then it should be joined to The Luck. Ask anyone in town, they would agree with you.'

She turned her back to him and went on stirring the pan, a satisfaction in the set of her shoulders. He didn't rightly understand it but, as far as he was concerned, the whole affair had put the life back into her, so he was content to be ignorant.

You might say that, for the next few months, contentment lay over Gil and Olive like a thick wool blanket. As winter took hold of the town, they worked side by side in the store – Gil lighting the big stove each morning before Olive came down, then, in the afternoons working out back on the new building. By Christmas the new storeroom was complete and Gil turned his attention to preparing for the new baby. Beattie had offered up the crib that had been Conrad's – fashioned of course by Tom Darling – but Gil had declined, gracefully he hoped, explaining his intention to set to and make his own. He and Mimi – she wasn't as easy to put off as Beattie – were working on it together: he the carpenter, she the seamstress. Beattie had to content herself with wool and knitting needles, steadfastly ignoring the fact that the baby would be born in June.

Chapter 20

'Olive's looking well, isn't she?' Beattie said. They'd just got into bed and Darragh, recognising the conspiratorial edge to her voice, wondered if he could get away with feigning sleep. A small snore maybe – hush her up. He felt a sharp elbow in his ribs.

'Darragh.' She was whispering now, the fact that they were alone in a house that was several miles from its nearest neighbour, seemingly lost on her.

'What, Beattie?' he said, pulling a fake yawn, settling the covers around his shoulders.

'I said, Olive's looking well. Quite big. Quite up front, you know ... the baby.'

'Well, that's how it's supposed to be, isn't it?' he said.

'Still a while to go, though, I guess,' Beattie said. She was waiting for him to fill in the blanks but he wasn't going to do it. He played it like he didn't know what was eating at her. He did know, of course: from what he could work out half the town knew – or at least thought they knew. He'd heard the rumour: Michael Kelly and Olive. He refused to entertain any part of it. Gil seemingly had risen above it, going about his business with his usual sunny smile and Olive ... well, who knew what Olive was thinking.

'Darragh.'

'Beattie.' There was nothing else for it. He turned to face her in the bed and, deciding there was only one way out of another troubled night, dealt his trump card.

'Wonder how Rose is getting on. Heard anything from her?'

Beattie's face lit up instantly.

'Rose,' she said. 'Oh, yes ... let me tell you what she had to say ...'

Darragh was asleep long before she finished.

Although she wouldn't have admitted this to her grandmother, Rose was making the most of Olive's pregnancy, relieved that the focus was shifted from her – and the expectation of another wedding – to her sister. The problem, if that's what you wanted to call it, was that she wasn't keen on a grand wedding affair. But deeper than that, on some murky level where the truth lay, she'd accepted Michael Kelly's proposal but was in no hurry to be married. She was still living in California, her work increasingly exciting and important to her. But Kelly was a different story – his determination put her in mind of some hero out of a storybook; his work on the cabin, the land, his new job at the woodyard: he tackled it all like it was a quest and she was the prize. Vida was not much help.

'Why marry at all?' Vida had said. 'I mean, we're not in the fifties now, are we?'

'We might not be here,' Rose said, 'but Oaklake's a different story. It's old fashioned. Quaint.'

'Quaint?'

'Yeah. Think *Little House on The Prairie*.

'My God,' Vida said. 'And you're aiming to live there?'

'Well, that's where Kelly's job is ... and that's where the cabin is ...'

'And what about you? This is where your job is, where your life is. There's more to life than following your husband around, Rose. You know that, don't you?'

Rose shrugged. She didn't know what to say. Part of her longed for a life in Oaklake, setting up home in the cabin, perhaps starting a family, but the other part of her, maybe the bigger portion, had her face turned towards California. She was getting a name for herself on important circuits – not just stage productions now but work with film companies. She had a flair for wardrobe management and production that was already marking her out. Her diary was filled until mid-spring. So, she didn't have time to get married. That is what she was telling Michael anyhow. He'd have to wait because she simply didn't have time.

It wasn't really working.

'We could just marry quietly, Rose,' he'd suggested during his last visit. 'We don't need to do it in Oaklake – let's be modern – let's do it here in California. Your mother's here, your friends. Come on – it would be easy. What do you say?'

She could never find an answer that placated him, was relieved when she saw him off on the Sunday evening, waving at the back of the car as he headed back to Oaklake and the woodyard, her mind already on her sketchbooks and swatches of cloth. And her thoughts. Beneath the level of truth, in a place so deep she couldn't pick at it, lay the real heart of her hesitation: Olive. Rumours have wings of their own and the one that had travelled from Oaklake had cast a long shadow over her. She'd intended to bring it up with Michael but found she didn't have the words to frame the question. As she walked back up the stairs to her small apartment she determined that she would stall Michael until June – until after Olive's child was born.

When Olive went into premature labour in the middle of May, Pearl Clodagh nearly bust a blood vessel in her haste to get to the store. Beattie, pale from her sleepless night tending to Olive, was serving behind the counter.

'Beattie!' Pearl said, dragging a couple of bedraggled looking toddlers behind her. Her face was lit up – fired up no doubt with the anticipation of the newsy day ahead.

'You ever think of journalism, Pearl?' Beattie said, flicking a damp cloth over the counter.

'Say again, Beattie?'

'Or photography perhaps – you know, one of those folks who speeds off to snap accidents, misfortunes?'

Pearl managed a watery smile. 'You OK, Beattie?'

'Me? I'm fine, Pearl, just fine. How about you? Come in for anything special?'

Pearl flicked her eyes at the counter and at the shelves at Beattie's back.

'Flour,' she said. 'Clean out of self-raising – got to do some baking, tins are near empty. You know what it's like with young ones.'

Here it comes, thought Beattie. You had to hand it to the damn woman.

'So … I heard that Olive was …'

'How much you want, Pearl?' Beattie said, the flour scoop in one hand, a large paper bag in the other.

'Oh. Fill the bag, Beattie, thank you. Yes, as I was saying, I heard that …'

Beattie banged the bag onto the counter. A small cloud of flour rose in the air. 'Anything else?'

'Er, no. I think that's all, but …'

'I'll put it on your account then. Bye Pearl, must get on.' Beattie turned away and went into the storeroom without waiting for the woman to leave. She waited till she'd heard the ring of the shop doorbell then opened the door at the foot of the stairs that led up to Gil and Olive's living quarters. She listened for a couple of minutes. It was quiet. Too quiet. She could hear a soft murmur of voices, but none of the hollering and cursing that had marked the night hours. She padded carefully up the stairs, paused at the kitchen door for a moment then went in. Mercy McPhail – the town midwife since time immemorial – was at the table opposite Gil. They were both slumped over mugs of coffee.

'Everything OK?' Beattie said, a small feather of anxiety catching the back of her throat.

'She's sleeping,' Mercy said. 'Getting ready for the next haul, I'd say.'

Beattie walked over to the bedroom and peered through the open door. Olive was laid back on a heap of pillows, her nightgown up round her waist, the heft of her belly rising and falling steadily under the tangle of damp sheets. She was snoring lightly.

'You think it'll be soon, then?' Beattie asked. Her palms dampened at the thought.

'Soon enough,' Mercy said. 'I've sent for Doctor Pete to be on the safe side. Her being a mite early, you know.' She didn't catch Beattie's eye.

Doctor Pete didn't make it in time. Beattie had just started back down the stairs when she heard Olive start up again. Something halfway between a cow in trouble and a Friday night bar fight, then a loud bang – something heavy landing on the floor. Gil appeared at the top of the stairs, rubbing his head, his face the colour of chalk.

'You go in, Beattie,' he said. 'I'll watch the shop.'

'But you should be ...'

'No. She doesn't want me there. She's cursed me flat out of the room. Threw the damn water glass at me.'

Beattie entered the bedroom cautiously. Mercy raised half an eyebrow in her direction. She'd seen it all before. But Beattie was taken aback – the memories of her own labour, of Conrad's birth, generally involved visions of soft, clean linen, fresh flowers by the open window, her own self smiling serenely throughout ...

'Good God, Beattie,' Mercy said, busy laying out a row of stainless steel bowls of varying shapes and sizes. 'This girl puts me in mind of you. The night you had Conrad? I swear I thought I wouldn't hear a damn thing again. Howl? I thought you was birthing a damn wolf. Now, is that crib ready?'

Beattie skirted the room towards the window, keeping a good distance between herself and the bed where Olive writhed like an animal caught in a trap. The girl's hands were clutching at the mattress, her head thrashing from side to side, teeth bared. Beattie took hold of a dampened flannel and moved towards the bed. Mercy put up a cautioning hand.

'Leave her be, Beattie. She's getting there her own way.'

'But look at her,' Beattie said. 'I mean ... is she OK?'

'She's fine ... she's doing just ... oh, wait a minute, here we go ...'

Olive suddenly hushed up and opened her eyes. 'It's coming,' she said. 'It's coming. I can feel it coming out.'

'OK, girlie,' Mercy said, brushing down her white apron, 'let's have us a look.'

Beattie hung back, suddenly afraid. 'Shall I get Gil?' she said after a few minutes, anxious to be anywhere but that bedroom – her own great-grandchild near born and her wanting to run.

Mercy, busy between Olive's knees, didn't look at her. 'Yep. Get Gil,' she said.

Beattie took the stairs as fast as she could, calling Gil's name as she went. He appeared at the storeroom door.

'Is she all right?' he said. 'Is everything all right?'

'Go up,' Beattie said, standing to one side of the stairs. 'Mercy said to go up. She's nearly there.'

Gil charged past her, two stairs at a time, got through the door just as Mercy was wrapping the baby in a white towel.

'Congratulations, Daddy,' she said, motioning him to come forward. Olive lay in the bed like a half-broken thing, one arm dangling limply over the mattress, the other flung back above her head. Her eyes were half closed.

Mercy handed the baby to Gil and led him over to Olive. 'It's a boy,' she said, beaming at them both.

'A boy,' Olive croaked. 'Let me see him, Gil.' Gil lay the child carefully on Olive's chest and watched as she pulled back the towel, her finger tracing the small forehead and nose, stroking the damp head. 'He's got his daddy's hair,' she said, then blew out a long breath and collapsed back onto the pillows.

Chapter 21

Ruaridh McKenzie, born almost four weeks early, was as near to a perfect copy of his father as it was possible to be. It was evident, even to Pearl Clodagh, who was at the store twice daily until Beattie finally relented and took her up to see Olive and the infant, that the golden sheen of the child's hair and the turquoise of his eyes marked him out as Gil's boy.

Rose arrived in town a week after the birth. She'd gone up to The Luck to find Beattie before going to the store.

'How come Michael's not with you?' Beattie said.

'He doesn't know I'm here yet. Thought I'd surprise him.'

Beattie said nothing. Considered her youngest granddaughter.

'He been to see the baby?' Rose asked, her finger idly trailing through a line of spilt sugar on the kitchen counter.

'Not yet,' Beattie said. 'Waiting for you, most likely.' She was lying. Michael Kelly had been over but Olive had sent him away. Too tired, she'd said.

'So ... what's he like. Is he ...'

'Fair hair. Just like his daddy,' Beattie said.

Rose's hand went to her throat. She let out a small puff of air, like she'd been holding her breath. 'Fair hair ... like Gil's ...'

'Just like Gil's,' Beattie said, smiling. 'Come on, why don't the two of us get over there. Olive is busting to show him off.'

Beattie had made that part up. Olive wasn't busting to show the baby off at all. On the contrary, it seemed she was busting to do anything that didn't involve him – serving in the shop, working out back in the storeroom – anything that left her unhampered and in peace. She'd taken to motherhood like some errant ewe: wandering off and leaving the child unattended, ignoring his cries for her milk, oblivious to Gil's attempts to interest her in bathing and dressing him. Beattie was filling in best she could and Mimi was helping out every morning, but it was clear as day that things weren't right.

Beattie was at her wits' end.

Olive was sitting behind the counter staring out at the street. She jumped up when they walked in.

'Olive. You did it! Congratulations!'

Rose put down a cardboard box on the counter and half waltzed up to her sister – her smiling face flushed pink, her arms outstretched. Olive stepped back and looked out the window again. She knew what she should be doing, what she should be saying, but try as she might she could find no button or lever to set it in motion.

'What you got there?' she said, untangling herself from Rose's embrace.

'It's for you, of course,' Rose exclaimed. 'You and the baby. Come on ...'

She watched as Olive opened the lid.

'Some of it's shop-bought,' she said. 'Although I made a couple of outfits myself, and I ...'

'What's this?'

Olive had heaped the clothes on one side and was holding up a large tub.

'Baby Formula,' Rose said. 'Everyone uses it in California. Much easier on the mother, they say ...'

Olive was perusing the labelling on the tin. 'Well, how do you fix it?' she said, on her tiptoes now and rooting in the bottom of the box. She came out with a pair of glass feeding bottles.

'There's rubber teats in there as well,' Rose said. 'I didn't bother with the sterilising compound – you with the brewing gear and all.'

Olive flicked a look at the shop clock. 'Well, let's get one of these things charged up – I figure he'll be wailing any minute now.'

Rose looked around. 'Well where is he, then? Where've you got him hidden?'

'I expect Mimi's got him upstairs. Or Gil.' She left the heap of clothes on the shop counter and took the tub of milk powder and the bottles through to the back room.

Rose looked at Beattie. 'Is everything OK?' she asked. Beattie fixed a smile on her face and nodded. Figured if she didn't give her concerns a name they might just go away.

When old man Riley had announced he would not enter into any land-selling deal, Olive had let the matter slip from her mind.

It was the dumbest thing she'd ever done.

While she'd quietly gloated over the failure of his plans, Michael Kelly got quietly on with his fallback plan. He spent weeks fixing up the fences around his fields, coppiced a small standing of oak that had choked the living daylight out of one corner of Riley's field, then set to and drained a boggy section of ground that miraculously improved the Riley land that stood at the other side of the fence from it. Then, one Saturday, still in his work gear because he figured that would give him a head start, he swung into The Ponderosa knowing full well that Riley would be sitting at the bar, most likely scanning the room for a volunteer to fill his pint glass. Kelly slid onto the bar stool next to him and leaned onto the bar like a man in dire need of some sustenance.

'You been mighty busy, Mr Kelly,' Riley said, tipping his empty glass towards him.

'You have got that right, indeed you have, Mr Riley,' Kelly said, waving over to Walter behind the bar. He waited till the ale arrived then lifted his glass to Riley. Riley snickered like an old ewe then took a long pull on his ale. He was not a big drinking man – largely owing to the fact that most of the town had tired of buying his ale for him and he was too mean to buy it for himself.

'You not hoping you've got me reconsidering?' He had a high-pitched voice which edged anything he said with a touch of comedy. It had been his undoing for most of his life. The blame for this he laid squarely at Miss Turbot's door: being short of sopranos for the school concert one Christmas she'd shuffled him across to sing with the girls – a move that had sealed his fate and reputation. Even now – with a wife and five children (all girls) he felt betrayed by his own voice. He saw it on everyone's face each time he spoke up – that flicker of amusement at his expense.

'Reconsidering?' Kelly wiped the ale froth from his chops. He allowed a frown to crease his forehead, just for a moment, then belted out a loud laugh. 'Reconsidering. Oh yes. I get you. Hah. No, not at all, Mr Riley. I would not hope that at all. I recognise you for what you are – a man of your word and,' he emphasised the word with a slap of his hand on the top of the bar, 'a mighty fine man at that.' Riley squinted at him, not sure if he was being praised or ridiculed.

'Noooo,' said Kelly, rubbing his chin like some old timer. 'Fact is – all the work I've been putting in, I'm about near out of cash ... mmh, indeed I am ...' He took another swig of his beer and waited. He wanted Riley to digest what he was saying before he tackled his main topic.

'Out of cash, you say? What, a strong-working feller like you, out of cash?' Riley's thin lips, frothed with ale, formed what was supposed to be a smile. This was bad news as far as he was concerned. Sure, he'd beaten off this Kelly feller – and Olive O'Grady, for Pete's sake – but money was money and he was waiting for one of them, preferably both of them, to come back at him with a better price. His own missus was in the family way again and, one way or another, he needed to add onto the farmhouse.

'It's sure looking that way, but ... ah well.' Kelly drained the rest of his glass then picked up his hat, making as if to leave. 'I did have another idea ... but no ... it's foolishness.' He fitted his hat onto his head and held out his hand to Riley. 'Well, very nice to bump into you, Mr Riley. I'll be seeing–'

'Another idea?' Riley said. 'What say we fill our glasses and you can tell me about it?'

Kelly had to turn away to hide the grin on his face.

Three pints later Kelly had it in the bag. Riley's reluctance to sell the land had, Kelly said, been very wise. And forward thinking. Because the modern way, he'd explained, leaning in as if imparting some secret information, was not to sell – but to rent. It was the way, the very best way, to make some regular money but still maintain your assets. Riley had swallowed it whole and not only shaken on it, but had made Walter leave the bar to find a sheet of paper so he could record what Kelly had offered and get him to sign it. Consequently, Monday morning saw the pair of them waiting outside Mart Joly's office, each eager to get the deal clinched. It was official within the hour: Michael Kelly was to rent Riley's land for two years at a price that had kept Riley awake the last two nights for fear of losing it.

Chapter 22

It took a few days for the news to filter through to Olive. Not because it wasn't talked about but because her head was no longer working properly. Sure, she could hear what people were saying to her, she could listen and nod, if she had the patience, but it was like her mind could no longer make sense of what was being said. As if there was a sheet of glass between her and everybody else. And all the time a sound like cold wind blowing across an empty desert, distracting her, putting her on edge. Solitude was the only remedy and she sought it constantly. The infant (she could not bring herself to call him by his name – *Ruaridh*, for God's sake. What was Gil thinking? A Scottish grandfather was one thing, but *Ruaridh?*) she avoided at all costs. His wailing was the only thing that pierced the glass, leaving her half demented, her fists clenched while he hung onto her nipples, the sound of him sucking driving her to angry tears. Rose and her baby formula had offered her a way out and she'd taken it. Sure, she was half aware of Beattie's concerned looks, but she didn't have the energy to care. To be left alone and be quiet – that's all she wanted.

So she went back to her horses.

It was early morning, a jagged blue mist still hanging in the air above the top meadow. Olive had slipped out of bed – again – leaving Gil sleeping, then left, not checking on the infant for fear of waking him. She'd driven up to The Luck and parked at the end of the track, walking up to the stables and surprising the horses. She'd saddled Champion and followed the trail up to the treeline.

All the time like she was in a dream.

She rode until she reached the end of the forest then pulled the horse to a halt, dismounted, turned to survey the fields below, then breathed. Breathed in like she was trying to burst her lungs, like she was trying to fill herself, push back the hollow that was burrowing her insides away. It gave her some relief but it was only ever short lived. She knew it would disappear as soon as she returned home: the demands of the infant, the confines of the house squeezing her till she thought she would suffocate.

It was a flash of white that caught her eye – down below, by Riley's fence. A glimpse of something white moving along the hedge that divided the two farms. She raised her hand to shield her eyes and squinted down the field. The hedge was too tall and wouldn't allow her a good view. She climbed back onto Champion and urged him down towards the hedge, dismounted again before she got there then crept the rest of the way, edging along the thick greenery until she came to a patch thin enough to see through onto Riley's field.

Olive stared in amazement. Riley had got himself a stallion. A mighty fine one at that. She leaned as far through the hedge as the fence would allow to get a better look at the creature. He was just about the most handsome horse she'd ever seen. A racer by the look of him. She made a soft shushing noise and held her hand out through the hedge. The horse ignored her.

'Fine looking fellow, isn't he?'

The voice came from nowhere. Olive let out a small shriek and leapt away from the hedge.

'Who the hell is that?' she said, her ire already up and spoiling for a fight. 'Who's there?'

Michael Kelly's smiling face appeared at the other side of the hedge. 'Morning, Mrs McKenzie.' He tipped his hat and gave a small bow, beaming the whole while. Olive stepped back and leaned against Champion's flanks – more to reassure herself that her head hadn't finally thrown all its spanners and left her seeing things that weren't there.

'You're up early,' Michael Kelly continued, the smile never leaving his face, amused no doubt by the fright he'd given her.

'And yourself,' she fired back, still leaning against her horse.

'What do you think of him, then?'

'Who?'

'The stallion. What do you think of him?' Kelly made a soft clucking noise with his tongue and to Olive's surprise, and annoyance, the creature came straight over to him.

'A fine beast. A beauty,' she said. 'When did Riley get him?'

Kelly put his hand to the stallion's mouth, let him nuzzle. 'Riley? Oh, he's not Riley's.' His eyes glinted with amusement. 'I thought you would have heard by now – that's how this place seems to work ...'

'Heard? Heard what?'

Kelly pushed his hat back from his forehead and paused. There was some theatre in it, Olive thought.

'Riley's rented me the land ... he's rented me it for ...' His smile beamed triumph.

Olive didn't hear the rest of what he said, her head suddenly full of the sound of breaking glass. She jumped up onto Champion, reined him around and galloped back to The Luck.

Olive did not talk to Gil about Kelly's deal with Riley for two reasons. First off, the realisation that the man had got the better of her rose like acid in her throat every time she thought about it. But second to that ... second to that was the way she'd felt on seeing him. The way some small fire had kindled itself in her belly and she'd wanted nothing more than to build it some more, set it ablaze ...

One night, Gil had woken early and found her lying awake beside him, her forehead creased like she was wrestling with something.

'You OK?' he said.

'Fine. Shhh. Don't wake the child.'

He turned on his side towards her. 'Looks like you're puzzling over something.'

'Well, I'm not.' She let out a short sigh, impatient already at his questioning, and turned away from him, pulling the covers up over her shoulders. To her dismay he shuffled closer to her and curled himself against her back.

'Gil,' she said. 'Don't.'

'I'm cold,' he said. She could feel the smile in his voice. 'I need a bit of warming up.' He put his hand on her waist, let it slide up and down on her hip, slowly working her nightdress up her thighs.

'Gil.' She tried to relax, tried to coax the passion that used to boil up in her so readily. But she felt nothing and even as she turned onto her back and tried her best to welcome Gil, to be a wife to him, she imagined herself a desert: stretched out, parched and arid. Endless. When it was over and Gil was sleeping, she cried. She heard the infant stirring in his crib and automatically held her breath, willing him to settle. He didn't. So she watched the sun coming up from her seat at the kitchen table, the soft pinks and peaches lighting the pots on the shelves like they were jewels, moving across the walls like slow magic, burnishing the infant's head until it gleamed gold. He looked up at her as he pulled on the teat of the bottle, his eyes locked onto her face in quiet consideration. She looked away from him. Felt nothing.

Gil got accustomed to Olive's absences. The first time he'd woken and found her gone a chill like a winter morning wrapped itself round his heart. She wasn't right. Anyone could see that. He and Beattie and Mimi were filling in all the gaps but Olive herself was a gap that no one seemed able to fill. Not even him. He'd paced the landing back and forth, panic poking the inside of his chest, until the boy had woken and distracted him and caught him up with all the things the morning demanded.

She was with the horses, she said, when she'd shown up at the store just after 8am, twisting her hair back and pulling her apron on, her cheeks pink and shining. There was some air of defiance about her and in his relief he didn't remark on her absence and he supposed she took his silence as some kind of agreement because from then on he woke each morning to find the bed empty, her clothes gone from the chair.

For a couple of weeks Olive confined her riding to the pastures that lay at the top end of the lake. She had no interest in Michael Kelly or what he was up to on Riley's land.

This is what she told herself.

She rode each morning, drawing the fresh air and open space into herself like she was a battery running low. It was what got her through the rest of the day: the effort of being civil to Gil, the demands of the damn customers, the tedium of the infant. Each night she lay in bed, the sheets clenched in her fists, feigning sleep and pining for the next morning. Eventually she got to a point where she thought she could make it work. If she could have those two hours of freedom each morning she could manage it, look like she was doing OK, be some sort of mother.

She was wrong.

It was a Sunday morning. The infant had been awake in the night again. 'Teething,' Beattie had declared earlier that week, like it was something to rejoice over. So Olive and Gil had taken shifts, walking the wailing child up and down the landing, rubbing his gums, cooling his cheeks. Then they'd all slept late. It was gone 8am when Olive woke. She lay quietly listening to Gil's steady breathing knowing it was time to get up and over to the horses, but there was a heavy pull to her that seemed to keep her fastened to the bed. She pulled the covers up to her chin and settled back into the bed. She couldn't remember ever feeling so tired, so weary, so ... She was on the verge of dropping off to sleep when the realisation hit like an unexpected bullseye. She slid noiselessly out of the bed. A ribbon of cold panic crept from the pit of her belly to the tip of her breast bone then threaded itself through her ribs and broke loose like a cage of released birds. She steadied herself on the small chest by the door as she tore off her nightgown and yanked on her clothes. Downstairs she stomped her feet into her boots, shoved open the door and fled out into the cold air. Brittle leaves clattered down from the oak that framed the backyard, cracking under her feet as she pushed through the gate. She made it as far as the truck, cast her eyes around like an escaping prisoner then doubled over and heaved up onto the dying grass.

Pregnant. She was goddamn pregnant. The thought sank like a stone and lodged in her belly.

She crawled into the truck and lay across the seats, her guts still pitching, her mouth sour. Hot tears coursed down her cheeks and down into her neck and hair.

She couldn't do it again.

She wouldn't do it again.

Chapter 23

She couldn't let the child take hold. She couldn't let Gil know.

These were Olive's only thoughts as she rode out each morning, spurring Champion on and on, ignoring his confusion and uneasiness, galloping him like they were escaping wild water, feeling the jolt of the saddle with each stride, welcoming the thud of the leather against her pelvis.

But each morning she woke and the pitching bed and the sour weight in her belly told her the child was still there.

She took to getting up earlier, long before it was light. This allowed her to get a good way towards The Luck before her pitching stomach forced her to the side of the road, roiling and throwing up into the dirt, and it allowed her to ride further and longer. But it wasn't safe. One morning, she'd just got the truck back onto the road when Henry's van came up behind her. He was on his run out to the mail office. She waved at him as he overtook her, her hands clammy from the thought that thirty seconds earlier he would have caught her hanging onto the tail board of the truck, holding back her hair, heaving her guts up.

As it happened, Henry most likely would not have noticed anything. His own thoughts were full of a new venture – one dreamed up by his sister, Maudie, it has to be said, but involving himself and his brother, Pastor Gracie.

Beattie, on the other hand, was a different story.

'What do you reckon is going on there?' she said to Darragh one morning. She'd been up since 5am, labouring over a pan of new pickle. Her eyes were still streaming from the onions.

Darragh was busy with the newspaper. He didn't answer.

'Darragh,' she said, banging the wooden spoon against the pan. He glanced over the top of the page.

'What's that, girl?'

Beattie pointed the end of the spoon at the window. 'Olive,' she said. 'She's out there. Again.'

'Well, I thought that's what she did most mornings now,' Darragh said, anxious to get back to his crossword but aiming not to show it. 'She's been at it awhile, hasn't she?'

'She has,' Beattie, replied, 'but not like this. She was already on the hill when I came down at 5am and she's still not back. And look at the weather. It's freezing.'

'Well ... I ... I guess that's just Olive. She, well ...' Darragh smiled, not sure what to say, his pen itching to get going again.

'Well it's not right,' Beattie said. 'It's not right and she's not right. I'm going to take myself down to the stables and find out what the hell is going on in that girl's head.'

Darragh nodded and glanced back at the crossword.

'Darragh,' Beattie said, belting the spoon against the pan again. He dropped the pen on the table.

They were halfway down the lane and almost at the stables, the pair of them breathing hard, stamping their feet against the cold when they saw it. A plume of lilac smoke rising above the plantation at the top of the meadow, a thin column spiralling upwards and drifting down onto the trees.

Beattie stopped and grabbed Darragh's arm. 'What the hell is that?' she said.

Darragh followed the direction of her waving arm.

'Smoke,' he said. 'Looks like Kelly's having a burn. Most likely that hedge he cut back last week.' Beattie nodded. Placated.

They walked a little further, Beattie's eye fixed on the haze of smoke. He could hear her mind working. She stopped suddenly.

'But I thought Kelly was away?'

'What?'

'I thought you said Kelly was going away. He was off to see Rose. Isn't that what you said? He was going to see Rose yesterday. Staying in California till the weekend.'

Darragh stared at her. She was right. Kelly was away. He looked up again at the trail of smoke. It was no longer lilac, no longer falling lightly down onto the trees. It was black and rising into the air like something wild and hungry.

Olive was beat. She'd been out for longer than ever before and could not keep herself upright in the saddle for another minute. She didn't have the strength to dismount or, she suspected, the iron in her legs to stay upright. It had been more than two weeks and still the child was holding on. She couldn't keep it up much longer, she knew that. Gil was going to notice something – or Beattie. She leaned forward and rested her head against Champion's neck, his damp mane against her raw cheek. She let herself hang there, arms dangling limp against the horse's sides, her breath steaming out into the freezing air, and let Champion wander his own path. He was thirsty, she knew that. He was thirsty and likely aiming for the trough. She ... she just needed to close her eyes for a moment, catch her breath, just ... just for a moment or two ...

She knew something was wrong before she even opened her eyes.

The smell.

There was a smell in her nostrils that she couldn't work out. Acrid and sweet. She hauled herself upright in the saddle and rubbed at her face. Champion was wheeling beneath her, his head low and weaving.

'Whoa, boy.' She leaned forward and stroked his neck but he pulled away from her, his head straining, his eyes rolled up.

'What is it, boy?'

She hauled in the reins but he fought her again, yanking back against her, his front legs rising and flailing. She looked round, trying to clear her head and get her bearings. She'd been asleep. The sun was up. Her clothes were cold and damp. She didn't know what time it was, she didn't know where she was, she ...

Champion suddenly reared up on his hind legs, and let out a high quivering scream. Spittle foamed against his bared teeth. Olive clamped her knees to his flanks and wrapped her hand in the reins. He lifted her up through the air, level with the hedge then higher than the hedge and suddenly she could see. She was at the hedge above Riley's land. Michael Kelly's stables were nestled in the bottom corner of the field. They were in her sight for less than a second, but there was no mistaking it: a thin curl of smoke was twisting from one end of the low building, spiralling up into the morning air.

Without thinking, Olive spurred Champion forward and galloped him along the line of the hedge. There was no gate, she knew that, but she had to find a gap, she had to get down to the stables. If Kelly's horses were in there ... if... Her head spun at the very thought. She urged Champion on, her eyes frantically scanning the hedge and watching the smoke. They reached the end of the field: the hedge was full thickness all the way – nothing that would allow them through. Champion knew what was needed before she even asked him. He wheeled away from the hedge in one smooth curve and thundered flat out back up the meadow towards the woodland, then, without breaking step he swerved into a turn and charged back down towards the hedge. Olive gulped in a lungful of air and tucked herself against his neck, bracing. It was higher than they'd ever jumped before, and wider. But she trusted him. She could feel it in him: in the lengthening of his stride, the smooth run of his spine. He could do it. They hurtled on and, as his feet left the ground, she closed her eyes and relaxed, felt the steady pulse of his blood against her ribs, the smooth ripple of ready muscle against her belly, and they rose, soared like they'd grown wings and were aiming for heaven itself. She opened her eyes and it was like they had broken through into some other world. All was silent and still as they glided through air that seemed to hold them aloft, that seemed to her to waft warm on her cheeks ...

And then they landed, like a fresh miracle, in Riley's field. Champion didn't break stride. He ran like a river in flood, rushing forward, covering the ground like it was disappearing before him, the beat of his hooves a drum announcing their arrival. The closer they got the faster he ran until Olive could hear it: a sound like hell itself: terrified hooves battering wood, Kelly's horses shrieking like tortured souls and the steady crackle of a fire that was just starting to enjoy itself.

Olive reined Champion round and leapt down from his back. She was running towards the stables as soon as her feet hit the earth. A plume of smoke rose, lilac and innocent looking, from the far end of the building. It was twisting up through the frozen air and falling like cobwebs on the frosted trees and, for a moment, Olive thought that she was mistaken – that she would round the end of the stables and find Michael Kelly cooking his breakfast on a campfire.

But it wasn't a mistake, the noise told her that: a din that rose into the air like it was issuing from some nightmare. Olive ran to the double doors and pulled blindly at them, shouting out to the horses inside.

'I'm coming, I'm coming.'

The doors didn't give. She rattled them again: nothing. She charged at them with her shoulder but they stood firm. They were barred from the inside.

Olive ran to the other end of the building, calling out to the horses the whole time, trying to keep the panic out of her voice. She had to get to them, she had to save them.

She rounded the end of the stables and pulled up sharply. The doors were chained and padlocked and fingers of black smoke were rolling from under them, dark and ominous, a ghostly carpet spreading soundlessly across the ground. There was a steady, rhythmic thud issuing from inside the building – as if some great machine were at work.

Ulysses.

The stallion didn't know her but she called out to him all the same.

'I'm coming, boy. I'm coming.'

She looked around frantically for something to smash the

padlock off but the ground around her was smooth and well kept – no rocks, nothing that she could use. She cast her eyes further, to the hedge near Kelly's cabin; he'd been doing some cutting back, the trimmed lengths still laying on the ground, ready to be collected up for burning. She charged off towards it and, halfway there spotted what she needed: Kelly's axe was lodged, ready for work, in a sawn-off stump. She yanked it out and fled back up the slope towards the stables.

She ran up to the door and grabbed the padlock. She held it for a split second then dropped it with a scream. She looked down at her hand, the hot metal had branded a sear of livid red across her palm. She leaned her cheek towards the door and felt the heat from the other side. She couldn't risk opening it and feeding the fire. She had to think of something else. She ran round the back of the building, fighting back the tears, swallowing down hard to stop the scream that was lodged in her throat, and spotted her only chance. A small window. She frantically cleared the glass and peered inside. The inside of the building was dark and gloomy. Kelly's mares had broken out of their stalls and were gathered together by the barred door. She couldn't see Ulysses but she could still hear him. Smoke hung heavy in the pitch of the roof and, in the far corner she saw the unmistakeable glow of fire.

Olive stood back from the window, and, ignoring the pain in her left hand, hefted the axe and brought it, wedge end first against the glass. It shattered instantly. She used the blunt edge to clear as much of the frame as she could then she hauled herself through on her belly. The mares were weaving frantically in front of the barred doors. She took a breath or two, choking as the smoke hit the back of her throat and the top of her lungs, then slowly walked over to them, her voice soft and low, murmuring calm easy words, anything that came into her head, anything to quiet them. They saw her and paused, steadied slightly. She carried on, carefully working her way through them, acting like everything was OK, like there was nothing to be worried about. She got to the door and felt for the fastenings, praying there was no padlock. The wood was rough under her burned hand but she kept on until she located the broad plank lodged between two metal staples that held the doors fast. She gripped one end of the plank and slowly edged it loose. The mares were working themselves up again, but she kept on, soothing them with words that meant nothing, like a mother's lullaby, comforting, promising safety. She dragged the plank back until it was free then laid it on the floor. She pushed against the doors – nothing happened. She pushed again, trying not to panic. The doors didn't budge. She bent down and felt along the bottom ledge. She found it straight away, the metal rod that held the door fastened against the floor. She slid it out slowly, not wanting to bolt the horses. There was the same fastening on the other door. She pulled it up and the doors gave instantly. She hurled herself back and watched as the mares burst past her in a single mass and galloped off across the meadow. She hung over for a few moments trying to steady her breathing. Her lungs felt full and too heavy, like they were filled with mud. Her eyes were stinging and fogged – she rubbed at them and saw the blood on her hands. She suddenly had the impression that she was dreaming: that none of this was actually happening, that she was about to wake up beside Gil ... and then she heard the noise and remembered.

Ulysses was still pounding at the doors of his stall but by Olive's reckoning he had slowed down. She hauled herself up and staggered towards him. The door she had opened had released the mares but it had also granted the growing flames what they desired the most: oxygen. The fire was no longer a warm glow in the corner of the building, it was now licking itself into shape, growing taller, fingering the doors of Ulysses stall, seeking out the timbers of the roof. She would never get the stallion through a burning door. She had to put it out. She frantically scanned the stalls. Water. Kelly had to have water on hand. A tap? A bucket? The light coming through the open doors was not enough to entirely cut through the gloom. She ran back and dodged into one of the mare's stalls, spotted the bucket lying on its side. She cut through into the next stall – the bucket was in the corner – and half full. She grabbed it and ran over to the fire and poured it as close as she could at its spitting base. The fire hissed for a moment then ignored her. She ran for another bucket, then again – forwards, backwards – the sound of Ulysses' hooves drumming her on. Then suddenly, he stopped.

Olive threw down the bucket and shouted for him.

'Ulysses. Ulysses.'

There was no reply.

Olive turned her attention to the door. It was alight now, slender flames stroking the boards. It was fastened with a heavy metal bolt – two heavy metal bolts. Olive cast her eyes around the floor searching for the axe. She dragged it over, hoisted it over her shoulder and brought it down onto the first bolt. Her aim was perfect – the bolt smashed into pieces and fell from the door. Ulysses let out a loud shriek and started kicking again, pounding furiously at the other side of the door. She swung the axe again, mistimed the strike and missed her aim. By now the door was truly blazing. She backed away from the heat while she repositioned the axe then launched herself forward and brought it down like she was felling a tree. The bolt budged but didn't come loose. Olive staggered away from the fire, rocking on her feet. She hoisted the axe again and tried to swing it. It fell from her hands and she fell forward onto her knees only inches from the fire. She scrabbled upright, tried to get on her feet. She couldn't do it.

'Ulysses, Ulysses,' she shouted. 'Come on, boy, come on.'

The beating of his hooves intensified until it seemed like the whole world was drumming in her ears. She hauled herself up from the floor and tried to get out of the way. To get out of the way of the door. He had to get out, she had to move out of the way, she ...

The doors to the stall suddenly burst open and Ulysses reared up at her like some mythical monster, his eyes bulging, his nostrils flared. Olive stumbled backwards to avoid him. He thundered past her, catching the blazing door as he ran. The door caught Olive full square. She looked down at her boots, not sure what had happened, surprised for a moment that she was still standing. Then her knees buckled and she dropped to the floor.

Chapter 24

Beattie was gripping the wheel like she was steering a ship through a storm, yanking the truck round every corner, ignoring every rut in the road.

'How's that smoke looking?'

Darragh twisted himself round in his seat. The track to Kelly's place twisted like a snake and the horizon shifted with it.

'Like we need to get there,' he said, bracing himself against the metal dashboard. 'Put your foot right down on that pedal, girl.'

'Oh my Lord,' Beattie said as they broadsided into the yard. She leapt from the truck and ran towards the cabin. Kelly's mares were milling by the front porch, breathing hard, their heads low. The stallion was a few feet from them swaying on his legs. His white coat was grey and streaked with soot, his mane shrivelled to uneven stubble. Beattie leaned forward, her hands on her thighs, trying to catch some breath. 'Thank God they managed to get out,' she gasped. 'But how on earth did they manage to ...'

'Beattie ... look.'

Beattie turned her eyes towards Darragh and clamped her hand across her mouth.

'Oh, no ... that can't be ... It can't be ...

Champion was running across the meadow, his tail straight out, his head too high. Screaming.

'Olive.' Beattie yelled and charged past the cabin towards the stables. She took it in without breaking stride: one end of the building was truly alight, flames wrapped round the timbers, jealous and greedy. Darragh overtook her, curving past the flames, running flat out to the doors at the other end of the block. Both doors were flung wide, smoke like thunder clouds billowing out and rolling across the frosted grass. He yanked off his shirt and threw it in the rain barrel then wrapped it round his head and face.

'Darragh.' Beattie's voice rang out above the crackle of the fire and the crash of falling timbers. 'Darragh ... she's there ... she's there.'

Beattie shot past him and disappeared into the smoke. He took a deep breath and stumbled after her. Olive was lying on her belly a few feet in from the doorway. Her one arm was outstretched, the other under her face as though she were sleeping. Darragh grabbed her shoulders and turned her onto her back. Her head lolled loosely. She didn't make a sound.

'Beattie, I've got her. Get out now, get ready for me ... I'm bringing her out.'

He scooped his granddaughter up, clawed his way blindly through the smoke and staggered towards the doors. Beattie grabbed him the second he was through and propelled them all forwards, pushing, pushing until Darragh almost pitched forward.

'It's OK, it's OK,' he yelled. 'We're clear, Beattie. Let me put her down.'

He laid Olive down on the cold grass, every cell of him urging her to wake up, to open her eyes. To be all right. 'Olive, Olive.' He was shaking her gently.

'Is she breathing?' Beattie yelled, her voice faltering.

Darragh leaned his ear to Olive's face, water dripping off his hair. He couldn't tell. He couldn't calm himself enough to listen.

'Darragh.' Beattie was on the ground next to him. She held her hand over Olive's mouth. Rocked back on her heels, crying.

'She's breathing ... oh thank the Lord, she's breathing ...'

'Get some water from the barrel,' Darragh said, flinging his wet shirt to Beattie. He leaned over and cradled Olive's head in his hands. Beattie got down beside them and dribbled water onto the girl's lips.

'Olive, it's me ... it's Grandma. Wake up. Please, wake up, Olive. Oh, Darragh ...' She had to stop and turn away. The girl's face was blackened, her hair singed jagged by the fire, her hands bloody and raw.

'Oh, my Lord,' she heard Darragh say. 'Beattie, quick, get the truck. We've got to get her to hospital.'

Beattie turned back and looked.

Olive's belly was drenched in blood.

Olive lay, the next twelve hours, like someone gone from the world: pale and motionless in the hospital bed, the air tanged with wood smoke, the sheets and pillows smudged with soot. She didn't move a muscle, neither when the doctor and nurses tended to her, Beattie wailing in the corridor outside, nor when Gil burst into the room wild-eyed and shaking.

When she did wake, sometime in the middle of the night, her eyes went to Gil, slumped in the chair beside her bed, and her hand went to her belly. She could feel it beneath her night gown: a thick layer of bandaging, tight against her flesh. And a stinging rawness that ran from one hip to the other. She shifted slightly in the bed.

'Olive, thank God. Oh, thank God.'

Gil leaned in towards her and buried his head into her hair. She could feel his tears running into her neck. She pushed him away gently.

'Gil ...' Her voice rasped against her throat.

'It's all right, love, it's all right ...'

'But ...' she looked at him, searching for something in his face that might give her an answer without asking the question.

'Did ... did I ...?'

He nodded. 'You did, Olive, you did.' He was smiling.

'I did?'

He nodded again. 'You saved them, Olive, you saved them all.' The words came out with a sob. 'Good God, I can't believe you did it ...'

'I saved them? What do ...'

He took hold of her again. 'Kelly's horses,' he said. 'You saved every goddamn one of them.'

Olive pushed him away again. She looked at her hands – one was heavily bandaged, her fingers black and grimy against the white sheet. She laid the other on her belly.

'But this ... what happened?'

'Oh,' he said. 'You got cut. You got yourself cut. They had to stitch you up.'

'Stitch me up? That's ... that's what this is?' she patted her belly.

Gil nodded and swiped the back of his hand across his eyes.

'You'll be good as new in no time. That's what the doctor said. Good as new.'

Olive turned her face from him. 'I need to sleep,' she said.

She turned carefully onto her side and let him rearrange her pillows and pull up the covers, tucking her in like she was his child. She listened as he turned down the light then settled himself back in the chair. Then she stared out into the darkness.

The child was still there.

Olive woke next morning creased and aching like she'd been folded in a closet all night. Gil's chair was empty, a teacup marking the place he'd been. She could hear voices outside the room, busy feet walking past the door, a trolley rattling up the corridor. She ran her tongue across her lips. They were no better than two dried out crusts. She turned her head towards the small locker by the bed: someone had left a pitcher of water and a small glass. She raised her arm towards it and immediately felt the pull against her belly. She stopped and sank back against the pillows. Remembered.

The child, she thought, the child is still there. And to her amazement, the thought made her smile.

Michael Kelly and Rose arrived later that day. Olive was napping – exhausted by the endless attention from Beattie, Darragh, Mimi, Gil. They'd taken it in turns to mind the infant so she had yet to see him but she was nursing some measure of hopefulness on that front: there had been some shift in her, some awakening that lent a tenderness to her thoughts about seeing him again, and about the new life that had clung on inside her. This is what she was thinking when they arrived.

Rose walked through the door like it was her first day at school, Michael Kelly behind her, unsure, peering over her shoulder. Olive gave them a dry smile and a small wave with her good hand.

'Oh my Lord,' Rose said, rushing over in a swish of silk and fresh air. 'Just look at you ... oh, Michael, look at her ... oh, Olive.' She broke down in a flurry of tears, her hands lighting on Olive's face, her hair, her bandaged hand.

'Am I that bad?' Olive said, trying another smile, feeling the splits in her lips widen.

'Oh, I'm sorry,' Rose gulped. 'I'm sorry, Olive. No, it's me ... it's such a relief ... it was such a shock ... and we've been travelling since Beattie rang ... Michael?' She straightened up and moved away so Michael Kelly could approach the bed. The look of concern on his face set Olive's stomach afloat.

'Have you been up there?' she said. Her tongue was like a lump of perished rubber in her mouth. Kelly shook his head.

'Came straight here,' he said. 'To thank you.' He took her hand. His eyes were full of tears.

'Don't you go blubbering on me as well,' she said. 'Beattie's near drenched these sheets twice ...' She forced a laugh which landed a bit high and awkward. It tensed her belly and she felt the twinge of the stitches.

'Oh, are you OK?' Rose said, nudging Kelly back out of the way.

'I cut my damn belly open, apparently.' Olive said, patting the sheets. 'Getting through that window most likely. That was some good forethought, Kelly, putting a damn window in your stables. A mite unusual, I have to say, but damn useful.'

'Oh, Olive, you poor thing.' Rose took hold of Olive's hand again, stroking it like it was a pet rabbit. And that's when Olive saw it.

The wedding ring.

Rose caught her eye instantly. 'Michael,' she said, turning towards him. 'I wonder if you might be able to persuade them to make us a cup of coffee?'

As soon as he was out of the door she turned back to Olive.

'Beattie doesn't know,' she said, her face pink at the mention of her grandmother's name. 'We were going to tell her this weekend, but now, all this ... it's probably ...'

'It's OK, Rose,' Olive said. 'It's OK. I won't say anything about it.'

She was concentrating on the feel of Michael Kelly's hand on her own. How the touch of him had set her heart banging against her ribs. But now, here they were – him married to Rose and her pregnant.

Two secrets, she thought. *Which one will Beattie rumble first?*

Chapter 25

It was decided that Olive should stay put in the hospital for a few days. Give her chance to recuperate, the doctor said. This was fine by her. Although it wasn't the recuperating she was in need of as much as the chance to figure herself out. She stayed mostly in bed, watching the weather from the window, letting herself doze on and off, waking each time with the same question. This change that had come over her, this thrill that she felt each time she thought about the new baby. Did she still feel it? The relief, each time to discover that yes, she did. She'd started rehearsing the conversation with Gil, grateful in part that she'd not managed a quiet moment with him since the night of the fire: he never arrived alone, always with Mimi or Beattie and the infant, or all three of them, a crowd round her bed, filling every bit of space, taking all the air out of the room. She would lay under the covers, awkward and centre stage, smiling, joining in even, but always some portion of herself standing back, watchful and guarded from some quiet place inside, concentrating on the new baby.

In terms of the infant – *Ruaridh* – she had detected an encouraging degree of softening towards him. She'd held him, at least. Stiff armed and tentative, sure, but that was because of the stitches across her belly, but once, when he'd smiled up at her and held his stubby hand out to touch her face, she'd leaned in and kissed his forehead. Without even thinking about it. She'd sat back in time to see Beattie smile over at Gil and a rush of something that felt like shame slicked over her like cold water.

Nonetheless, she'd taken it as a good sign. Something she could build on.

But she needed to talk to Gil.

This is what she was turning over in her mind one afternoon

when Rose waltzed in through the door. She was on her own. The cold fresh air came in with her, her cheeks were like two polished apples. She looked like an advert for good health.

'Rose, how come you always look like you just stepped out of a damn film?'

'Oh, don't be silly,' Rose said, whipping off her coat and squaring up her dress.

'Silly?' Olive said, sweeping her two arms over her own shabby self. 'I reckon I could raise the bar for Halloween this year.'

'Don't exaggerate,' Rose said. 'You look just fine. A little frayed round the edges perhaps ...' She turned her attention to the large bag she'd brought in with her. 'Anyway, I've come to take you in hand.' She rolled up her dress sleeves and unzipped the bag. Olive watched.

'I'm not wearing no fancy clothes if that's what you're toting ... oh.'

Rose turned. She has a large pair of scissors in her hand. They looked suspiciously like Beattie's dressmaking scissors.

'What the hell are you aiming to do with them?'

'Olive.' Rose pulled a stern face. 'Have you actually taken a good look in the mirror?'

'Well, I've taken a look. Might not call it a good look.'

'And this?' Rose ruffled Olive's hair – what was left of it. She pulled a large hand mirror out of the bag and gave it to Olive.

'Well yes, OK, it's looked better.'

Later that afternoon Olive lay in bed pondering her new haircut – and Rose's account of the wedding. Michael Kelly had eventually won her round, apparently, persuaded her that a small, quiet, *modern* wedding was the way to go. Sure, Olive and Gil's do had been just grand, but did she really want to go to all that fuss and organisation? Olive wasn't convinced that Rose hadn't wanted a bit of fuss, that she hadn't somehow been sold short. She'd pulled a small set of photographs out of her bag, *I've not had time to put them in an album yet*, and Olive shuffled through them. Rose and

Michael Kelly arm in arm, laughing: Rose's dress falling like soft layers of petals, her hair curling round her face, Michael Kelly's face lit like it was polished, in a suit that made him look like someone going to the races. And Vida. Olive pulled the photograph closer.

'She's still so young, isn't she?' Olive said. Her mother's face smiled out at the camera. Olive searched her features trying to detect some degree of regret or shame, any damn thing to indicate remorse for leaving her and Rose behind, for abandoning them. But there was none. On the contrary, Vida had a look that seemed to suggest deep contentment, like life had taken her to the place she wanted to be and she was happy there.

'You OK?' Olive suddenly became aware that Rose was watching her. 'Vida ... you've not seen her in an awful long time ... she's ...'

'I don't feel any need to see her, Rose,' Olive said, putting the photographs down on the bed.

'I believe she would like to see you ... now, you know ... now you've got the baby.'

Olive let out a snort. 'She's a mite late for showing interest in babies, don't you think?' The irony of her words brought two blotches of colour to her cheeks. 'She ever talk about our pa? About Conrad?' she said.

'No, not really.' Rose said.

'You see any photographs of him?'

'No. A few postcards, that's all. But ...' Rose paused and considered her sister. 'She told me ...'

'What?'

Rose's hand went to her throat as it always did when she was feeling indecisive. 'She ... erm, she told me he looked like Darragh.'

'So, when you going to tell Beattie? Or has she already guessed?'

Rose smiled and sat down on the edge of the bed. She fished inside the neck of her dress.

'She already knows,' she said, drawing out a small golden locket. 'She stomped around and cried for a while ... and then she gave me this. It's just like yours, look.'

Rose held up the chain and swung the locket towards Olive. A scrolled 'R' set in a filigree of intricate gold. Beattie had had them made when the girls were young and then stashed them away, her mind, even then, on what their futures would hold. She'd given Olive hers on the morning of her wedding, laid her hair to one side and fastened the clasp with her rough, clumsy farmer's hands, setting them both off in a bout of laughter that tailed off into tears. Olive knew that Beattie had been looking forward to the same moment with Rose. She was more than up to the fuss and organisation. Michael Kelly might have considered that.

Olive glanced at the clock on her small table. Half an hour and Gil would be arriving. The thought of it made her breath catch. He'd wanted to bring Ruaridh with him but she'd insisted he come alone. She'd seen the disappointment, and worry, in his face, but she needed him on his own to tell him about the new baby. She daren't wait any longer, felt like she had to act while this new feeling, this excitement, was still upon her. She was afraid it would disappear, afraid that if she examined it too often it would blow out, like opening a door to see if a candle was still lit at the risk of snuffing the damn thing out. Gil would make it real. He would wrap the whole thing up and keep it all alight – her, the baby ... So she lay still, letting her mind skim the surface of her feelings but not allowing herself to go too deep. There'd been another welcome shift in her too, she'd noticed it while Rose was with her. The bed was pitching less and her stomach seemed to have settled. She reckoned her body was easing into the pregnancy in a way it never had the first time round. She considered this for some time, starkly aware of her concerted attempts to unseat the baby, the fact that she didn't deserve this. Then she tucked the feeling away like it was some important document that was going to guarantee future security and let herself drift off to sleep.

She woke – or thought she woke – to Gil leaning over her, his lips against her own. A long, lingering kiss that tasted of – *tobacco?* When she opened her eyes Michael Kelly was smiling down at her.

'Thank you,' he whispered, then gently cupped her cheek in his hand, raised a finger to his lips, and turned away.

'Sorry I'm late,' Gil said.

Olive sprang up in the bed, her eyes scanning the room for Michael Kelly as Gil breezed in through the door. He launched into a long-winded tale about dropping the infant off with Beattie and getting caught up in talk about Rose and Michael Kelly. He was full of the telling of it until Olive could stand it no longer and put her hand on his arm and shushed him up.

'Sorry, love,' he said. 'How are you feeling?'

'I ... I'm fine.' She put her hand to her mouth, traced the curve of her cheek. 'I was dreaming ... I think.'

She hoisted herself up in the bed and fixed on a smile. 'The doctor says I can come home soon. Tomorrow maybe.'

Gil nodded. He knew that already. What he didn't know – what had had him gassing away like a fool – was why she'd asked him to come on his own.

'So ... well ... I...'

Gil narrowed his eyes and waited. His heart already weighing the options.

'I ... I...' She blew out a loud breath and took hold of his hand. 'Gil...'

'For God's sake, Olive, just tell me. What?'

She moved his hand and lay it on her belly.

'I'm pregnant.'

Gil snatched his hand away. 'You're ... you're pregnant. What ... I mean ... when did you ... how .... oh my Lord, you're pregnant.'

He caught hold of her and pulled her towards him, burying her face in his chest, the thud of his heart against her face.

That was when she felt the first twinge. She thought nothing of it, took it to be the stitches across her belly. Until Gil released her and she leaned back against the pillows, laughing, her face wet with tears. Then the pain came again. Low down in her belly, a grumbling kind of pain, lower than the dressing. Followed by a darting pain across the tops of her thighs. Olive clamped her hand to her stomach and let out a sharp gasp as pain like a hot knife thrust through her lower back and into her belly.

'Gil ... get me up, quickly. Get me up. I need to get to the bathroom.' She threw back the bed covers and swung her legs out, clamping them together as she walked, squeezing against the heavy weight that was bearing down, pushing out of her pelvis, a twisting pain that made her want to scream out. But she didn't scream out. She held it in. She held it all in. Recognised it for what it was. She didn't deserve to cry out. Because she didn't deserve this baby and this – this was her punishment.

And it was swift. A sheet of pain like a bolt of lightning struck her as she lowered herself onto the toilet, then a sudden gush of hot blood, followed by a dull pressing ache in the lips of her vagina, another flow of blood, a sudden urge to urinate.

And then it was over.

She leaned forward and let her head hang down. A bead of sweat tracked its way down her nose and onto the floor. Her nightdress clung to her back like a wet sheet. Gil was kneeling beside her, rocking on his heels, his hand on her shoulder.

'Is ... is ...'

'I just need a moment, Gil,' she said.

He staggered to his feet. 'I'll go get the nurse,' he said, 'I'll go and get ...'

'No.'

'But Olive ...'

'Gil. No. Don't get the nurse. I'm all right. I'll be all right. Just give me a minute.'

Olive gripped the edge of the wash basin and pulled herself to her feet. The room set off in a circle and she sat down again. Cold sweat pricked her forehead.

'Olive.'

She looked up at him and the room reeled again. 'I'm OK,' she said. Her voice came at her from far away.

‘I’ll go get someone …’

‘No.’ She lifted her head again, squinting against the light bouncing off the white tiles, trying to locate his face. Everything was so bright. She was so cold. ‘I’m sorry, Gil. There’s no baby. I made a mistake.’

Chapter 26

They kept it to themselves: Olive didn't want a fuss and Gil wanted to do whatever would make her happy.

But grief stalked them.

In his quiet moments Gil revisited the memory of Olive's announcement, rolled it around in his mind like it was a fine taste in his mouth. Pregnant. Another child. It was just what he wanted. He hadn't known until she said it, but it had set up a need in him that he wanted to satisfy. He couldn't broach it with Olive. She'd eventually sprung back, but something had gone out of her – or taken a step back. It was like she was there in person but watching from behind a pane of glass. Everyone thought it was the after-effects of the fire: the shock, smoke on the lungs, the overexertion, and the two of them played along with it. But when they were alone in bed, the day done, the infant asleep, they curled into one another, silently watching the moonlight play across the bedroom window, the oak in the backyard dealing a shadow show against the wall, and he imagined their unspoken thoughts spiralling up into the cool air, and falling back down on them. Soft strands that would stitch them together more tightly than before.

But Olive's mind was a patchwork that didn't want to fit together. Her thoughts would not line up in any order that gave her peace. She set to on some task only to find herself wandering away from it, the job half finished, some other necessity catching her attention, then just as soon losing its grip on her. She went through the day but achieved nothing. The infant was a constant of course, somehow threading it all together. But they were loose threads: despite herself, the longing for the lost baby did not translate into easy love for the one she already had. What it all boiled down to was a feeling that she had to tread carefully at all times: there were too many gaps in her mind, too many chances to slip through and find herself skidding towards places she should not go. The fire, the lost child. Michael Kelly.

On top of it all Beattie's eye was on her like a weathercock in a north wind. No matter how much she ducked and weaved it seemed that Beattie was always just behind her. Or just ahead.

'So how long do you think before Rose comes down to the cabin ... you know, moves down here?' Beattie said. She'd roped Olive into some early-morning cleaning. They'd spent a solid hour rubbing the counter with beeswax and lemon oil, Beattie's concoction, then buffing it up with a pair of lambswool dusters. It was shining like an altar.

'No idea,' Olive said. 'But Pearl Clodagh's gonna get it if she plonks her kid's backside on here.'

She allowed herself a half smile: for all his griping about what to call the place, Kelly's timber masterpiece had been named for him. The Cabin. He'd never shake it off. He might come up with some fancy moniker – nail it to the gate post even – but Oaklake being Oaklake, the place would always be The Cabin.

She was running her hand back and forth over the wood, letting her fingers trace the grain, circling the two knots that made the surface uneven and had to be avoided when displaying goods, hoping that Beattie was going to drop the subject.

'Well, I reckon it won't be long,' Beattie said.

Olive didn't say anything.

'Before she comes down here I mean ... settles in at The Cabin?'

Olive felt her shoulders rise up a notch. She knew what was coming.

'Well ... I reckon it won't be long before they're, you know ... thinking of starting themselves a little family.'

Olive braced herself but it still got through. Like a sharp arrow through an unguarded gap. She'd thought about it already, lying in the dark beside Gil. How would she feel if – when – Rose got pregnant?

‘I don’t know,’ she said. It struck her that she might have added “I don’t care” but she knew it wasn’t true. There was no doubt about it, if Rose had a child she would be like the Madonna herself. She would sew outfits, she would bake cookies, she would ... she would be perfect.

‘Well, I’m going to talk to her about it,’ Beattie said. ‘After all,’ she stopped and sniffed. ‘It’s not altogether right, now that they’re married and all ...’

Olive waited. Beattie was fussing with the oilcloth.

‘What’s not altogether right?’

Beattie smoothed the oilcloth with her big hands. ‘Well him. Michael ... living here on his own. Rose up in California. It’s not right, is it?’

Olive gathered up the dusters and took them to the door for a shaking. She didn’t want to think about Rose – or Michael Kelly.

‘I guess it must be *modern*.’

Beattie let out a snort and started hoisting boxes back onto the counter. She was still hurting about the wedding, still struggling to work out how something she’d been relying on had simply wriggled away.

‘You’re likely right, though.’ Olive said it just to see Beattie’s face brighten. ‘Modern or not, some things just don’t change.’

The truth, though, was that things *were* changing. The new decade was almost upon them and with it a growing feeling that someone had lifted the stone that Oaklake crouched happily beneath and shone an unwanted light down on them. The old folksy ways they were so fond of were starting to look like something else. Backwardness perhaps. The outside world was creeping in. Some of it was welcome – the new highway north of Picker’s Flag for example, made getting around a whole lot easier. But it made them a whole lot more accessible. Vulnerable. New folks were arriving – with their different accents and their different ways. Picker’s had taken the worst hit – dam workers from up north – rough fellers, light on working, heavy on drinking. The monthly town meetings took longer and left folks with a feeling of mild unrest, a feeling that things had somehow gotten out of kilter. Peace of mind seemed harder to come by: small groups of neighbours hung around after the meetings, still chewing over some unresolved worry, more often than not waiting to talk things over, generally with Gil.

Olive wasn't sure how it had come about: there had been no official election but it seemed that Gil, having agreed to chair the meetings, had then by some default found himself called on for all manner of problem-solving reasons. Sure, it was his evenness and good humour that did it, plus the fact that he was generally available at the store but Olive found that she did not like it – the fact that he could be whisked off at any given moment – to debate the finer points of Clodagh's gripe with O' Reilly or to have a chat to some youngster hell-bent on trouble. It left her at home with the infant, restless and on edge, unable to settle until he returned.

As a result she'd taken to working out back in her brewing shed – dodging up and down the stairs to check on the boy every once in a while then returning to her kegs, keeping herself busy and keeping her mind quiet. This is where she was, one Thursday evening, Gil out on some hand-holding mission in town, her stomping around the brewing shed, her breath pluming out into the malty air. She was muffled up in one of Gil's jumpers, the neck pulled up over her chin, mixing a new vat of barley and malt, stamping her feet against the cold floor when she heard the click of the gate catch.

'I'm in here, Gil.' she shouted. She didn't leave off from her stirring. His footsteps rang across the frozen yard. Now, she thought, she'd be obliged to pin back her ears and listen to some tale of misery ...

'Well, hello there, Mrs McKenzie.'

Olive spun round, dropped the spoon into the mash.

'Kelly,' she said, yanking the collar of Gil's sweater off her face. 'What in God's name are you doing here?'

He gave her a smile that advertised all his teeth.

'Come for some advice,' he said.

'Oh,' she said. 'Well you'll have to come back later.' She turned her back on him and fished the spoon out of the mash. 'Gil's out. Dealing with some matter or other. Don't know when he'll be back.'

'It's not Gil I'm wanting. It's you.'

Olive dropped the spoon again. 'What?' she said, not turning round. She could feel the heat in her cheeks. She leaned over the vat to retrieve the spoon. Kelly chuckled.

'I said, it's you I want ... some horse advice ... I ...'

Olive straightened up and turned to him. 'Oh. Horse advice. Well, OK ... fire away.'

Kelly chuckled again. Olive detected some discomfort in it. 'I suppose what I really need is a consultation. It's complicated ... well, no, not complicated exactly, but erm ...'

'Is it Ulysses?'

'It is.' He raised an eyebrow at her. 'How'd you know?'

Olive sniffed. 'Stands to reason. What's the problem?'

Kelly shuffled on his feet. He glanced away from Olive. 'Well, er ... his manliness, his, erm ... *interest*. It seems to have taken something of a knock.'

Olive stepped towards him. 'He's lost his urge, you mean. His urge for the mares?'

'Well, yes. That's it. You have it right there.'

'I'll give it some thought,' she said and turned back to her stirring because she knew the pleasure his request had granted her was written all over her face.

Chapter 27

A couple of weeks later, November already lending a chill to the air that had folks fearing the worst for the months ahead, Darragh was loading the stove with fuel before heading up to bed when Gil burst in through the door.

'Where's Beattie?' he said, his breath half gone out of him from rushing. He had the baby in his arms. The infant's face was red as a tomato.

'Get Beattie,' Gil said, unhooking the blanket from his son. 'He's not well, the boy's not well.' He rubbed his free hand back and forth through his hair, his eyes glittering with tears.

Beattie appeared at the kitchen door, still pulling at the straps on her wooden leg. She took hold of the baby and started unfastening his clothes, pulling off layers of vests and woollens until she got him near naked.

'Get me some warm water and a cloth,' she barked at Darragh. 'Water only just warm – tepid. How long's he been like this, Gil?'

'I don't rightly know. Olive's had him all day, I was working out back, I ...'

'It doesn't matter. Get me the thermometer, Darragh, then go get the truck started. This child is cooking up, we need to get him to the hospital. Where's Olive?'

'She's not here ... ' Gil said.

'No worries, we can pick her up on the way through town ...'

'She ... she's not there,' Gil said.

'What?'

'She isn't there. She's not at home. She ...'

'It doesn't matter,' Beattie said. 'Come on. Let's go.'

By the time they were halfway to Picker's Flag, Beattie was sure. The child was breathing wrong, the skin on his chest was showing dark spots. Her daddy had lived through it and had drummed the warning signs into her. Brain fever. The very thing that near killed her, left her with half a leg.

'Drive faster, Darragh,' she shouted.

She hoped the noise of the engine muffled the panic in her voice.

'So where's Olive?' Beattie whispered. She'd sat on the question till it was pricking her backside. The three of them were hunched on a hard bench outside the small room where two doctors and three nurses were tending to Ruaridh.

'She went out,' Gil said. 'She said she was going out. I thought she was in the ale shed doing a brew but she wasn't there. I couldn't find her ... I don't know where she went. I had to stop looking ... the boy ...'

Beattie frowned at Darragh. 'Out? But why? Why would she be out so late? And where? Where would she go?'

'I don't know,' Gil said, his voice strained like it was coming through a chink of wood.

'You don't know? But what kind of answer is that, Gil?'

Darragh gave her arm a squeeze, shook his head at her. She was having none of it. 'I said, what kind ...'

Beattie broke off as the door to the small room opened and one of the doctors emerged. The expression on his face landed on Gil's heart like hammer. He leapt to his feet, clutching at the doctor's arm.

'Is he all right ... is he going to be all right?'

'It's too early to say, Mr McKenzie. All I can say is thank the Lord you got him here so quickly. We'll know by the morning, but the child has got a long night ahead.' He looked at the three of them then up and down the corridor. 'Is the child's mother here?' he said, clearing the embarrassment out of his throat with a small cough.

'She's on her way now,' Beattie said, springing to her feet. 'She was out visiting when the child took ill. I'm meeting her with the truck.' She managed a smile but it slid off her face too quickly to be convincing. It seemed to her that things could not be more wrong. How could Olive be off some place that Gil didn't know? How could that possibly be?

'We better set off for her now, Beattie,' Darragh said, backing her lie up so solidly it made her want to cry.

She gripped Gil by the shoulders. 'We'll be right back, son. We'll get Olive. We'll be right back.'

Gil watched the two of them until they rounded the corner at the bottom of the ward. He felt like he was in water up to his neck, he couldn't feel the floor. He wanted Beattie to take him by the shoulders again and hold him up, keep holding him up. He'd not told Beattie the truth – he knew where Olive was. And he was not the only one who knew it.

'Oh Lord, she's not there,' Beattie said, before Darragh had stopped the truck. The store was in darkness.

'I'm still going up to check,' Darragh said. He knew she was right but it was more a need to get away for a few moments. The fizz of Beattie's panic was starting to cross over to him. The whole journey home she'd gone back and forth over the what ifs, throwing questions at him that he couldn't answer. He needed a few minutes to think – and to work out how to tell Beattie where he thought Olive might be. He walked carefully round to the back of the store. The sight of the door swinging open on its hinges – witness to the panic of Gil's leaving – whipped a tight band round his guts. He turned on the light and called out for Olive, embarrassed by the lack of conviction in his voice.

'Olive?' He was play-acting in case Beattie was coming up behind him.

'Olive?' He sang her name out one more time then turned and shut the door behind him.

'Well?' Beattie said, before his backside was on the seat.

Darragh shook his head. 'I reckon it might be worth trying The Luck,' he said, reversing the truck back up the street. 'She could have gone there if she came back and found Gil and the boy gone, although ...'

'Although, what?'

Beattie swivelled in her seat so she could see Darragh's face. He was scuppered and he knew it.

Darragh concentrated on turning the truck round but she'd got him. Like the moon coming out from behind a cloud and lighting up the very thing you were trying to hide. He wiped his mouth with the back of his hand and leaned forward in his seat, peering out into the dark. He was going to have to tell her.

'Darragh.' Her voice put a squirm in his belly.

'She's likely round at The Cabin ...'

'The Cabin? What the hell do you mean, The ...'

Darragh took a deep breath and shot the words out fast. 'The Cabin, with Michael Kelly.'

The first time Darragh had come upon Michael and Olive – the pair of them sat together at Kelly's kitchen table, a mess of paperwork spread out before them – he'd been embarrassed and awkward, quickly excusing himself and near enough tripping himself up to get back through the door.

'Oh, hello there, Grandpa,' Olive said, her casual tone unknotting him some. 'You might be able to help us out with these.' She waved her hand at the papers scattered on the table.

'What is it?' Darragh said, lowering himself onto a chair and unfolding his spectacles. He was buying himself a bit of time, wondering if Beattie was aware of the ... the situation.

'Plans. Kelly's building some new stables.'

Darragh glanced over at Michael Kelly. Stables was no news to him. He and Michael had already discussed the matter at length – in fact that was the reason behind the visit – Darragh had come up with a new idea and he wanted to talk it out with Kelly.

'Well, I ... well, yes, I might be able to help. What's holding you up?' He fixed his glasses on and picked up the piece of paper nearest to him. He'd seen it before. What he hadn't seen before was his own granddaughter – the wife of another man, the mother of a young baby – sitting at the table with a man who wasn't her husband as if it were the most ordinary thing in the world. But he held his tongue, and his nerve, till it was almost suppertime, then got up from the table.

'You want a lift back home, Ol?' he said, making a big show of looking at his watch.

She was making notes on of one of the drawings. She didn't even look up. 'No. I've got the truck. I'm fine.'

So he hadn't mentioned it to Beattie and it had been rolling round his guts like a bad apple ever since. He'd avoided going over to The Cabin for a few nights until Beattie noticed and asked him what he was up to. He'd almost told her then but backed out at the last second, telling himself he was making a fuss over nothing. Darragh knew her mind wasn't entirely made up about Michael Kelly – she tolerated him helping the feller out with the woodwork because it was going to benefit Rose in the long run – but she had concerns about the man that he failed to see and this would have trumped the lot. So he'd gone, walking instead of driving. He'd approached the front door cautiously then, realising his possible error, made a great performance of walking into one of the feed buckets on the doorstep. It was no matter because Olive was not there. Neither was Michael Kelly. Darragh had paused on the threshold and listened, then backed out quickly for fear he might hear some noise he didn't want to hear. He flicked his eyes to the bedroom window – there was no light on. He didn't know if that was good or bad.

'Darragh.' Michael Kelly's voice boomed out from the small barn. 'Thought I heard someone clanging around.' Kelly was smiling but his face was slick with sweat and his hair was damp and strung with lengths of hay.

'Michael,' Darragh said. 'You OK?'

'Fine, fine. I was just away up to The Cabin now to get some coffee on. Olive's in the barn.'

Darragh's cheeks near dropped off his face.

'In the ...'

'Yeah, she's in the barn. We've been having our first go ... go on.' Kelly ushered him on but Darragh's feet were not for moving. 'Darragh, go on in, I'll bring you some coffee down. We might have more luck with the three of us ...'

'Well, I told Beattie I'd not be long, I might just start back ...'

'Grandpa ... is that you?' Oh, good Lord, Darragh thought, rubbing his hands on the front of his pants.

'It is,' he shouted.

'Well, can you get yourself in here, then – we could do with an extra set of hands. This feller's just not taking the bait.

Darragh walked into the barn as slowly as he could. Kelly had strung some lighting up and, despite the chill of the evening, the effect was warm and cosy. Olive was perched on a bale of hay, leaning back against the wooden planking of the stall. A tall, slender-muscled mare – one Darragh had not seen before, was standing a few feet from her. Kelly's stallion was on the other side of the barn, pulling hay out of a net.

'He's just not interested,' Olive said, pushing her hair back from her face. 'We've been trying for near two hours and it's like he doesn't know what he's supposed to do.'

'And you didn't think to tell me this, Darragh? You didn't think to tell me that our granddaughter' – she put some theatrical stress on the word – 'our own granddaughter, is spending her evenings with another man? No. Not another man ... her sister's husband, her brother-in-law, while her own husband and child sit at home wondering where the hell she is,' – her voice was gaining some pitch – 'and what the hell she is doing?'

'It's not like that, Beattie ...' His ears were stinging.

'It's not like that? Darragh, what the hell were you thinking? You should have come straight to me. I should have known about it. My God.' She swiped at her forehead with her coat sleeve. She should have known about it – there was the truth of the matter – but the wedding, the baby, the store: she'd got herself so wrapped up in it all she'd failed to see what was happening. She turned the key in the ignition and hammered the truck forward, wound down the window and let the freezing air blast over her cheeks.

Chapter 28

Gil leaned forward on the bench and let his head rest in his hands. His back ached from sitting but every time he got to his feet he set off walking the corridor, his heart picking up a pace that left him jittery and tearful. He listened to the murmur of voices from behind the door, the occasional splash of water, opening and closing of drawers. They were working on Ruaridh, that's all he knew. *Working on him.* Like he was a puzzle or a broken-down car. He could feel his head throbbing through the palms of his hands, a low monotonous vibration that went up a notch if he looked at the lights. It was not pain as such – he could have settled for pain – it was a low hum, like voices, that had nowhere to go except whirl round his head till he felt like he might tear it off.

Olive. He hadn't told Beattie the truth. He'd known where she was. Same place she was most evenings, it seemed. She was with Michael Kelly.

'It's horse business, Gil,' she'd said, first time he raised the matter.

'That's what you call it, is it?' he'd thrown back.

She'd charged out of the room at that and he hadn't gone after her. He'd been ready to let it lie but she'd burst back in a few minutes later, her cheeks crimson and her eyes wet.

'So this is how it is, Gil,' she said. 'You expect me to hang around the house on my own every evening while you go out round town sorting out everyone else's business.'

He wasn't expecting that. 'But Olive ...'

'But Olive? But Olive nothing. It's most nights, Gil, straight from the supper table more often than not. And I'm here ... on my own ...'

'But you're not on your own, Olive, you've got ...'

'I've got the infant. In bed. Sleeping.'

'But I thought ...'

'You thought what? That I could occupy myself embroidering pillow slips? That I could take up goddamn knitting?'

'Well no, no ... I thought ...'

He'd got no further. She'd slammed back out. She didn't give a damn what he thought. He'd stood at the kitchen sink, watching the leaves dropping from the oak in the yard. He'd thought it might be a good thing – her having some time alone with Ruaridh, a chance to tie them together some, but he'd known, known the first time that he'd come back to an empty house, that she was unhappy. And he'd ignored it.

He'd been over at Henry's: there were changes afoot with the mail service and Henry had got himself het up and wanted Gil to go over the documents with him. He'd been a while and when he came back he found the kitchen empty. Ruaridh was sleeping in his crib but Olive was nowhere to be seen. He'd tracked her down eventually, lugging sacks of barley around in the brewing shed, dust and chaff dancing in the dim light of the filthy lamp.

'Ol. What you doing down here?'

She'd given him a queer look.

'Thought I'd get this place sorted,' she said, peeling a cobweb off her sleeve. 'Thought I might get a brew going. It's been a while. And there's nothing else to do.'

She'd turned her back on him and carried on. He should have done something then, stopped getting so caught up in other folk's business, started to concentrate on his own. But he hadn't. He'd let it ride. Even when Darragh had taken him on one side, he'd not listened – not really. Told himself it was fine, that she was still healing, that everything would work its way round. It hadn't. It had just got itself a whole lot more knotted up. He'd got back from a call one evening and gone straight to the brewing shed, intending to give her a hand or to talk her into coming up into the house – but he'd found the shed closed up and dark. He'd gone up the stairs with a smile on his face and some sense of ease in his chest. The kitchen was warm and lit up. Mimi was at the kitchen table, a length of fabric draped over her knees.

'Olive's just popped out,' she said. 'She'll not be long.'

Gil studied his mother's face.

'Out?'

'Yep. Horse trouble.'

'Horse trouble ... but ...' Gil scratched at his head. Olive had backed off her horse work before Ruaridh was born – the sickness had made it impossible. Sure, she'd taken up the riding again but, the horse work ...

'Who was it?' he said.

Mimi didn't answer.

'Ma. Who did she go to?'

Mimi put her needle and thread on the table and looked at him. 'It was Michael Kelly, I believe.'

Gil lifted his head and looked down the corridor. He could hear voices and footsteps approaching. The doors at the end suddenly flew open and Olive hurtled through, followed closely by Darragh and Beattie.

'Where is he? 'Olive was shouting. 'Where the hell is he?'

A nurse stepped out from behind a desk and caught Olive by the arm.

'Mrs McKenzie?'

Olive shrugged her off and continued up the corridor towards him. Her hair was hanging loose, her boots leaving mud trails on the floor.

'It's all right, Ol,' Gil called, striding towards her. 'It's all right, they're in with him now, they're getting him sorted ...'

'Who's in with him?' She was level with him then past him in a rush of cold air. He went after her.

'The doctor, the nurses ... they're ... Ol. Olive, no, you can't go in there ...'

She didn't hear him: she reached the door, pushed it open and disappeared inside. Gil ran after her but stopped outside the door, too nervous to follow her in. He could hear her voice inside, high pitched and indignant. She was scared. She wouldn't come over well, he knew it. She would have their backs up and standing their ground and them working on Ruaridh. He took a deep breath and put his hand against the door, then thought better of it, stepped back, pulled at his hair. He could hear the doctor's voice, a calm deep bass against Olive's high yapping. The door suddenly swung open and one of the nurses, her hat slightly off centre, came out.

'You might want to go in, Mr McKenzie,' she said, smoothing her apron back down. 'Your wife is a little ... a little overwhelmed.' She put her hands up as Beattie stepped forward. 'Sorry. Parents only at this point. But you're more than welcome to wait out here.'

Beattie cast her eye over the bench, then fixed it on the nurse. The woman cleared her throat and stepped behind Gil. Beattie moved forward, hands on her hips.

'You telling me I can't see ...'

'Beattie, the nurse is right,' Gil said. 'You and Darragh get on home – there's nothing to do here but wait.'

'Listen to Gil, girl,' Darragh said, taking her by the arm. 'Let's go back and get some sleep. We can be back at first light.'

Chapter 29

First light, as is often the way for folks subjected to a long night of sleeplessness and worry, brought a degree of hope and ease that could not have been imagined during the heavy dark hours, hours measured out by the stern click of the clock and the soft churning of the radiators.

Young McKenzie – for that is how the doctors and nurses referred to him – survived.

But he paid a price.

It was small compared to the one that the young Beattie had ended up paying, but it was a price nonetheless. The rage of the temperature and the pressure in his brain affected his eyes: when he awoke the next morning, his temperature and rash subsiding, his left eye had taken on a heavy and unequal look. He opened his eyes and Gil burst into tears. Olive, on the other hand leaned closer to the bed and gave the child a long, considered look.

'There's something wrong with his eye.' She turned away from the cot towards Gil. 'Look here, look at his eye. It's not proper. It wasn't like that before ...' she hesitated a moment, her hand at her throat. 'Was it? Gil. It wasn't like that before?' She didn't rightly know. She'd spent as much time avoiding the child as she'd spent with him. She hunched back over the cot and looked again. 'Do you think he's all right?'

'Of course he's all right. The fever's gone, he's woken up. He's all right. We've got to let Beattie know.'

But Olive was still considering her son's face. He sure didn't look all right to her. Looked to her like his brain had taken some damage. The thought pulled some kind of plug in her and everything she'd pledged in the night, the promise to polish up her mothering, to quit going out in the evening, to stop avoiding him – it all drained away. She stepped away from the cot.

The following week, after they had been allowed to take Ruaridh home, was rough as a ploughed field. Beattie was like a hound on scent – alert to every sound or move the lad made. Gil eventually stepped in: she meant well but her concern was adding a degree of electricity to the air that had them all twitching.

'Leave him to me and Olive, now, Beattie,' he'd said. 'He's fine. We'll be fine ...'

'But ... but what about ...'

'Beattie, honestly. We'll be fine.'

He didn't want to hear what she had to say, her concerns about Olive. He knew he had to do something, sort it out, tackle Olive, but he was becoming increasingly aware that whilst he was first choice when it came to solving other people's problems, he was hopeless when it came to confronting his own. It was a dilemma that left him staring at the ceiling when he should have been sleeping, sometimes watching the slow progress of the clock, sometimes studying Olive as she lay, a straight and tidy line in the bed, trying to fathom out what to do.

Mimi and Beattie were pecking at him, the pair of them full of answers, the main one being to start thinking about a second baby.

They had no idea.

As confused and angry as he was about Olive's dealings with Michael Kelly, the image of Olive in hospital was burned into his memory: the light he saw in her face when she told him about the new baby – the grey shadow that seemed to drop on her like some old curtain when she knew the child was lost. He knew what folks in town thought of her: sure, they admired her – but they gave her a wide berth. They only saw what was uppermost: the wire in her, the sharp edges. They didn't see what lay underneath, they hadn't seen her propped up, pale as milk, on the pillows, biting back the tears. Only he had seen that.

Even so, he doubted himself. The way she had of looking past his shoulder or simply walking away when he was talking to her, the harshness that seemed to flavour all her dealings with him. Night-times she lay rigid and still on her side of the bed, aiming chill waves of disapproval, like arrows, towards him if he got too near. She was the same with Ruaridh. 'Young McKenzie' she was calling him now, like he was still in hospital, like he was still the property of the doctor and nurses. When she did nurse him, she handled him like he was damaged goods. But Gil could cope with that. He had faith that things were bound to improve on that front. What he couldn't cope with was the fear that she would suddenly leave the supper table one evening and announce that she was headed over to The Cabin, her face dark with defiance, challenging him to speak up. He'd be left staring at the remnants of their meal, the kitchen quiet and empty, Ruaridh sleeping and him unable to do a damn thing about it. The scene haunted him, the jut of her chin, the obstinate set of her shoulders, the sound of her boots on the stairs as she left. But still he could not bring himself to raise the matter with her.

So he decided to speak to Michael Kelly.

'I'm popping out for a short while after supper, Ol,' Gil said as they were closing up the store. She threw him a black look across the counter.

'Oh?'

'Just to give Darragh a hand. He asked me. He's set on overhauling the boat. Needs a hand pulling it up. I won't be long, I ...'

'It's OK,' she said, not looking at him.

Darragh was in on it. Gil had taken the chance and talked to him, told him what was on his mind and Darragh had been all for it. This was largely due to the fact – and Gil was not strictly privy to this – that Beattie had been leaning on him to tackle Michael Kelly himself, to warn him away from Olive. The very thought had had him out of bed before sun up, out on the farm working up a sweat on unnecessary tasks.

'You sure? I could ask Mimi to stay over a bit longer.'

'Excuse me? What are you suggesting, Gil? That I'm not capable of looking after my own child? That I might sneak off somewhere? That I might ...'

'Ol, I'm not suggesting anything. It's just ...'

'For God's sake, Gil. Stop fussing over everything. Just go. Go and get the job done. I'll still be here when you get back.'

Gil parked the broom and headed out the shop door, her eyes burning into his back the whole way.

He knew he couldn't take off straight away; he had to time it right.

He glanced across the street as he walked, letting his eyes drift on the woodyard office. Michael Kelly would be inside, finishing up the day's paperwork, maybe checking the clock, getting ready to close things down for another day.

Gil knew this because he had been observing him.

Most days he locked the office door, pocketed the keys and headed for his truck, perhaps stopping for a moment's chat with whoever happened to be on the street. Occasionally, and Gil was hoping today wouldn't be one of those occasions, he pocketed the office keys and headed for The Ponderosa. When that happened Gil had to lose track of him.

Gil fired up the engine, switched on the blowers and settled down to watch Kelly's office door. It was five thirty straight: the man ought to be showing himself at any time. Gil could see Olive on the verandah swiping the mop back and forth over the boards. There was a degree of vim in her movements that spelled trouble. All the more reason to get things sorted – to sit down with Michael Kelly and reason him, gently, away from her. He watched a while longer until he suddenly realised Kelly had left the office and was in the street chatting to someone. Gil squinted his eyes and his heart dropped. It was old man Riley.

Gil watched as Kelly patted old Riley on the back and set off walking. He tracked him, willing him towards the truck, away from The Ponderosa. It was the truck, Kelly was heading for the truck. Gil let out a loud breath and pulled the pickup onto the road, cruised down to the gas station and waited for Kelly to drive past. He sat for a couple of minutes, then a couple more, his eyes fixed on the road. He let another while go by then drove back into town. Kelly's truck was still parked in the street.

From what Gil could see the truck was empty. The lights sure weren't on and there was no plume of exhaust jetting out into the evening air. He glanced towards the woodyard office: the window blinds were down, the place in shut up darkness. Gil checked over his shoulder – there was no sign of Olive – pocketed the keys and headed up the street towards The Ponderosa. His intentions were not entirely clear: mainly to look through the window as he passed and see if Michael Kelly was inside. If he was inside then that was that. He'd have to leave it: the business he had on his mind required some privacy, a quiet spot where he could discuss the situation with Kelly in a reasonable fashion and lay out his request. The possibility of having to walk away lent him a degree of relief.

'Well, Mr McKenzie. Hello there.'

Gil stopped abruptly and turned. Michael Kelly was emerging from the narrow alley way that ran between the pharmacy and Mimi's workshop. He was carrying a parcel under one arm.

'I've just come from your ma's place,' Kelly said, patting the package. 'She is one clever woman and that's for sure.'

He pulled up beside Gil, his eyes glittering with what seemed to be delight at their chance meeting.

'Now you're not heading in there, by any chance?' Kelly said, smiling, nodding his head towards The Ponderosa. Gil fancied he detected something of a challenge in his tone.

'I am,' he said. 'You coming?' Then strode off without waiting for an answer.

'Well, sure,' Michael Kelly said. Gil could hear the smirk in his voice.

The Ponderosa was warm and dimly lit and low on clientele. Old man Riley's bar stool was empty but his full glass sat on the bar waiting for him.

'I'll get us a drink,' Gil said, motioning Kelly to the booth at the far end of the room, close enough to the fire to feel its benefit but away from Riley's flapping ears.

When Gil got to the booth Michael Kelly was unwrapping the package. If it was a stalling tactic then Gil was glad of it because the confidence that had urged him into the bar seemed, just as urgently, to have left him. He watched as Kelly pulled at the string and folded back the brown paper.

'There we are,' Michael Kelly said. 'What did I tell you? Your ma is one hell of a woman. Just look at that.' He unfolded a pair of pants – work pants by the look of them. 'Just look at that finish ...' Kelly was running his thumb along the leg seam. 'And look, look at this. Have a feel, go on, Gil, have a feel. Look how she's lined them. Boy oh boy.'

Gil leaned across the table and felt the pants. His mother had lined them with soft wool. He nodded at Kelly. 'Warm.'

'Warm indeed,' Kelly agreed, running his hand across the fabric.

At that point Gil had given up on the idea of tackling Kelly. The Ponderosa, after all, was not the place. He took a sip of his whiskey and relaxed into his seat. Michael Kelly was still fussing with the parcel.

'Aha.' Kelly pulled out a second pair of pants and held them out. It seemed to Gil they were identical to the first pair but a good deal smaller. Kelly's eyes were flashing with pleasure.

'Oh yes,' he said, looking over at Gil. 'These are perfect. I reckon she'll love them, yes?'

'Rose?' Gil said, taking another sip of his whiskey.

Kelly let out a loud peal of laughter. 'Rose?' he said. 'Rose in a pair of wool-lined pants? Oh my Lord.' He laughed again then picked up his own glass. 'No, they're not for Rose.' He considered Gil over the rim of his glass. 'They're for Olive. It gets damn cold in that stable.'

Gil stared at him. 'I beg your pardon?'

'Olive,' Kelly said, his eyes creased with a smile. 'Before your boy took ill ... she reckoned we could use some warmer togs.'

It was the 'we' that did it.

Gil grabbed his whiskey and slung it back in one gulp then thumped the glass down on the table. 'Well, she won't be needing them,' Gil said. 'Because here's the thing, Michael, she won't be coming to the stables any more. I don't want her coming round and I don't want you seeing her any more.'

Kelly took a small sip of his whiskey and smiled at Gil over his glass. 'You don't want her ...'

'I don't want her coming over, Kelly. It's not right. You're a married man. She should be at home with me ... and the child.

Kelly raised his eyebrows and swilled his whiskey. 'And Olive's said that, has she?'

'It doesn't matter who's said it. That's the measure of it.'

Kelly shook his head slowly and rubbed his chin, chuckling to himself like he was puzzling over some humorous anecdote. He put his elbows on the table and leaned closer. 'Gil,' he said. 'You reckon Olive's gonna take notice of something like that?' He leaned back and smirked.

'What you saying, Michael?' Gil said. The fire suddenly seemed too hot, the room lacking in air. He shrugged his jacket off and loosened his collar.

'What I'm saying,' Kelly started, then paused to take another sip of his whiskey. 'What I'm saying, Gil, is that Olive doesn't strike me as the telling kind. If you know what I mean.'

'I don't give two damns about what's striking you, Michael. What I'm saying,' he emphasised the 'I' with a sharp slap on the table. 'What I'm saying ...'

'Gil, Gil, calm down, young feller. Don't go getting yourself heated up. I didn't mean to upset you. Damn it man, we're related. It's OK. I've heard you. Olive won't be coming over any more. I won't be seeing her any more. There. I've said it. Look ...' He started to get to his feet. 'Let's seal it with another drink.'

Gil pulled himself up and tugged his jacket back on. Kelly's good humour was making him feel churlish. 'Not for me. I've said what I wanted to say. I'll leave it at that.'

'Well, let me walk out with you, Gil. C'mon. We walked in as friends, we should be walking out the same way.'

'Suit yourself, Kelly,' Gil said sliding out of the booth and heading for the door. For some reason he could not fathom it felt that Kelly had the upper hand. Old man Riley turned from the bar and winked at him and Gil wondered how much he'd heard.

Outside, Kelly stepped in beside Gil. 'It's a funny thing though, isn't it?'

'What's that?' Gil was trying to calculate how long he'd been gone: whether he could go straight back home or whether he needed to hang it out a bit.

'Well, you know. How I ended up with Rose and you ended up with Olive.'

'Funny? What's funny about it?' He was getting damn weary of Kelly's voice.

'Well, think about it. You – a city boy, Rose out in California ...'

'What? What you talking about, Kelly?'

'And Olive. Well, I know she has the store and all, but let's face it, she's a farm girl at heart, a horsewoman. I sometimes think ...' he paused and gazed up at the sky like he was in some damn movie. 'Hah, no ... it's just nonsense ...'

'You sometimes think what, Kelly?'

'Oh, I don't know that I should be saying it. ..'

Gil waited. There was a toying look on Kelly's face, like a cat ready to spring a mouse. He quickened his pace and left Kelly behind.

'Well, OK then,' Kelly called. 'Sometimes I think I should have stuck with Olive and let you have Rose.'

Afterwards, Gil would reckon that was the point the street seemed to tip and some rush of wind, or maybe electricity, spun him on the spot, propelled him towards Kelly and drove his fist clean into his jaw. One second Kelly was smirking at him, the next he was flat on his back in the street. He scrabbled himself half upright but Gil kicked his arms out from under him and he went down again.

'For God's sake, man,' Kelly said, rolling onto his side and tucking his head into his arms. Gil stepped back and aimed his boot at Kelly's back. It connected with a sickening crunch – his heavy work boots against flesh and bone.

'My God, Gil, stop it. Get a hold of yourself.' Kelly's voice was muffled. No longer, it seemed to Gil, so sure of itself. He'd never in his life hit another person. He'd never hit anything, but now, at this moment, he felt like he might go on kicking Kelly and never tire of it. The thought terrified him.

'Get up,' he shouted. 'Get yourself up off the goddamn ground.'

Kelly rolled onto his knees and staggered to his feet. His face was bleeding. The parcel had come unfastened and the two pairs of pants lay in the dust. He bent down and tried to scoop them up. Gil pushed him out of the way and grabbed them. He took hold of the legs of the smaller pair and ripped them apart then threw them into Kelly's face.

'You stay away from Olive, you hear? You stay the hell away from all of us.'

Chapter 30

When the news broke, a good week later, it added two hours to Henry's mail round. The telling of it left him nursing a fierce jaw ache and croaking like a frog, his vocal chords damn near welded together.

Michael Kelly was leaving town.

Gil and Beattie were late in finding out, mainly, they decided afterwards, because Henry would have assumed their prior knowledge of the matter, Michael Kelly being family and all. It took a visit from Pearl, her two cheeks nipped red with the pleasure of the unanticipated excitement. Gil listened to her account of the matter for a few minutes, her mouth moving at a speed that had him at first mesmerised and then suddenly afraid of what it might reveal. What if someone had seen the tussle between him and Kelly? He'd somehow moved to calling it a tussle, the deeper part of him knowing it had been no such thing. He'd lumped Kelly on the chin when the man wasn't expecting it and then – and this was the part he couldn't swallow – he'd kicked the man when he was down. The shame of it weighed on him like a bellyful of cold grease. But the thought that someone might have witnessed it, that Pearl was working her way up to revealing him as a spineless bully, had him making excuses to leave the counter and head for the cool stillness of the storeroom. He closed the door behind him and closed his eyes, listening to the rise and fall of Pearl's chirping, trying to dispel the image of Michael Kelly curled up on the ground, his boot headed towards the man's defenceless back.

'What you doing out here?'

Gil straightened himself out and searched for Olive's voice. She emerged from behind a pile of wooden crates, pushing her hair from her forehead with the back of one hand.

'Oh. Just taking a breather,' he said.

She raised her eyebrows.

'Pearl,' he said. 'Pearl's just come in.'

'Hmph.' Olive bent down to the crates again. 'I'll be needing the small crowbar for this lot.'

'Yeah.' Gil didn't move. He studied Olive for a few moments. 'She's got some pretty big news.'

'Doesn't she ever.' Olive was on the move, heading along the aisle away from him, the order book in her hand, making a big deal of perusing the shelves.

'True.'

He watched her a mite longer, aiming to pick his time. She turned to look at him.

'So?'

'So ... apparently ... well, apparently, Michael Kelly's leaving town.'

The words hung there for a moment, Gil not sure of which way they were going to land. Olive whacked them back.

'Thought everybody knew that.' She turned her back on him and returned to scanning the shelves. The boards under Gil's feet rippled.

'What?' he said. 'You already knew?'

'Of course I already knew.'

'But ... but how?'

She spun round and flung the words at him.

'Because he told me, Gil. He damn well told me.'

'What? ... What did he tell you?'

The words came out small and choked for he neither wanted them aired or answered. If Kelly had told her about the *tussle* ... He leaned against the stack of shelving hoping that his want of support might show itself as nonchalance. She considered him over the top of the order book for a few moments then pushed past him and out into the yard.

If Gil figured that Kelly would go quietly – that some overriding sense of integrity would have him saying his quiet farewells and hitting the road – he was wrong.

A couple of days later Henry came in with the invitation. There was to be a barn dance. The whole town was invited. Rose was coming down and then, according to Henry, the pair of them were going to return to California together. No doubt, Gil thought, hand in hand and heading into a peach melba sunset. A slick of meanness seemed to settle in his insides. Olive, when he told her later that afternoon, seemed indifferent. Whether it was to the news or to him he couldn't tell. Beattie was ecstatic.

'I guess we'll have to go,' Gil said, after Beattie had left for the day. A finger of bile poked his gullet.

'Why wouldn't we?' Olive said, shaking her apron then rolling it into a smooth bundle. Seemed like she'd not looked him in the eye for days. He'd decided Kelly must have told her everything, from the ripping up of the pants to the crack on the jaw. He'd decided that he didn't damn well care. Kelly was looking for it and he got it. If she thought he was in the wrong then she'd have to damn well speak up.

'Looks like there's going to be bunting.' Olive nodded towards the front window. Beattie was staggering towards her truck with a large crate. Gil shook his head.

'I reckon we might even see the Annie O'Grady rolled out,' Olive said. 'It'll be just like the wedding all over again.'

'More like the goddamn Michael Kelly show,' Gil said. He clicked off the shop lights. 'I'll see you upstairs,' he said and left her in the gloom. He paused at the kitchen door, his hand on his heart, a jab of acid like a shard of ice against his ribs.

Everything Gil predicted about Kelly's leaving turned out true. The man was centre stage all night, soaking up the limelight like it was the California sun.

Gil sat at the back of the barn with Ruaridh, guarding him, or guarding himself, he wasn't sure. He watched the whole performance, for that was surely what it was, until the lad suddenly struck up grizzling and he had an excuse to leave. He turned at the door and scanned the barn for Olive. He spotted her at the food table, empty plate in hand. She was talking to Michael Kelly. Gil paused for a few moments, rocking the boy and watching.

'Gil. You want me to take the lad?'

Beattie was at his side, her eyes following the direction of his own gaze.

'No.' he said, dragging his eyes away from Olive. 'I'm going to get him back home. He's had enough, I reckon.' He glanced back across the barn. It seemed to him that Michael Kelly had shifted closer to Olive. She was leaning her head in towards him.

'Well, I'll go and let Olive know,' Beattie said. 'I was aiming to get myself a plate of food anyhow. I'll send her on, shall I?'

Gil was watching Olive again. 'Send her ... no ... don't worry, Beattie, I can manage the lad. She'll come when she's ready I guess, so ...' He glanced down: Beattie was gone. He searched the barn for her and saw the top of her head. She was already halfway to the food table, elbows out, moving through the crowd like she was on oiled wheels.

So Gil missed Kelly's final moments of glory: the speechifying, the handshaking, the tears for God's sake. But he heard about it from Beattie the next day. He'd hauled himself out of bed, leaving Olive to sleep and drove over to the barn. Beattie was already there.

'Well, looks like he's gone.' She was winding in a length of bunting, looping it round her open hand and elbow.

Gil didn't say anything.

'You talk to Olive yet?'

He shook his head. He'd not spoken to Olive at all. He'd settled the lad the night before then propped himself up on pillows, intending to wait up for her. When he woke it was light and she was asleep beside him.

'She's still sleeping,' Gil said.

'Well, shame you had to go early. I hung on till the end, had to – you know how Darragh gets with all that jigging music, he …'

Gil closed his ears and let Beattie's chatter wash over him and concentrated on rolling the tarpaulin that had been the backdrop to Kelly's stage. He'd volunteered for the clearing up: there was something about the task that appealed to him. He might not have been able – or willing – to say what that was but maybe something akin to a good bonfire on New Year's Day.

With Kelly gone he could relax. He and Olive could move forward. Given time he might raise the notion of a second child. Hell, they might even have a third, a fourth. Maybe move into The Luck, build a bit of extra space there, raise the noisy, spilling over brood that, in his youth and stalked by the loneliness peculiar to an only child, he'd always imagined.

'So you don't know if she agreed?' Beattie was standing beside him, a bundle of table cloths heaped against her chest.

'What?'

'Olive,' Beattie said. 'Do you know if she agreed. Did she take Michael up on it?'

'Did she … I don't know what you're talking about, Beattie.'

Beattie's face creased into a frown. 'Well, you need to talk to her, Gil. Michael's asked her to keep things going at The Cabin while he's gone – the horses and all, you know – wants her to consider some kind of partnership. That's what they were talking about at the table last night when I … you know, when I went over.'

Gil let the tarpaulin drop.

He drove fast, the window wound down, his head whirling like it might spin off. Why had he left early? Why hadn't he gone over to Olive himself? Why had he not dealt with the damn matter like a man? And why, for God's sake, had he not given Michael Kelly a better beating when he'd had the chance?

Gil took the stairs two at a time and burst in through the kitchen door. Olive was at the table, Ruaridh beside her in his high chair.

She took in Gil's expression and the flush of his face and scowled back at him.

'I figure Beattie's told you, then.'

'She's told me about Michael Kelly, if that's what you mean.'

She took a slurp of coffee then banged the mug on the table. 'If that's what I mean? Of course it's what I goddamn mean. For Pete's sake, Gil. Couldn't you for once, just once, say it straight. Say what's on your mind, instead of ...'

Ruaridh's face crumpled up and he let out a wail. 'Oh, for Christ's sake.'

Gil crossed the kitchen and lifted the lad out of his seat.

'Well, I don't want it, Ol. Whatever Kelly has said to you, whatever he's goddamn proposed – I don't want any of it.' It came out too mild. Olive shook her head at him. Near enough let out a laugh.

'You don't want any of it. You? What about me, Gil? What about what I want? Have you figured that in?'

Gil gazed down at her. 'I figured you've got me. You've got me and the boy. And the store. That should be enough, Ol. That should be enough.'

She let her head drop forward, put her hands over her eyes. When she looked back at him her face was wet with tears.

'That's the problem, Gil. It's not.'

Chapter 31

It was Beattie who sorted things out. Whether she'd already spoken to Darragh about it or whether she'd simply concocted the story on the spot, Gil wasn't sure. The fact was when she came into the store later that day the atmosphere between him and Olive was sagging like a rain cloud fit to burst. Beattie took one look at them and spilled out the news: Kelly had asked Darragh to look after The Cabin; to tend the horses until they were moved to California.

'Darragh jumped straight at it, of course,' Beattie said, before either of them had a chance to say anything. 'You know how thick those two are. Green blood, according to Darragh. Hah. Anyway, he's chomped on about it all morning, he's over there now, he's full of ...' She stopped suddenly and considered the pair of them. 'You two OK?'

Gil had stopped mid-task: the flour scoop in one hand, a paper sack in the other. Beattie's news – this sudden resolution to his problem – had left him half stunned. He closed his mouth and swallowed hard.

'Fine, Beattie. We're fine, thanks.'

'Good. Well, where is he? Where's my favourite boy?'

'Oh, he's out with my ma. They're taking a stroll. They're likely going back to hers.' He glanced towards the shop clock, caught sight of Olive's face. 'They'll maybe be there now.'

'Well in that case, I'll take myself over there. I'm parched.'

As the shop door closed behind her, Gil thought he heard the first clap of thunder.

He turned, ready to take whatever tongue-lashing Olive was going to send his way.

She wasn't there.

They hobbled through the rest of the day until Gil, his face near frosted off with the iciness of her, decided that sometimes the best way to let a thing mend is to quit picking at it. So he stopped trying to fix things between him and Olive and let her be, kept himself busy and waited till she thawed on her own account. By Monday morning things were flowing a little easier, but Gil was still keeping a safe distance. Consequently he was out sweeping the shop verandah when Sheriff McCleavy turned up. Gil watched him approach.

John McCleavy was a man who took his job very seriously. On the one hand it had earned him a good deal of respect, on the other – largely due to a predilection for all things cowboy – it added an element of entertainment to all his dealings. The folks in Oaklake took him seriously enough but, back in Picker's Flag where he rested his spurs, he was, even at the tender age of thirty, viewed as something of a relic.

He ambled over in the manner of a feller just off his horse, his sheriff's star pinned to his waistcoat, the light bouncing off his fancy boots.

'Well, howdy there, Gil.' He touched his hand to the brim of his Stetson.

'Morning, Sheriff.'

'Taking yourself some air, I see, and I sure don't blame you.'

'Don't see you out this way too often,' Gil said.

'Well, ain't that the truth, Gil. Ain't that the truth.'

'So, you need something from the store? We're not strictly opened up yet but ...'

'Well that is mighty kind of you, Gil, but no ... that's not what I'm here for.' He pulled up alongside Gil, hooked his thumbs in his belt loops and surveyed the street. He nodded his head towards the woodyard office.

'You family to this Kelly feller?'

'What?'

'Michael Kelly. You and him. You're family, right?'

'Well, yes. Olive and Rose, they're sisters so, yes, we're related.'

'And I hear there was some celebrating for the feller on Saturday night, some hoedown?'

'A hoedown. There was. He was leaving town ... he's left. For California.'

McCleavy reached inside his waistcoat and slotted a pack of Lucky Strikes out of his shirt pocket and let this information settle in. He shook one out of the packet and lodged it in the corner of his mouth then offered the packet to Gil.

'Not for me, thanks.' He watched as McCleavy pulled out a pack of matches and lit up, squinting his eyes against the first shot of smoke.

'Good sense,' McCleavy said, taking a long drag. 'Should never have took the darn things up myself.' He turned to consider the street again. Gil worked his finger round his collar. This was the thing about McCleavy: he had a slow way of working that left a man worrying and Gil suddenly found that he was worrying.

'So, what is it that brings you out this way, Sheriff? See more of your pa, generally speaking.'

McCleavy picked a thread off his tongue then looked at Gil. 'Pa asked me to come over. You know how he is sometimes.'

Gil nodded. Walter McCleavy – mainly due to a nervous disposition that had his mind closing down at any trouble more vexing than a lost cat – had never risen above the station of Deputy.

'So, this hoedown? You were there?'

'I was. Everyone was. I reckon the whole town turned out.'

McCleavy gave a slow nod. 'You stay all night?'

'Well, no. Not all night. I had to take my boy home early – he got unsettled.'

McCleavy nodded again. 'You see anyone in the street when you came home?'

'No,' Gil said. 'Why?'

'And you stayed home?'

'I did. Look, Sheriff. What the hell is this all about?'

McCleavy tossed his cigarette out onto the street and tipped his head towards the woodyard office. 'Got a call from Danish this morning. Went in early. Things was just as he left them 'cept the safe door was open and the cash tin was gone.'

'What?' Gil heard the words but couldn't line them up in any order that made sense. 'So ... so who ...?'

'Well, here's the thing, Gil. I had a long chat with Danish and ... well, you know sure enough. There's only three fellers got the workings of that safe – Danish himself, Michael Kelly ... and you.'

Chapter 32

Anyone investigating the history of Oaklake might, at this point, tap the page before them and declare this was the time things began to change. It was not so much the town itself – for that never grew in terms of size due to an alteration in the railroad route – but the people and, as a consequence, the feeling of the place.

News of the burglary went round the town like a steel bearing in a pinball machine. And it rang everybody's bell. For a day or so talk was all about who was responsible but the consensus was soon settled. The Lindo family. New to the area. Rough types hauled up in cheap trailers north of Picker's Flag. Far as anyone knew – because everyone was keeping their distance – the family consisted of two brothers, their beaten-down wives and a clutch of skinny kids. John McCleavy had no proof it was them and, short of finding them with a cash tin, how was he going to prove anything? Nonetheless he was damn sure they were the culprits and the town quietly agreed.

This apportioning of blame, whether it was right or not, gave most folks a degree of relief. Not enough, however, to allow them to rest completely easy in their beds. Within a day or two half the town was talking about fixing shutters to their windows or putting up fences or fixing doors on their porches. It was a welcome upshot for Danish: the money he'd lost was nothing compared to the windfall orders that were appearing in his letterbox each morning. When he thought things couldn't get any busier, there was another burglary, quickly followed by a third and a fourth and, although they were all over in Picker's Flag, Pearl Clodagh boosted his coffers further by talking her man into purchasing a house dog – a good barking dog. The Creaseys followed suit, swiftly followed by the pharmacy and before he knew it Danish had struck up a sideline in dog kennels.

There was a new bustle about town. Folks eager for news – good or bad – found themselves chatting in the street to neighbours they didn't usually bother with. Pearl Clodagh, always keen to be first off the blocks when it came to some new titbit, took to loitering outside the mail office waiting for Henry to get off his rounds and The Ponderosa started opening an hour earlier to accommodate the surge in clientele.

But it was the store saw the biggest change. It became the unofficial meeting place for anyone wanting to catch up on burglary gossip. The place was jammed from the moment Gil pulled up the shutters till he closed the doors and turned the key in the lock. The town women, usually touting a string of kids too young for school, drifted in and congregated in the aisles, by the counter, round the stove, anywhere there was a square foot of space.

It drove Olive mad. The takings didn't improve but fixing the place up at the end of the night took twice as long. Gil, on the other hand, welcomed it: Olive's thawing was taking some time and the constant presence of customers forced her into a warmth towards him which – if not completely sincere – was a marked improvement to her general coolness. The subject of Michael Kelly had not been raised between them again; not in connection with The Cabin, nor in connection with the burglary. They had stepped around the matter and left it behind them like a pile of horse dung in the road. Darragh, increasingly helped by Beattie, was full-on minding Kelly's cabin, but he never spoke of it to Olive and she never enquired. All this might have boiled down to some reassurance for Gil: the problem of Michael Kelly was solved, now all he had to do was wait for Olive to come round. Instead he found himself lying awake at night drawn back to the conversation they'd had the morning after Kelly's party and the fear that he was not enough for her – that he and Ruaridh would never be enough – had him in a cold sweat.

The solution came to him early one evening. Olive had already gone up and he was sweeping the shop floor. As he started on the horse tack aisle he saw that someone had overturned a couple of tea chests and formed a pair of makeshift seats. He stood back and looked at the arrangement and the idea dropped in.

Simple as that.

He put the broom down, switched off the lights and went upstairs. Olive was on the chair in the bathroom, paddling her feet in a large bowl of salt water. He wandered in and perched on the side of the tub.

'Ol, I've had an idea.'

She gave him a quick look. 'Well, I hope it involves my goddamn feet,' she said. 'I swear I can feel the bones coming through.' She wriggled her toes in the water and grimaced.

'I could give you a foot rub?' He said. He was taking a chance, but the thought of his idea was buoying him up.

'Depends what your idea is,' she said.

He paused for a moment.

'A tea room,' Gil said. 'I reckon we should open a tea room. All them ladies we're getting in ...'

Olive lifted her feet out of the bowl and planted them on the towel. She gave him a long look.

'A tea room?'

He nodded. His words had put some light in her eyes but he wasn't sure if that was good or bad.

'A tea room. Good Lord, Gil.' She stepped off the towel and padded into the kitchen. Gil waited a moment or two then followed her wet footprints across the wooden floor. She was at the kitchen table, rooting through the drawer.

'Well ... what do you think, Ol?'

She swivelled round and gave him a crooked smile.

'What do I think? I think you've hit the nail on the goddamn head. But we've got to plan this thing properly. You fetch us a pen and some paper, I'll get the coffee on. A tea room. Good Lord, Gil, we could double our takings.'

The tea room, it turned out, was the cure. The added ingredient that Olive needed to shift whatever it was that was stuck in her gullet: the lost child, her reluctant mothering, Michael Kelly – her goddamn dissatisfaction with everything. It couldn't be said that she blossomed as such, but there was a detectable unfurling. Gil felt the benefit most. In the privacy of their own rooms they'd sit, elbow to elbow, and pick over the day's work. The harder they laboured the more content Olive grew and the closer they became until, a few months after the opening of the tea room, Gil could barely recall the anxieties of the previous year. Their marriage became the thing he'd longed it to be.

He knew other folks might not have seen it the same way but regardless of what the town folk thought – and he knew what it was – it seemed to him that he and Olive fit together like the pieces of an engine. She might have been the steel piston hammering away at whatever job she was at, but he was the oil easing the work along, smoothing things out. He would have struggled to explain himself but it was as if everything had slotted in together and life had taken on a degree of richness that had been lacking.

This was not just in terms of him and Olive – it was something bigger than that. The burglary – for that had surely been the catalyst – had stirred things up and, when the dust had settled, it seemed an unaccountable change had taken place. It was like the town had suddenly come of age, like someone had set to with a cloth and polished it up. Gil and Olive weren't the only ones to expand their business: Danish, flush with the new influx of money, had put up another timber shed and taken on two new apprentices and Mimi had space added onto her workshop and started a line in frocks brought in from California. It wasn't much but, together with the new tea room, it gave the place a feel of success, of things moving forward. There was even talk – and the mere idea of it had Pearl Clodagh clucking like a chicken – of a picture house. All in all, he thought, things were looking up.

Later, he'd blame that thought for tempting fate.

Chapter 33

It was late August, the tail end of a Friday afternoon and Olive was out front clearing lemonade glasses. Gil and the boy had gone off with Beattie and Darragh. An air show two counties east. Darragh's idea, of course. She was considering a minute's sit in the sun when she noticed a woman walking down the street toward the store.

'Rose,' Olive said, as the woman drew nearer. 'What in God's name are you doing here?'

Rose didn't answer the question. She smiled, stepped up onto the verandah, touched Olive's arm as she passed then plonked herself down on a bench. 'Look at this,' she said and swept her arm in a wide arc. 'Look how smart it is. I hardly recognised the place.'

'Well, you know. Not California I suppose, but, yep, the place is on the up. So what brings you here? Beattie never mentioned it.'

Rose considered the empty glasses on Olive's tray and ran her tongue over her lips. 'Is that lemonade?'

Olive nodded. 'You thirsty?'

'Parched,' Rose said. 'Road's dusty as hell.' She lifted her hair off her neck a moment then let it drop again. She'd still not answered the question.

When Olive got back with two glasses Rose was dozing. She put the drinks on the table and settled on the bench opposite her sister. Rose had taken off her jacket and, without it, it was plain to see she'd lost some softness and gained some edges. Her wristwatch hung loose like a bangle. She woke suddenly with a small yelp and a look on her face that put Olive in mind of a spooked mare.

'You OK?' Olive said, passing a glass over. Rose rolled it against her forehead, massaging the beads of condensation into her hairline.

'Sure,' Rose said.

'Sure, sure?'

Rose managed a small laugh. Something like herself but ten parts diluted. 'Sure, sure,' she said.

'Well you don't look it. You're as scrawny as me.'

'What?' Rose straightened herself up and smoothed her dress down. 'No I'm not,' she said. 'I'm like I ever was.'

Olive raised an eyebrow.

'Olive! Stop it. I'm fine. Honestly. Now ...' she paused and drained half the lemonade. 'Tell me – what the hell has happened to the town?'

So Olive parked the question and caught her up on the news, starting with the burglary – which she figured Rose knew about but said it anyway – and finishing with the rumours about the picture house. When she'd ended Rose sat quiet for a minute or two.

'Darragh and Beattie don't know I'm coming,' she said.

'Oh?'

'I didn't really want them to know ... yet. I ... I'd appreciate it if ...'

'No need to worry. They're out of town. On a jaunt. Coming back tomorrow.'

'Oh, well that's OK then.' Rose's face smoothed out like the news had settled something.

'So, you want to stay here – at the store? There's plenty of room. Gil and ...'

Rose shook her head. 'No. I'm heading over to The Cabin. There's a few things need sorting out. I, well ... no, that's what it is. I need to sort a few things out.'

'So, where's ...?' Olive started, and then found she couldn't go on.

'Michael's not coming,' Rose said. 'He's busy.'

Olive picked up her glass and took a long sip to mask the colour rising in her cheeks. 'You're staying for supper, though?'

'No, I've brought something with me. I plan to get straight over there. Get started, you know.'

'You need a lift over?'

Rose shook her head and pointed up the street. 'I drove down. Spur of the moment thing. Look, I'm going to get going.'

Olive nodded. Curiosity was crippling her. 'You sorting out anything in particular?'

'Well, kind of,' Rose said. She stood up and picked her jacket off the table. As she pulled it on the sleeves of her dress rode up and Olive understood. Or at least she thought she understood. A plume of bruises stained the insides of Rose's upper arms: a sickening mixture of yellow and purple against the vulnerable white of her skin.

'I was hoping you might come over, give me a hand?'

'Well, OK, yes, I can do that ... but Rose ...'

'I'll see you later, then.' Rose stepped off the verandah. She walked a few steps then turned back to her sister.

'Come on your own, won't you?'

Olive only nodded: a feeling of dread had risen from her chest and choked up her throat.

It was gone seven o'clock when Olive pulled the truck into the yard at The Cabin. She allowed her eyes a swift scan of the place. Darragh's handiwork was plain to see: a tidy order everywhere. The doors and window frames were fresh painted and the path up to the door had been picked out with edging and planted with low shrubs. The place had the look of a child's drawing or a toy farm. Every inch of it bore witness to the amount of time Darragh – and likely Beattie – spent there. The thought rankled her.

The drive over had worn her out: her mind flitting from one crazy notion to another, trying to fathom the reason for Rose's visit. She couldn't even call it a visit – more like a sudden appearance. Too sudden. Something was wrong, that was a certainty – but what? The bruising she'd seen led her in one direction but her mind kept tugging her back to the fear she kept shut away – the fear that one day someone would ask her straight about her and Michael Kelly and she would have to come up with an answer. It wouldn't be Gil – she knew that much. Most likely person would be Beattie.

The last person she wanted it to be was Rose.

On the drive over, trying to divert her mind, she'd pictured her arrival at The Cabin: she'd find Rose in the kitchen, a pail of sudsy water by her side, a cloth in her hand and her head in a cupboard. The picture vanished as soon as she pushed the front door open and stepped into the hallway. She paused, waiting for some sound to point her in the direction of Rose. But there was only silence.

'Rose?'

She opened the kitchen door and went in. The room was neat – and empty. No food on the table. Olive went back through the hall and into the small parlour. *The best room,* Kelly had called it. Olive flicked her eyes round the room. She'd spent no time in there. Two armchairs were pulled up to the cold hearth, a small sofa tucked underneath the window. There was no sign of Rose. She backed into the hall and considered the stairs.

'Rose?'

She waited a moment then slipped off her boots and started up, taking each step slowly. She paused on the landing and leaned a moment on the window sill. The Cabin had two bedrooms. Kelly and Rose's, the one with the balcony, was to her left. This was information she shouldn't strictly know, information that would dress her up in a bad light whether she was deserving of it or not. She stepped carefully into the room – the bed was neatly made and empty. Olive crossed over to the dressing table, passing the balcony doors on the way and that's when she saw Rose.

'Rose,' she shouted.

It was more from relief because it was obvious her sister wouldn't hear her. Olive ran back down the stairs, pushed her boots on and flew out into the yard. She ran towards the stable block, slowing only when she got to the hedge. She made herself stop and wait till her breathing slowed down then walked towards her sister.

'Rose?'

Rose turned, the spade still in her hand. 'Olive! What time is it?' Her face was streaked with dirt and her hair, half pinned up and half loose, was hanging over her eyes. Her forearms were glazed with sweat. She started brushing the soil from her hands then hurriedly tugged down her sleeves.

'What you doing?'

'Doing?' Rose let the spade drop. 'Oh, I ... I ...' She cast her eyes around the patch that Darragh had obviously got started. 'Nothing,' she said. 'I didn't know Grandpa had done all this.' She indicated the neat rows of planting: corn already waist high, beet leaves glowing red and warm in the late sun.

'Me neither,' Olive said, staring at the spade by Rose's feet. 'Looked like you were digging.'

'Digging? Me?' Rose said. She swooped down and picked up the spade. She let out a small laugh, nervous and shrill. 'I was just tidying. It looked so, so inviting. Too long in the city, I suppose.' She let out another piercing laugh and walked past Olive. 'Come on. Let's go up to the house. I've got a quart of fresh orange juice in the pantry, and let me tell you, one thing California is good at is ...'

Olive let her walk on. She looked over at the spot Rose had been.

'Olive, come on.'

Olive dragged her eyes away from Darragh's patch and went after her sister. She caught up with her in the yard. Rose turned at the sound of her footsteps.

'I miss all this,' she said casting her arm in a dramatic arc.

Olive nodded. Strictly speaking Rose had never lived there. There was nothing to miss.

'Well, not just this,' Rose said, like she'd read Olive's thoughts. 'Oaklake, you know. You and Gil, Grandma and Grandpa, I ... I miss it.'

Olive slowed her pace and hung back slightly, suddenly fearful that Rose was about to cry. She could shoulder most things, but tears? Tears had her shutting down like a bear in winter.

'Come on,' she said, overtaking Rose without looking at her face. 'Let's see if this California juice is as good as my lemonade.'

They'd sat at the kitchen table for over an hour, Rose making small talk – a good deal of it – prattling on about Vida, her work, California. She made no mention of Michael Kelly, nor got any closer to explaining her sudden arrival in town. Olive could feel herself getting cranked up. She scraped her chair back from the table and took their glasses over to the sink.

'Rose,' she said, ignoring the fact that her sister was still in full flow. 'You said you'd come down to get something sorted out?'

Rose paused mid-sentence. 'Something sorted out? Did I? Did I say that?' The nervous laugh was back. 'Well, yes of course I did. I did say that, but, hah ... I've done it. I've done the sorting out. So we, we can just sit here and jaw away.'

Olive considered her sister. She'd got that look again, wild eyed and panicked. Like an animal caught in a trap.

'What's going on, Rose?' She left the sink and, steeling herself, draped her arm across Rose's bony shoulder. Rose made a small noise like a stifled hiccup then collapsed in tears.

What it boiled down to was that Rose didn't know what was going on. She said this over and over, her face buried in her hands while she rocked gently back and forth. It seemed that California life wasn't suiting Michael Kelly – he was away a good deal, often for a week or two at a time – returning unexpectedly, usually full of good humour – but sometimes not. Sometimes sour and argumentative. Always broke. She was working extra hours to stop them from getting behind on the rent but nothing she did seemed to satisfy him.

'Have you asked him about it?' Olive said. 'Have you asked him what's wrong, where he's going off to?'

'I asked him once, a few days ago,' Rose said, lifting her face and looking at Olive. 'He didn't like it. He ...'

Olive glanced at Rose's arms. 'He hit you?'

Rose hung her head again and her hair fell over her eyes. 'No, he didn't hit me. He was ... rough.'

'Rough?'

Rose's voice was a whisper. 'Forceful, you know. Not gentle.'

Olive sat down next to her sister and closed her eyes.

Here it was: the memory she'd kept clamped down inside of her for years. Threatening to let loose and fly up through her throat and into the air.

She'd been so young. Michael Kelly so … so mature. After it had happened she told herself it was fine. He was an experienced man, knew how these things went. But she'd had nothing to compare it with, not until she'd married Gil and realised that what had happened in the woods with Michael Kelly was not strictly normal. She'd enjoyed it – that was the shaming thing – she'd responded to his wildness with her own – biting into his shoulders, clawing at his back, pulling at his hair. But afterwards she'd kept herself covered up for days. Her arms bore the marks of his hands and her backbone was scraped raw. Turned out that was nothing – surface stuff that went away. Not like getting married to Gil and then finding out she was pregnant.

'You OK, Ol?' Rose had dried her eyes and was staring at her.

'I'm fine. Fine.' She swallowed hard and pushed the memory back down. Forced it back into its box.

'I'd better go,' she said, knowing it was the wrong thing to do, knowing she should sit with Rose, talk some more. But she needed to get away. 'I'll come back tomorrow,' she said, already halfway to the door.

She climbed into the truck and let out a long breath.

It was in the past. It came to nothing. It meant nothing. But she was a liar and she knew it because, despite Gil and the boy, despite the store and the tea room, and despite him being married to her sister, every fibre in her body still keened towards Michael Kelly. Every moment in his presence she'd felt the draw of him, knowing that one look, one word, would have had her in his arms, sweating and flailing like a drowning woman.

And she hated herself for it. Because he'd never touched her again. She'd rescued his mares, built his stables back up and even, before Beattie had stuck her oar in, agreed to manage The Cabin when he went to California. She'd done all those things because of what it might promise: some contact with him, some possibility that the spark between them might suddenly catch hold and burst into flames.

Chapter 34

Olive pulled the truck off the road and looked at her watch. It was almost 10pm. She'd told Gil she was going back to see Rose. Didn't tell him Rose didn't know she was coming. Far as she was concerned Rose's explanation had cast some light on her sudden appearance, on the bruising – but it had left the matter of the spade, the digging, unaccounted for.

The light had all but gone – a wash of afterglow on the horizon silhouetting the row of pine trees that had stood there since she could remember. The air was warm but she pulled on her jacket and set off through the oak planting towards The Cabin. The light in Rose's bedroom was on but, although the balcony doors were open, the room was concealed by a lace curtain that lifted slightly, moved by some small night breeze. Olive stepped carefully through the yard and positioned herself by the hedge. She could hear the horses moving in their stalls – fancied they could maybe catch the scent of her. She stood for a while longer then hunkered down on the ground and watched the bedroom.

At 10.30pm Rose appeared at the balcony door. She pulled back the lace curtain and stepped out onto the wooden boards. Her hair was loose. She leaned her head forwards and let it hang then took a brush to it – long slow sweeps from the nape of her neck to the ends, lifting it so she could reach it all. Olive had to look away. It was a ritual at once familiar and private. When she was finished, she caught the length of it into a ribbon and tied it at the nape of her neck. She looked like a child fresh from the tub and ready for bed. She stood for a while against the wooden railings, looking out at the sky, her nightdress blowing softly at her ankles then disappeared back into the bedroom. A few minutes later the light went out.

Olive hauled herself back up and let the blood get back into her legs, then, casting a quick glance over her shoulder, headed for Darragh's vegetable patch. The spade was leaning against the fence. She took hold of it, then, positioning herself in what she thought was the right place, considered the ground. Darragh was a thorough gardener: all around her the earth was soft and tilled. She crouched down to feel it, wishing she'd taken a chance and brought the flashlight. There was no obvious mound or disturbance that betrayed Rose's activity. Olive tried the spade in a couple of places, feeling the give of the soil. Third time she fancied she met less resistance. She trod down on the spade and lifted out a load of soil. Then another. She bent down and felt the shallow depression she'd made and, happy she was in the right spot, pushed up her jacket sleeves and stepped on the spade again. Rose, it seemed, was more able than she appeared: after five minutes or so digging Olive stood back to take off her jacket and grab a breather. She'd dug out a decent pile of soil but there was no sign of Rose's cache. She kept going a while longer, thinking maybe she'd got things wrong – maybe Rose had just been digging.

And then a dull clang of metal against metal.

She flung the spade down and dropped onto all fours. The hole was deep and the sides were soft. She leaned in carefully and felt for the bottom. She dragged her hand slowly over the damp soil, sifting small stones through her fingers until she felt the cold edge of a box. A metal box. She lowered herself onto her belly and reached in until she could get both hands on it, then drew it out. As she got to her feet, a light went on behind her. She spun round. Rose was standing at the edge of the patch, watching her.

'Put it back, Ol,' she said.

Olive looked down at the metal box in her hands. Her heart was going like a freight train. 'What is it?' she said, trying to keep her voice even.

'It doesn't matter what it is. Just put it back.' She was threading her way towards Olive, the flashlight strobing Darragh's rows as she moved. Rose drew level with her and took hold of the box. As it passed between them Olive suddenly recognised it for what it was.

'My God,' she said. 'It's ... no, surely not ... not Michael?'

Rose nodded then dropped the cash box back into the hole. The flashlight lit up the lettering painted on the lid: 'Property of The Woodyard, Oaklake'.

Chapter 35

The knowledge of Michael Kelly's treachery did not sit easy with Olive. Rose had sworn her to secrecy then set off for California before the sun was up, leaving The Cabin free of all traces of her visit – like she'd never been there at all.

But Olive was struggling: the knowing of it sat like a live thing, crouched in her gullet, waiting for its chance to escape. The image of the cash box, the neat painted lettering, disappearing as they shovelled the earth back over it then smoothed it down, haunted her. She'd ventured back to the site as soon as Rose had gone. Gazed for a while then, before turning away, snapped a small twig off an overhanging branch and stuck it in by the fence to mark the spot.

A gravestone of sorts.

The thought had alarmed her and sent her rushing back to the store where she sat waiting for Gil and the others to return and restore a sense of ordinariness to the day.

But that night, and the ones that followed, held her captive: hopelessly wakeful and replaying the events of Rose's secret visit like a never ending movie reel. The closing scene – Rose in her nightdress hefting the spade like some deranged sleepwalker; the two of them, heads together, smoothing the ground to hide their dark handiwork – had her gripping the sheets in her fists and clamping her jaw down, holding back the words that were clamouring to be spoken and seal Michael Kelly's fate.

He was a thief. Michael Kelly was a thief.

And she was a goddamn fool.

More than once she'd had to excuse herself from Beattie's company because she could feel the words swelling in her mouth, like something that couldn't be swallowed. Her jaw ached with the urge to hawk them up and lay bare Kelly's deceit, but she said nothing. She drew a line under the truth about Michael Kelly and forced him from her mind.

Turned out this was the right thing because the truth, as the saying goes, showed up all of its own accord.

The letter arrived a few weeks after Rose's visit. Henry, thinking he could knock a couple of minutes off his round, but mainly hoping Darragh might open it there and then and douse his curiosity, delivered it to The Cabin, rather than the woodyard office as the address required.

'It's for Michael,' Henry said, as Darragh scrutinised the envelope.

'Yes. I can see that,' Darragh said, and slipped the thing into his shirt pocket. 'I'll take it up to The Luck. Beattie'll likely deal with it.'

Henry allowed a small pause. 'There's an address on the back,' he said, fixing his eyes on the inch of pale mauve envelope sticking out of Darragh's pocket. 'And a name.' He allowed another small pause then threw in his last card. 'Irish, I think.'

Darragh let out a sigh and pulled the letter back out of his pocket. He turned it over and pulled it up to his eyes.

'Looks like you're right, Henry,' he said. 'Galway. Yep. Michael's family is there. Most likely from his mother.' He drew the envelope closer and inspected the neat writing. 'Ah, yes. I'm right. Mary Kelly. It's from Mary Kelly. That's his mother.' He grinned at Henry then stuffed the thing back in his pocket.

Darragh waited until the plume of dust from Henry's van was almost out of sight, then he parked his tools and cranked up the pickup. He needed to get to Beattie. He needed to show her the letter, because he and Michael Kelly had done a whole lot of jawing about the old country and this much he knew – Michael Kelly had no sisters and his mother's name was Ellen.

Beattie took one look at the letter and set the kettle on the stove.

'Beattie, we can't ...'

She dealt him one of her lip-sealing glares then turned her back on him. Five minutes later the envelope was open and the single sheet of paper, a matching mauve, was in her hands. She set off reading out loud:

My dearest Michael, I hope this letter finds you in the best of health. Things here are good but quiet, and not so easy without you by my side, I find myself wondering …

Beattie left off reading out loud and scanned the rest of the sheet quietly, her lips moving silently over the words. She got to the end and looked at Darragh.

'Well, I'll be damned,' she said.

'What?' Darragh said.

She dragged out a chair and sat down heavily. 'I don't believe it,' she said.

Darragh snatched the page out of her hand and started reading. It wasn't long. Nor particularly interesting. Until he came to the final words:

So hurry home soon, my darling boy. Your loving wife, Mary.
Ps the girls send their love.

'Rose,' Beattie whispered. 'We've got to go to Rose.'

She waited for his objections, for him to try and talk her out of it, but he put the letter back in its envelope and tucked it in his pocket.

'Go pack some things, Beatt,' he said. 'We'll make an early start of it.'

Beattie was on stakeout. She cradled her mug of coffee and, from her perch in the diner window, perused the front of Vida's apartment. The blinds were down, like they had been the night before when she and Darragh had turned up, saddle-sore and numb from travel. She'd left Darragh sleeping in the cheap room they'd managed to hire and slipped out early to grab herself a coffee and a front row seat. She was braced so tight it was like her chest was bound up with wire and would allow no space to breathe. This was not just on account of Rose, although Lord knows how she was going to tackle that one. No – it was Darragh.

He'd cried. She'd found him sitting on the edge of the bed with the open suitcase empty beside him. He'd looked up at her and his face was wet with tears. It damn near finished her. They'd run the thing ragged – her having to haul in her temper in favour of salving Darragh's wounded heart – until there was nothing left to do but get in the pickup and start driving. She'd spent the entire journey tuned to a pitch just short of humming. The only thing keeping her lid on was the thought of getting Michael Kelly in a tight corner and clobbering him black and blue.

'More coffee, ma'am?' The waitress was beside her, her smile and uniform still early morning fresh.

'Well, yes. Thank you. I will,' Beattie said. The girl was itching to talk.

'Looks like you've had a long journey.'

Beattie looked down at her crumpled skirt. Her two shoes dull with farm dust.

'Oh, I'm sorry,' the girl said. Her face was going from pink to red.

'No, no. Don't worry yourself. You're right. We drove up last night. I left my husband sleeping – thought I'd get an early start, you know.'

The girl nodded and looked over at Vida's windows.

'You visiting?'

'Planning to,' Beattie said. 'Waiting for a decent hour.'

The girl put the coffee jug down and struck a pose that had Beattie wondering if she was one of these wannabe movie stars that Rose talked about.

'You not visiting Vida by any chance?' she said, in a theatrical whisper.

Beattie didn't know what to say.

The girl picked the jug back up. 'Aw. OK. Never mind. Just thought ... you sitting there watching that building an' all, thought you might be waiting for Vida ...' She started back towards the counter. 'Because if you was, she's not there. She's away.'

'Away?' Beattie said.

'Yep,' the girl said, wandering back to the counter. 'She's away. I believe her daughter's still there though.'

Beattie managed to keep her backside clamped to the seat a few minutes longer then got up to leave.

Beattie had never visited Vida. Last time she'd seen her, apart from the pictures of Rose's wedding, was when she'd turned up at The Luck – staying long enough to deposit her two girls – like they were a couple of parcels – then taking off without a backward glance. Never had the time, she would say to anyone who asked (most likely Pearl Clodagh). Never had the courage was more like it. She kept all that stuff, that past history, under lock and key: it was too raw for her to unravel so she bundled it altogether, shoved it in a dark place and kept away from it. She'd concentrated on the positives. Conrad's disappearance had granted her the care of his two baby girls. Positive. Rose had a safe haven in California. Positive. Think positive, act positive, stay positive. That was her motto. She'd survived by sticking to it and avoiding anything that might threaten it. Like visiting Vida.

All the same and despite this sudden revelation that Vida wasn't home, Beattie found herself unable to approach the apartment. She crossed the street then turned sharply left, avoiding the entrance way. When she got to the end of the block, she crossed the next quiet street and pounded on. What if the waitress was wrong? What if Vida had returned in the night – if she rang the door and it was Vida's voice that answered? What if she was invited up and she couldn't refuse and she had to go in ... and ... and see ...

Beattie put her hand up to her chest and made herself stop. She tucked into a shop doorway and tried to steady her breathing. This was why she'd stayed away. It was too risky. Oaklake, the farm, the store: they were safe, nothing to rumble her peace of mind. But here? She could feel it already: her armour chinking open, the small threads she'd managed to tuck away poking out. And every one of them leading back to Conrad.

She drew the letter out of her jacket pocket and considered the envelope. There was a girlishness to the neat loops and curls of the handwriting that made her want to weep. She'd near memorised the message inside. The poor young woman, waiting for her husband's return, like some war wife, when he ... when he had abandoned all thought of her and his babies and turned his attentions to ... to her Rose. Plucked her no less. Plucked her and now ...

Beattie shoved the letter back in her pocket. She was going to have to deal with this. No matter what it cost her. She pulled her jacket round her then fastened every button. It wasn't exactly armour but it would have to do. Then she stepped out of the doorway and turned back the way she'd come. By the time she got back to the apartment entrance she was ready for whatever was going to come her way.

Later, when she was back at the guest house, propped up on the bed and relating the morning's events to Darragh, she recognised the irony of the situation because what came her way was Rose.

'I was just about to buzz,' Beattie said to Darragh. 'And there she was – walking towards me on the other side of the door.'

What she didn't say was that the moment almost had her on the floor. It made no sense, but there it was: as Rose crossed the lobby – her image superimposed on Beattie's own reflection – she'd thought it was Conrad. The fair hair, something about the eyes, the lift of the chin. Rose's own reaction didn't help: at the sight of Beattie's face she stopped in her tracks, her hand against the glass, her face a study in alarm. They'd stared at each other for a few moments then Rose, fumbling with the catch, yanked open the door.

'Grandma. What's wrong?'

'Well, for a moment I couldn't speak,' Beattie said. Darragh raised an eyebrow at this but said nothing.

'She thought there was something wrong with us, you see, thought perhaps you … never mind. Anyway …' Beattie took a long breath. 'She took me up to the apartment. Up to Vida's apartment.'

Darragh shifted on the bed in order to get a better view of Beattie's face.

'Was there …? Did … did you see …'

'There was nothing,' Beattie said. 'No photo of him, nothing. Not a thing to say he ever existed.'

'So what did you do? What happened?'

Beattie had followed Rose into the apartment, her eyes firmly glued on her granddaughter's back. She didn't want to be caught unawares by some chance photograph or some memento that might knock her off course.

'Come through here, Grandma,' Rose had said, and they went through into what was obviously Rose's own room. A row of soft dresses dangled on hangers hooked over a makeshift rail. The bed was covered with the spread that Beattie and Mimi had made. A wedding gift. Beattie lowered herself onto a chair. Rose perched opposite her on the end of bed, like she was readying herself for bad news.

'What is it, Grandma? What's brought you here like this? Is it … is it Grandpa … is something wrong with …'

'What? Oh. No. Nothing like that. He's fine. Everyone's fine.' Beattie stopped because she couldn't find the words. She unbuttoned her jacket and pulled the letter out of her pocket.

'Oh.' Rose looked at the envelope and burst into tears.

'She already knew, Darragh. The poor girl already knew. There was another letter, see – she'd found it in Michael's suit pocket. Confronted him.'

'Another letter?'

Beattie nodded her head. 'She came across it a couple of weeks ago. He'd been away, come home rolling drunk. She'd stripped him off and put him to bed and set about cleaning his suit. Found the letter.'

'And it was the same?'

'More or less. Anyway, she woke him up, tried to get some sense out of him. Said he was impossible so she left him sleeping. Went out and walked a few blocks trying to, you know, get her head clear before she tackled him again.'

'And what did he have to say for himself?'

'Nothing. When she got back, he'd gone.'

'Gone?'

'Gone. His clothes, his shoes, his papers – everything – gone.'

'But how? Did he leave a note?'

'No note, no money, nothing. Nothing at all. Actually ...' Beattie drew in a long breath and turned to Darragh. 'That's not strictly true. He did leave her something.' She shook her head. 'She's pregnant, Darragh. The poor child is pregnant.'

Chapter 36

As beginnings go, this was none too promising. The pill and free love were not part of Rose's world. Her bigamous husband had abandoned her, pregnant, to a community which still prized marriage, family and stay-at-home mothers above all else. Nonetheless Rose squared up to her predicament in a manner that gave everyone a run for their money.

It's just a matter of perspective, Grandma. That's what she'd said. Beattie had puzzled over that one because the only damn perspective she could see was a pregnant young woman without a husband. She'd had to quash her impulse to scoop the poor girl up and carry her back to the safety of the farm and accept defeat. Short of admitting she wanted to hide the girl away until 'the event' was over, she'd had to back off and concede that Rose's insistence at staying in California was, in terms of Oaklake and gossip, a workable option.

I've got my work, Grandma, and this grand place to live. And Vida. Vida will be here to help out.

Beattie had let out a small snort. Vida help out? That sure as hell cut no mustard with her. But she'd acquiesced. It would at least let them off the hook for a short while, allow some time to get used to the idea and decide how to play it. So they'd left, Rose waving like a mad thing from the sidewalk, the waitress from the diner staring out the window, a tea cloth dangling loose in her hands.

'What you thinking?'

They'd been driving near enough two hours and barely spoken a word. Darragh didn't reply. Fact was he wasn't thinking, he was concentrating. There was a weight on his chest like water pressing against a dam. Keeping his hands fast on the wheel and his mouth clamped shut was the only thing holding it back. If it broke now, before he got back to the farm, before he got back to a place he could sit and damn well mull things over ... and there was the problem, right there, because the only place he wanted to be was at Kelly's cabin. Tending the horses, titivating the new vegetable garden, mooching round in the peace and quiet. He blew out a small sigh then closed his mouth tight again.

Beattie left it. She was all talked out anyway. She bundled her sweater up and laid it against the window then settled her head into it. She didn't sleep but there was some relief in pretending.

By the end of the week Beattie had the thing straight. Scrubbing and cleaning was the secret. To her mind there were few problems that couldn't be unknotted by a long stint with a stiff brush and a bucket of soapy water.

'You expecting the Queen of England or something, Beattie?' Gil had said. Third day in a row he'd gone down to open the store and found her on her hands and knees working her way down one of the aisles.

'Ha-ha,' she'd replied without leaving off.

Next day he'd come down and found her in the tea room. The mop and bucket were propped by the door and she was at a table, staring into a cup of coffee. She jumped when he walked in.

'Just finishing or just starting?'

'What?'

Gil nodded towards the mop.

'Oh. Finished. I'm all done. Got it all straight.'

Gil waited for her to go on but she didn't. She picked up her cup with both hands and peered into it.

'You want to tell me what's going on, Beattie?' She met his eyes for a moment then looked away.

'Beattie?'

'Nothing's going on.'

'Nothing's going ... Beattie, the whole place is shone up like it's new built and the only portion I've seen of you all week is your backside stuck out over that damn scrubbing brush, so don't tell me that ...'

Beattie put her cup down and stifled a sigh. There was some new weariness about her, a heaviness that had been cast over everything she set about. Sure, she'd worked the thing through, but every part of her was weary and aching.

'Sit down, Gil,' she said, pulling out the chair beside her.

It was the look on her face that made him hesitate.

By the end of the day Gil, Olive and Mimi were privy to Rose's predicament: Gil was tasked with breaking the news to Olive, whilst Beattie had taken herself round to Mimi's workshop to chew the thing over. Olive and Gil, full-on in the store and tea room, didn't get any real opportunity to talk until later that night when, in the safety of the dark bedroom, they hammered it out. Olive followed Gil's lead, slating Michael Kelly up and down and left to right until it seemed they'd left no portion of his character – or his blackguard deeds – unsullied. But it wasn't until Gil was sleeping that she let herself really consider the matter. She and Gil had trounced Kelly every which way yet not once had she crossed the line – the line she'd drawn over the bruises on Rose's arms, the hidden cash box. She'd kept that information back, telling herself she was protecting Rose. But now, as she lay watching the moon, she let herself consider the truth: the news of Michael's desertion had had her sliding through the gaps she usually skirted round, gaps took her down fast roads and dropped her in a place where Michael Kelly turned up and whisked her away.

For the next couple of weeks there was a degree of breath-holding that left the five of them distracted and on edge. Henry's daily visits had Beattie flapping like a waterlogged duck and Olive and Gil took to listening in to Pearl Clodagh in the tea room. There was a plan of sorts: if the news should break they'd concentrate on the positives:

Rose's pregnancy, and on no account be drawn into talk of Michael Kelly. This served them well until, about a week into October, they discovered they'd overlooked one major consideration.

Darragh was behind the small shed, resting on his spade when he heard the sound of an approaching engine. His first thought was that Beattie had nabbed him. He flung the half cigarette he'd been enjoying and rubbed the back of his hand across his mouth. Being caught smoking would be one thing but being caught at The Cabin – tending Michael Kelly's property no less – would be an act of treachery worthy of some lengthy verbal pasting. Fact was, despite Beattie's disapproval, he'd been visiting the place regularly – by his reckoning The Cabin was insurance for Rose and needed keeping it in order in case she ever decided to move back. This was the main line of argument should Beattie ever tackle him. Next line – though less solid, was that he liked to make sure Riley's youngest was making a good job of looking after the horses. The fact he was less likely to mention was that he didn't want to see his new kitchen patch grass over and all his hard work going to nothing.

It suddenly struck him that it couldn't be Beattie. She was on her way to California. She'd left before the sun was over the top pasture, her and Mimi, the pair of them decked out in new togs like a pair of road trippers. The thought gave him a moment's relief before he realised that if it wasn't Beattie then who the hell could it be? He turned his head and listened to the note of the engine. It had the low throaty growl of a large truck, more likely some kind of wagon. He gave a slight nod when he caught the hiss of air brakes as the driver pulled to a halt.

Darragh leaned the spade against the shed and crept along the back wall. The view of The Cabin was poor but good enough to see a tall feller climbing down from the cab of a dusty Dodge. It wasn't close enough to read the licence plate. Darragh squinted against the sun as the feller walked quickly towards the house and disappeared inside, leaving the front door wide open.

Darragh ran his tongue over his dry lips.

Was this the Lindo brothers, right here in Oaklake?

He'd heard a whole lot about them but he'd never had sight of them. He chanced another quick look at the truck. The windshield had a layer of dust that denied any view of the cab, but he figured if one of them had gone inside then one was surely sitting in the truck keeping lookout. If that were the case how could he get across the yard without being seen? Darragh raked his hand through his hair and tried to line up his thoughts. Whoever was in the cabin figured the place was empty, so if he could get over there and apprehend the feller he would, at least, have the element of surprise. That was one fact in his favour. Try as he might, however, he couldn't think of another. Seemed to him to be a whole stack of other facts that cautioned against showing himself: first off he wasn't a man given to any form of confrontation: secondly he'd chosen to walk over to The Cabin that morning so had no means of escape other than his own two legs and lastly he was approaching his sixtieth birthday and was pretty much committed to reaching it in one piece. Also – apart from a garden rake and a spade – he wasn't armed.

Before he got any closer to deciding what to do he heard the slam of a door. A couple of seconds later the truck engine rumbled back into life.

He must have got what he came for, Darragh reasoned, willing the feller to reverse out of the yard and leave. He didn't.

Darragh flattened himself against the shed wall as the truck passed. California plates. The driver dropped the revs as he manoeuvred the tilt of the corner then headed towards the stables. Darragh grabbed the spade and followed, tucking himself tight against the hedge. He didn't rightly know what he was expecting to do but digging up a few taters no longer seemed like an option.

Chapter 37

Darragh turned up at the tea room just as Olive was closing up. He bust in through the door like his pants were on fire.

'Gil here?' he said. There was some wild look on his face that she'd not seen before.

'No ... he's over with Danish, he's ...'

'Good,' he said, and motioned her to sit down. She hesitated but he caught hold of her arm. 'Pour us both some of that coffee, Ol. I need to talk to you.'

'I thought it was the Lindos,' Darragh said. He was taking his time stirring sugar into his coffee. 'Thought it was the Lindos come to rob the place.'

'But?' She could feel herself hotting up.

'But it wasn't.' He paused for an awful long time and it suddenly struck Olive that he looked tired. And older. But she couldn't help herself: if he had something to tell her then why make a three-course meal of the thing. She sat back in her seat, feigning an air of indifference, trying to swallow down the impatience striping the back of her throat. Darragh eventually stopped stirring his coffee and laid the spoon down on the table.

'It was Michael. Michael Kelly.'

She stared at him. 'M ... Michael? But what ... what did ...'

'He'd come for the horses.' He delivered the words like he was banging in nails. His eyes wouldn't meet hers.

She made herself wait. Counted out the seconds, tried to shut out the noise of the wind that seemed to be howling round in her head. Darragh surely had it wrong. Michael had surely gone to The Cabin hoping she would be there ...

'The horses. Did you ... did you talk to him?'

'Didn't get much chance,' he said. 'He loaded the horses then took off like his tail end was burning. Seems he got what he wanted and left.'

He was studying her face, trying to measure the effect of his words.

'You understand what I'm saying, Ol, don't you?'

She started to get up out of her seat but Darragh put his hand on her arm.

'Ol.'

She ignored him. Turned her head as if she was watching the street. In truth her eyes were swimming and she could see nothing but some blur of colour.

'Ol?'

'What?'

'You've got to let him go. He's no good. He's not who we thought he was.'

'Yes, but, did he ... did he ...?' She leapt up. It was one thing knowing you were a fool, another to realise that someone else knew it too.

'I told him, Ol, told him to stay away from us all. To stay away from you ... I ...'

She was halfway across the room, her face burning like it had been torched.

'Ol.'

She would not turn, would not let him see her. At that moment she hated them all. Gil, Darragh, Beattie, the child – the whole goddamn lot of them for trapping her there.

And Michael Kelly for leaving her behind.

Olive's hating went unnoticed. Apart from a sudden revived interest in brewing – not just the ale but various soda recipes for the tea room – she went about the place in her usual manner: brusque, short-fused and speedy, so no one gave her a second thought. Rose, of course, was a different matter: it seemed to Olive that as the weeks passed, her sister's situation became less of a predicament and more like the event of the goddamn century.

'She's swelling like a goddamn peach,' Beattie declared, every time she returned from California. The sheer joy of it all was near enough sweating out of her. She and Mimi were full on with needlework preparations and Darragh was knocking up a new crib.

It was cutting Olive to pieces. She'd been trying. She'd not said anything to Gil but she supposed he must have figured things out for himself – the new warmth in the bedroom. But nothing came of it. Her monthly crampings, heralding the tarry flow, flushed away whatever hope she nurtured and, save the confused thoughts of Michael Kelly which lay embedded deep, shrivelled and hard as a nut, her belly remained empty.

She squared up to it in her usual way – kept busy, but her mind, quiet enough while she was labouring, threw a switch as soon as her head touched the pillow. Each night, while Gil lay sleeping beside her, she sped down tormented tracks that by-passed the anger, the hurt, the what-ifs and dropped her in some fairy-tale place where, daytimes, she and Michael Kelly worked side by side raising racehorses and, night-times, slept tangled and spent in each other's arms.

The worst thing was no one really seemed to notice. If Rose was the ripe peach, full of hot promise, then Olive was last year's husks – empty and weightless, blowing around alone.

Turned out this was not true.

Darragh was watching Olive, watching her like a hawk. From a distant perch it has to be said, for fear of alerting Beattie, for he knew that, despite being buried to the hilt in Rose's affairs, Beattie's nose would have no trouble sniffing out any undue interest in Olive.

The fact was, he'd not told the whole story. Not told Olive – or Beattie. No, he'd kept some things to himself.

The truth largely.

This was because he didn't know what to do with it. Some days it felt like it was trailing behind him like a shadow that didn't fit, other times it sat like a damp weight in his chest.

He'd stood by as Kelly had loaded the horses, sure there was some explanation that would square everything up. He'd taken the man on like he was his own blood. A mistake had obviously been made and it just needed Michael to tell it the right way.

'You'll be going back to Ireland, I suppose?' That's what he had said, hopefulness coating every word.

Kelly had let out a snort of laughter. 'Ireland?' he said, like it was the funniest thing he'd ever heard. 'No, I'll not be going back to Ireland, Darragh ...'

'But what about your ... your wife and ...'

'Mary?' Kelly shook his head. 'No, I'll not be going back to Mary. I've moved on from all that.' He shook his head again and smiled like the thought was just too amusing to contemplate and Darragh had felt it then, some heavy dampness settling in his chest – his heart suddenly submerged and far away.

'But Rose, you've ... you've not moved on from her?' He waited, praying for the right answer. It didn't come. Even the mention of the child she was expecting didn't take the steel out of Kelly's eyes.

'I can't do it, Darragh. I'm going away.' He was leading the last mare into the truck. Darragh stood by, his hands hanging loose by his side. If Beattie had been there, she'd have run Kelly off. Very likely run him down, given the chance but he, all he seemed capable of was standing like his all strings had been cut.

Kelly checked the horses one last time then jumped down and closed the truck doors. He strode past Darragh and climbed up into the cab. The truck was moving before he wound down the window and called out. Darragh had to jog alongside to catch the words over the noise of the engine.

'I'm headed to New Jersey. Got myself a position at the racing stables there.' He'd glanced down then and smiled. 'Let her know, will you?'

'What? Who? Rose?' Darragh, shouted.

Kelly laughed. 'No,' he said. 'Olive. Let Olive know.' Then he cranked up a gear and left in a swirl of dust and grit.

Darragh stood for a long time, breathing in the dust and the engine fumes, watching the road until the truck disappeared from sight. Then he turned his back on the place and left, vowing he would never breathe a word of it to anyone, convincing himself that if he left it unspoken then nothing could ever come of it. But whatever conviction he managed to heap together in the day simply toppled over at night and had him lying for hours while tormenting possibilities paraded through his head.

What if Kelly came back for Olive? What if he sent word to let her know where he was? What if she already knew and was just biding her time? But the thing that had him in a sweat was that every question had the same answer: she would go, she would disappear and he would lose her – just like he lost Conrad. So he formed himself a plan. Later he would wonder if this was where he mis-stepped; whether it was his arrogant notion that he could protect Olive that caught him out. Because, while he was busy watching over her, Fate was busy with plans of its own.

Turned out he was watching the wrong person.

Chapter 38

James William Kelly was born a couple of months later, three weeks early but smiling, according to Beattie who had arrived at the hospital just as Vida, swaddled in some flowing silk concoction and late for a filming fixture, was leaving.

'She'll be a while yet,' Vida said as Beattie, still in her farm clothes, shot past her in the corridor. She'd set off as soon as the call came, stopping only once to ring Darragh and tell him to get a shift on with the crib.

'Just as well I didn't stop,' Beattie said. Again. Darragh could feel his eyes drooping. She'd only been back a few hours and he'd had the story front and back three times over.

'I nearly passed out when he suddenly appeared,' Beattie said. 'I had no idea things was so advanced. Rose was so ... so composed ... so serene.'

Darragh managed a muffled grunt as he slid further down the bed and pulled the covers over his ears.

'I guess she'll likely be visiting soon, bring young James down. Well, in fact I guess she'll likely be considering coming back home now ... hah, yes.' Darragh could feel her nodding. He closed his eyes and left her to it.

As it turned out James Kelly did not get to see Oaklake until he was nearly three years old. This was not by design as much as plain circumstance: Rose's work took off to an extent that she began referring to it as her *career*. Beattie was not strictly sure what this meant but it furnished Rose with the means to rent her own place and take on live-in help: a young woman who filled in as a cook, housekeeper and childminder and who was happy to accompany

Rose when she was working. *On location,* she called it. Consequently they saw little of her. Heard plenty – she was on the telephone every Sunday to update them on young Kelly – but they only saw her and the boy if they took to the road and paid her a visit.

This didn't sit well with Beattie although it did offer certain advantages. Chief of these was that it was less of a trial for Olive, because Olive and Gil were trying for another baby. Although Beattie didn't have this first hand – she'd got it from Mimi who'd got it off Gil – the news had granted Darragh a degree of respite from his secret concerns about Michael Kelly and Olive. They were trying, but nothing was happening. The subject could not be broached but the problem, as far as Beattie was concerned, was plain as the nose on her face: Olive was skinnier than a starved rat and wound tight as a bowstring. She thrummed around the place tight-lipped and snappish, putting everyone – including the customers – on edge. On top of this she seemed to regard her boy, young McKenzie, like just another job in an endless list of jobs. She dealt with him same as if he was a box of groceries to pack or a delivery to sort through: always thorough and efficient but like she was already thinking of the next job on the list. No, it was pretty obvious to Beattie, you could see why any child might not want to hole up in Olive's cold belly.

Gil, prompted by Mimi, had eventually stepped in and suggested they take on some help in the shop and tea room: someone who could lighten Olive's load a little, allow her more time on the brewing. However he'd dressed it up it had worked: Olive spent less and less time serving and more time out back, on her own, so by the time Rose's visit was announced, they were all breathing easier.

'Will she be stopping by the store first?' Olive asked.

Beattie had come by to pick up some last-minute supplies and young McKenzie.

'No, she's coming straight over to the farm,' Beattie said. The crease in Olive's forehead smoothed out, so Beattie took a chance.

'You nervous?'

'Nervous?' Olive squawked. 'Why the hell would I be nervous?'

'Well, you know. You've not seen her or ... well, I mean ... you've not ...'

'For God's sake, Grandma, we do speak on the telephone, you know. We do actually *talk* to one another.' A thread of spittle flew from Olive's mouth. Her colour was up, her two fists balled up against her skinny hips.

Beattie knew this wasn't strictly true but she backed off anyway. She picked up her bags and stuck a smile on her face.

'So, where's my boy, then?'

Olive shrugged her bony shoulders. 'No idea. Upstairs, probably. Or in the tea room, traipsing after the Clodagh girl.'

Beattie pressed her lips together and regarded her granddaughter. There was the problem with Olive, right there: she was so damn hard. *The Clodagh girl.* Why not call the child by her name? Why not soften up to a degree and damn well get on with people?

'What?' Olive was glaring at her. The crease across her forehead was back in place. Sharp, like it was cut in.

Beattie gave her a long look then shook her head.

'It doesn't matter,' she said, and turned to leave.

But it did matter. The way Olive conducted herself. The girl was so goddamn angry all the time. And cold. She and Mimi had talked about it, part despairing, part marvelling over how Gil put up with it, how he put such a happy face on it all. It amused folks in town, she knew that much. It was common knowledge: Gil McKenzie could light up anybody's day with just a smile, but Olive – meet her on the street and folks would absent-mindedly check the sky for clouds, wonder whether or not they'd remembered an umbrella. It was like she trailed a chill wind behind her, charging along with a face that always betrayed her haste and discomfort. On top of that she carried a sour vinegary smell, as if she'd just emerged from a long pickling session.

And yet it worked. That's what Mimi had told her. When Olive and Gil were alone – it all worked. Beattie didn't know if it was the truth or whether Gil was just trying to reassure his mother.

The thing was, though, it didn't matter a damn what she thought – it wasn't like she could change anything. Seemed to her that change came around of its own accord anyway. You just had to look around to see the truth in that. The town, for example, was no longer the place she and Darragh had settled. Too big – that's what her and Darragh reckoned. Too many folks you didn't know. The railroad had let them down but, after the road between them and Picker's Flag got re-laid, folks started drifting in. Building land was cheaper, the town was quiet – quaint, that's how visitors always referred to it. Well, it hadn't lost that but it had, it seemed to Beattie, lost something. A clutch of new houses had gone up and, soon after that, the school house got extended to take in the extra youngsters and before long the place felt less – she and Darragh struggled over this one – less familiar, less like home.

This wasn't helped by the Lindo family. They'd stuck fast. More than that, they'd swelled their ranks. The two ratty trailers they'd arrived with years back had been dragged to the back of their plot and been replaced by two less beat-up models but, other than the erection of a shanty-looking washhouse, there was never any sign of real building work. This offered an element of hope to folks in both towns, the hope that one morning they might drive by and the whole damn camp would be gone. The truth was the presence of the Lindos, in a place that was neither here nor there, kept everyone quietly on edge. They were an unknown quantity, not to be trusted – and not wanted. Like all edge-dwellers – wolves, coyotes, predators – they inhabited a place in folks' minds that spelled out threat. Self-sufficient, disregarding of society but constantly watching – and waiting.

Darragh and young McKenzie were on the verandah swing, on lookout. Beattie, intent on tackling Rose's visit like it was some kind of homecoming, was working the old iron range like it was a troop kitchen. It was nerves – Darragh knew that: the girl's sudden announcement had set her on edge.

'It's probably nothing, of course ... no reason for it at all.' That's what Beattie had said the night before – and the night before that – after she'd exhausted the various imagined motives behind Rose's sudden decision to visit.

'She most likely just needs a rest, Beattie. That's all it is, girl. Now go to sleep. Looks like you've got a lot of pan rattling to do in the morning. Come on ...'

He'd rolled onto his back and slipped his arm under her neck and drew her head onto his chest.

'I can hear your heart,' she'd said, then, within a couple of minutes, had drifted off to sleep.

Darragh had lain a long time, watching the shadows rippling across the ceiling, his ears tuned to the night sounds of the sleeping farm: the low rustle of leaves in the empty yard, the soft tick of the clock in the kitchen below them, the occasional stirring of the horses.

She could hear his heart. He wondered if she would sleep so soundly if she could really hear what was in there. He doubted it because there were many nights it stole sleep from him. Sometimes it was thoughts of Michael Kelly, hovering like some sharp-sighted hawk, fanning his imagination and fear, ramping up his old worries over Olive. But other nights – and these were the best nights and the worst nights – he let himself imagine the water lapping at the lake's edge. On those nights he would take a deep breath and slowly loosen the strings round his heart. He would let it fall open and, with careful fingers, sift through the layers of sand until he had him in his sights once more.

Conrad. The boy lay curled in his heart like a shell.

'Darragh, are you falling asleep?'

Darragh twisted his head slowly round so she could see her mistake. He slid his arm free and raised a finger to his lips. She peered over his shoulder at the sleeping youngster. 'I'm going to put him to bed,' he said. 'There'll be plenty of time for him to meet his cousin in the morning.' He tucked the lad into his arms then hauled himself off the swing.

'I won't be long,' he whispered as he squeezed past. She had a smudge of flour on the end of her nose which should have made him smile – instead it made her look tired, frail. Made him want to wrap her up and put her somewhere safe. Seemed to him they'd gone from raising their own child to their two grandchildren and now here he was, hauling his great-grandchild up the stairs. It was taking its toll.

Darragh drew back the covers and slipped the lad under the sheet, arranged the blankets up to his chin then perched himself on the edge of the mattress. The bedroom was warm from the kitchen below and for a moment he thought he might just lie down beside the lad. Rest his eyes, let his thoughts wander. They were getting old – there was the truth of the matter. He and Beattie, swinging along like they were still in their prime – fooling everyone but themselves. Although that wasn't the reality of it; it wasn't so much being fooled as being willing to look the other way, go along with things. Out of necessity of course, he could see that: Gil and Olive didn't intend to ask too much, expect too much. No, they just needed the extra help – always too much for them to do. But now, Rose on her way with the youngster. Young Kelly. What if she was to leave him at The Luck, like Vida? What if they were suddenly expected to rev up their engines again and take on the raising of another child?

Darragh let go a sigh and looked down at young McKenzie. The lad was sprawled on his back like a flatfish, his hair flopped back from his forehead, his two hands thrown back on the pillows, palms open like he was ready to receive some secret night-time blessing. The boy was a shrunk down version of his father, no mistaking that. Especially now, with his eyes sealed fast, his lashes near brushing his cheeks – no unruly eye to make suggestions that had no bearing on the truth. The fever had marked him but it had let him go. Like Beattie. Took more from her, of course. Not that you'd know: she'd risen to her challenge like it was nothing, like missing a leg was nothing. He'd never heard her utter a word against it – either good or bad. But now he'd clocked the small changes in her: a small weariness that showed in the bend of her back, the slack droop of her cheeks when she was sleeping. Couldn't say anything, of course. Could only watch as she mustered herself each morning, forcing a spring into her step that she neither felt nor trusted. And that was his problem, right there: she would rise up to whatever presented itself – another youngster to care for, another shift at the store – she would rise up and meet it, overcome it with a willingness that left him half-hearted and flailing in her wake.

Sometimes – and these times showed up more and more frequently it seemed – he felt a pull that he was finding difficult to ignore. The pull to rise above things, to get himself to a place of peace and quiet where he could get a look at the bigger picture, where he could spy whatever might be coming towards them.

He eased himself up off the bed, arranged the covers closer round the boy's neck and trod quietly down the stairs. He lifted his jacket off the peg in the hallway and went into the kitchen. Beattie looked up from the mixing bowl.

'You going out?'

'Thought I might wander down the barn. Look in on the Annie O'Grady,' he said, watching her face closely.

She narrowed her eyes a cinch. 'The Annie O'Grady?'

He nodded, still trying to gauge how his words had landed.

She put down her mixing bowl and dusted her hands against her hips.

'I'd better go and get the bunting.'

He didn't care that Beattie had read him wrong. The air in the barn offered a still quietness that eased him. The plane, covered in old tarps, waited like some great sleeping bird. He tugged at the corner of one cover and let it slide to the floor, then circled its tidy shape, kicking lightly at the tyres, running his hand over the metalwork, tracing the worn lettering of his mother's name.

He rested his backside on an old crate and pondered his idea. It wasn't an idea beyond doing, he reasoned. Advancing years might tug at your bones if you were lugging a bundle of fencing tack or coaxing a bunch of feisty cattle through a gate, but in the air: why, that would be a different matter altogether. Beattie would doubtless take some talking round, but ...

Chapter 39

It turned out that Beattie took no talking round at all – not because she was for the idea, but because the events that unfolded over the next couple of days robbed her – robbed everyone – of any belief that what was decided, known, hoped for, what was expected, held dear or planned, was as nought in the stony face of Fate.

Rose's arrival, the grand welcome, went as planned. They would look back, some point much later, and give thanks for that.

'It went well, didn't it?'

Beattie and Darragh were in bed, laid flat out, side by side like a pair of worn-out stretchers.

'Perfect,' Darragh said. 'Perfect.'

It was offered up in the spirit of a full stop – a good thick line drawn under any talking so that he could turn his attention to some serious shut-eye. There was silence for a few minutes which allowed him some hope. Then Beattie shuffled onto her side and he could feel her gaze burning into the side of his face. He faked a low snore but she was having none of it.

'What did you think of Olive?'

'Olive?'

'Yes, you know. What did you make of it?'

He wanted to pretend that he didn't know what she was talking about, but couldn't.

Olive.

She'd spent the entire evening with her eyes fixed firmly on Rose's youngster, like she couldn't pull herself away from looking at him. At one point, towards the end of the evening, she'd even had the lad on her lap.

'It was good for her,' Beattie said. 'They do say it's good for a woman's *hormones ...'* – she whispered the word. 'You know, if you're trying for a child. It gets things *stirred up in the right direction.'*

Darragh waited. Lay in the dark waiting to see if she was going to say the rest of it. She didn't, but it didn't matter because they'd both seen Olive's reaction when Rose pushed young Kelly forward to meet his aunt, seen the colour leave her face and the gasp escape her lips.

'My God,' was all she managed, but everyone knew what she meant: the child, down to the shine on his dark curls and the mischief in his eyes, was the image of Michael Kelly.

The morning after the party came and went with an easy ordinariness that boded nothing, other than another enjoyable afternoon and evening. Rose was up early with the boy, gliding round the kitchen gathering up dishes that had been left, re-setting the stove and fussing round Darragh and Beattie in a way that left them both quietly pleased.

'Feels like you've never been away ...' Beattie said, slurping a mouthful of coffee.

Darragh nudged her foot under the table but she avoided his eye.

'And the boy ... just look at him there ...'

The three of them considered the lad, sprawled on the floor with Beattie's two cats, basking in a pool of sunlight that lit the wooden floor the colour of marmalade.

'Look how happy he is here.'

'He's always like that, Grandma,' Rose said, a smile in her voice. 'I swear there isn't a difficult bone in that boy's body.'

Beattie changed tack. 'Look at him with the animals, though. Something of a farmer in him, I'd say.'

Darragh booted her under the table. She swung her chair round so he couldn't reach her. No point pretending as far as she was concerned: the girl had come back with the boy – damn fine welcome they'd put on – but they were all still clueless as to the reason for her visit.

'So,' Beattie said, clearing her throat and drumming her fingers on the table, like she was about to make an important announcement. 'We were just wondering ...'

Darragh let his head drop into his hands. Bad enough she was dragging it out of the girl, but to implicate him as well. 'Wondering if you came down for any particular reason, Rose?'

Rose swung round to look at them.

'The Cabin,' she said. The look on her face was hard to read.

Darragh saw Beattie's face light up. The joy of being right.

'The Cabin!' she exclaimed, her two hands dancing now. 'You and the lad coming back to The Cabin, well that's just ...'

'Oh, Grandma ... no that's ... that's not what I meant.'

Rose crossed the kitchen floor, put down the dish towel and pulled out the chair next to Beattie. Something serious in her expression now.

'I'm here to put it up for sale. The Cabin. Michael. He's asked me to sell it. He ... he needs the money.'

Darragh was up and out of his chair. 'Michael?' he thundered. 'He ... he wants you to ... I don't believe it. I ... when did you speak to him?'

'He's been contacting me this last while. Letters. He's, well. I've seen a lawyer, got myself some advice, you know. Said the best thing I can do is change the papers and put them in the boy's name. That should work but Michael,' Rose hesitated and glanced down at young Kelly. 'Michael is being ... erm ... disagreeable about it.'

'Disagreeable?' Darragh shouted. There was a noise like a steam kettle going off in his head, like something in him might just blow. Beattie tugged on his arm and nodded towards the boy, put her finger to her lips. He pulled his chair back out and sat down.

'Tell it, Rose,' he said. 'Tell us what's going on.'

The story was a simple one and soon told. Michael Kelly had contacted Rose a few months earlier. A letter. It was a benign kind of note, asking after her, the boy. It bore no return address so she put it in the bin and forgot about it. Until a second letter turned up. This one carried the address of some legal firm in New Jersey and was plain enough: their client, Michael Kelly, was keen to realise the value of his assets – namely The Cabin, Oaklake – would she be kind enough to forward the land deeds and documents forthwith. She'd replied, after consulting her own lawyer, that no, she would not.

'That's when he started writing to me himself,' Rose said. 'Two or three times a week. I stopped opening them, they were ...'

'Disagreeable,' Darragh said. He spat the word out like a piece of gristle.

Rose shook her head. 'More than that, I guess. They were ... well, I showed one to the lawyer and ... threatening. That's what he called it.' She paused and drew in a breath. 'Anyway. I took no notice of it, then ...' she glanced down at young Kelly again and lowered her voice, 'Then we got back from work one evening – we'd all been out on location – and the door to the apartment was bust in and the place was torn apart. Sorry.' She was regarding the pair of them, their mouths hanging open like a couple of stunned fish. 'I'm sorry, Grandma. I didn't want to come and tell you all this. There's nothing you can do about it. It's my problem, I'm the fool here.'

Darragh jumped to his feet again.

'Nothing we can do about it? Goddamn it girl, you imagine we're just going to stand by and let that, that ... imposter, take everything from you, from you and the boy? I tell you now, that is not going to happen. I will chain myself to the goddamn doorpost before that man gets his hands on it. Damn it, I'll burn it to the ground rather than see him set a foot in it.'

'Darragh.' Beattie pulled him back into his seat. 'Sit down,' she said. 'You're alarming the boy.' He looked at her, rubbed his hands over his face. Because here it was. Coming for him again. Just like he'd feared. The call to shake himself into some action he was not equal to, to rouse himself up and start hauling again.

Chapter 40

Rose had insisted on going to The Cabin alone. She took the boy: wanted him to see the place, reasoned that if things didn't work out and Michael got his way, then at least the child might have some memory of what had been.

'You won't be long, though?' Darragh was pacing the kitchen floor. His blood was still up and not for settling.

'I'll not, Grandad. Honestly. We'll be there and back.'

'But what if …' He couldn't say it. *What if Michael Kelly was there busting the place up?* 'Let me run you across there,' he said, swiping the truck keys off the hook. 'It won't take a minute.'

'Really, we'll be fine. We're up for a walk, aren't we, young man?' She held out her hand and the lad slipped his small mitt into hers.

Darragh watched the pair of them till they were out of sight then took himself off to the barn. He busied himself with the Annie O'Grady – she was almost ready for action now – and tried to conjure up the quiet of the night before. It was no good: the silence just seemed to amplify the pounding in his head until it was as if the tin walls were thrumming like some giant drum. Eventually he gave up tinkering with the engine and dragged one of the tarps across a stretch of old hay and lay himself down. Michael Kelly: the man had been nothing but a threat from the get-go and he'd been too blind to see it. He'd welcomed him, for God's sake, admired him, sought out his company, considered him a son … The stupidity of it brought tears to his eyes, because now here he was, worrying about what the feller was going to land him with next. He'd worn himself down with his quiet surveillance of Olive, but Rose? Now he was being called up to protect Rose too.

I should go after her, he thought. *I should go after her.*

But he didn't. He fell asleep.

Darragh opened his eyes, unable for a few moments to recognise his whereabouts. Some scent in his nostrils that didn't sit right with the fact that he'd been sleeping. He shifted himself and the creak of the tarp had things placed. He rolled onto his hands and knees then, with an effort that made him thankful no one was watching, straightened himself out. He put his head on one side and listened. He could hear nothing save the background swing of the yard: an orchestra of creaking and banging so familiar his ears generally ignored it. He could hear no voices.

He dragged open the barn door and slipped out into the day: the late day, judging by the fall of the sun. The truck was gone and the yard – save for the dogs eyeing him from their pitch on the back porch – was empty. He'd been in the kitchen long enough for the kettle to boil up, when the dogs set up barking. He looked out and saw the truck coming up the track. Beattie. No doubt Rose and the boy with her, parched most likely. He got two extra mugs down from the shelf and pulled a tumbler from the cupboard.

Beattie came in through the door, an armful of boxes balanced against her bosom.

'Ha ha – you're back,' she said. 'How was it?'

How was it? He put the kettle down. 'How was what?'

'The Cabin. You were gone so long I was minded to come and find you all. Then Olive called and ... you know what it's like, needed an extra hand at the tea room. She plonked the boxes on the table and looked at him. 'So how did it go? Where's Rose?'

'She's ... I thought she was ... I was in the ...' He stopped himself. How could he tell Beattie he'd not gone to The Cabin with Rose, that he'd fallen asleep in the barn instead? His hand sought the edge of the table and he clung onto it for a few moments as the churning of his insides rose to such a pitch it seemed the only thing keeping him upright was the iron fist clenched around his throat. She should have been back by now, her and the boy – they should have been back. What if he'd been right? What if Michael Kelly was at The Cabin? What if ...

'Darragh?'

Beattie's voice came through like she was far away – like he was a child dreaming maybe, or she was calling up from the farm to the top field. He released his hold on the table, steadied himself for a second then, lifting his hat off the hook by the door, walked out into the yard. The dogs clamoured round his legs but he paid them no heed. He slid into the truck, started the engine and pulled away. Beattie banged on the window. He rolled it down, without stopping.

'Darragh ...'

'Rose,' he said. 'She's not back yet. I'll go fetch her.' He wound the window up so Beattie wouldn't see the tears in his eyes and bumped the truck down the track.

Rose wasn't back. He'd been sleeping. Rose wasn't back. He'd been sleeping.

He wound the window down again and tried to pull some air into his chest but the rush of wind and dust, the rattle of the wheels on the road only made things worse. He put his foot down on the pedal and drove. All he could do was drive, keep driving, get to The Cabin. Find Rose.

There were no lights on. That was Darragh's first thought as he swung the pickup into the yard – his entrance faster than he realised, kicking up a spray of grit and releasing a screech of tyres that hit him like a tuning fork and wound his nerves to such a pitch he thought something in him might shatter.

He got out of the cab on legs he could no longer feel and hobbled round to the front of the cabin.

The door was wide open.

He went through like a man sleepwalking, Rose's name half formed on his lips, his ears keening for any sound that might offer some relief, that might make it all stop, wake him up from the nightmare he seemed to have fallen into.

But the room was silent – and empty. He turned to leave,

creeping, for some reason, like he might disturb something. And then, like an axe falling or the thud of the hangman's trapdoor – he saw it.

One of the kitchen chairs was lying on its side, splayed across the floor in front of the stove.

He backed out of the room, shouting her name now. Over and over, louder and louder, until he was screaming like a man demented. He staggered across the yard, clawed his way along the hedge and half ran, half stumbled his way to the stable block. The doors were bolted and padlocked, he could see that before he even drew level with them. There was no way she could be in there but he hammered and hollered all the same, a great booming sound that echoed in the growing gloom and followed him as he ran to the other end of the building, hoping, hoping ... but no. The locks were in place, rusty with disuse. Nothing, nothing to give him any ...

'Grandad.'

Darragh spun round, his eyes flicking round the yard, along the hedge, up along the edges of the field.

'Rose?' He cupped his hand behind his ear. 'Rose, is that you?'

He yelled her name again then stopped, willing some reply to come back to him. There was nothing. He started away from the stable block, his ears stretching for some sign, some clue that might set him in the right direction. He noted with some surprise that his clothes were damp, wet even. Rain: the steady fall of it already a dancing distraction on the tin roof. He drew alongside his old vegetable garden and stopped to get his breath. There was no planting there to speak of – hadn't been for years – just a mess of self-seeded weeds. Still, it struck him that there was some evidence that the ground had been trampled. He stood at the edge of the patch then walked a few steps in, his feet automatically picking a path between the greenery.

The spade was leaning against the back hedge. The ground in front of it was freshly dug.

It was more than he could bear. Darragh turned and ran.

He ran till he thought his heart might burst, the rain washing into his eyes and his mouth, blinding him, choking. He broke into the yard, his breath pulling like an overrun mare, stumbled to his knees, dragged himself upright, half running, half scrabbling towards the pickup. The door was open. He threw himself in, slammed the door against the rain and turned the key.

'Grandad.'

Darragh froze. He turned his head slowly, sure that his reason – whatever was left of it – had now truly cut him loose.

'Hello, Grandad.'

Young Kelly, his damp hair stuck against his pale forehead, was curled like a young pup on the passenger seat.

Chapter 41

They never found her. That was the short version of it, the one that appeared in the newspapers sporadically – even after the heat had gone out of the thing. 'Rose Kelly, aged 23, mother to James William, aged three years, disappeared from her home (this mistake they always allowed because of the misplaced comfort it offered) in Oaklake on October 27th and has never been seen again.'

The longer version took more digesting and depended on who was telling it.

The boy knew nothing. It seemed he'd come inside from the swing and wasn't able to find his mother. He'd gone upstairs and, still unable to find her, got into bed. He woke to someone shouting, went outside, saw the truck and, because it was raining, got in. That's as much as they could get from him before Vida arrived. She stayed just long enough to make them feel deficient, inadequate in some fundamental, guilty way, then whisked him back to California.

Walter McCleavy was knocked sideways: unnerved by the sudden limelight he called in reinforcements from Picker's Flag then, after two days searching yielded no results, brought in more officers from up county. They scoured the place, left to right, top to bottom for another three days but found nothing. *As if she's been spirited away,* McCleavy told Darragh, his face bled of all colour like it was one of his own he was searching for. The dug-over earth, the spade – an image that would wake Darragh for months – added to the mystery but yielded nothing. The rain had continued all night and any footprints that might have been of use were long gone.

The folk of Oaklake wove their own version of things. Some had it down for the work of a stranger, perhaps some hobo secretly camped out at The Cabin, disturbed by Rose's unexpected visit. Others, who remembered, quietly agreed that Rose had simply run off – left the boy behind for someone else to raise, just like her own mother. The majority, however, McCleavy included, lay the blame at the Lindo brothers' door. Problem was, despite determined searches of their property and questioning sessions that lasted through whole days and into the night, no corroborating evidence could be found.

Darragh, after his sessions with McCleavy and the other officers, spoke about it to no one save Beattie. They'd quarrelled, the pair of them. The first few hours after Rose had gone, both pale and sick with adrenaline, they'd gone off at different tangents. Darragh's heart told him that Michael Kelly was the man they needed to find but Beattie, against all the evidence Rose had told them, declared it too unlikely because she'd already laid the crime at the Lindos' door. He'd stomped out of the kitchen and down to the barn where the sight of the tarp stretched across the hay, evidence of his neglect, his own guilty part in the story, clobbered him and set him back to work on the engine. Next morning he and Gil dragged the Annie O'Grady out into the yard and an hour later he was airborne, circling the ground above The Cabin, following the weave of the road, the river, tracing the edges of the oak planting. The lake.

He circled twice. First time he thought he saw tyre tracks at its top edge: coming out from the trees and stopping at the water. It was hard to see properly – the rain still lashing at the Piper's windscreen, so he took her around again. By that time the water below was trammelling like an incoming tide. He took the plane down lower, still not sure if it was tracks. Closer up he reasoned it might be shadow, or simply the lay of the ground. Nonetheless he contacted McCleavy as soon as he landed and followed the patrol car over to the lake. The rain was hitting the pickup like he was surging through a river. He kept his eyes on McCleavy's tail lights, trying to keep his mind quiet, trying to remember the exact spot he'd seen the tracks. They found nothing but the thought that he'd been mistaken or led them to the wrong place had him airborne the next morning before Beattie realised he was out of bed. He retraced his route of the night before, flying the plane as low as his guts would allow him. McCleavy's tracks were plain to see, even in the churned-up mud. He tracked the edge of the woods, tracing imaginary lines to the shore of the lake, but nothing snagged his eye. He pulled the plane higher, took it over the woods, squinting his eyes at the ground below until his neck burned from looking down. But the land below yielded nothing. On the third and fourth day he mustered what courage he had left and took the plane over the lake, back and forth in sweeping loops, his guts creased with the fear that he might see something in the water, some floating trail that would settle his heart and break it in the same instant.

He kept it up for weeks, until Beattie asked him to stop.

Poor Beattie. She blew round the place like a flag left too long in the wind. Worn thin and frayed at the edges, she went through her days with a look of confusion on her face like she'd misplaced something or lost her bearings. She'd borne it as long as she could – Darragh taking to the sky – she'd even gone up with him a couple of times, but it had made her feel worse, afraid that she'd never get her feet back on solid ground. When she asked him to park the plane up, quit looking, he'd merely nodded. Beyond her fear for Rose, which crouched over her like a thing with talons, waiting some place just out of sight, ready to swoop down and carry her away, was her fear for the boy. She couldn't quit thinking of him. Whisked off and out of her sight. Living with Vida, for God's sake – Vida taking care of him – as if she'd have the first notion. Her cheeks still felt the sting of the woman's accusing glare as she packed the lad into the back of her car.

It wasn't our fault, she'd wanted to say.

So how come some part of her felt like it was?

How come some damn part of her felt like they had it coming? Like they'd had their quota of good – thank you very much – and now it was time to deal with another portion of bad. Because that's how she'd got to seeing it. No damn positives in this helping, no silver linings she might drape over it all and shine it up. No – just a plateful of bitter despair that no one could stomach.

Within a few days though, her distress over the boy got overtaken by a growing concern for Olive.

Rose's disappearance hit Olive harder than any of them. She came to a standstill and nothing could get her going again. First couple of days she sat on a kitchen chair, staring down at her hands, acknowledging no one. They didn't know what to do with her. She quit eating, quit speaking, quit the store and the Tea Room – she took on the look of someone ready to leave this world for the next. The doctor was called in but could only talk about pills – or a quiet stretch somewhere away from home. They'd all paled at the thought.

Gil and the boy hovered around her but it was like she couldn't see them, like she'd slipped through some veil, was stranded in some desolate place that no one could reach.

Remarkably it was Pearl Clodagh who came up with the answer. It didn't strike Beattie like the answer when Pearl first raised it, but after a couple of weeks watching Darragh circling the skies like a soul lost its way and Olive draining out to nothing in front of her eyes, she was willing to give anything a try.

'It will do the trick, Beattie, you mark my words.' Pearl had delivered it with a nod and a knowing wink, then turned on her heels and towed her batch of youngsters out the door.

'We'd have to check with Vida first, of course,' Beattie said.

Gil was gawping at her like he couldn't quite take in what she was saying.

'What, you mean ...'

'Well, yes ... why not? The boys would be near enough in age ... like brothers, even.' She was trying too hard, she knew it, could hear the false edge of optimism in her own voice.,

'But, Beattie, how ...?'

'Well, we'd just do it ... if Vida was agreeable of course.'

'And Olive,' Gil said. 'You haven't mentioned Olive.'

'Well, Olive's the whole point of it, Gil.' Beattie said. 'Good Lord, if we don't find some way to pull her out of this ... this ...' she couldn't find the word. Her brain was like some over-trawled stretch of water.

'Depression.' Gil said.

'Well, yes, OK – *depression*. If we don't find some way ...'

'I'll talk to her,' Gil said. 'You talk to Vida first, then I'll talk to Olive.'

It turned out Vida was agreeable. Enthusiastic even. It had been one thing marching off with the boy, steamed up with anger and disbelief, but another thing altogether trying to work, entertain the young thing *and* maintain a respectable social life.

Gil, given the go ahead by Beattie was left to tackle the subject with Olive. He waited till the evening when the lad was in bed then opened a bottle of ale, shared it between two glasses and went out to the front verandah. She was staring out at nothing, her hands loose in her lap. She gave a slight nod when he put the glass down in front of her but didn't speak. He took a long haul on his ale then launched into his piece. Said it all quick so she wouldn't have a chance to say no, or walk away or – worse still – laugh at him. To his amazement, his utter, utter amazement, she gave a small shake of her head – then smiled. *Smiled.* Gil wasn't sure if that was good or bad but he soldiered on and before he knew it Olive was nodding. *Yes, let's do it,* she said, quietly. *Let's do it.*

By the end of the week it was settled. Young Kelly was to return to Oaklake and be placed in the care of Gil and Olive. In the absence of a consenting parent they could not apply to adopt him, but would, to all intents and purposes, raise him as their own.

By the time the day of the child's arrival came, Olive was like a thing just born: up and moving round the place like some new invention, as though something had been washed away and she was ready to start over.

It would be fair to say that Olive's transformation and the subsequent arrival of the youngster dealt them all a degree of respite, some measure of positive distraction from the ongoing search for Rose. They threw themselves at the task of settling the youngster in, fussing and fretting over him like he was something fresh planted and tender and quietly laid the investigation down, shucking it off like they were taking some brief rest from an overloaded pack.

In terms of the investigation, the county sheriff and his officers had been eventually pulled away, leaving the local officers to continue alone. This arrangement was playing havoc with McCleavy's insides: he'd never entertained no fancy notions about chasing down murderers. Or finding missing women. Hell, the woodyard burgling had near enough burnt a hole in his guts and the Lindos – just considering going out to their camp had acid crawling into his throat. Truth was, without the support of the county men – or his son, John, who had been side-tracked by Picker's Flag business – he didn't have a clue what to do. He covered this by spending most days driving around in the patrol car, re-examining various spots at the lake, crawling around the grounds of The Cabin, gathering 'evidence' from folks in town, but mainly he was just waiting for time to pass. Waiting for some other *incident* to come up that would require his attention and grant him permission to quietly – and apologetically of course – leave the whole sorry business behind him. Because he knew, like everyone else in town, that whatever had happened to Rose Kelly, she sure as hell wasn't coming back.

Chapter 42

And so it was.

Time moved on, measured at first by the usual markers: Christmas, Easter, Thanksgiving, and then by years: one year, two, three, but Rose Kelly never returned. And the mystery of her disappearance was never solved.

The boy inched his way upwards, Michael Kelly's stamp on his features but a considered, ruminating way of doing things that spoke more of Rose. That he was the apple of Olive's eye was plain to everyone, including the youngster himself. He didn't possess any knowledge of what Olive had been like before his arrival, so if someone had tried to explain to him how much softening, how much warming it had brought about, he would have struggled to imagine it. Because no one would disagree that Olive, for all the improvement, was a woman for whom breathing – along with every other tiresome thing the day demanded of her – was a chore. This particularly included any dealings she had with her own son, whose every act, every word, seemed to fall short or hit the wrong note. Lacking any instruction on the matter, Kelly was left to draw his own conclusions. He became something of an observer, generally tagging along with whatever it was McKenzie was doing: mostly keeping out of Olive's way.

Years later, when time had moved on, leaving a different trail to unravel entirely, there were two memories of his early life he considered significant. The first was laid down when he was around seven years old and McKenzie still ten.

The rumours of a picture house, started years earlier, had finally come to something like fruition. Not in Oaklake itself, like folks was hoping, but just the other side of Picker's Flag. That was the first disappointment. The second was, rather than the uptown, modern cinematic experience laced with popcorn and ice lollies that everyone had privately envisaged, it was housed in a converted grain barn – the barn sitting at the back of Dora Dwight's farm, Dora being sister to Henry the mailman. The main thing to know about Dora was that she was widowed young and childless and that the only thing she loved more than money was Jesus. This may seem unimportant but it was not, because any child in Oaklake who wished to see the Saturday afternoon show had to attend Sunday School the week before in order to secure a place on the bus. There was no dodging out of this because Dora herself was in charge of the Sunday School sessions. Strictly speaking there was no bus. It was Henry's mail van, tricked out either side with a line of old feather pillows and eiderdowns and just enough room to accommodate a dozen kids who generally arrived in Picker's with swollen eyes. However, it was generally considered that this – the sitting through two hours of Dora's class, plus the sneezing gauntlet of Henry's van – was a small price to pay and Sunday School attendance went up and Saturdays became a whole lot more exciting. It was one such day that stuck itself in Kelly's mind.

Olive had granted the two of them time off from their Saturday chores to reap the reward of a Sunday afternoon of hymn singing. It was their first visit and, because Henry had taken it steady – having learned the hard way about Avril Clodagh's tendency towards queasiness, they arrived a mite late. As a consequence the Picker's kids had taken all the prime seats – these being wooden benches, and the Oaklake kids were left with the straw bales: serviceable, but capable of working up a good leg rash if you weren't wearing your long pants.

Anyhow, on the day in question, the barn door was pulled to and fixed closed, the projector rattled into life and the curtain/bed sheet that hid the glory of the big screen was hoisted back with invisible hands and three dozen kids fell silent for the cartoon. McKenzie was chewing his way through a strip of toffee – an entrepreneurial extra courtesy of Dora – and Kelly was cracking peanuts when

Popeye, led in by a tune so jaunty it had them off their seats, burst onto the screen, his chops and muscles bulging. A roar went up for black-whiskered Brutus, but it was the moment that Olive, accompanied by a chorus of loud kissing noises and wolf whistles, slinked into view that had Kelly's eyes popping. He leaned forward on his bale and looked closer for surely, there on the screen before him was McKenzie's ma. He spun round in his seat to see McKenzie's face but he didn't seem to have registered anything. Kelly was mesmerised. Surely, he reasoned, Mr Walt himself had chanced through Oaklake and, after glimpsing Mrs McKenzie; the scraped-back hair, legs that dangled like two bits of string from her skirts, had gone home and fashioned Olive Oyl. He could be forgiven of course for lack of knowledge with regards to her demeanour: his Olive was soft and droopy, the one they lived with was sharp as a whittled stick. He considered Popeye's features more closely to see if he could back up his theory, but no – the sailor man was nothing like Gil – or anyone else he'd ever seen in Oaklake. He sat back on his bale, figuring that he would bring it up with McKenzie when the show was over. As it turned out, the chance to do this never arose owing to the portion of hard labour that went with the privilege of being in the audience – namely a full hour clearing up the barn – followed by a spell of lounging about outside waiting for Henry. The time, depending on your age, was used up either throwing stones at the fence post, chatting to girls or making a stand against the Picker's boys. Kelly and McKenzie were generally drawn to the stone-throwing, but that day, for some reason, McKenzie thrust his hands in his pockets and wandered away. Kelly watched as he sauntered up to a couple of the older boys. The Lindo brothers. Kelly didn't know it at the time but they were set to become the second significant memory of his younger life.

Kelly's memory of the two Lindo boys was complicated: it ran like a coarse thread through more of his young years than he liked to admit, refusing to lay flat or knit itself in. The reason, he figured, when the two had gone from his life and he had room to reflect, was because he'd never really let them close, not like McKenzie had. Sure, he'd gone along with it all, but he wouldn't have if McKenzie hadn't pulled him along. The truth was he'd always been frightened by the Lindos. This, considering the general attitude in town, was not an unnatural thing. However by the time he was ten and old enough to understand some of his history, some of the rumours attached to the older Lindos and his vanished ma, he developed a fear of the entire family that had him finding reasons to stay at home on Saturdays. This meant that McKenzie went into Picker's Flag on his own, an acceptable enough arrangement until the day Henry's bus returned to Oaklake without him.

'Didn't turn up,' Henry said, to Gil. 'Waited long enough and he didn't show.'

It transpired that McKenzie had been catching a ride on Henry's cinema bus, but not actually going to see the picture show. It had been going on for weeks. Months maybe.

'So what are you doing with yourself in Picker's if you're not seeing the show?'

Gil had managed to get his son on his own. Last thing they needed was for Olive to get her tyres pumped up over it.

'Nothing,' McKenzie said.

'Nothing?'

McKenzie nodded and sprawled himself over the table, his head resting on his arms like he was planning to take a nap.

'Well, what kind of nothing? Who you doing it with?'

McKenzie let out a long sigh and hoisted his head off his arms like he was hauling a sack full of rocks. 'God, Pa. I'm not doing it with anyone. We just ... we ...' His voice pitched between bass and treble, his Adam's apple like a new landmark and Gil wondered when it had all happened, how it had all happened. This transformation.

'We?'

'Hell, just a bunch of us, you know. We just hang around. It's nothing.'

'McKenzie,' Gil tapped the lad on the shoulder. 'Sit yourself up. I'm not sure what's going on here. I know you're an age now – I understand, things get different when you're fourteen but ... you're not doing anything you shouldn't be doing? You're not associating with those Lindo boys are you?'

'God, Pa. The Lindo boys. You kidding me? Hah.' He cranked himself up from the chair, straightening himself out slowly like his bones didn't fit together any more then slouched past Gil, sluicing him with a waft of boy sweat that near brought tears to his eyes.

So Gil chose to leave it. Didn't say anything to Olive, let things go on as before. Only thing he did – out of some need to lay his own mind at rest – was take a trip into Picker's the following Saturday. He parked in the main street and scanned the road for the Lindos' vehicle. It was there sure enough, pulled up crooked outside the pool house. Gil walked over and looked in through the window. The place seemed empty. He pushed in through the door and saw them leaning in the corner. The two Lindo boys, a couple of other lads he didn't recognise and a young girl who looked like she shouldn't be in there. But no one else. He threw them a small nod then left.

McKenzie walked back in from the restroom just as Gil was getting back into the truck.

If Olive noticed the changes in McKenzie she didn't get down to discussing it overmuch. Beyond shrugging her shoulders or rolling her eyes she treated him just the same; sharp, impatient, mostly indifferent.

'It's his age,' was all she would say, when Gil eventually brought it up. 'All boys are surly at that age. He needs his space, Gil. Leave him be. Quit fretting over him.'

Gil rode along with it, decided she was right – the boy was finding his feet, growing up. It was only natural. Just a phase.

Beattie and Darragh weren't so confident. Teenage boys: they'd had some experience in that department.

'They gonna need to rope that boy in some, I reckon.'

They had finished up for the day and were parked on the front porch watching McKenzie, hunched like some double-jointed bird over the propped up hood of one of the old farm trucks.

'Don't I know it,' Darragh said.

'Like seeing him all over again, isn't it?' Beattie said.

Darragh nodded but didn't say anything. She was right. Could have been Conrad out there, working himself into a sweat and getting nowhere but mad.

'What's his chances of fixing that thing?' Beattie said.

Darragh gave a short laugh and pushed his hat back from his forehead. 'None,' he said. 'None at all. The boy don't know it yet but his wits ain't in his fingers, they're in his head.'

'What's he say he wants it for?'

'Get to Picker's and back. Seeing his buddies.'

Beattie left it a minute or two. 'I'm not so sure of that, are you? I mean ... do they know, do Gil and Olive know how much time he's spending over there?'

'Guess so. Like you said. Reckon they need to reel him in some.'

They sat in silence watching the boy. It went without saying, no chance that Olive would intervene – she was probably happy he was out from under her feet, although happy wasn't strictly a word you would use in relation to the woman. She saved the small measure of goodwill she seemed to have been dealt for young Kelly – and for Gil too, they supposed, because *he* always seemed happy enough. But McKenzie – he'd had to be content with her crumbs.

If anyone knew the truth of what was going on it was Kelly.

Night-times, their beds too close to give him any choice in the matter, he was held captive by McKenzie's stories, whispered through the air between them: stories that kept him awake, staring into the dark long after McKenzie had shuffled off to sleep. The

Lindos weren't what folks had them down for – that seemed to be the point of every tale. Their misdemeanours – their proclivity for violence and lawbreaking were, according to McKenzie, mere high spirits, daring escapades. Innocent fun. He had them in his head like comic book heroes – lovable villains who seasoned the otherwise bland world of Oaklake with a portion of excitement.

So Kelly listened, but he believed none of it. What he believed was that McKenzie had his head on back to front. The boys were Lindos. Nothing good could ever come from them.

A couple of years later he changed his mind. The first reason involved a girl. The second involved money.

Chapter 43

That Kelly's journey towards adulthood was going to be a smoother affair than McKenzie's was evident from the get-go. The boy went to bed early one evening – some slight hoarseness at the supper table which they put down to being out too long in a cold wind, and came down to breakfast the following morning with a voice deeper than Gil's. Next thing they knew he was putting on inches faster than a stick of rhubarb and sprouting whiskers: nothing like the few threadbare stragglers drooping limp on McKenzie's upper lip – the ones he secretly stiffened with salt water each morning – but a proper thicket that threatened the bathroom drainage. By the time he was halfway through fourteen, the job, it seemed, was near finished: like he'd done with being a boy and was all set to be a man. The next part was inevitable.

'Who *was* that?

'What?'

McKenzie was walking ahead, his usual watery slouch like his bones might just suddenly fold up on him.

'In the back seat,' Kelly said. 'Who was it sitting in the back seat?'

McKenzie pulled to a halt and swivelled round, his head on one side and a grin across his hairless chops. This was their new routine. Kelly would wait up after school, walk as far as the lane then kick dirt until he heard the steady thrum of old man Riley's new Ford. McKenzie would unfold himself from the front seat, drag out his college bag and the two of them would walk the mile into town.

'Who was that in the back seat?' McKenzie said. 'You fooling with me here, young feller? Ha, I don't believe it.' He dropped his voice down low to match Kelly's deep bass: 'Who was that in the back seat?'

Kelly let it ride. McKenzie mooched on for a bit longer then pulled up again.

'You know who it was.'

This was the way of it. McKenzie never told you anything straight: you had to wait him out. Kelly watched as McKenzie loped off again. He could tell from the back of his head he was still grinning. He let him go.

'It was Rachel.' McKenzie had stopped just past the bend, his book bag dangling from one arm. 'They've gone enrolled her in the college. The *secretarial* class. Reckon the old man needs someone to keep all his paperwork in order.'

'What? Rachel? Rachel Riley?'

'The very one.' McKenzie booted a stone off the road.

It could be said that Rachel Riley entered Kelly's life like a new star showing up in the sky, but this would be high talk because he'd known the girl most of his life: been through schooling with her, seen her most weekends in the town, seen her in church, hell, even seen her in Dora's hymn-singing sessions. But seeing her there in the back of the new Ford, her hand on the back of the driver's seat, leaning forward to say something to her daddy, her hair like a run of water, was like he'd looked up and seen her, really seen her, for the first time.

'She goes into Picker's every Saturday, you know.'

Kelly forked a piece of potato into his mouth and ignored McKenzie. They were taking an early supper on account of a new brew being ready for bottling – a wet and gassy affair that required all four of them and generally whipped Olive up into a lather – but was manageable if they were able to sample the goods. Experience had dealt them a measure of stealth that generally allowed a mild level of inebriation – not enough so's Olive and Gil would notice, but enough to lend the occasion a level of fun it otherwise lacked.

McKenzie booted his foot under the table. 'You listening to me, Kel? I said ...'

'What?'

'What?' McKenzie said, a loose grin sliding round his face. 'Rachel. She goes into Picker's. To Dora's, every Saturday.'

Olive cleared her throat noisily. Generally her first warning.

'So?'

'So? Well, just thought you seemed a mite interested in that direction earlier.'

'Well, maybe you thought wrong.'

McKenzie shrugged his shoulders and held his hands out. 'Maybe so, but it sure looked to me like ...'

'Quit your teasing, boy, and eat up,' Olive said.

'Just saying,' McKenzie said, without looking at his mother. He put down his fork – a sure-fire way to rile her up, speed being of the essence on bottling nights – and made like he was staring off into the distance, which took some doing, seeing as the curtains were already pulled to. 'Takes her two brothers with her. You know, to see the picture ...'

'McKenzie,' Olive rapped her knife on the table. 'I said quit it.'

She glanced across at Kelly and the colour in his face gave her the truth of it.

'Good for her,' Kelly said. Sounded unconvincing even to his own ears. He avoided Olive's eyes. She'd have him rumbled for sure: not an hour earlier he'd questioned her about the likelihood of taking on some paid work – in the store maybe, or over with Darragh and Beattie at The Luck, because, if he was going to ask Rachel Riley out – and that was a sure damn thing – he was going to need some money behind him. He might only be fourteen but he knew, same as everyone else, that if you were interested in a girl then you needed some moneymaking enterprise to back you up. He didn't imagine one would present itself quite so soon.

'Kelly, wake up.'

Kelly opened his eyes. There was no light at the window but he could make out McKenzie, bent over him, half dressed.

'What you doing?'

'We're going out.' McKenzie's breath was warm and stale on his face.

'What?'

'I said we're going out. Come on.' He hauled back Kelly's bed covers.

Kelly pulled them back up.

'What you talking about?'

'We've got us a job. Come on, Kelly. For God's sake, man, get up. They're waiting for us.'

He whipped the bed sheets right down, grabbed Kelly's pile of clothes and threw them at him. Kelly swung his legs over the edge of the mattress and grabbed McKenzie's wrist.

'What you on about, Mac? Who's waiting for us?'

'The boys,' McKenzie said. 'Get a move on. We don't want to be late.'

Kelly sat for a moment or two, his head fogged from being pulled out of his sleep.

'What boys?'

'Just a couple of lads from Picker's. For Christ's sake, Kel, get moving.'

'But ...'

'But what?' McKenzie stooped down so his mouth was a few inches from Kelly's ear. 'You want to earn yourself some money, don't you?' he hissed. 'You're so interested in that Riley girl, I heard you talking to Ma – asking about some work, earning yourself some money. So come on, here's your chance.' He straightened up and paused for a few seconds. 'Hell, I thought you'd jump at it.'

This wasn't strictly true. The job McKenzie had signed up for – signed them both up for – needed more than one pair of hands. He had been pretty certain, when he agreed to it, that Kelly might baulk on him – largely down to the fact that the Lindo boys were involved.

But Kelly's sudden need for a bit of moneymaking had put things in a new light, made his agreeing a whole lot more probable.

Kelly started pulling on his shirt.

'What the hell kind of work is it, Mac? It's the middle of the goddamn night.'

McKenzie nudged the boy's boots over to him, watched as he leaned to tie them.

'Not entirely sure. Easy money. That's what they said. We'll see soon enough, come on.'

McKenzie lifted the casing of the bedroom window, hunched himself over and threaded himself backward through the space. Kelly watched as he disappeared, his two hands gripping the sill then peeling off one at a time to let him make the drop to the yard below, then, taking one last look at his bed, he followed.

They walked side by side down the unlit road, the night sky low and heavy over their heads.

'You OK?' McKenzie said.

Kelly didn't answer. His feet were for turning back. Further they got from town, harder it got to keep going forward.

McKenzie, like he could read what Kelly was thinking, juiced up his pace. He broke into a slow trot and disappeared into the dark, the soft slap of his shoe leather against the dirt track the only sound that Kelly could hear until, unnerved to be alone, he picked up his own stride and fell in alongside him. They ran until the end of the lane was in view then slowed up some. The moon showed itself for a short moment and revealed the road ahead.

'There's no one there,' Kelly said. 'Thought you said they was waiting for us?'

'They are,' McKenzie said. 'They will be. Damn it, Kel, they're not going to be in plain sight are they? Come on.'

They continued until the lane ended at the side of the road then McKenzie opened his jacket and pulled out a small flashlight. He aimed it across the road and pressed it on and off. A short burst of light against the fence opposite.

‘Damn it, Mac, why didn’t you get that thing out earlier?’

‘Sshhh.’ McKenzie cupped his hand behind his ear. Somewhere further up the road an engine purred into life. He turned towards the sound and flashed the beam one more time.

‘Told you they was waiting, didn’t I?’

Kelly stood himself one side of McKenzie and looked down the road. He could hear the vehicle, the growl of the engine low and malevolent like some waiting animal.

‘How do you know it’s … shit …’ A dark shape suddenly loomed through the gloom. Kelly grabbed hold of McKenzie’s arm. ‘What the …’ The vehicle rolled towards them. A pickup. Beat to hell.

‘Mac. You are not serious. Is that the Lindo boys?’

McKenzie shook his arm loose and moved towards the truck. The passenger door creaked open. Kelly stood at the roadside, his two feet taken root, his head like it had flown off some place better.

‘Kelly.’ McKenzie’s voice came out of the dark. ‘*Kelly.*’

The pickup had come forward some and there was McKenzie, slid in beside the two Lindo boys, the three of them jaundiced and unearthly in the cab light, holding the door open.

‘For fuck’s sake,’ he hissed. ‘Get in.’

Chapter 44

Afterwards, when he was back in his bed, the sky outside the window leaching towards dawn, Kelly let his mind run through the night's events. Like he was recounting some dream except, there, in his hands, was a ten dollar bill. Ten dollars: for a spell of rowing and carrying. A couple hours at the most and that included walking back. The Lindo boys – McKenzie didn't introduce them and that suited Kelly – did some jawing then got out, lugged a sack off the back of the pickup, handed it to McKenzie, and got back in the truck. There was some more talking then the one in the driver's seat called him over, stuck his hand out the window and passed him a couple of banknotes. Kelly stuffed them in his jeans then followed McKenzie into the trees.

'Where we headed?' Kelly was following hard on McKenzie's heels, his eyes on the soft bump of the sack, the beam of the flashlight scanning the way ahead.

'Just keep up for God's sake and quit warbling.'

Kelly held his tongue till he'd gauged they'd cut about halfway through the forest and were coming out the other side: the lake side.

'We not burying it in here, then?'

'Nope.'

'We sinking it then?'

McKenzie swung round. The torch beam skittered across the quiet trees.

'You serious? Are we sinking it? Hell, Kelly. Get your damn head on.'

'We not headed for … for the island?'

'That's exactly where we headed.'

Kelly turned his face so's McKenzie couldn't see it. The island. The very thought had his heart shifting through its gears. Certain things in his life loomed over him: the Lindo boys, being alone in the dark – and the island.

'So ... what's the plan?'

'You'll see when we get there. Now quit talking.'

They carried on in silence until they got to the water's edge. The boat was tucked under a sweep of low willow, shucked up on the gravel. McKenzie motioned Kelly in, handed him the sack, then pushed them out onto the water. He took up the oars and, without a word, struck up rowing.

Kelly considered the sack, propped up like a small bale of wool in the bottom of the boat.

'What do you reckon is in there?'

'Reckon we don't get to know that. Reckon we just keep it safe till they need it again.'

He considered McKenzie, pulling on the oars like it was no bother at all, like they were just extensions of his own arms. Then he made himself look over McKenzie's shoulder.

'So, what's the plan?'

'You'll see when we get there. Hush up, Kelly.'

'But ...'

'Hush up, goddamnit.'

Kelly looked over McKenzie's shoulder again. An outline of trees jagged and black against the backdrop of night sky, a sense of the water shallowing out some as they drew nearer. He'd visited the place only once before: a family picnic with Beattie and Mimi. He was small – six or seven maybe. They'd toured the place like it was their own private museum: walked round Tom Darling's old shack, his woodshed, still stacked with wood, then Beattie had hauled up the trapdoor off the root cellar and they'd all peered down into the blackness. Nothing untoward occurred but his mind had conjured it up in nightmare dreams ever since. Dreams of being lost. Lost and alone, waiting to be found. Calling out for his mother. Waking up to find her gone and being alone. Alone and trapped on the island.

'What the hell's wrong with you now?'

'Nothing. I'm ... nothing.'

'Then what you look like that for?'

'What?'

'Like you gonna pitch your guts any minute.'

Kelly hauled himself up straight, rubbed his hands over his face. 'I'm OK, it's just ... just ...' He couldn't help himself. 'What if we get lost? What if we can't get back?'

'Kelly, have you lost your goddamn mind? Get ready. We're near enough there.'

Thing was they hadn't got lost and they'd got back. Here he was, lying in his bed like nothing had happened, ten dollars richer and, if McKenzie was right, plenty of opportunity to do it again. And McKenzie was right. The arrangement, as they took to referring to it, went on for a couple of years. Kelly's part in it was lifting and carrying. He never got involved with the talking side of things, kept himself apart from the Lindo boys and let McKenzie deal with them. For a long while this suited him and allowed him a peculiar angle on the situation, one that, in his mind, cast him as McKenzie's helper rather than an accomplice. His job was to lug the stuff into the boat then, when they got to the island, lug it over to the shack. Once he had it parked by the trapdoor his only job was to hold the flashlight while McKenzie hauled the stuff down into the root cellar.

As time went by, however, the stack of ten dollar bills under his mattress thickened and Kelly got to thinking about how he might put it to use. His schooling days were finished, he and Rachel were a regular item and he was working full-time, apprenticed to Earl Dracup. On top of that the living quarters above the store seemed to have shrunk: the bedroom he shared with McKenzie had fit fine when they were both boys, but now it squeezed the air out of him. It was time, he realised, to start thinking about doing up his ma's old place.

McKenzie couldn't have landed more different. But he'd known that from the get-go. There was no cosying down involved in his plans. As soon as his pile of money got thick enough he took off into Picker's and rigged himself out with the Clodagh's cast off Chevy. He took to driving to college straight after breakfast and arriving home just before supper was on the table. Then he'd be off again – hanging out, shooting pool, driving the roads with his buddies – getting back late, shuffling round the bedroom in the dark. He and Kelly took to living separate lives: apart from the *arrangement* the only thing they shared was the stale air in the bedroom and then only for the few hours McKenzie was in his bed.

The set-up for drop nights was always the same. Kelly never knew when it was coming, just got woke by McKenzie, then they'd be off, out the window and through the woods like they were on their way to some common day job. Then one night the set-up changed.

'I seen the boys today,' McKenzie said. They'd gone through supper and were set doing the dishes. Olive and Gil were out back, sampling one of Olive's new ales.

'OK.'

'They gonna need us tonight.'

'Oh.'

'Said they been having a clear out. Aiming to get it moved quick. Said we'll need the Chevy.

'Shit. Like how much stuff is it? I'm figuring that cellar must be near full.'

McKenzie shrugged. He picked up the pile of plates he'd dried and carried them to the cabinet. 'I'll be at the end of the lane. Usual time, OK?'

'What? Where are you ... so ... you mean for me to come on my own?'

'Only to the end of the lane, goddamnit. Jesus Christ, Kelly. You know the goddamn routine well enough.'

It was true. He did know the routine and this was nothing like it. This was *out of the ordinary*. He emptied the bowl of water into the sink and watched the dirty suds disappear.

'So why the change?'

'What?'

'Why the change. Why ... what you doing if you not coming back here first?'

'Don't matter what I'm doing, young feller. Only thing matters is you get your butt down the lane. OK?'

Kelly ran the water a few seconds. *Young feller.* Talking to him like he was still in school, like he was some little kid.

'You seeing someone in Picker's, then?'

'None of your business.'

'Well your ma figures you ...'

'I don't give a damn what my ma thinks. You think she cares a damn what I do?'

'I reckon she's interested. I've heard her talking to your pa.'

McKenzie laughed but it made him sound sad. 'She don't give one damn about what I do. Never has, never will. But it's not like I care. I got plans of my own and they sure don't involve hanging around this place.' He banged the cabinet door closed like that settled the matter then hung the dish towel over the stove rail. 'See you at the end of the lane.' And he was gone.

Kelly didn't bother trying to sleep. He lay on the top of the bed covers, dressed, other than his boots which were paired up on the rug. He watched the light leave the sky, stealing the colour out of everything until all was left was shadows and silhouettes: the dark hunch of McKenzie's empty bed, the black fingers of the oak out back.

He didn't want to do it: there was the truth of it. Not just now, this moment. He didn't want to do it at all. Sneaking around in the dark for the Lindos. Hiding their stuff when God only knew what it was. It wasn't just the fear – for that part had never left him – the dark, the island, the goddamn Lindo boys. No, it was more than that. He'd grown out of it. Wanted to be done with it.

Problem was McKenzie. No way he felt the same.

He lingered on the bed a while longer then, half fearful, half hopeful he might drop off to sleep, decided to make an early start. Get the damn thing over with.

The lane seemed a whole lot darker without McKenzie to follow. He'd brought the flashlight but, out of some superstitious feeling, dare not use it. He kept to the edge ready to duck into the trees should someone chance along, creeping, like some night-time criminal – and that surely was what he was, what the Lindo boys had made him. He shook his head. He wasn't fool enough to believe that. The Lindo boys had offered him the opportunity and he had damn well taken it. But now he needed to quit. For one thing, how long could a person's luck last out? That they'd never been caught, never even raised Olive's suspicion, not even when McKenzie went and bought the goddamn Chevy, was some miracle. By the time he reached the end of the lane the decision was near made: he was going to do this last drop then talk to McKenzie, tell him he was out of it.

He waited at the edge of the road. He'd prepared himself for the fact that McKenzie wouldn't be there, that he'd have to wait on him in the dark, but some low drum beat threading itself through the roadside trees suggested he was wrong, that his luck was in and the Chevy was already there. He took the flashlight out of his jacket and walked out into the road a little way looking down towards the drift of music. Sure enough, the Chevy was parked further up the road, tucked in under the trees. McKenzie had the interior light on, a warm yellow glow that put a degree of confidence back into Kelly's legs. He pushed the flashlight back into his jacket and made his way towards it. He was about to step out of the roadside undergrowth and onto the road when he pulled up short. He drew himself further back into the low branches and peered out at the Chevy. McKenzie was not alone. There was someone else in the car with him.

Kelly's first thought was to retrace his footsteps and take himself back home, tell McKenzie he'd fallen asleep. His second thought, which he dismissed straight off because it involved sneaking through the dark trees, was to creep up on the car and surprise McKenzie and his girl. As it turned out he didn't get chance to consider a third option because the Chevy doors suddenly swung open, loosing the music into the night air. McKenzie got out one side and the passenger got out the other. They walked round the back of the car then set off down the road. Kelly waited a few moments then followed. He got as far as the Chevy when another car engine rumbled into life. He dodged back into the trees and watched as a low slung car, a coupe maybe, slid slowly past, its headlights off, the tyres picking out every piece of loose gravel. He couldn't make out the driver.

Kelly waited until McKenzie was back in the Chevy then scooted himself back through the trees towards the end of the lane. He stood there a few minutes waiting for his breathing to settle then stepped out into the road and switched on the flashlight: two short bursts of light against the fence. McKenzie replied with a flick of the headlights.

The Chevy doors were still open. McKenzie was in the driver's seat, one foot on the road, a cigarette hanging loosely from his fingers.

'Why are you so goddamn early?

'Could ask you the same thing,' Kelly said, getting into the car and slamming the door shut. He tested the air for some tell-tale scent, some trace of perfume maybe or hairspray.

'Thought I saw another car going by.'

McKenzie ignored him.

'Few minutes ago, thought I saw a car go past?'

McKenzie tossed his cigarette out into the road and swung round in his seat.

'Sounds to me like you seeing things, young feller.' He gave a loud yawn then pulled the lever at the side of his seat. It reclined back. He stretched himself out and settled into it. 'Wake me up when the boys get here,' he said, then closed his eyes and turned his back on Kelly.

Kelly waited until McKenzie's breathing had levelled out then twisted round in his seat. He flicked on his flashlight and scanned the back of the car. He wasn't sure what he was expecting to see, but it sure as hell wasn't a suitcase.

'What the hell you doing now?' McKenzie said. His voice was muffled by the crook of his arm.

Kelly switched the beam off and turned back in the seat. McKenzie shifted and settled himself back down. Kelly looked over his shoulder into the back of the car. Sure enough, jammed behind the driver's seat – a small brown suitcase: the one that had perched on top of the bedroom wardrobe for as long as he could remember.

He considered McKenzie, stretched out like he didn't have anything to worry about other than a spell of shut-eye. That was the thing about him: always so goddamn relaxed. Nothing ever seemed to get to him, not even the constant pecking he got from Olive. It was like he ambled through life, always smiling, always the same dopey look on his face. A face that people trusted. This was why the Lindo boys had chosen him, Kelly knew that much. He wound down the window and breathed in the night air. Some small breeze carrying the scent of the forest floor flowed in and lifted the stack of papers heaped on McKenzie's dash. A couple of them fluttered onto the floor. As Kelly bent to pick them up the car was suddenly lit up. He jerked upright in his seat and shook McKenzie.

'They're here, Mac.' He quickly scanned the envelope in his hand. All he managed to see before he shoved it back into place was McKenzie's name and a California stamp.

Chapter 45

That night in the Chevy figured in Kelly's thoughts for a long time afterwards. He didn't mention it to the police when they questioned him a few weeks later, but when he was in his bed, the room missing the steady beat of McKenzie's breathing, he played it over and over like a movie, trying to tease out some clue as to what came next, to spot the moment when the plot suddenly up and changed.

The Lindos truck had pulled alongside the Chevy and McKenzie got out, stretching himself and popping his knuckles like some animal just out of hibernation.

Kelly waited till he'd disappeared round the back of the truck then snatched up the envelope. It was opened but empty. He leaned forward and grabbed the pile of papers off the dash. He rifled through them clumsily, not knowing what he was looking for. Halfway through he stopped. It wasn't the letter itself that pulled him up because it was too dark and he was too stirred up to read it, it was the insignia across the top of the sheet. Los Angeles Police Department. Kelly clamped his hand over his mouth. The letter dropped to the floor and McKenzie's head suddenly appeared at the window.

'You planning to stay in there all night?'

Kelly kicked the sheet of paper under the seat and hauled himself out of the car. The back of his throat was clenched like a fist. The Los Angeles Police Department? Christ almighty. Were they onto them? Had they discovered their dealings with the Lindo boys? He followed McKenzie on legs that didn't want to hold him up.

'What's up with him?'

The youngest Lindo was pointing a finger at him.

'Needs more sleep,' McKenzie said. Laughing.

'Yeah? Thought I'd heard he was seeing the Riley girl? Wouldn't of thought he'd be wanting much in the sleep department when ...'

Kelly stepped forward. 'We gonna get this done, then?'

The three others looked at him and then looked at each other.

'Jesus Christ, he speaks. The kid actually speaks.'

McKenzie threw him a weak smile. 'The young feller's right. We better get this done. Come on.'

There hadn't been much stuff to haul. Not like Kelly had imagined. A clear-out, McKenzie had said. He'd thought a truckload would be coming their way. But no. It was one box. A packing crate. Too heavy for one person but easy enough with two. Kelly barely remembered the journey to the island, his mind blowing backwards and forwards over the letter, the image of the police insignia flaring behind his eyes like a warning.

Things went like they usually did until they got to the trapdoor.

'I wonder what's in there?'

Kelly stopped in his tracks?

'What?'

McKenzie tapped the side of the crate with his shoe. 'Wonderin' what's in there.'

'You said it yourself, Mac, we don't get to know that, we just ...'

'That was a long time ago,' McKenzie said. Then he brought out the crowbar.

Jewellery. The crate was full of it. Kelly figured they must have looked like a couple of pirates, the two of them, crouched in the dark, McKenzie dipping his hands into the crate over and over, gold, silver, jewels, sieving through his fingers. Kelly's nerve eventually gave way and he grabbed the lid and tried to slide it in place. McKenzie held it back.

'One last feel,' he said, then thrust his hands deep into the glittering trove. He pulled out a small necklace, fitted with a locket. He considered it for a couple of moments then pushed it into his shirt pocket. 'OK,' he said. 'Put the lid on.'

After that it was like things happened too fast, like too much happened at once and he could never line it up straight in his mind. He kept going back over things but got to mixing up one trip with another until he could no longer make a true account of anything in his mind. But this much he knew: that *was* the night everything had changed. He'd not known it right away: they'd got back to their beds like always and, when he woke next morning McKenzie was already down in the kitchen and the suitcase was back on top of the wardrobe. Like nothing had happened. The feeling lasted about five minutes.

'Goddamnit, McKenzie ...' Olive's voice sliced through the air. Kelly slid out of bed and started pulling on his clothes. Things generally went better on a morning if he was in the kitchen. Like some kind of buffer between McKenzie and his mother. He pushed open the kitchen door just as the plate hit the floor.

'Mac ...'

McKenzie was at the sink, holding onto the edge of the draining board. He had a look on his face that Kelly had not seen before.

'Come in, young feller,' he said, making a slight bow. 'You're just in time for the show.' He picked a plate off the drainer and hurled it across the room.

'Mac.' Kelly stepped into the room. 'What's going on?'

'What's going on? I tell you what's going on, young Kelly. What's going on is my mother here,' he indicated Olive, wedged in the corner by the pantry cupboard. 'My mother here and I are having a little discussion ...'

'Well ...'

'Wait, wait ... we are having a little discussion about my inability to do the dishes the right way ... in fact ... in fact ... about my inability to do any goddamn thing the right goddamn way. He hurled another plate across the room.

Kelly looked across at Olive. Her face was the colour of old milk.

'Where's Gil?'

'Gil?' McKenzie yelled. 'You mean good old Gil? Why I guess

he's down in the store or the tea room – doing as he's goddamn told. Like what else would he be doing?'

'Come on, Mac,' Kelly said. 'You need to get out of here.'

'I need to get out of here?' McKenzie let out a high laugh. 'Ha. You took the words right out of my mouth, young feller. Right out of my goddamn mouth.' He turned to look at Olive then swiped the rest of the crockery onto the floor. 'I'll try better next time, Mother. I truly will.' Then he slammed out the door.

Chapter 46

Kelly never raised the plate-throwing incident with McKenzie and, as far as he knew, neither did Olive, but it hung between the three of them like some damp blanket that would not air. If she had spoken to Gil about it then he could see no evidence of it, but the difference in Olive's dealings with McKenzie was another matter. Whether it was out of fear of McKenzie or for her crockery was hard to say but she quit her picking and adopted a manner that was civil, if not warm.

In the end it didn't matter. None of it mattered, because nothing she did – nothing anybody did – seemed to satisfy McKenzie. Next few weeks it was like someone had lit a fire under his ass and he wouldn't budge off it. Kelly quit trying to talk to him – too afraid of what he might hear, but he'd come to the conclusion that the letter he'd seen in McKenzie's car had something to do with it. More than once Kelly had woken in the night and looked over at McKenzie, seen him lying there awake, the locket dangling from his fingers, but he never spoke about it. Once, he'd done a quick search under McKenzie's mattress but quit halfway through, too nervous of what he might find. So they all went along with it, like a group of folks being led along a cliff by a blind man. Waiting for the fall.

When it came it wasn't what they'd anticipated.

'You ever think about your ma?'

McKenzie's voice drifted out of the dark. Kelly turned over in his bed.

'My ma?'

'Yeah.' McKenzie had the locket out again, dangled over his head, watching it spin.

'Well, not really, I suppose. I don't really remember her.' Kelly waited, but McKenzie said nothing more. His eyes grew heavy and he turned back onto his side.

Next thing he knew McKenzie was shaking him awake.

'The boys?' Kelly muttered, rubbing his eyes.

'Don't you know it. C'mon roust your ass.' He was already hauling up the window.

It was straight forward. A standard kind of drop, apart from McKenzie's dealings with the boys – more curt than usual – and some swaggering edge to him that put Kelly in a quiet stew. When it was over and they were back in their beds Kelly could not sleep. The letter – and the fact he'd still not said anything about quitting lay heavy on him. He must have fallen asleep because at some point in the night – it was still dark, that much he remembered afterwards – McKenzie shook him awake again.

'Christ's sake, Mac, what the hell you want now?'

'My shoes,' McKenzie said. 'My good shoes. I reckon I left 'em in the boat. I'm going back for them. OK?'

'Christ almighty. OK. What the hell you need to wake me for?' He rolled back onto his side and pulled the bed covers over his head. 'And leave the goddamn window open, don't go waking me again ...'

And that was it. When he woke next morning the window was still open. McKenzie's bed was empty and the suitcase was gone.

First couple of days they did nothing. Olive reckoned he was over in Picker's with his buddies. *Cooling his heels.* Kelly held his tongue. He could have mentioned the letter, the suitcase, but he didn't. The third night of lying in bed, his eye on the window as if McKenzie might suddenly appear, he got up. He knew what he had to do. Didn't want to do it but he needed to know McKenzie was OK.

By the time he reached the edge of the lake, sweat was running down his back. The boat wasn't there. This, he reasoned, was a good sign.

He looked out across the dark water, his eyes scanning the low hunch of the land, searching for some back-up, some small lit-up glow that would tell him he was right: that he'd get over there and McKenzie would be camped up snug as a bug in the old timer's shack. But there was nothing. He walked a little way further along the lake shore and loosed old man Riley's boat from its moorings, fixed the oars then, without giving too much consideration to what he was doing lest his nerve quit on him, pulled towards the island.

He knew as soon as he landed that McKenzie wasn't there. There was no boat for one thing. And it was too quiet. That made no goddamn sense at all, he knew that, but the place *felt* empty. He switched on the flashlight, keeping it low to the ground and traced the path to the shack. He swung the beam across the window and door and called McKenzie's name. He waited a moment then pushed open the door. The place was empty. He backed out and swept the torchlight across the dirt. The trapdoor lay open: a dark invitation he was in no mind to accept. He called out again and played the flashlight over the black yawn of the cellar, then waited. His heart was drilling a hole in his chest. He walked slowly to the trapdoor and got down on his knees, pulled in a lungful of air and aimed the torch beam down into the cellar.

It was empty. No one in it.

Nothing in it.

Kelly hooked the flashlight to his jacket and lowered his feet onto the ladder. He wiped the sweat off his hands on the back of his pants and started down into the darkness. He stopped before he reached the bottom and ranged the beam around the cellar. It was truly empty. Everything they'd stashed, the boxes, crates, sacks, Christ knows what, was gone. He made the last couple of rungs and stepped down onto the dirt floor.

There was nothing to say they'd ever been there.

He shone the flashlight one last time and fixed his feet back on the ladder. He was halfway up when he saw them. McKenzie's good shoes. Lodged on a narrow shelf behind the ladder. Neatly arranged, side by side, as if he'd just stepped outside and was expecting to return. Kelly stretched his arm between the rungs and picked them up. He lifted them over his head and set them on the ground while he climbed out the rest of the way. He took hold of the edge of the trapdoor and eased it back into place. The metal ring clattered as it landed and the sound disturbed some roosting bird, sent it skittering through the trees, taking his nerve with it. He gave one last look around then shoved the shoes inside his jacket and headed back to the boat.

Afterwards, when he was back in his bed, he realised he'd made a mistake. He ought to have left a note. He'd examined the shoes – even pulled out the leather linings – expecting some word from McKenzie, some message. But there was nothing. He considered going back, maybe rowing over there in the daylight, checking the place over properly and leaving some food in case McKenzie was camped up some other place on the island. But he didn't.

Chapter 47

A couple of days after his trip to the island, near enough a week since McKenzie had gone, Kelly was on the back porch kicking off his work boots when he heard raised voices in the kitchen. He listened at the door: Gil and Olive, the only time he ever heard harsh words spoken between them.

'It was you, Olive. You never quit pecking on the boy.' Olive was banging the pans on the stove.

'Pecking on him? You knew what he was up to with those boys. It didn't bother you?' Kelly took hold of the doorpost.

Olive knew about the Lindo boys?

He crept up the stairs, closed the bedroom door behind him and pulled his bundle of money out from under the mattress. He riffled through it then stuffed it back in, pushing it all the way to the wall. He cracked open the door and leaned against the frame and listened, dreading some further revelation yet unable to pull himself away. After ten minutes they'd said nothing more about the Lindos so, led mainly by gnawing hunger and the smell of supper, he clomped down the stairs and into the kitchen. Neither Gil or Olive looked at him. He busied himself setting the table, filled a pitcher of water. Once the three of them were seated he took a deep breath and jumped in.

'I've been thinking about taking a trip over to Ma's old place. Maybe start fixing it up ...'

Olive and Gil stared at him.

'What? What's brought this on?' Gil said.

Kelly didn't have a ready answer – he forked a pile of beans into his mouth to buy some time. Olive and Gil watched him chew.

'Well?' Olive said, once he'd managed to swallow the beans past the lump in his throat. He felt his face colour up.

'It's just ... erm ... it's just that me and Rachel ... well, me and Rachel, we ...' He took a deep breath and ran at it. 'Me and Rachel, we're looking to settle next year ...' He couldn't finish.

Gil grinned. 'Looking to settle next year, son? That's the first I've heard of it.'

Kelly grinned, sweat running down the side of his face. Truth was it was the first he'd heard of it himself. It had just come out – the shock of Olive's knowledge of their escapades with the Lindos and the fear she might discover, and confiscate, his ill-gotten gains, had propelled him into panic talk. More to the point Rachel was not privy to this sudden development. He bolted down his supper then excused himself and hotfooted it over to the Riley place, practising his speech all the way, mortified by the notion that she might think him a fool and turn him down. She didn't, but reckoned that they'd need to keep it to themselves a while because her pa would no doubt see fit to clamp a whole lot of stipulations to the idea. So she jumped in and got a head start on the stipulating – the main thing being Kelly *had* to get the house fixed up good first.

Turned out those stipulations saved his bacon.

A couple of nights later, when Kelly returned home after spell of ditch clearing, he found the house quiet and empty. He washed himself down at the tap and fixed up some supper from what Olive had left out. He was at the table, jawing through a slice of ham, when he saw it – the shotgun – propped up against the cabinet. The sight of it quelled his appetite. He left his plate and went quietly up the stairs. Gil and Olive were talking in bed. He paused outside their door for a moment.

'That you, Kelly?' Gil suddenly called.

Kelly started. 'It's me,' he said. 'Everything OK?'

'Sure is,' Gil said. 'Goodnight, son.'

'Goodnight.'

Kelly lay listening for as long as his eyes would allow him. He could hear nothing clearly but something about the pitch of their voices, some underlying note of anxiety told him that Gil was lying. Something was wrong. Tired as he was, sleep brought no relief. The night plagued him with dreams of McKenzie; he was in the old timer's cellar, trapped with no ladder, he was running along the railroad tracks, the engine hot on his heels. He woke twice to the sound of his own yelling, twisted in damp sheets, panting like a young dog.

When he came down into the kitchen next morning the shotgun had gone. He glanced over at Olive. Her face carried its usual stony look: chin jutted out, scowl fixed on her forehead. He took his place at the table. There was no sign of Gil.

'Gil not here?' He was taking a chance starting up any conversation: it was largely accepted that Olive was not partial to morning talk. She ignored him, put a plate of eggs and bread in front of him and walked out of the kitchen.

'Everything OK?' Dracup said, as Kelly got into the pickup.

'Fine,' Kelly said, settling his work bag and lunchbox on the floor.

This was his new routine. Earl collected him at the end of the track each morning, seven thirty on the dot. No leeway or else he got left behind. The original arrangement was that he'd been taken on as an apprentice, but after a couple of months he'd demonstrated such a knack with wood and nails that Dracup had put his wages up and more or less treated him as a partner. Unless he was late for the truck, in which case he generally lost a day's wages.

Dracup pulled out a filthy handkerchief and snorted into it. A wet trumpeting that turned Kelly's stomach. He'd keep it up all the way to the workshop.

'Heard the Lindos came calling last night.' Dracup said, dragging up a beakful of snot.

Kelly swivelled in his seat. 'Say what?'

'The Lindo boys,' Dracup said. 'Old Henry was driving by, soon after suppertime. Saw them talking to Gil.'

Kelly wound down the window and let the air play on his face.

The Lindos? The image of the shotgun leaning against the cabinet danced before his eyes. He felt the eggs and bread bunching up in his guts.

'You know what they was after?' he asked Dracup.

'Was going to ask you the same thing.'

Kelly worried the thing to death all day. It was a hard thing to admit but McKenzie's departure, mystifying as it was, had provided him with some kind of solution in terms of quitting the arrangement with the Lindos. Leastwise that's what he'd assumed. Now, the two of them showing up saying God-knows-what to Gil and Olive.

When Dracup dropped him off he took the mile into town at a half run. He was drawing level with The Ponderosa when he spotted Gil. He changed course and trotted over.

'Got some fire in those heels tonight, son. You seeing Rachel?'

'Yeah ... no ... I mean ... Gil. What's going on? Dracup said the Lindos came calling last night. Henry saw their truck.'

'The Lindos? News to me, son. Reckon Henry's eyes are failing. What would the Lindos want here?'

Kelly considered this answer. He could give a number of good reasons as to what the Lindos might be wanting – top of the pile might be having their stuff back. Close second might be McKenzie's hide. Second thoughts, they might just settle for McKenzie's hide.

'But the shotgun,' Kelly said. 'When I got in last night, the shotgun was by the cabinet. And the both of you were in bed.'

Gil laughed. 'I'd been cleaning the darn thing. Been in town yesterday – Naylor lost a couple of ewes. Reckons it was coyotes. Asked me to take a look.'

Kelly considered Gil's face. He had never known him to lie, but then again the man was as good as a real pa to him: it was a father's place to lie if it smoothed things out. In any case, Kelly did feel a sight smoothed out so he let it be. When he got back from ditch clearing later that evening however, the shotgun was nowhere to be seen. He got to bed and lay a long time trying to work out what the hell was going on, praying that McKenzie would come back, praying that the Lindos wouldn't come looking for him.

A couple of days later his prayers were part way answered. The radio was on full blast when Dracup pulled the truck up beside him. Dracup leaned over and threw the door open.

'Get in, quick. We're on national radio.' Kelly tuned his ears in to what was being said, grappling with the presenter's East Coast accent.

'A double shooting? In Picker's Flag?' he said to Dracup as soon as the presenter moved on.

'The Lindos,' Dracup said, swiping at a bead of snot swinging from his nose. 'The Lindos got it last night. In their beds.'

'They got it? What do you mean, they got it?'

'They got shot,' Dracup said. 'As in they got shot dead.' There was a certain amount of excitement in his voice.

'Sh ... shot dead? You joking me on, Earl? Who in God's name would ...'

Christ almighty.

'Who in God's name would ...'

'Think about it, son. There'd be plenty contenders happy to see 'em gone.'

It was true, and if the news was right Kelly could foresee some quiet celebrating going on in the town. He might feel that way himself – should feel that way, but ... some cold hand slipped itself into his heart.

The shotgun.

What if Gil had gone and done it? Or Olive – a damn sight more likely than Gil. What if the Lindos had come calling like Henry said and ... and ...

The rest of the day swam by in a sickening stream. His mind lurched through different scenarios, pulling him along like some chained captive. At dinnertime he listened to Earl, trying to catch hold of some of his excitement, trying to find the relief he himself should be feeling. The Lindos were gone. But nothing held: the vision of the shotgun – leaning against the kitchen cabinet – swam in front of his eyes. He got no relief until they were on the road back home.

Dracup switched on the radio as soon as they struck out, cruising the channels till he picked up some news. The pair of them leaned close to the dash and listened for a mention of Picker's. They were just coming to the long straight before the town when the story came on.

'Close the window, Kelly, I can't catch what the feller is saying.'

They missed a good deal of the details due to some crackling problem, but right at the end the presenter said, loud and clear, 'State police now believe the killings may be linked to a local man …'

Kelly felt the blood drain from his face.

'Did you hear that, what that feller just said? Linked to … turn it up, Earl …'

Dracup fussed with the dials.

'Police are now searching for … shotgun …'

The radio went back to crackling.

'Damn and blast it.' Kelly said. 'What the hell did they mean, looking for a local man?' His mind was charging ahead. Visions of Gil being led away in handcuffs.

'Tune it in, Earl. Tune the damn radio back in.'

'… searching for disappeared two weeks ago and …'

'What do they mean, "disappeared two weeks" … my God, they can't think …' He couldn't say it.

Dracup reached for his handkerchief. 'Sounds like that's exactly what they're thinking, son.'

'You mean … McKenzie?'

'Guess so. I'm sorry son.'

Chapter 48

Kelly got Dracup to let him out the truck a mile or so before the turn into town. The police were looking for McKenzie? The thought of it sucked the air out of his lungs. He tried it every way but couldn't get it to fit. Sure, McKenzie had gotten some mean streak about him these last few weeks – but shoot the Lindos?

By the time he got into town he had it laying straighter in his mind. The news story was nothing but nonsense – East Coast nonsense. Chances were McKenzie would turn up, hell he might even be sat in the kitchen when he got back.

He saw it as he approached the backyard. There was something in the mailbox. Henry generally made one delivery a day and either Olive or Gil would come down and pick it up. A second delivery was not usual. Kelly opened the box and drew out a package – whoever had put it there it had not come from the mail office. It was wrapped in a piece of sackcloth and tied with string. A square of paper was lodged beneath the cross of the string: his name was on it – scrawled in a looping hand that he recognised straight off.

It was from McKenzie.

He tucked the thing in the front of his overalls and crossed the yard, his head swivelling this way and that like he was being observed. He was halfway up the stairs when he heard voices from the kitchen. He listened outside the door a couple of seconds then went in. Olive and Gil were at the table, Olive's face the colour of old snow, her eyes circled black.

'Ah, here he is now.'

Kelly looked toward the voice. A state trooper was leaning against the stove. He stepped forward, holding out his hand. 'And you must be young Kelly?'

Kelly looked at Gil. 'Don't worry, son. The officer just needs to ask you a couple of questions.'

'Sit down, sit down,' the officer said. There was some oiliness about the way he spoke. A slight hiss in his voice.

Kelly took a seat and felt the edge of the package nudge his ribs. It brought heat to his cheeks.

'Like your pa said, son, just here to ask you a couple of questions.' The officer paused for a couple of seconds then launched in.

'So, you heard anything from McKenzie?'

Kelly swallowed hard then looked the officer in the eye. 'No sir. I haven't heard from him at all.' The officer stared back at him.

'You sure of that?'

'I'm sure.'

The officer took a small notepad out of his pocket and wrote on it. Then he stared straight at Kelly again.

'You any idea what happened to the shotgun?'

Kelly spun round to look at Gil. 'The shotgun?' He craned his neck and looked at the cabinet. 'It was right there,' he said, pointing at the stove. 'It was right there last time I saw it. Gil?'

'I already told the officer, son. That's where we left it. It's gone. Disappeared.'

'Disappeared?' It came out strangled and high-pitched. Kelly rubbed at his throat.

The officer eyeballed him again. 'Your folks say it disappeared sometime yesterday ...'

'Well, that's what we're supposing, Officer,' Gil butted in.

'Sure, sure ... that's what you're supposing.' The officer had turned slightly to address Gil but spun back again to face Kelly. 'You wouldn't know anything about it disappearing, son?' He had a smile on his face but his eyes were narrow and cold.

Kelly leaned back, feigning some semblance of confidence, then remembered the package in his overalls and hunched over the table again. The move made him look shifty.

'I don't know anything about no shotgun. Last I saw it, it was leaned right there.' He pointed to the cabinet.

'And you see anyone round the place last night or the night before?'

Kelly considered for a moment. He'd seen nothing. But the package. McKenzie had left him a package. That could only mean one thing – he was still around. And Henry – Gil had spun him a line about the Lindos visit, he was sure of that. What if the boys *had* come calling, asking questions? What if McKenzie had found out and ...

'Taking some thinking about, son. You got something to tell me?'

Kelly sat up abruptly and knocked against the table, rattling the pots. He saw Olive's face tighten: her nerves were near busting through her skin.

'I didn't see anyone,' Kelly said. 'I didn't see a soul.'

The officer blew out a long breath like he was disappointed. Shook his head. He leaned forward, fingered the brim of his hat that lay on the table in front of him.

'So, you know the Lindo boys at all?'

'Know of 'em ... like most folks. Don't search them out ... I ...'

Gil butted in again. 'Officer – just wondering if you could use a bite to eat? Just about our suppertime and ... well you know what building's like. Hungry work.' He glanced at Olive, nodded in the direction of the stove. She looked at him like she didn't know who he was then suddenly sprang up and grabbed the skillet and disappeared into the cold pantry. The officer considered Kelly a while longer then tucked his notebook in his pocket and picked up his hat.

'No, not necessary. I've taken up enough of your time. I'll be getting myself back.'

Gil and Kelly walked him out then watched as he crossed the street towards the police truck. He pulled open the door then paused and turned to look at them.

'Appreciate your help in this matter, Mr Kelly,' he shouted.

'Mighty grateful for your help.' His words echoed round the street and carried, Kelly imagined, clear across the town and across the surrounding farmland. He turned to Gil but Gil quietened him with a small shake of his head then led the way back into the kitchen.

Supper was agonising: Gil and Olive barely spoke, like they didn't have the words necessary to discuss what had landed at their feet, like they didn't have the strength to hold their heads up. McKenzie – a suspected murderer, his name on the national news.

Kelly excused himself as soon as he put his fork down and went up to his room. The package was warm in his hands when he pulled it out from his overalls. He turned it over, felt the shape and size of it – then carefully unfastened the string and unwrapped one end of the sackcloth and looked inside. He sat on the bed and, his hands slippery with sweat, emptied the package onto the cover. Ten-dollar bills – a good deal of them. He picked the wad up and brought it to his nose and sniffed it. He ruffled it with his thumb, loosely calculating how many notes there might be. Upwards of a thousand dollars he reckoned. He fanned the bills out, hoping for a letter or even a short note – some kind of explanation – and a small package slipped out – a sheet of paper folded tightly around something small to form a packet. Kelly eased it open.

The locket fell onto the bed. He stared at it for a moment then picked it up and held it in front of his face, watching it spin, mesmerised for a while by the arrows of late sun it spun on the walls. He smoothed out the paper. One word scrawled in pencil.

Yours.

He wiped his hands on the bed cover and prised open the locket. The picture of his mother smiled back at him.

Next morning was like the circus had suddenly pitched up in town. The place was choked with TV trucks and police cars and it seemed like everyone was out in the street aiming for a ringside seat. Macy Creasy, decked out in a new frock, got herself interviewed on national TV, and Pearl Clodagh, surrounded by her string of kids, posed for *The Western Listener*. By mid-morning it was like there was no air left in the place, no space to breathe or think – at least that's how it felt to Kelly. And thinking was what he needed to do. He stuck it for most of the day then got word to Earl that he needed to take a couple of days off, packed up some food and a couple of blankets, left a note for Gil and Olive and set off for The Cabin.

It was drawing in dark when he got there. He had no plan other than to sit some place quiet and think. He'd brought McKenzie's package and the locket with him. Not because they weren't safe at home but because he'd got some nonsensical notion that they might help him work out what had happened, that he might be able to *feel* where McKenzie was, that they would somehow lead him to him. He tracked through the long grass round to the back of the cabin and lowered himself onto the wooden seat of the apple tree swing. He closed his eyes and waited a moment, trying to feel something, to conjure up some memory. This is where he was when his mother disappeared, apparently. That's what he'd told them: three years old and a lost mother. He waited some more, his hand wrapped around the locket, willing some thought, some remembrance to swim through the layers he'd piled over it all. Piled over it because he'd had everything he'd needed – Olive, Gil, McKenzie. Beattie and Darragh. He'd not felt the loss. Never felt the need to understand. But now.

He traced the lettering on the front of the locket then prised it open. He eased out the photograph and examined the back of it, hoping for – *what?* Some sign that would tell him he was wrong? That would convince him McKenzie hadn't recognised the locket and understood its meaning – understood that the Lindos had been involved in Rose's disappearance. That he hadn't decided to deal out his own portion of justice.

There was no denying it: it was the locket started things off. McKenzie's mean moods, his shouting and hollering, his sudden change towards the Lindos. And now here it was, in his own hands. Delivered like a gift. Or an explanation.

The police were right: it had to be McKenzie. He'd stole the Lindos' stuff then sneaked back to Olive and Gil's, swiped the gun and ... the thought lodged at the back of Kelly's throat like a lump of gristle. He couldn't swallow it and he couldn't spit it out. He got up from the swing and stood awhile looking out over the long meadow then turned and made his way back to the cabin. He paused before going through the door and scanned the hedges and fields, traced the length of the track and the turn towards the stables.

'You out there, Mac?' he half shouted. His heart hammered at the possibility of a reply. He left the front door unlatched and lay most of the night waiting for some sound to tell him that McKenzie had come back. Come back to face the music, perhaps, or just come back to say goodbye. But when he woke next morning he was still alone. He stood in the empty kitchen awhile then took his coffee out into the yard. McKenzie was gone. There was the truth of it. Guilty as hell and gone. Police had it right. They must have.

Chapter 49

Ten years later

It was unseasonably warm. Only an inch or two into April but the sun acting like it was July or August. Talk in the store was of crops coming too soon, the blight of late frosts and, because the river was busting along like a freight train, the likelihood of flooding. In short, the usual calamitous conversations enjoyed by farmers across the region.

It was driving Olive crazy. All the damn day long. *They got anything better to talk about?* She fixed her smile on first thing in the morning but come lunchtime it was hanging off. Gil was no help, no help at all. *It's a small town, Ol.* That's all he had to say about it. *A small town and small talk comes with it.* A small snort was all that ever earned.

'I'm going out back, Gil.'

'Yes, yes ...' he glanced up from his newspaper.

This was how it went these days. She'd disappear out back, some task in the storeroom or the ale house, pulling her away from the endless griping while he settled himself behind the counter, generally with a cup of coffee, waiting for the afternoon customers. He looked out over the street. He'd not be seeing more than a handful – old timers mostly, folks who still bought their goods in town as opposed to driving out to the new shopping mall in Picker's Flag. The place had near enough cut the store's takings in two and showed no sign of easing up. Progress, it was called. Apparently. Problem was it never seemed to show its face for long in Oaklake. There'd been moments – times when it seemed like things might take off, that the place might expand beyond its small boundary – but they never lasted, like they were lined up and ready at the start line and the starter's gun never went off. Or they didn't hear it. The race was always won by some other place: Picker's got the new highway, the Infirmary, the factories and now, now they'd got the shopping mall, complete with a goddamn Woolworth's store. And Oaklake? All they had was what they'd fashioned themselves: the store, the woodyard, the pharmacy, The Ponderosa. Mimi's dress shop was long gone. The tea room too.

Gil knew it wasn't just the mall, of course, or the Woolworth's store, because business had dropped off long before then. It seemed the cloud that got cast over McKenzie and the Lindo shooting never really cleared and, although folks had been polite enough early on, over time many of them backed away: always a friendly wave as they passed by the front verandah, but pass by they most often did. It irked the hell out of Olive and, truth be told, him too, because no one rightly gave a damn about the Lindo brothers, either then or now. Main point was they were gone, and good riddance. But McKenzie? – McKenzie was a different story. He'd never returned – either to clear his name or face whatever music was waiting for him – but there'd not been a single day Gil hadn't thought about him, hadn't wondered where he was, what kind of man he'd become. Never been able to talk to Olive about it, of course. He'd tried, in the early days, but she'd shook him off, seemingly content to go with the common consensus – that the boy was guilty. It was apparent, she'd once said, that the O'Grady family had been singled out for bad luck. Conrad, Rose, McKenzie – all disappeared. The Luck? she'd snorted. That turned out to be the wrong goddamn name. He'd done his best to disagree with her – until the business with Beattie and Darragh came along and sealed it.

The shop bell cut through his thinking.

'Gil?'

McCleavy was at the door, a set of eyeglasses dangling from his neck.

'Walt. What's going on?'

'Well. Most likely nothing but ...'

He beckoned Gil out onto the verandah.

'What do you make of that?' He pointed a bony finger across the town.

Gil didn't need the eyeglasses to see it. A thin column of smoke was rising from the island.

'Kids,' he said. 'Most likely kids, Walt.'

He handed the glasses back and waited while McCleavy took another long look. He was rattled and Gil knew it. Olive considered the old man a nuisance, always round, asking for Gil's opinion or advice. He needed to quit, she said. The job had gotten too much for him.

'Don't worry about it,' Gil said. 'It's nothing. It'll be gone in a couple of hours.'

Gil was in the house searching out his own eyeglasses when McCleavy's truck pulled into the farmyard. They'd shut the shop up early: town was empty, seemed no point to hanging around. He watched McCleavy hobble his way across to the house, scattering the chickens and raising the curiosity of the dogs, then went out to meet him.

'You seen it's still going, then?' McCleavy wheezed, hand on the gatepost.

'Yep,' Gil said. 'About to take another look now.'

Gil raised the glasses to his eyes and took a long look out at the island – at the brazen column of smoke rising through the trees. Thicker now and black. Like whoever it was was burning something that oughtn't to be burned.

'That's some campfire,' Gil said.

'You still think it's kids?' McCleavy asked. The question set a wild gallop in his chest.

'Most likely,' Gil said, wiping his forehead with the back of his hand. The heat had been troubling him of late. Some unnatural heat that seemed to have nothing to do with the weather.

‘Think we need to take a look?’ McCleavy said.

Gil nodded. ‘I’ll get my coat and go down for the boat.’ He steadied himself against the gatepost a moment. ‘Might get myself a cup of water first.’

By the time Gil got to the lake McCleavy was pacing. He hobbled up to the truck, took Gil’s arm and steered him to the water’s edge.

‘Look,’ he whispered. ‘Riley’s boat is gone. Gone from the post ... and look.’ He indicated the patch of shore where the boat generally rested. Gil pushed his hat off his forehead.

‘OK,’ he said. He knew what McCleavy was thinking – same thing he was thinking: last time a boat had gone missing was when McKenzie had disappeared. He wandered away from McCleavy to let the memory land. He took his hat off and let the lake breeze play over his face. *McKenzie.* Near enough ten years to the day. He felt it rising up in his chest like something long submerged. A mix of hope and alarm. He breathed deep to pull it back down.

‘I’ll likely row over on my own,’ he said to McCleavy.

McCleavy nodded. ‘I’ll come out if you’re not back smart,’ he said, steadying the boat, then giving a weak shove to cast Gil off. ‘I’ll have my eye on you,’ he shouted, holding up his own eyeglasses. ‘I’ll be watching you.’

Gil pulled on the oars and let the boat take him into the quiet cool of the lake. When he was three quarters of the way there, he rested a minute. The usual heft of his arms seemed to have deserted him and the feverish feeling that was only pricking earlier now seemed to be rolling through his body in waves. He considered the column of smoke and the green of the island, its edge now close enough to land a stone. He shivered, not sure if it was the fever or the thought that McKenzie had indeed returned, that he was waiting for him on the island, ready to let loose whatever tale he’d been holding onto these last years. He took up the oars and started to pull towards the shore.

He hadn’t pulled many strokes when the first rock bounced off the side of the boat. He looked round, alarmed, the confusion of the situation unsettling him. Another rock glanced off the edge of the boat and landed at his feet. He pulled the boat around and sculled back a few feet.

'Who's there?' he called.

'Get away from here,' a voice called out, accompanied by a volley of smaller rocks.

Gil pulled further away and watched as a huge man appeared from the waterside greenery. He was as big as a bear. And completely naked. One thing was for sure: it wasn't McKenzie.

'Whoa, feller,' Gil called. 'What the hell's going on? I mean you no harm.'

'I told you,' the voice boomed back. 'You get away from here.' It was accompanied by a sizeable boulder that would have taken the bottom of the boat out but landed, fortunately, several feet away. Gil pulled away to what he considered to be a safe distance.

'Who are you?' he hollered. The giant moved out of sight then lobbed another rock which, despite the distance between them, still came close.

'You needing any help, feller?' Gil shouted back. Despite the strangeness afforded by the situation the habit of civility still outweighed the alarm he was feeling. On top of that the fever, now a constant beat in his head, seemed to be lending the occasion something of a dreamlike quality.

'I said, you needing any help over there?'

'No.'

Gil half ducked, waiting for the hail of stones, but the man said nothing more.

'You maybe needing some food, though?' he called. The giant moved back into sight.

'I could use some grub,' he said. 'But you bring it. Just you.'

Gil picked up the oars and rowed steadily away.

Chapter 50

Halfway back Gil slowed and let the boat slide to a halt. He was aware that McCleavy was watching but the need to rest was overpowering. What he wanted most was to lie back in the boat and sleep but that for sure would have brought McCleavy skittering across. Instead he gazed over the boat's edge and down into the dark water.

He and Olive used to do the same in the days after the accident.

They would row out, mostly at night because that somehow felt more fitting, then sit wrapped in blankets, the lantern between them, peering down into the water. On occasion Gil would imagine he could see the dull lights of the plane shining up at them, a foolish fancy but one that allowed him to swing the lantern lightly as if signalling back. He never knew what Olive made of that because she'd remained tight-lipped as ever. But he knew Darragh and Beattie's deaths had left a kink in their lives that no amount of talking would ever straighten out.

Over the years the need to visit lessened, then disappeared altogether – what had happened became part of the story of the place. The story of Oaklake. Hell, he'd told it himself often enough – curious visitors, travellers and the like. *How come the place is called Oaklake, but the lake itself is called O'Grady's Lake?* There were two answers to the question – the short one and the long one. Most folks in town offered up the short version: the lake was named for Darragh O'Grady, one of the early settlers in the town.

The long version still hurt.

When Rose disappeared something in Beattie and Darragh failed to recover. They still had Olive of course – and Gil and young McKenzie, but the loss of Rose hit them dead centre. They made up for it some ways through Kelly – they doted on the boy, and he on them, so when McKenzie then upped and disappeared Kelly became the centre of their world. He and Rachel popped out babies like it was the sales and Darragh and Beattie slipped into a world of babyminding and helping out that suited them no end, and for a long time they seemed to dodge any ill effects of ageing. Then, one winter, Darragh went down with a chest cold that he could not shake. It dogged him for weeks until, as spring was starting to show and he was looking about as exhausted as a person can look, Kelly insisted he visit the doctor. The suggestion caused something of a row – Darragh not being the kind that ever went to the doctor. Kelly, however, towed him along and, mindful of the fact that Darragh was likely to abscond, went into the consulting room with him. The doctor came to his conclusion after a brief examination. It was obvious – Kelly could see that now: in the stark lights Darragh was as white and transparent as the paint on the walls. It was a cancer – probably in some way attributed to his crop dusting days. Chemicals. They drove back to The Luck in silence. Darragh didn't say anything until they'd got through the gate and were heading up the track.

'I need you not to tell Beattie, son,' he said.

'But ...'

'And don't tell Rachel or the youngsters either. This is just between me and you.'

What Kelly didn't know – what no one knew except Darragh – was that Beattie's mind was not the thing it used to be; there had been some portion of softening. It wasn't an easy thing to put your finger on, but she was changed in her way of reasoning – and her memory kept letting loose and leaving her stranded halfway through a sentence or a task. It was this that had kept him from the doctor: he knew that the constant rasping in his chest was not a natural thing – it was filling him up like sawdust and choking the life out of him, but he couldn't let it win – he had Beattie to consider. So, when Kelly returned him home he took things easy, drank the medicine that the doctor had given him and, for a couple of weeks, seemed to be breathing easier and showing some improvement. Then the improvement stopped and it was like the ground had suddenly tilted behind him and he couldn't get any purchase on it and he was sliding backwards. Rock bottom showed up unexpectedly a few days later: he had just climbed back into bed, cold sweating after a vicious bout of coughing and realised that Beattie was not there. He hauled himself upright and went looking for her. The back door was swinging open, so out he went, calling her name. He heard her before he saw her – stomping down the track, her nightdress blowing backwards, her thin hair loose in the wind, hollering at the top of her voice. Darragh staggered across the yard and started the pickup. He drew alongside her but she was oblivious – she was muttering now, her hands twisting this way and that. He drove ahead then parked the truck and walked slowly back to her.

'Beattie,' he said, his voice weak with fear. She looked at him and went to walk past.

'Beattie,' he said. 'Where are you going?'

She didn't stop. 'To get the boy,' she said. 'I'm going to get the boy. You know what he's like. If I don't get him from school he'll be straight to the lake ...'

'Beattie ...' he took hold of her hand.

'Darragh ... no ... I have to get him, I'll be late. Come on.' Then she put her hands to her mouth and shouted. 'Conrad ... Conrad.'

Darragh managed to get her back home. He dried her off with a towel then got them both into bed. When he was sure she was asleep he let himself go. It was like switching off a light.

When he woke the next morning she was leaning over him – dressed and spruced up. She set a mug of coffee down on the cabinet then sat down on the bed. She had something in her hand. Darragh saw that it was his own handkerchief – blood-spotted and telling a story of its own.

'I need to ask you something,' she said.

Darragh hauled himself up on the pillows. He wasn't sure if she was truly herself or not.

'Ask away,' he said.

'I want us to go up one last time.'

'Go up?' he said. 'Go up where?

'Go up. Up in the plane. I want to see The Luck one last time.'

Darragh took her hands in his own and looked in her eyes.

'What do you mean?' he said.

But he knew what she meant.

And that is what happened. The long version. On a warm spring morning Darragh O'Grady, a man dying of lung cancer, wrangled the Annie O'Grady out of her wraps and into the air, and on that same warm morning he and his darling Beattie, wrapped in blankets and rugs, flew across their farm, circled Oaklake town, waved down at the sleeping Kelly place, then headed out to the lake and, hand in hand, crashed down into the water.

Gil trailed his hand in the water. His head was beating like the full sun was on it. He dipped his hat and let it soak a moment, arranged it low on his forehead then took up the oars and fixed for the shore. McCleavy was hollering before he'd reached the last stretch.

'Starting to get a bit jittery there, Gil,' he said, as Gil landed the boat.

'Some stranger,' Gil said, as he tied off the boat. 'Didn't recognise him, he ...' Gil stopped. The last thing he wanted was to alarm McCleavy. 'He looks like he could use a bit of help.'

'Help?' McCleavy yelped. 'What kind of help?' He was shifting from one foot to the other.

'Well, he has no supplies for one thing,' Gil said. 'Said I'd take something over for him. I was wondering if you might ask round, get a few things together.'

McCleavy's face dropped a few creases. The old feller hove to labour like a clock to ticking and Gil knew it.

'Well, sure?' he said. 'What time you coming back?'

'Six o'clock,' Gil said, but McCleavy was already striding away.

Olive was in the kitchen when he got back, cooking. She was scraping the bottom of some big pan like she wanted to take the copper off. Moving to The Luck after Beattie and Darragh had gone had loosed something in her. Whether it was being able to get right away from the store or being back in the place she was raised – or her taking on with her horse work again – Gil never knew. Nonetheless, life with her was a darn sight easier.

'What was all that about? You were gone a good stretch.'

Gil flopped down at the table and waited for the wave of heat that seemed to have some grudge against him pass. Olive left off the banging and scraping and sat down beside him.

'You OK?'

Gil wiped his forehead and smiled at her. 'I'm fine. A shade feverish. I'll be good by morning.'

'Well, why don't you go have some rest – I'll call you when food's ready.' Her words caused him more alarm than he would have cared to say. He felt bad – but did he look that bad?

'No,' he said. 'I have to go out again.'

Gil and Olive set out for the lake ten minutes before six. Gil had rested and eaten and was already feeling a whole lot better.

'I'm coming over with you, Gil,' Olive said, 'Give you some back up.'

'No need, Ol. The feller is no threat. Needs a bit of help that's all.'

Somehow the story he had spun McCleavy had become, in his mind, a reasonable explanation. Truth was, of course, that he'd never got near the stranger on account of the bombardment of rocks. If the man was in need of help he had a rum way of asking for it. However he had agreed to take supplies over and that was what he was going to do.

'We need a signal,' Olive said. 'We need some kind of signal in case you need assistance. I can be ready with the eyeglasses, I can row over in Riley's boat.'

'Olive, the man is no threat. He was naked, for goodness sake.'

Olive let out a hoot. 'Well – if the feller strikes up with any nonsense come straight on back ...'

She spent the rest of the drive looking out of the window, chuckling to herself. When they pulled up at the lakeside McCleavy was there with his eldest grandson, loading sacks into the boat.

'You OK now, Gil?' he said. 'You were looking a tad peaky earlier.'

'Fine. I'm fine. Too much sun I guess. You've done a good job here,' he said, indicating the stash of supplies piled in the boat. 'A few togs too, I see?'

'Yes well ... I, erm ...' he cleared his throat and glanced sideways at Olive. 'I saw through the eyeglasses. The fellow is, erm ...' Olive raised her eyebrows at Gil and walked back to the truck: he could see her shoulders shaking.

Gil rowed steadily. His strength seemed to have returned and the heat that had plagued him had backed off. McCleavy had done a good job – he could see at least two plate pies and someone had put up a couple of bottles of beer. As he got nearer the island he lessened his pull on the oars and let the boat slow to a halt: he was hoping for a better reception than before but wasn't counting on it. He peered across the water – the light was dropping faster than he'd anticipated. There was something in the water a way ahead of him. He rowed cautiously nearer, then called out.

'Hey, feller. Where are you? I'm back. Brought you those supplies.' He listened for a reply. There was nothing. He rowed closer to the craft until he could see quite plainly it was a raft – rough in its making – but laying smartly enough on top of the water. A length of rope trailed from its one side. Gil traced its length to the shore and saw him, the stranger, crouched behind a stand of low shrubbery. He put his hand to his mouth and shouted louder.

'I've come back. I brought your supplies.'

'Put them on the raft then go.' The same booming voice.

Gil pressed on. 'Do you need any medicine?'

'I said, put them on the raft – then leave.' A large flat stone came skating across the water towards him.

'OK, OK,' Gil said. 'Give me a minute.' He transferred the sacks onto the raft then moved away a good distance. 'I'm coming back tomorrow,' he yelled. 'I'll come in the morning, OK?' There was no reply but Gil could see the raft was on the move. 'And no more darn rocks, OK? I'm being neighbourly here, no call to be hurling rocks at folks.'

That said he pulled away and headed back home.

Chapter 51

Gil never got to go back next morning. He lay awake half the night swinging through extremes of temperature, one minute huddled under the bedclothes trying to still his clattering teeth, the next swabbing sheets of sweat off his face and chest. Olive slept through it all but took one look at him when she awoke – his hair plastered down, his nightclothes in a damp pile on the floor – and declared he was going nowhere. He didn't argue. He had no memory of ever feeling so ill. Mimi came over so Olive could go off to the store.

'I told the big feller I'd be back this morning, Ol.'

'And you'll be doing no such thing.'

'I'll most likely have shook it off come lunchtime ...'

'Have you taken a look at yourself in the mirror?'

He hadn't. Was waiting for her to leave before he chanced trying his legs out.

'Where's my ma?'

'Out back. Putting the washing to dry.'

Gil let his head flop back against the pillows. It was a good sleep he needed, that was all. A good sleep and a bite to eat. He'd be up and running before the day was out.

He was right – to some extent.

When he woke – a couple of hours later – he felt good. Normal. There was no heat in his head, the sheets were dry and he felt hungry. Ravenous. He swung his legs off the mattress and padded over to the bathroom. He splashed his face with cold water, cleaned his teeth for a long time then went back to the bedroom. Mimi was waiting for him, the folded bed sheets looped over one arm.

'I've not seen you sleep like that since you had the measles.'

'Hi, Ma, you OK?'

'I'm just fine, son. How about you? Are you OK?'

He sat down on the edge of the bed. 'I feel good. Slept it off whatever it was.'

Mimi nodded. She wasn't so sure. She'd spent most of the morning watching over him. It had taken her aback, him lying there, so far under he was almost out cold. He'd lost weight. It had been a while since she'd last seen him in any state of undress but he was thinner and something about that had set up some pulse of worry.

'You want something to eat?'

'I reckon I do. I'm starved.'

'Good.' Good. Yes, hunger was always a good sign. Went with recovery.

'I'll see you in the kitchen, then.'

He'd aimed to be back before Olive got in from the store. His mother's food restored him (and him eating it, her) to such an extent that they agreed she should go back to town. He was fine. Fully recovered.

'Call in at the store and tell Ol I'm OK,' he said, as she was getting in the car. 'Tell her she needn't hurry back.'

As soon as her car was out of sight he went back into the kitchen and unhooked the pickup keys from the wall. He'd told the feller he'd go back over and that's what he intended to do.

The trouble started on the way back. He'd gotten over there without a hitch, taking it easy on the oars. It seemed like the feller had been waiting for him: he was sitting cross-legged on the bank, fully clothed, thankfully, swigging from a bottle of beer.

'Reckoned you wasn't going to turn up,' he hollered as Gil swung the boat in the last few yards. He got up in one surprisingly nimble movement and met the boat at the water's edge. Pulled it in like it was made of paper.

'You brought any more of this?' He waggled the half-empty bottle in Gil's face.

'In the boat,' Gil said. 'Brought you some of my wife's ale. She's pretty well known for it.'

The feller leaned over the side of the boat, grabbed the box and tucked it under one arm.

'Come on, then. Let's get ourselves out of this sun.' There was some kindliness to the remark that made Gil think that perhaps he'd been wrong about the man. The stone-throwing and all. The feller had been in a fix and maybe not shown his best side.

'Well, likely I'll get myself straight back, I ...'

'No, no,' the feller said. 'I've got some questions to ask and strikes me you might be the feller to answer them.'

So Gil had gone along with it. Sat out the back of Tom Darling's old shack drinking beer and listening. Afterwards he wasn't sure if it was the beer or the sun, but, as he was rowing back, trying to work out how the hell he was going to tell Olive what the feller had said, he felt a flicker of heat move from the base of his spine, up through his chest and into his head. By the time he got back to The Luck sweat was pooling in the notches of his collar bones and Olive's car was parked up in the yard.

He didn't get away with it lightly, either from Olive or from whatever it was that was ailing him.

'You've been out.'

It wasn't a question.

He drew a glass of water at the kitchen sink and rolled the cold condensation over his forehead. What he really wanted to do was strip off his shirt, maybe hose himself down in the yard. Or maybe just lower himself to the floor, right there where he stood, and close his eyes. Sleep.

'I said, you've been out.'

Gil reached out for the kitchen chair and steadied himself down onto it.

'Honestly, Gil. What the hell you thinking? Just look at you ...'

He didn't hear any more. It was like someone suddenly pulled the plug. Switched him right off. When he woke, he had been magically transported from the kitchen into the bedroom. The room was half dark, the window open. He listened for a moment then pulled back the bed covers.

'You can forget that right now.'

Olive was perched on the chair at the other side of the bed, her small face peering out from the shadows.

'Ol.' He sank back into the bed, grateful to be lying flat again. He put his hand to his abdomen. 'Did I hurt myself?'

Olive got off the chair and hoisted up his vest.

'Where?'

Gil peered down at his belly. There was nothing to see but there was a pain like someone was screwing up his guts from the inside.

'You hungry maybe?'

It made some kind of sense but it wasn't anything to do with hunger, he knew that.

'Maybe,' he said. He closed his eyes again. 'Ol,' he said, 'I need to talk to you ... that feller ... he said some strange things. He said ...'

When he opened his eyes she'd gone. He could hear her downstairs, the tap running, cupboard doors opening and closing. He didn't know if she'd heard him out or not.

Turned out it didn't really matter.

Chapter 52

It was a week or so later, early evening, the sun still warm. Kelly was out on the new road. His eldest son was coming up ten years old and itching to get behind the wheel. Considering the general advantages this would offer, Kelly had been taking him out each day after supper and letting him drive the long straight between Oaklake and Picker's Flag, pausing at the entrance to Arnold's Farm to try his hand at backing up. They had just come out of one such manoeuvre when Kelly noticed a car – some miles away – but approaching at what seemed to be some lick. As it drew nearer he recognised it for a state trooper.

'Better let me behind that wheel, son,' he said, nodding up the road at the racing vehicle. They watched as it came close, slowed to a crawl, then pulled up alongside. There were two cops in the car – the driver was adjusting his hat, fixing to get out: his partner – aviator shades glinting – was in the passenger seat, staring out through the windshield, still as a statue. Kelly let out a groan: there were a dozen and one things wrong with the pickup and this pair, judging by the city shine on them, were going to take pleasure in finding them all.

'Sorry to bother you, sir,' the officer said, 'Wondering if you seen any strangers over this way?'

Kelly considered his answer. There had been a stranger for sure, but by all accounts he'd moved on.

'Real big feller. Dark hair,' the officer said.

Kelly scratched his head, not sure whether to speak up. He held his tongue.

'Truck driver said he gave such a feller a ride. Dropped him off a mile or so from Picker's Flag.'

Kelly took the out. 'Ah, Picker's Flag. No, we're Oaklake folk,' he said, nodding at his boy. 'Just headed back there now.'

The officer put his hands on his hips and gazed down the road.

'That's the thing see,' he said. 'Big feller said he was aiming to get to Oaklake.'

'Ah,' Kelly said. 'When did you say this was?'

'Week before last? Truck driver dropped him off Tuesday.'

'Right. OK. Could make sense then.' Kelly nodded his head as if he were recalling some detail. 'We did have a feller camped out on the island. Didn't see him myself. Stayed a couple of days I believe and then moved on.'

The officer had produced a small notepad. 'Did anyone get to talk to him?'

Kelly thought a while. Gil was still ailing, barely off his bed. 'Well, Gil McKenzie spoke to him but ...'

'Gil McKenzie ...' the officer was scratching on his notepad. 'Will I find him in town?'

'Thereabouts,' Kelly said. 'The Luck. Just the other side of town. But ...' The officer was already headed back to his vehicle. 'Gil's sick,' he shouted. 'He's down with some kind of fever.'

The officer threw him a back-handed wave and hauled himself back into the police car. Kelly and his boy sat still as it cruised past. The second officer paid them no attention at all.

Next morning Kelly was up early – but not early enough. When he went out on the porch to fetch wood for the stove – him still in his night vest – the state trooper was parked out front waiting for him. He dodged inside, pulled on a shirt then went back out. The officer already had his hand on the gatepost. Kelly shaded his eyes: it was not the same guy – this was his buddy – younger, taller, mirrored shades. Looked mean. Almost looked familiar.

'Good day there, Officer,' Kelly said. 'Early start you have on you this morning.'

The officer said nothing, unlatched the gate and approached the house.

'You still looking for help with that stranger?' Kelly's voice came out crooked on account of a sudden dryness in his throat.

'OK if I come up?' the officer said. He didn't wait for an answer and stepped onto the porch. His boots shone like good coal.

'Coffee's on,' Kelly said. 'Bring you some out?'

The officer nodded and took a seat on the old armchair – the one the dogs favoured. Kelly left him there, watching the sun coming up over The Luck. When he came out with the coffee, he set it down on the rail and settled himself on the bench. Neither he or the officer spoke: the sight of the sun coming up over The Luck required all the breath a man had.

'Worth coming to Oaklake just to see that,' Kelly said. The officer took up his coffee and said nothing. For a feller who turned up unexpected he didn't have a whole lot to say.

'The place is looking good,' he said, eventually. The words made no sense.

Later, when Kelly was considering it, he couldn't remember exactly what order things happened after that. The feller had taken off his aviators and turned to look at him. The intervening years had added a few lines but the droop of his eyelid pointed him straight out.

'My God.' Kelly's voice was a whisper. 'McKenzie ... is ...' The officer slipped off his hat and his hair, lit up like the sun itself, clinched the deal. Kelly got up from the bench and staggered over – hand outstretched – not so much a greeting as a need to touch the man, make sure he was real.

'Dear God,' Kelly said, holding onto McKenzie's hand. 'How the hell ...'

McKenzie smiled and Kelly felt some tug in his guts that went way back. 'I didn't know where you were,' he said, his voice cracking. 'I didn't know where you were.'

'I'm sorry,' McKenzie started. 'I always meant ...' He stopped abruptly as Rachel stepped out through the door, shading her eyes, a youngster in her arms. McKenzie stepped away from Kelly and put his hat and aviators back on. 'That's very good of you, Mr Kelly,' he said. 'So I'll meet you by the lake around 3pm? You can show us where the feller was camped.'

Then he strode through the gate, leaving Kelly clutching the porch rail. McKenzie looked back before he reached the car and, seeing that Rachel had gone back inside, put his finger to his lips. Kelly nodded and went in.

'What was that about?' Rachel asked.

'Still looking for that feller that was camped out.'

'Gave me something of a shock, seeing him there.'

Kelly nodded. She'd always had the knack of saying the right thing.

Chapter 53

Kelly's mind ruled him for the rest of the day. No matter what task he set to he found himself paused and gazing, following some train of thought that never took him anywhere. As a consequence he was at the lake early – he parked the pickup and wandered down to the edge. Riley's boat was back in its usual spot, like nothing had happened. What had happened? What was he going to tell McKenzie? What would McKenzie tell him? The questions thrummed his head until, at last, he heard the state trooper crunching down the track. With some relief he saw that McKenzie was not alone – he was back in the passenger seat and his buddy was at the wheel. There'd be no room for talk.

'Good of you to do this, Mr Kelly,' the officer said. 'I seen Mr Gil McKenzie like you said. He's informed me as to what took place.' He scanned the lake as he spoke, eyeing the water like a man afraid of getting wet.

'This it?' he said, slapping the hull of the boat. Kelly nodded.

'You taking us across in this?'

'That's the plan,' Kelly said, glancing across at McKenzie.

'It'll be OK, Huey,' McKenzie said. 'The water don't look too deep.'

Huey got into the boat and clamped his backside to the plank like a magnet. At the first pull on the oars, he let out a small whimper. McKenzie motioned to Kelly to quit rowing.

'I got this on my own, Huey,' he said. 'I'll go across with this feller and take a good look. You dig around on this side.'

Huey was out of his seat and clambering over the side before Kelly got them back near the shingle. He splashed the last few feet and sat down on the shore, face slicker than a newborn pup.

'Got a strong aversion to water,' McKenzie said, as Kelly pulled them back into deeper water. Kelly glanced back: Huey was on his hands and knees throwing up his guts.

'Mind if I row?'

They exchanged places and Kelly watched as McKenzie settled himself and took up the oars. He handled each one like it was a good instrument he'd been longing to play. He picked out a gentle rhythm and lulled the boat out onto the lake. Kelly didn't speak: the queue of questions he had lined up had somehow snagged themselves into a ball and stopped up his throat. McKenzie was rowing like he was pulling something back into himself, sucking each breath in deep and blowing it out hard, like a man starved of air. His eyes were closed.

'I heard about the plane crash,' he said, and rested the oars.

'A while back, now,' Kelly said.

McKenzie was peering down into the water. 'They still down there?'

Kelly nodded. 'There's a stone for them in the churchyard, but we held the service out here. On the shore.'

'Christ.' McKenzie dipped his hand into the water.

'Was it like the papers said ... an accident?'

Kelly waited a moment or two. There been some part of him that had expected McKenzie to show up after the accident. Thought he wouldn't be able to stay away.

'Darragh was sick,' he said. 'And Beattie was failing. Her mind, it was ... letting her down.'

'So you saying it ... it might not have been an accident?'

Kelly shrugged. He could feel it in himself, the urge to punish McKenzie for turning his back on them all, for leaving them to pick their way through.

'I don't know, Mac. Who can say for sure? There was no note. But, well ... I reckon it was intended. Darragh only had weeks left.'

He still felt the catch in his throat. Darragh. Beattie. His world half emptied after they'd gone.

'Christ. So my folks, they're at The Luck now?'

Kelly nodded. 'Seemed like the rightful thing to do, Olive being the only O'Grady left.'

McKenzie raised his eyebrows at that then picked up the oars again and pulled away. 'I've always pictured you at the farm,' he said. 'Figured you might've ended up with it.'

'Nah. Like you saw, Rachel and me fixed up my ma's old place.'

'And I see you got yourself a youngster or two?'

'We got five. At the moment.'

McKenzie let out a hoot of laughter. 'Five? At the moment? What the hell you hiding in your britches, Kelly?'

Kelly shook his head. He was still digesting what McKenzie had said. *I'd always pictured you* ... There was some consolation in it.

'How about you, you got any youngsters?'

McKenzie shook his head. 'Ain't got around to anything like that.'

'So, you aiming to tell me what happened?' Kelly said.

'Been a long time wanting to,' McKenzie said. 'But it's going to have to wait some more – the story's not ready for telling yet. I've got business here needs sorting.' He nodded towards the island, put his aviators and hat back on and, to Kelly's eyes at least, seemed to disappear.

The truth was, McKenzie had a struggle going on in his mind that he'd not anticipated: after years of banishing all thoughts of Oaklake, his folks, The Luck, they were now tugging on his sleeve like a child who wants to get home. He'd not intended to ever come back and when the call came through, and Huey announced where they were headed, his heart had struck up a gallop that he couldn't rein in. They'd been tracking the big feller for some time – right across the state and, when they'd reached the border, McKenzie thought they'd be called back. But the information from the truck driver convinced the Captain they were closing in and he sent them on. McKenzie felt something change the minute they crossed the state line. It was as though some thirst in him had suddenly been quenched: the fields, the hills, the farms – he rolled down the window and breathed them all in. Then, when he'd seen Kelly, and the sun coming up over The Luck, the thirst started up again big time. He knew he wanted to come back. But, like he'd told Kelly, there was business needed sorting and it was his place to sort it.

'Do folks still come over here?' he said, as they threaded their way through a path that was more of a memory than a real thing.

'Kids, on occasion. Nothing more than that.'

'Huey said my pa came over and spoke to the stranger?'

'I believe he did. Don't know what was said.'

'You catch any sight of him?'

'Nope. Heard about it from old McCleavy, though. Said the feller was butt naked.'

'Yeah. That's what Huey said. Figures, though.'

'You know who the feller was, then?' Kelly said.

'Feller's a fist fighter. A fraudster. Been setting up fights across two states. Done plenty of winning and plenty of embezzling. Takes off with the monies while the last fighters are slogging it out. That's how we knew we nearly had our man: truck driver said the feller he picked up was wearing some odd-looking clobber – like a woman's robe.' McKenzie left out the part about the last fight, the one that had ended with the opponent – a young kid barely out of school – dead. He veered off the path and headed in the direction of the old shack. Kelly hadn't been out on the island since the time McKenzie had disappeared. In all the years that had passed by since then he'd never imagined the two of them like this – edging their way round the wire fence again, keeping clear of the old well. The trapdoor to the cellar was just visible through the scrub grass up ahead. Kelly slowed to a halt and watched as McKenzie light-stepped it up to the shack and peered through the window.

'Better not come too close, now,' he said to Kelly.

'But he's gone. Gil said the feller was gone.'

'Evidence,' McKenzie said. 'Might be evidence needs preserving.'

Kelly stood back and watched. He didn't know a whole lot about police work but it seemed pretty obvious to him; the feller had left a burned-out campfire, some plates, a couple of bottles. McKenzie was poking around like a dog on scent.

'Folks sent him some supplies over. Gil brought them out.'

'Yeah, Huey said.' McKenzie nudged a bottle with his boot. 'My ma still making this stuff?'

Kelly shrugged. 'I believe so. Although it could be an old batch.'

McKenzie took a handkerchief out of his pocket and picked the bottle up. There was no label on it. He took a bag from his pocket and slipped the bottle in.

'Fingerprinting,' he said. 'Come on – I seen all I need to see. Let's go.'

Chapter 54

Kelly took the oars and McKenzie let him. They were silent most of the way back, like they had a lot to think about that didn't particularly need airing. Kelly was shortening the oars, ready for the final length, when McKenzie took off his aviators and spoke up.

'My pa,' he said. 'Huey said he looked real sick.'

Kelly nodded. 'That's right. Doctor's not sure what it is but it's sticking around too long to be good.'

McKenzie let this settle. 'Can you fix it for me to see him?'

'I can take you round there now if you like.'

'No ... no. Not like that. I need to see him on my own. I don't want to see my ma.'

'You two never did get on, did you?'

'Hell, that's one way to put it. Anyway,' McKenzie draped his arm over the side of the boat and let his hand trail the surface of the water, 'you and Rachel must have got yourselves tied up fairly quick – five youngsters and counting ...'

'Yeah.' Kelly ignored the sudden change of subject. 'It was on account of your ma.'

McKenzie let out a snort. 'Tell me something that don't surprise me.'

'No. I mean, it was on account of something your ma said to Gil. After you'd gone. I overheard them.' Kelly stopped himself. Ten years waiting for answers and now he wasn't sure he wanted them.

'Well, go on. Tell me. What did she say?'

'She knew. She knew about us and the Lindo boys. I heard her say it to Gil. So I figured ... well, I didn't rightly figure, I just panicked. Thought she was going to confiscate my money, you know, my earnings. So I asked Rachel if she'd, you know ... consider marrying.'

McKenzie's face lit up. 'And the rest is history.'

'Yeah, something like that.' There was some part of the memory that still embarrassed him.

McKenzie concentrated on the patterns his hand was pulling through the water.

'Well, you had it wrong, cousin. Not that it's done you any harm. You and Rachel and your ... your brood.' He gave a laugh, harsh and metallic.

'Well, I heard her good enough. I heard what she said. "You know what he's up to with those boys, Gil." That's what she said.'

McKenzie shook his head then half turned so he was looking across the lake rather than Kelly.

'It was me she was talking about. She saw *me*. Us. Me and Clifford Ortez. Far as I remember you never met him. We knocked around at the pool house. We were parked down the lane, sitting in his car.' He gave a short laugh. 'Thought she'd caught us doing something *unnatural*.'

'What?' McKenzie's words had added an unintended pitch to his voice.

'You know.'

Kelly gave him a tight smile but couldn't think of anything to say that wouldn't betray his embarrassment.

'I don't believe it,' he said at last.

'No,' McKenzie said. There was some amusement in his face that was unsettling.

'But she ... well you weren't though, were you ... you know, doing ...'

'God, no, course we weren't.' McKenzie eyes lit up with amusement. 'But if she'd come by ten minutes later we might have been.'

'Wha ...'

'Don't tell me you never knew?'

'Knew?'

'Never knew I was ... *unnatural*.'

'No. What do you mean? Of course I didn't know. Good God, Mac.'

'Well my ma did. Or reckoned she did. And she sure as hell didn't like it. Or like me.'

'That's why you went, then?'

McKenzie nodded slowly. 'Had no choice. Me and Clifford – we had plans. Law enforcement. We wanted to be cops. Problem was he got accepted and I didn't.' He touched his left eyebrow. 'This goddamn eye,' he said. 'Failed my entry medical. So then – and I guess this is where it all went wrong, or right depending on which way you look at it – I figured if I had enough money I could get my eye fixed then re-apply. Which I did.'

Kelly glanced at McKenzie's drooping eyelid.

'I know, I know. Had the operation, it was successful. I re-applied and got in. Couple of years later the slackness set in again. I was kinda happy – I'd missed it in some stupid way – but anyway I was in and there was nothing they could do about it.'

'And ... and what about you and ...'

McKenzie smiled. 'Cliff? Me and Cliff?'

'Yeah.'

'We're good. Flatmates, buddies. That's what we call it. No sense in broadcasting it. It's easier out west, but still not that easy.'

Kelly took a long breath in. 'Christ, Mac. I'm sorry.'

'It's not your fault, Kel. It's not anyone's fault but ... ' he shook his head. 'My ma, you know. She didn't make things any easier.'

'What about Gil?'

'I doubt she told him. Well, if she did he never said anything to me. Anyway ... I took off soon after that.' He looked off across the water.

'And now you're back.'

'Yeah,' McKenzie said, putting his aviators back on. 'Now I'm back.'

Huey was watching as they pulled up to the shore, twitching like a dog with fleas. He held out his arm as McKenzie climbed off the boat.

'You OK there, Mac?'

'Fine, Huey – I'm fine.'

'Find anything?'

McKenzie held up the bag and bottle. 'Feller had this. Thought we might get his prints off it. Tie him in tight.'

'Captain'll favour that.'

'Judge, too, if we hook him this time.' He turned to Kelly. 'Appreciate your help, sir. And if you could set up that meeting we talked about. We'll be in touch. We're staying over at the … where we staying, Huey?'

'Belle Royale. Opposite the …'

'Yeah, I know where it is,' Kelly said. A sudden weariness seemed to have sapped him. He leaned against the boat's edge and watched the car drive off. After a while he quit trying to make sense of it and went home.

McKenzie had set him an impossible task: getting Olive away from Gil was going to be like prising the shell off an unripe nut. She'd not left his side this last week, watching his every expression for signs of decline. It was like she was afforded of what was going to happen but she was damn well going to prevent it. She hovered over Gil, sleeves rolled up, hair tied back like she was fit and ready to fight whatever was coming their way.

Kelly took his leave straight after he'd cleared the supper table. Rachel was busying the kids to bed. He'd spun a concerned tale about one of the horses, said he was going round for Olive.

'I'll not be long,' he yelled up the stairs. She appeared on the landing, the baby still damp from the bath, clean and soft as rising dough. She looked done in, her six months gone already, but more beautiful by the day as far as he was concerned. Her dark hair fell like a thick curtain around her face as she peered over the bannister. He felt bad for deceiving her.

'Sorry, love. I'll stoke us a good fire when I get back. Rub your feet for you.'

She rounded her free hand over the bowl of her stomach and

smiled. 'I know all there is to know about your foot rubs, Mr Kelly – and where they lead.'

He could hear her calling the twins to the bath as he closed the door behind him and headed out into the dark.

Chapter 55

The reception desk at The Belle Royale was busy and Kelly had a good idea as to why: Lori Flynn. New to Picker's Flag and setting most folks alight with her modern hairdo and forward outfits: she graced the polished walnut like a wanton figurehead; hair and breasts tumbling, a lilt to her voice that sparked visions of dark and energetic liaisons.

He pushed his way through a flock of loitering bellhops, waiters and porters and presented himself before her.

'Well, hello there, Mr Kelly,' she said, her voice dripping warm and dangerous. She had made it her business to memorise the name of every man in the locality, a feat which, although admirable in its show of memory, had not endeared her to many women. 'Don't often see you over this way. Can I be of some service?'

Kelly leaned in, not particularly wanting his business broadcast. Lori took this as an invitation and dropped towards him, back arched like a gymnast, her bosom, barely held by the small arrangement of lace and frill across her chest, presenting itself at a distance that threatened suffocation. He stepped back, knocking into a porter who was hanging like a hound, loon-faced, trying for a front row view.

'Sorry, fellers,' Lori said. 'Got work to do here.' She waved her one hand as if trying to work a ring loose and the fan club dispersed. 'Sorry about that,' she said, leaning over the desk again. 'These young fellers ...' She paused and caressed a long hank of golden hair. 'That's why I prefer an older man,' she said, running the tip of her tongue across her top lip. Kelly felt the colour rush to his face. She smiled, arching one brow.

'You got the troopers staying here,' Kelly said. 'Needed to speak with one of them.'

'Ooh, yes,' Lori said. 'The troopers. Which one you wanna speak to?'

'Tall one. Blond hair?'

'Mmhhh. I know the one.' She arranged her hair over one shoulder and took up stroking it like a cat. 'Moody. Mirrored shades. Yeah, just my type.'

Kelly was fast losing concentration. 'Can you get him down for me?'

'Sure,' she said. 'Whatever you want.'

Kelly retreated to a small table by the fire and, when he was sure Lori wasn't looking, wiped the sweat from his face. He got straight to his feet when McKenzie – full paraphernalia on – appeared at the foot of the stairs.

'You OK?' McKenzie said. 'You look a little steamed up.'

'Reception,' Kelly said, nodding towards Lori who had her two eyes fixed on McKenzie.

'See you later, Officer,' she called. 'Don't forget what I told you. I'm off at nine.'

Kelly bolted out the door leaving McKenzie to fend for himself.

'You're not going to have a whole lot of time with your pa,' Kelly said, as he pulled the pickup onto the road. 'Olive's not going to want to leave him. I'll keep her as long as I can, but she'll soon see there's nothing wrong with the darn horse.'

McKenzie didn't speak for a long time, then he blew out a long breath.

'Perhaps this isn't a good time. Maybe I should wait a while. Come back another day you know ...' He pulled down the window and let the night air in. A thin line of sweat trickled from his hat band, past his ear. He wiped it with his shoulder. 'I'm afraid to see him, Kelly. I never intended this. To come back, find him ailing. I never imagined ...'

'You'll be fine.' Kelly couldn't say what he was thinking: that there was likely going to be no second chance to see Gil – that this was it.

Kelly slowed the pickup as The Luck came into view.

'I'll drop you here. Make your way up to the barn then wait till I drive off with Olive. And watch the clock – I swear she won't stand more than a half hour away from him. I'll see you back in the barn.' He pulled away, McKenzie's ashen face reflecting in the mirror for a moment then disappearing into the trees like the moon dodging behind a cloud.

McKenzie watched from the side of the barn. His ma – hurry and aggravation in her every step – crossed the yard with Kelly, her black bag clutched to her chest, the yellow beam of the flashlight swinging across the ground. She was saying something he couldn't make out, but the sound of her voice set off a flutter in his chest. He watched Kelly drive through the gate and onto the road then crossed the yard and stepped up onto the porch. The light was on in the kitchen – he pushed the door and went in.

In terms of memories, the room offered up the best of both worlds: Beattie's big mixing bowls still crowned the top shelf – most likely because they were too high for reaching – and the table that Darragh made the winter they were first wed still lounged crooked on the rug that Beattie cursed and sweated over that same winter. But the chairs by the stove were Gil and Olive's, the coffee pot on the stove was the one he'd known from home, the butter dish, the wood basket. It caught him unawares – the relief at seeing it all. The relief that it was all still there, his life was still there – ticking away in a place he thought he would never see again. Like it was waiting for him. He crossed the kitchen to the stairs, took them steadily, his knees unstuffed and weak. The door to Darragh and Beattie's old room was ajar, lamp lit and cosy. McKenzie forced himself forward, paused at the door to calm his breath and went in.

The window was open some. Gil was laid on his side, facing the cool breeze that was lifting the curtains and stirring the fringes on the lamp shade. He shifted in the bed as McKenzie came in, twisting his head to get a better look.

'That you, Ol?'

McKenzie didn't answer but walked a little closer so his pa could get a look at him.

'Ah. Officer. You back again?' He shifted some more, the effort setting off some dark discomfort that etched his face with shadow. He hauled himself up the bed, groaning softly as he arranged himself against the bolster. There was a wrong odour about him – sweet and cloying.

'Sit down,' Gil said, motioning towards the chair.

McKenzie stepped forward into the soft pool of lamp light and took the chair. His pa looked over at him.

'You not the same officer?'

'I'm not. You saw my partner Huey ...' McKenzie removed his hat and looked at his pa. ' I'm Officer McKenzie.' Gil still didn't cotton on. McKenzie didn't want to rush things but he had lost a grip on the time – he couldn't say if he'd been two minutes or twenty. He moved in closer. 'Pa, it's me. McKenzie.'

Gil pushed up from the bolster. 'McKenzie. My McKenzie? What you saying? Come here – let me take a look at you.' He grabbed McKenzie by the wrist and pulled him in. The sudden touch released some lever in McKenzie. Gil, hoisting himself up some more, took hold of the boy's face. 'Look at me,' he said. 'Look at me.'

McKenzie wiped his eyes against his sleeve and looked at his pa. Gil considered him for a moment or two then ran his hand against the grain of his hair, touched his thumb to McKenzie's eyelid. Then he leaned into the boy's neck and wept. McKenzie would have stayed like that forever but Gil eventually pulled away, his one arm clamped against his belly as he lowered himself back onto the bolster, breathing deep, his face bunched against the pain. McKenzie set himself on the edge of the bed and waited.

'Your ma is out,' Gil said, his breath still coming stiff and wary.

'I know that,' McKenzie said. 'Kelly fixed this for me. I figured I wasn't wanting to see her just yet. Or her wanting to see me.'

Gil nodded.

'I have things I need to say,' McKenzie said, the imminence of his speech, it not rehearsed to any degree of confidence suddenly forcing him back to his feet.

'When I went away, Pa ... I ... I.' The words were not going to come easy. 'When I went away ...' He flopped back down on the bed.

Gil took his hand. 'I figure I might know why you went away, son. But ... but you never sent word. You left us wondering, me and your ma.'

'My ma? I'd say she never gave me a second thought. You know how she was with me.'

Gil covered his eyes with his hand. It was a gesture of such hopelessness it brought tears to McKenzie's eyes.

'It wasn't just that, Pa. I had to stay away. The Lindo boys. The shooting was all over the radio. Seemed to me like there was only one person they were interested in – and that was me: the jackass who stole their stuff and disappeared. But it wasn't me, Pa – I needed to tell you that. I worked for them a while and then I lost my wits and stole their stuff, but I sure as hell didn't shoot them. I was two days gone from Oaklake by then, but when I saw that news in the paper – I quit sleeping at night. I just kept going. I'm sorry.'

'That's why you've come back then, son – to confess your innocence?'

McKenzie got back to his feet. There was an agitation in him that he was finding hard to get a hold of.

'No, Pa. That's not why I'm back.' He indicated his uniform, struggling with the aggravation of trying to explain himself. 'I'm a trooper – got sent over this way tracking that stranger. Never intended to come back ...' He stopped at this, the expression on Gil's face tripping him up. 'I would've come back at some ... look, I'm sorry, Pa.'

Gil patted the side of the bed. 'Sit down, son. You've come back. I've seen you. That's all that matters.' He sank back against the pillows.

'So, you're a trooper?' His voice had no strength, like he was just this side of sleep.

'Yep. A while now. Been tracking this feller a couple months. He's run us across two states. Never thought he'd run us here. I understand you spoke with him?'

Gil reached for the water pitcher on the side table. The effort drained the colour from his face.

'Well, he was a strange feller,' Gil said. 'Said some darn strange things too, like I told your buddy.'

'Hear he said he was an O'Grady?'

'He did. Said his pa was Conrad.' McKenzie already knew this, from Huey.

'Not possible, of course,' Gil said, 'and anyway your buddy tells me the feller is a hustler – reckons he picked up on some story and was chancing his hand.' Gil stopped talking and concentrated on pulling some air into his lungs. 'Funny thing, though,' he said, after a few moments.

'What's that?'

'His name. It was his name threw me.'

'His name? Feller's name is West according to our knowing. He signs in places as "West". Never heard of him using another name. Never used O'Grady.'

'Told me his name was Westerly.'

'Mr Westerly?'

Gil shook his head. A pearl of sweat flew from the end of his nose and spotted McKenzie's hand.

'No – Westerly O'Grady. Said his name was Westerly O'Grady.'

'And?'

'And it threw me. Conrad O'Grady was mighty fond of the sea. If any man was going to call his son for an obliging sea breeze I reckon it would be Conrad.'

'What did he want?'

'He wanted the farm.'

Chapter 56

A beam of light swung across the bedroom ceiling. McKenzie leapt up.

'Pa, I've got to go. Ma's back.' He bent down and kissed the top of his father's head then strode to the door.

'Why don't you stay – see her.'

'You know why, she won't want to see me. Never had any problem making that clear. But I'll come back, Pa.' McKenzie slipped out the door.

'Son ...'

McKenzie dodged back into the room.

'Don't leave it too long.'

McKenzie crept down the stairs and out onto the back porch. He waited until he heard the front door slam closed then crossed the yard into the barn. It took him by surprise. The emptiness of it: the tarp, usually draped across The Annie O'Grady, heaped in a corner, Darragh's workbench stacked with tool boxes.

'You there, Mac?'

Kelly was at the barn door. McKenzie could hear the low purr of the pickup engine.

'Come on. We need to go.'

McKenzie took another look round the barn then followed.

'How'd it go?'

McKenzie hadn't said a word since they'd left The Luck. He was staring out the windshield, his two hands loose on his lap.

'My pa's real sick, isn't he?'

'Yeah, I reckon that's so.' Kelly kept his voice soft. 'He was awake though? You got to speak to him?'

'Yeah. He was awake. We talked some. Christ, Kel,' McKenzie

raised his hands then let them drop again. 'When did it all get so … so fucked up?'

Kelly concentrated on the road. 'You gonna go back?'

'Yeah. Yeah, I'll have to go back. To see my pa, of course but … but I'll have to go back and …'

'And see your ma?'

McKenzie drew in a long breath. 'Yeah, I'll have to go back and see my ma.'

'Probably for the best, Mac, you know. Let go of the past and all.'

Let go of the past. There was no chance of that. Kelly didn't know it yet but the past was hurtling towards them like a runaway locomotive.

He went back a couple of days later. Him and Huey. Boots shined, shirts freshly laundered. Bolstered. They needed to ask a few more questions about when the feller – *Mr Westerly O'Grady* – had disappeared. Whether anyone had actually seen him leave. Problem was they'd picked up no reports about strangers hitch-hiking or walking, no sightings of him at the rail station in Picker's Flag. Seemed he'd truly disappeared. They'd tracked him easy enough across two states then he'd got to Oaklake and vanished like a puff of smoke, leaving behind his trash, the burned-out campfire and the empty boat.

'Did the feller say anything about where he was from, sir, or where he might be heading?' Huey was taking the lead.

'Said he was born in Honolulu. Didn't say where he was heading.'

'Anyone else get to speak to the feller?'

Gil shook his head. His face was bunched up with pain.

McKenzie stood at the other side of the bed, straight as a statue, his aviators shielding his eyes from the sun – and Olive. She was at Gil's side – smaller than McKenzie remembered. There was still a good measure of iron in her, he could see that, but something about her had diminished. She'd not looked at him once, was listening to what Huey was saying but had her eyes clamped on Gil's face. They'd met the doctor's car in the lane on their way up. It had taken the breath from him, the sudden thought he might be too late. The alarm had rushed him past Huey and into the bedroom, not thinking that she might be there, not thinking of anything except Gil. He'd let out a small gasp when he saw her at the bedside, Gil's hand loose on the covers, covered by her own.

'No.' Gil said. 'Far as I know it was ... just me saw him ... and ...'

'Gil,' Olive said. 'I'll do the talking.' She turned slightly to address Huey. 'The feller only wanted Gil over there.'

'So how did you all know that the feller had left?'

'Well, the boat was back. Tied up. McCleavy found it. He was all set to go over because ...' She turned back towards Gil. 'Well, because Gil was laid up. McCleavy said he'd go instead.'

'So he definitely went over? Even though the boat was back?'

'Far as I know.'

Huey ran his finger round his shirt collar. 'And your husband, Mr McKenzie ...' He nodded towards Gil who had drifted off into a half-sleep. Beads of sweat stood out on his forehead and the pillow beneath his head was circled with damp.

'Did he happen to tell you what this feller was wanting?'

Olive glanced at Gil then shook her head. 'He's been like this best part of a week. Sleeping.'

Huey nodded then glanced over at McKenzie. 'Want to add anything?'

'Nope.'

It wasn't true. There was plenty he wanted to add. But not now. Not in front of Gil.

He thought she hadn't recognised him.

Him standing there with his damn sunglasses on, like she couldn't see through him. *A police officer.* Well that portion had, surprised her. But the fact that he'd not come clean, introduced himself straight out. Well what kind of surprise was that? None as far as she was concerned. Just showed he'd not changed his colours. Furtive as he'd ever been. She'd waited till they were getting back into the patrol car.

'Where can I get you officers if ... if I think of anything else, or if my husband remembers anything else?'

Huey hesitated behind the open car door. 'Well, we'll be in Picker's Flag another night or so I guess. You can get us at the Belle Royale.'

She'd nodded then dashed back towards the house.

'Funny little woman,' Huey said, as he buckled in.

McKenzie said nothing. Watched her go. He was trying to figure out his next move. He needed to see her. There were things he needed to say. Things that needed saying. Especially now. Gil on his bed, waning like a tired moon.

He'd just got out of the shower when the phone on the bedside table rang.

'Lady down here asking to see you, Officer.' Lori Flynn from reception. He pulled the towel round himself and sat down on the bed.

'Well, who is it?'

Lori muffled the receiver while she asked the question.

'It's Mrs McKenzie,' she said. 'Olive McKenzie. From out at Oaklake?'

'What?' He jumped up from the bed. 'Well ... well, it's most likely Huey she's wanting to see – Officer Hughes, that is. He's in the room along from me.'

'No-o-o.' she strung it out like a musical note. 'She's asking for you ... specifically. Shall I send her up?'

'Send her up? No. Tell her I'll be down in a few minutes. I'll meet her in the bar.'

He listened to Lori's muffled voice again.

'No. She says she'll see you outside. She's got her vehicle parked directly out front. She'll wait for you there.'

Goddamn.

McKenzie got his uniform back off the hanger, slipped his boots on and grabbed his hat off the bed. He put his aviators on then, as he was walking down the stairs, took them off and put them in his shirt pocket. He was going to have to come clean. Now was as good a time as any.

He knew as soon as he saw her face. Lit up by the street light. Some nasty satisfaction etched on it. He paused to brace himself then, momentarily thrown by the idea that he was wrong and that she'd come to tell him that Gil had taken a turn for the worse, quickened his pace and let himself into her car.

'Is it ...?'

'No, it's not your *pa*.' She spat the words at him. 'Thought I didn't know. Thought you could stand there, by your *pa's* bedside and I wouldn't know it was you?'

He let her words float away. *It wasn't Gil. Gil was OK.*

'Is he OK? Is Pa OK?'

'Is Pa OK?' Her voice was a mocking sing song. 'What do you think? You saw him. You think he's OK?'

He shook his head. 'He looks worse. I ... I saw him already. A few nights ago.'

That let some air out of her tyres but she recovered quickly.

'So,' she said, swivelling round in her seat. 'You've come back all big and mighty, in your *state trooper uniform*. Like you're someone important, someone who never did any wrong. I daresay the police force don't know anything about your *past*. Or about your *appetites*.'

He considered her a few moments. The puckered skin around her mouth, the frown ironed into her forehead, her hair scraped back tight and mean. She was like some ragged bird flown up from hell.

'What?' she said. 'Cat got your goddamn tongue?'

'I know,' he said, softly.

'What's that. They not teach you to speak up in that goddamn police force?'

'I said, I know.'
'You know? Hah – he knows. You know what, for God's sake?'
He took a couple of slow breaths, let his heart settle back a little.
'I know about you and Rose.'
He fancied he felt all the air go out of her.

Chapter 57

It was the middle of the night when the phone on the bedside table rang again. A male voice on the other end, stifling a yawn.

'Call for you, Officer McKenzie. I'm putting it through right now.'

McKenzie hauled himself up against the pillows and fumbled for the lamp, a small click on the line then Kelly's voice.

'Mac, Mac ... is that you?'

'It's me ... what's wrong?' He didn't want Kelly to answer. It was Gil. It had to be Gil.

'Your ma,' Kelly said. 'You know where she is?'

'My ma? No. She was here, but she went ...' McKenzie moved the watch so he could see it. 'She went more than three hours ago, drove off ...'

'Was she OK? She hasn't come back. We don't know where she is.'

'She was OK,' McKenzie said. He heard the edge of doubt in his own voice. Olive had driven off all right. Stepped on the gas before he'd got out the car. Left him standing in the street.

'You don't sound so sure. I mean, what did she want. Why was she over there?'

McKenzie pushed the hair back off his forehead. 'I don't rightly know. She ... she, I'm not sure. Look, I'll come out there now. You at The Luck?'

'Yeah.'

'My pa?'

'Gil's not too good. That's why we need to find Olive.'

Kelly was waiting for him on the front porch. The light in the upstairs bedroom shone a patch of dim colour onto the yard below.

'How is he?'

'Resting. The doctor's been. Given him something for the pain.'

McKenzie scanned the yard: there was no sign of Olive's car. 'She's not back?'

Kelly shook his head. 'You two argue or anything?'

'No. Didn't get chance for anything like that. She'd come to tell me that she'd recognised me. She was, well, you know ... mean. Mean-minded about it all. She did all the talking, so I let her. Waited till she was finished, then I told her.'

'You told her? You told her what?'

'I told her I knew about her and Rose.'

Kelly studied McKenzie's face in the half-light. It hadn't changed a great deal in ten years. Leaner maybe, more man than boy, but there was no malice written in it.

'Her and Rose? My ma, you mean?'

McKenzie nodded. 'Don't suppose there's any beer in the house?'

Kelly got up and went in. McKenzie leaned back in his chair and propped his feet on the rail. He'd waited a long time to tell his story but he reckoned the time had come. By the time Kelly came back with the beer he had it straight in his mind.

'I went to see Vida,' McKenzie said. He rested his bottle of ale on the rail. 'A few weeks after I left, I went to see Vida.'

He'd been two months gone from Oaklake. Two months carrying a weight on his shoulders colder than a wet blanket. Fear. It should have been easy enough to put his finger on: fear the cops might pick him up, fear the Lindo family would come after him, but it seemed like it had spiralled out of all perspective. He was afraid all the time and of everything. Later he would come to realise it was a consequence of suddenly uprooting himself from a small town, a result of having no place he felt known or safe, but at the time, road weary and half starved, it felt like he'd been tipped out of a small pot and set down on a different planet.

His initial plan had been to get to the west coast and meet up with Clifford but he abandoned that as soon as he heard the news on the radio. The Lindo boys were dead. The police were looking for him. He wasn't that far from Oaklake at that point. He'd sold the Lindo's stuff, left a share for Kelly, then ditched the car outside some town whose name he couldn't remember. He spent the night in the back seat then simply walked away from it, trekked the short distance into town and bought another at the first car lot he came across.

He was driving mainly at night: daytimes he parked up by some mall or diner complex, trying to get some sleep in the back end of the station wagon. But his mind wouldn't let him be: every voice or car door had him upright, listening out like some spooked animal.

Then one morning, starved beyond all reason, he'd climbed out of the vehicle, crossed the parking lot and gone into a Dunkin' Donuts. Turned out it could have been the dumbest thing he'd ever done because, no sooner had he got settled in a booth, his hands wrapped round his first cup of coffee, than two patrol cars pulled up outside the door. Four officers – two from each car – bowled in through the door and took the booth opposite him. First off he'd kept his face turned away from them, concentrating on what was going on in the parking lot. When the waitress came over with his order he quietly asked if he might change his mind – have the order to go. He'd pulled on his cap and slid out from the seat. He was almost at the counter when the cop called out.

'Hey, buddy.'

He didn't respond. Acted like he'd not heard, leaned against the counter silently urging the waitress on.

'Hey, buddy.' The voice was closer. He had no choice. He turned his head. The officer's hands were extended in front of him, something dangling from his fist. McKenzie made half a move to offer up his wrists.

'You left your truck keys on the table,' he said.

'Excuse me?'

'Your keys,' the cop jerked his thumb towards the empty table. 'You left them on the table.'

McKenzie held out his hand and the cop dropped the keys into his palm.

'Thanks.'

'No problem, buddy. No problem at all.'

He got back into the station wagon and wept. Some of it was relief. Some of it was fear. But most of it – and this wasn't something that sat easy with him – was homesickness. He berated himself even as the tears were still coming but he couldn't deny it: as much as he'd yearned to leave Oaklake, its small-minded dreariness, its hopeless, empty nothingness, at that moment he'd have given anything to be back there.

He never knew if it was the weeping or the donuts that fixed him but after the brush with the cops something in him seemed to shift. They hadn't recognised him. Hell, they hadn't even given him a second look. He'd got back out of the wagon and gone and bought himself a newspaper. Read it from cover to cover and could find nothing except local news. Nothing about Picker's or Oaklake and nothing about him. He'd gone back for more donuts and coffee, sat himself where he could see the TV, watched for near enough half an hour and again, there was no mention of him. None at all.

By the time he was back in the driving seat he'd got himself a plan.

He was going to go and see Vida.

'You went to see Vida?'

'I did.'

'But why? And how did you know where to find her?'

McKenzie laughed. It had been easy. That's what happened when you lived somewhere like Oaklake. You forgot there was a whole different world out there.

'Cause she was family of sorts, I guess. She was in the directory. I called her up and she invited me round.'

He'd gone round. She'd made it clear from the get-go that she was headed out later that evening, invited him to stay over, laughed when he acted like he had somewhere else to be. Likely could see that he needed to talk.

'Stay for a shower at least,' she'd said. 'Prise your feet out of those fancy boots.'

There had been a relief in that. He'd swiped the boots when he emptied the Lindos' cellar. Left his own shoes behind, like it was some grand gesture. He realised his mistake soon after: they'd rubbed his feet raw.

He spent the evening watching the TV, mooching round Vida's place. She came in late, knocking around the place, clumsy with drink. She sat down on the couch beside him and shook him till he stopped pretending he was asleep. She wanted to talk about Conrad, about his seagoing, his disappearance. Showed him a handful of postcards: Nova Scotia, Hawaii. Honolulu. Then she talked about her babies – Rose and Olive – about leaving them with Darragh and Beattie and all and that's when she told him.

'It just sort of slipped out like she thought I already knew.'

'What?'

'Rose and Olive,' McKenzie said. 'Seems they weren't sisters.'

Kelly placed his bottle of ale carefully down on the table.

'They weren't ...?'

'They weren't sisters. Well, not full sisters. Vida said she was already pregnant when she took up with Conrad.'

'Pregnant?'

'Yeah. With Olive. With my ma.'

Kelly picked his ale off the table and took a long swig. 'So Conrad ... '

'So Conrad was father to Rose, but not to Olive. They were half-sisters.'

Kelly let out a low whistle. 'So who was the other feller? Who was Olive's father?'

McKenzie shook his head. 'Reckoned she didn't know. Seemed

to think it was quite the thing – not knowing which feller had left her expecting.'

'Good Lord. Did Conrad not mind?'

'That I don't know. Maybe he never saw the birth certificate, maybe he just assumed and she didn't put him straight. Sounded like he wasn't around all that much.'

'So, strictly speaking, Olive is not an O'Grady.'

'I know. Kind of amusing, isn't it?'

'Reckon she might not see it that way.' Kelly was quiet a few moments. 'So this is what you told her when you saw her earlier on?'

'Not exactly. I knew about her and Rose. That's all I got chance to say. She took off like someone had scorched her tail.'

Kelly got up from his chair. 'Wait here,' he said. 'I'll go check on Gil, then I reckon we need to go and find her.'

McKenzie swirled the last dregs in the bottle and tipped it to his lips. He'd told Kelly some of it, but not all. Figured he'd leave the rest of the telling to Olive.

Chapter 58

Olive was pulling on the oars slowly. It was dark but it seemed to her that things had never looked more clear.

He knew. All these years and her son – her own son, come back to deal her the hand that should have been dealt years ago. She quit rowing and let the boat drift to a halt. There was some kind of pattern to it if you thought about it. Some circle that had started and ended. Almost ended – because he knew about her and Rose. She drew the oars in and fixed them then cast her eyes over the dark water. So much to think about, to get straight. He'd be coming for her, that much was certain. Wanting the facts, the full story – the truth. And what would she tell him?

She'd gone over to The Cabin unexpectedly. Not insofar that Rose wasn't expecting her, but that she'd not fully intended to go there herself. She'd left the store and before she knew it she was steering the truck down the track towards The Cabin. She'd barely slept since Beattie had told her.

Rose was going to sell The Cabin. The idea of it had her mind derailed. If Rose was willing to sell The Cabin to appease Michael Kelly, what would happen if, *when,* she inherited half of The Luck? What would happen then? Would she sell it out from under their feet? Everything that Darragh and Beattie had worked for? She'd settled it in her own head years back. The Luck would surely be hers and Gil's. Rose had no use for it, she was settled in her own place, had a life, a child, a *caree*r. Hell, she had everything she wanted. There was no way she would want The Luck.

But Michael Kelly. She sure as hell hadn't allowed for that.

She'd initially pulled the truck into the yard then, suddenly struck by the fact that she didn't rightly know what she was going to say, took it further down the track and parked by the stables figuring she could say she'd come by to pick up some tack. She was walking back to the house, rehearsing this line, when she caught sight of Rose. It was the colour of her dress that snagged her eye – a drift of pale lemon through the waist high weeds in Darragh's old vegetable plot.

'Rose.'

Rose looked up, then looked down again at whatever it was she had in her hands.

'Don't tell me there's actual vegetables growing in there?'

'Olive ... I. Wait there a minute ...'

She'd had plenty of time to think about it afterwards and reckoned that was the moment – the way Rose turned away like a child guarding her schoolwork, or perhaps hiding some small household breakage – the moment she knew all her worries about Michael Kelly, about the havoc he was going to wreak on her own future, were going to come true.

'What have you got there?' She was on the plot now, ploughing her way through old corn, ropes of squash runners. Rose was ahead of her, her back still turned. She'd got to the fence – as far as she could go – then stopped. She turned round slowly and faced her sister. Olive took in the dirt on the front of her dress, a smear of mud across one cheek ...

The black cash box in her hands.

At first she'd misunderstood. Looked at the box, back at Rose's face.

'You going to shop him, then?'

'What?' Rose was coming towards her now, picking her feet carefully through the tangle of growth.

'The box. You gonna tell them what he did. Shop him to the police?'

Rose gave an uncertain laugh. 'Oh, I don't think so, Ol. That was a long time ago.' She brushed past Olive and out onto the track, banging the earth from her shoes.

'Not too long, when you think about it. I mean, I'm sure the police ...' She was following Rose back towards the cabin.

'Ol. I know you mean well, but that's not what I'm going to do. Michael wants The Cabin and chances are he's going to get it.' They were in the kitchen now, Rose still clutching the box to her chest, the table between them. 'Vida's lawyer's doing his best to get it tied up for the boy, for Kelly, but, well I don't know ...'

'Well, that sure as hell won't work,' Olive said. 'Seeing as the boy's a bastard.'

It was out of her mouth before she could stop it. Not that she wanted to stop it because it was the plain truth.

'Excuse me?' Rose put the box down on the table. 'What did you say, Olive?' She was staring at her sister, her face and throat flushed red.

'I said, your boy's a bastard – strictly speaking. So, legally ...'

Rose crossed the kitchen, held the door open. 'I reckon you should maybe leave now, Ol, before I say something I regret.'

After that it was a blur. Like a movie reel wound on over fast. She'd lunged for the box. That much she remembered. She'd lunged for the box then ran for the truck. Then she was in the truck, the box thrown on the seat beside her and the engine running. Rose was running towards her, shouting, her hair and scarf streaming out around her face, the truck door open. Rose reached inside and grabbed the wheel but she pushed her away. She pushed her away, yanked the door closed, stepped on the gas and ...

Whump.

A small sound really, like she'd maybe run over a chicken. Some such thing. She looked in the rear mirror and there she was. Rose. Face down in the dirt.

As she climbed from the truck a small piece of silk fluttered from where it was caught in the door.

'It was a mistake,' she whispered, but Rose didn't answer.

Then the movie reel sped up some more till it seemed she was no longer *doing* but *watching.* She watched herself pick up her sister's body, carry her to the truck, fasten her into the passenger seat, her head lolling forwards on a neck too broken to support it, her hair hanging down, a pool of gold in her lap. Then she drove, drove to the lake, got the boat and somehow, *somehow,* laid Rose in there. She got the hessian from the back of the truck, gathered up some rocks and rowed out. Then the scene changed. She was no longer on the water, tracing the ripples that marked the place, the place where ...

No. Now she was in the truck. She had the cash box in her hands, she was prising it open with a screw driver, her face beaded with sweat. What was it Rose had shouted?

Don't open it, Olive. You don't know what's in there.

But she had to open it. Bastard or no bastard, she wasn't going to let Michael Kelly wrest The Cabin from the boy. She prodded and poked at the thing until the lid flew open and the contents showered across floor of the truck. She leaned down and gathered them up.

Documents. That's what was in there. She smoothed the sheets out on her lap.

The deeds for The Cabin.

She closed her eyes and leaned back in the seat.

It wasn't until she was almost back at Oaklake that she saw the locket, Rose's locket, lying on the floor of the cab. Which was when she made her second mistake because, keen to examine the piece of paper that lay beside it, she tucked it inside her pocket and pulled the truck to the side of the road. The paper was yellow with age, folded in quarters. She unwrapped it carefully; two pieces of paper, not one.

Don't open it, Olive. You don't know what's in there.

It was a pair of birth certificates. Hers. Rose's.

She read them then let the two flimsy pages fall onto her lap.

The film reel stopped and she crashed back to earth.

McKenzie was speaking to Huey on the police radio, the mike up close to his mouth.

'Need you to check around Picker's Flag for me, bud. We're trying to locate Mrs McKenzie ... yes, yes. We're heading out that way now, but just need to check she's not stopped for a bite to eat, some bar or diner, you know? OK ... sure ... thanks.'

'You think that's possible?' The edge in McKenzie's voice had alarmed Kelly. Made him think there was something about the situation he'd not been told.

'It's possible,' McKenzie said. 'Maybe she just needed some time on her own to, you know, digest what I'd said.'

Olive picked up the oars again and started across the water. What she couldn't work out was how McKenzie knew – and whether he knew the rest of it. She lifted her hand to her neck and felt her locket.

It was the locket – Rose's locket – that had nearly undone her. There it was when she undressed that night – Gil asleep in bed, oblivious to the damp lake smell of her. It had dropped to the floor as she stepped out of her clothes – some warmth in it that nearly had her breath stopped. She'd deliberated long on what to do with it – go back to The Cabin, maybe, and drop it somewhere in the grass, or else dig a hole and bury it – but she could neither entertain the thought of going back to The Cabin, nor the notion of dropping it into the earth, so she hid it at the bottom of her jewellery box and there it had stayed. The burglary, years later, had solved the thing. Or so she'd thought.

It had been a couple of days after McKenzie had disappeared. Her and Gil were on the front porch, idling after supper, when a truck pulled up hard in front of the store.

'The Lindos,' Gil said, slipping his boots back on. 'Hello there, boys,' he said, as they strode towards the store. 'Don't see you out this way often. You in need of some help?'

The eldest Lindo had stepped forward. 'Well, I guess you could put it that way, feller. Seems you owe us a portion of money.'

Gil scratched at his head and smiled.

'A portion of money? Well ...' he gave a soft chuckle, ''Fraid you lost me there, boys. How do you figure that one out?'

'Your boy. He took off with our stuff.'

'Well, I don't know about that. You know anything about that, Olive?'

'Not a thing,' she'd said.

Then, as if providence itself had been waiting in line for this very moment, the late sun dropped below a broad swatch of cloud and caught the locket hanging at her throat.

The eldest Lindo glanced at his brother then took another step forward. 'Well, you don't settle this Gil, we'll be back to take what's owed.' He tapped his brother on the arm. 'Come on, we're done here.'

He rolled down the window as they drove off. 'Pretty necklace you've got there, ma'am.'

She'd waited till Gil was asleep then driven out to the trailer park. Turned out the Lindo boys knew a darn sight more than she'd bargained for. Brought up the matter of the locket – Rose's locket – straight away, grinning at her as they recalled lifting it from her jewellery box, their eyes lit up with some money-making mischief – until she pulled out the shotgun. She'd meant it as a warning, she'd not intended to harm them. But who would have believed her? She wasn't blind to what people thought of her. She'd tried her best after Rose – bringing up her boy. There was some redemption in that, surely?

The police radio crackled into life. McKenzie unhooked it from the dash and pressed the button on its side.

'How's it going, Huey? Any sign of her?'

'Nothing, Mac. You need me to come and meet you somewhere?'

'Nah, it's OK. I've got Mr Kelly here with me, we're almost at the lake now. Planning to take a quick look round then head back to the farm. Chances are she's turned up there already.'

'That's a good point, Mac,' Kelly said. 'Olive surely is back by now. Gil and all, you know? Maybe we should just go straight back.'

'We'll take a quick look first,' McKenzie said, swinging the car off the road and onto the track that led towards the lake.

Olive quit rowing. The moon had suddenly emerged from a patch of cloud, sending a beam, like a path, across the dark water. She shivered as it lit up the trees at the far edge of the lake. She fancied she could see the outline of the old shack. It had surprised her, a few weeks back, to find it still standing.

The stranger had been camped up there. He'd been suspicious of her at first, but happy enough when she'd explained who she was and produced the parcel of food – and the bottles of ale. She'd watched him as he ate and drank: he was the part of the circle that perplexed her the most. The way he'd turned up with McKenzie in tow, like they were both holding opposite ends of the rope and she was the bit that was going to join it together. *He wanted the farm.* That's what Gil had said. Westerly O'Grady: Conrad's son. Half-brother to Rose of course, but not to her. He'd shown her his papers. His goddamn birth certificate. Held it out to her, a smile on his face, like it was the winning ticket, like he thought she was just going to pack up her stuff and hand the farm over. It had been easy enough. Ale: men never could resist it. *I've made you a special brew.* That's what she'd said as he flipped the top off the second bottle. Didn't mention what was special about it.

Olive lifted her hand to her neck and unfastened her locket. She prised it open and considered the small photograph. What had she been – seventeen, eighteen? So much still ahead but, it seemed to her, her young face already betraying the dissatisfaction that had dogged most of her life. All of her life, truth be known. She'd taken the wrong path – known it the moment she met Michael Kelly. She shook her head. His name stuck in her gullet even now.

She thought of Gil, back at The Luck, the very life sweating from him: his hour of need and her not there. But she could brook no other solution: couldn't entertain the look on his face when he learned the truth about her, or stomach the thought of McKenzie laying it all out like the Sunday papers.

Some quick burst of light in the corner of her eye told her she didn't have long. They were coming for her. She watched as the headlights traced the edge of the lake, heard the slamming of doors, raised voices.

'Olive.'

'Ma.'

Some roosting bird took off, squawking across the water like a bad omen.

It was time.

She snapped the locket shut, slid off her shoes and arranged them side by side beneath the seat, then leaned forward and lay the locket in the bottom of the boat. She took one last look around: something royal about the colour of the night sky, she thought. Something royal, and maybe forgiving.

She closed her eyes and breathed it in, then slipped into the water without a sound.

Acknowledgments

A massive thankyou to all the staff at Honno Press, especially Rebecca John, whose guidance and expertise has been invaluable.

My thanks and gratitude to Lara Clough, Chris Kinsey and David Thorpe, Nicola Ratnett, Peter Barker, Rachel Bulbulia, Kathryn Dangerfield, Ciaran and Muiread O'onnell for all their teaching, advice and support.

Special thanks to Cheryl Christopher.

A very special thankyou to a very special man – my husband Paul – for his endless enthusiasm and love.

ABOUT HONNO

Honno Welsh Women's Press was set up in 1986 by a group of women who felt strongly that women in Wales needed wider opportunities to see their writing in print and to become involved in the publishing process. Our aim is to develop the writing talents of women in Wales, give them new and exciting opportunities to see their work published and often to give them their first 'break' as a writer.

Honno is registered as a community co-operative. Any profit that Honno makes is invested in the publishing programme. Women from Wales and around the world have expressed their support for Honno. Each supporter has a vote at the Annual General Meeting. For more information and to buy our publications, please visit our website www.honno.co.uk or email us on post@honno.co.uk.

Honno
D41, Hugh Owen Building,
Aberystwyth University,
Aberystwyth,
Ceredigion,
SY23 3DY.

We are very grateful for the support of all
our Honno Friends.